The

Broadcast

A mystery thriller

Liam Fialkov

The Broadcast

https://www.facebook.com/liam.fialkov.77
liam_fialkov@outlook.com

CONTENTS

CHAPTER 1

The Broadcast

A sense of optimism prevailed at the TXB headquarters in anticipation of the upcoming evening's event. As a result of the unique video clip that fell into their hands, the senior managers predicted the highest ratings in the network's history.

The advertising department built up viewers' expectations. During three weeks, they bombarded the airwaves with trailers that promised a TV program the likes of which had never been seen on the small screen.

As the hour of the broadcast approached, excitement grew and spread throughout the country, and people rushed home to catch what promised to be an earthshaking event.

A quarter of a century had passed since the killing that riled the nation. Still, the consequences of that murder trial—which bore all the makings of a quintessential Hollywood production—had yet to fade, and the emotional wounds it inflicted upon different segments of the population never completely healed. The trial, saturated with emotions and unpredictable twists, captivated people all over the country. It involved fame, wealth, power, sex, and interracial tension.

The defendant, accused of committing a horrific crime, was movie actor Pedro Gonzales, whose friendly face was recognized and liked across the United States. In the course of the trial, the public became acquainted with the slain victims: Melisa Robinson, Gonzales's golden-haired ex-wife and the mother of his son, and Adrian Parker, her friend with whom she had spent that tragic afternoon on July 9 in that fateful year.

The media had called it "The Trial from the Movies," and celebrated every detail in numerous sensational articles. The press and the public focused on the charming and charismatic actor, covering anecdotes of his life in the poverty-stricken neighborhood where he grew up through his rise to fame and wealth. Diligent reporters unearthed tales about his relationships with women that his good looks and considerable talent had brought him.

People everywhere remembered how they had a hard time accepting the jury's not-guilty verdict, despite plenty of evidence pointing to the contrary.

Angry individuals flooded radio talk shows with calls expressing their outrage over the quick and surprising ruling, which exonerated the Latino celebrity. The widespread opinion held that the outstanding defense team had played the race card to the jury, which was predominantly comprised of people of Latino background.

And now, lo and behold, twenty-five years later, the popular TV network announced, to the amazement of the public, that it was in possession of a filmstrip documenting the murder. People found it hard to believe that after such a long time, they would be able to see the incident with their own eyes and finally settle their lingering doubts.

An opinion poll funded by TXB discovered that the far-reaching implications of the affair raised interest and curiosity about the upcoming broadcast in most segments of the population. It included people who were not even born or were children during the trial.

Competing TV networks intended to play movie reruns at the time of the broadcast, knowing they couldn't compete with the enormous viewership that TXB had secured.

Beginning in the early evening hours, TXB-affiliated stations convened panels that debated the trial and its outcome. Of course, the panel discussions were accompanied by many commercials, earning TXB additional millions in advertising revenue.

The network scheduled the show to air after prime time at 10:00 p.m. and the promos displayed viewer discretion warnings which had the effect of further increasing excited anticipation. As the hour approached, parents hurried to finish their household chores and put their kids to bed.

Panels were divided into two camps. One side featured panelists who thought they were going to be exposed to an extraordinary and incredible revelation. On the other side were those who suspected a hoax.

***

Looking through the window of his twenty-eighth floor office at the TXB building in downtown New York City, producer Walter Lindsey watched the glimmering metropolis lights below. He saw traffic subside as the hour of the show drew near, but he wasn't sure whether it was due to the broadcast or perhaps because of the late hour. The 44-year-old seasoned producer knew that he had come across an incredible journalistic scoop, an extraordinary exclusive. Despite some doubts, he could not miss this great chance for ratings gold.

CHAPTER 2

Jonathan and Sarah

Engaged in their evening routine, Jonathan and Sarah fed their three dogs, eleven cats, and a large flock of chickens, ducks, and geese. All the animals appeared impatient and eager to receive their food.

Afterward, they turned their attention to their own meal. While preparing dinner in their large wooden house, which resided among tall sequoia trees, they did not hide their curiosity about the upcoming special broadcast.

Sarah was especially excited. She remembered the infamous trial that took place about twenty-five years earlier, and how she had followed it, riveted to the TV and radio. She was no more than fifteen years old when it happened, and now it seemed like it took place in another era.

Jonathan had not followed the events of the affair like Sarah had. During the trial, he thought the story received too much attention—that it had become a cynical, journalistic farce and was not really a "trial from the movies," as the media called it.

However, as the hour grew near, Sarah thought he seemed unusually restless.

Sarah reached out to him as they sat at the dinner table with all three dogs sprawled on the floor at their feet. "I wonder if the film TXB is going to air is real or some kind of hoax," she said. "And if it is authentic, where did they get it after all these years?"

As she did every evening during the week, she'd taken the time to prepare dinner from scratch after returning home from work at the clinic. She didn't like ready-made meals. "Your husband is spoiled," her friends teased her. But for Sarah, cooking was a way to unwind and relax her mind at the end of a busy day, so she prepared dinner even on days when she was overcome by fatigue, and she just wanted to sink into a comfortable couch.

Jonathan's response surprised her. "The film is authentic," he said confidently.

"How can you be so sure?" she asked, examining him while he focused on his food.

"Because it's Walter's project," he answered. "And I talked with him."

"So, what did Walter tell you?" Mention of Jonathan's brother piqued her interest. The two brothers had recently mended most of their profound differences, overcoming a deep-seated, long-term hostility, which had lingered for many years. Jonathan's big brother, who hadn't attended their wedding, had even come for a surprise visit and had been their guest for three days.

"He said it's his project." Volunteering no further details, he laid his plate on the floor for his loyal dog, Bono, to lick before it was put in the dishwasher.

Jonathan rose from his chair, which Sarah correctly interpreted as his disinclination to continue the conversation.

She watched him as he stepped into the living room. *Still as handsome as when I first met him*, she thought to herself, *and he is already over forty.*

She knew that when he dealt with personal issues—like his relationship with his brother—he tended to express himself in short, decisive sentences. Otherwise, he liked to speak and expand on theoretical matters. He acquired knowledge on topics that triggered his curiosity and imagination by employing his remarkable, self-directed learning capability.

***

They had bought their house at an incredible bargain price. A short ad in a local paper had caught Sarah's attention. "Must sell due to unforeseen circumstances."

"Why do you think it's so cheap?" She asked Jonathan.

"It's earthquake country," he responded, "They probably got tired of things falling off the shelves, it could get quite scary."

"Would it be scary for you?" She asked, carefully examining him.

"I don't think so," he said. "I would just have to get used to it."

"You're sure?"

"People scare me more than the earth."

"I always wanted to live in the forest," Sarah said.

"Well, this may be your chance."

She called the seller, who hadn't even bothered hiring the services of a real estate company, and gave her the impression that he just wanted to get rid of the property—and to get away from it as fast as possible.

When they had come to see the place, Sarah fell in love with the wooded surrounding. It made her feel at home right away. She recalled that when she was young, she had participated in demonstrations against forest logging and was not embarrassed to hug and talk to trees.

Jonathan liked the place because of the large wooden house that contained three bedrooms connected by a corridor. It included a rustic, country kitchen, and a spacious living room brightened by plenty of large windows.

They had not needed an expert eye to notice that the house needed renovation; there were a few broken shingles on the roof, and the wooden walls were crying out for paint. But they thought that with time, they could repair the damage caused by age and neglect and transform the house into a home, a nest where their love would blossom and their children would grow.

While touring the property, they had come across an old barn made of gray, uncoated bricks, which stood about thirty yards from the house on the other side of the unpaved parking lot.

"I can set up my repair shop here," Jonathan said to his wife.

Sarah nodded, seeing the potential of the barn as a place where he could repair his customers' vehicles and park the two antique cars that he hoped to restore, once he found the time.

The house stood in a rural region, on the outskirts of Corralitos, a small town in central California. The roads in the area were narrow and partially damaged, and in the last section leading to their land, the paved road turned to dirt, crossing a little creek over an old, narrow, concrete bridge.

Jonathan and Sarah knew that the property sat right on the San Andreas Fault. Still, one month after touring the property, they moved in and started to fix their new country home.

They had found that despite the somewhat dangerous location, there were other houses in the vicinity, and their residents were not frightened of the prospect that a strong earthquake could sweep them away. The tough people who lived in the area strictly guarded their privacy and didn't like anyone meddling in their affairs, which suited Jonathan and Sarah just fine.

CHAPTER 3

Sarah

When Sarah sat in front of the TV, curiously waiting for what was promised to be a remarkable broadcast, she briefly reflected on her own unresolved questions.

At sixteen years old, she was a typical teenager, cheerful and a good and disciplined student. Occasionally, however, she had outbursts of rebelliousness and audacity toward her teachers, which always came as a surprise, for them and also for her.

She woke up one morning, dazed and bewildered, unaware that her world was going to crumble. It took her a while to realize where she was, even though it was her old familiar room. She gazed at the posters of her favorite musical idols hanging on the walls around her. Somehow, they looked out of place and the colors seemed wrong.

She tried hard to remember what happened the previous night but couldn't evoke anything in her mind, as though a gap had opened in the time sequence of her consciousness.

Her bedroom door opened, and her mother entered without knocking.

"*Don't* think I didn't notice that you came home completely drunk last night," her mother snapped.

Sarah was confused and didn't know what to say.

"Such shameful behavior, young lady, will not be tolerated in this house." Her mother exited, slamming the door behind her.

What did I do? Who was I with? Sarah dredged through her memory. During lunch, she chatted with her friend Megan about meeting that evening. She vaguely recalled them sitting in the park, not far from her home. But what else did they do? Did she really get drunk?

She phoned Megan.

"What happened yesterday?" she asked, embarrassed. "It's strange, but I can't remember anything."

But Megan could only confirm that they had indeed met, sat in the park, drank a little beer and gossiped for a while. Nothing unusual. After about an hour, they separated and headed back to their homes.

Time passed.

Sarah never thought that the day would come when her parents would be ashamed of her—so much that they would want to send her away from them to a convent until the disgrace disappeared. They didn't believe her when she said she didn't remember what happened. They did blame her for destroying her life by getting pregnant at such a young age. They claimed that she'd brought shame on the family, that she had been inconsiderate toward them, and that she hurt their reputation as a good, Christian family.

Scared and confused, Sarah arrived at a convent called The Sisterhood of the Holy Cross, located on the outskirts of Phoenix, Arizona. Her parents offered to take her in their car—after they arranged the details of her stay, at least until she gave birth—but she preferred to take a bus, dragging a small suitcase with her. The long bus ride allowed reflecting on the recent puzzling developments. It seemed that just yesterday she had been an optimistic, joyful teenager, and now her world was clouded by uncertainty.

What kind of people—the question burned inside her—*are more concerned about their reputation, about their neighbors' opinion of them, than with their daughter's well-being?* She thought she might never forgive her parents.

The nuns received her with kindness and cordiality. A banner behind the receptionist's desk read, "God is Love." That warmed her heart.

She signed some forms that she didn't bother reading, and handed over a sealed envelope from her parents. She knew the letter contained signed forms, transferring legal guardianship from her parents to the convent.

Then she was taken for a tour of the grounds, shown the

facilities, and given precise explanations of what was expected of her. She went to sleep feeling encouraged and sensing that she had arrived in a community that accepted her as she was and forgave her despite her condition.

***

Sarah liked life at the convent. The sisters, led by the mother superior, treated her with empathy, accepted her with compassion, and didn't judge her for her actions and the circumstances that brought her to the convent.

The nuns and Sarah among them were required to lead an austere way of life, which included work and prayers from the early morning hours until bedtime. Sarah learned that staying busy helped her avoid overthinking about her situation, her ruined dreams, the upcoming birth, and everyone who had betrayed her. She saw the convent as a place of refuge and resentment over her exile gradually changed to gratitude.

She enjoyed the communal prayers and the singing of hymns. Gradually, she felt drawn to the religion itself. She observed that a few of the nuns radiated an inner joy, grace, and love that stemmed from their faith, so they believed, from God, Jesus, Mother Mary, and the Holy Spirit.

She tried to pray with her whole heart and found it difficult. Her parents, despite belonging to an evangelical Protestant denomination, lived a secular life and only visited church on rare occasions, mainly for social reasons.

During her childhood, Sarah had visited church on a few occasions but hadn't connected to the sense of sacredness that the pastor tried to induce. She hadn't found religion alluring, so she'd adopted a secular point of view, accepting that believing in God didn't make sense to her.

The nuns, old and young alike, showered Sarah with affection and compassion. She grew fond of her roommate, a kindred soul named Mona, a young nun with whom she felt a shared destiny. In her early twenties, pretty, and gentle, Mona harbored a deep inner pain. Sarah saw it in Mona's eyes and heard it when Mona cried at night when no one else was awake. A few times Sarah approached Mona, gently. She tried to offer help and lend an ear. But Mona wasn't ready to share.

Sarah felt, perhaps for the first time in her life, that she had arrived at a place where she was accepted for who she was, flaws and everything. She liked wearing a nun's habit: no need to stand out. She took comfort in being surrounded by women. She found that she liked not having men around. With men, she always felt how they would scan her with their eyes, as though undressing her in their minds and imagining her from a sexual perspective.

She was charmed and even slightly in love with the image of Jesus whom she perceived as a merciful and loving figure. She continued to pray with perseverance, read and pondered religious scriptures, and began to think that this was the life that was meant for her. She wondered if, in some mysterious way, she had arrived at the best place to fulfill her destiny.

As Sarah immersed herself in convent life, she started to observe several elements that bothered her. At first, the many paintings that decorated the monastery's walls portraying a crucified Jesus or happy, genderless cherubim flying in the sky above the Savior's birth, struck her as off-putting. Later she found manipulative passages in the religious literature that contradicted her common sense, annoyed her, and disturbed her yearning to achieve perfection and complete integrity in her new path.

One day when Sarah was required to clean and scrub the private living area of the mother superior, she discovered a small door hidden behind a book cabinet. Curious, she opened the door and entered a space quite unlike the modest dwelling of a nun. The hidden room contained soft couches, a large color TV, and a state-of-the-art computer. In an adjacent room, Sarah was surprised to find a small Jacuzzi.

Sarah recognized the hypocrisy between the mother superior's luxurious accommodations and the asceticism forced upon all the other nuns.

As Sarah surveyed the mother superior's lavish hidden chamber, she heard steps approaching from the corridor. Worried she would get caught snooping, her heart pounded as she hurried to escape from the room.

The charm and appeal of convent life faded quickly. Furthermore, Sarah found herself attracted to the few men who visited the monastery, guests and service personnel, and against her will, caught herself fantasizing sexual involvement with one of them.

***

Then came the most difficult experience of her short life.

The delivery of her baby, which took place at a hospital in Phoenix, was not as hard and painful as Sarah had feared. A short time after giving birth to a healthy son, she rested in bed, embracing the baby who was put to her bosom. As she was recovering and feeling elated and amazed by the abundance of love she felt toward her newborn son, she fell into a deep sleep, helped by the painkillers given to her to ease the delivery.

When she awoke, the baby was gone. Panic gripped her, along with an ominous feeling of dread.

"Nurse!" she called, trying to maintain a normal tone of voice. "Nurse, bring me my baby, I need to feed him."

A nurse, accompanied by the convent's mother superior, entered the room. Both of them wore somber facial expressions.

"What's going on here?" Sarah shouted, frightened. "Where is my baby? Bring him to me now!"

The nurse locked her gaze with Sarah's and held it. Her voice held both compassion and finality as she said, "Your son has been given to an adoptive family."

"No way!" Sarah protested. "He's *mine*, only mine! Not

anybody else's!"

"We've acted according to the contract that you and your parents agreed upon and signed," the mother superior said, her expression changing from somber to righteousness. "Sarah, you cannot give the child the life that he deserves."

Sarah screeched in outrage and flung herself from the bed. The open back of her hospital gown flapped as she ran down the hospital's corridors in a frantic state, searching in vain for her baby. The head nurse dispatched two orderlies to bring her back. They had a hard time restraining her. She wildly kicked and scratched, like a wounded animal, until they managed to overpower her. They immobilized her while a nurse injected her with a potent tranquilizer.

She wept when she woke and remembered the dream in which she saw herself turn to God and ask, "Why?"

When she returned to the convent, she felt lifeless, apathetic, and disinterested, as if the power of life had been sucked out of her. She refused to get up from the bed and lay there absorbed with self-pity.

For a whole month, she barely rose from her bed and refused to take part in the convent's activities, including prayers, and choir practice. Thoughts of heresy, rebellion, and revenge—directed at the mother superior—consumed her mind. But the bitterness inside her found no outlet, perhaps because she didn't have the strength.

The nuns allowed Sarah the indolence of her deep

depression, and her friend Mona brought food and smiles of affection to the room they shared. Her thoughts dwelled upon the son who had been taken away from her before she even had the chance to know him. Daniel, she called him, though she never spoke the name aloud.

Very slowly, the power of life returned to flow through her body and begin the healing process. One morning, she got up early and went for a trip outside the monastery's grounds. She spent the day in the surrounding nature trails, hiking aimlessly, immersed in deep thoughts. As evening approached, she climbed to the top of a rounded, grassy hill, where she sat on the ground for a long time. She looked at the mountains far away, and the city in front of her and she came to a clear realization that she was not destined to be a nun.

Later, she requested and was granted an appointment with the mother superior. When she walked into the office of the head of the convent, she saw that the place was decorated with crosses, statues, and ornate paintings. It all looked phony to her. Sarah looked at the woman with disdain and disrespect and saw her as the one responsible for the horrible despoilment she had suffered.

"I'm leaving," she announced, feeling contempt for the nun.

"Sarah, my dear," the mother superior looked surprised, "this is not the time for critical and fateful decisions. You have gone through an ordeal which you're trying to understand. One day you'll see that everything has a reason, and God wants only what's best for you."

"I didn't come to argue," Sarah said in an arid tone. "This is not the kind of life I want."

"If you leave now," the mother superior threatened, "you will never know the truth and the meaning of life. Nor will you find peace and harmony."

"Are you finding peace and harmony in your life?" Sarah rebutted, remembering the Jacuzzi, the computer, and the television, but she didn't bother telling what she knew. "At least I'm going to experience life, not run away from it."

***

When Sarah returned to St. Louis, Missouri, she felt no need to move back in with her parents. She moved to a rented apartment and turned away from religion. But despite the harsh experience of having her son robbed from her, she carried with her a subtly positive feeling, a tiny ray of light that endured from her time at the convent. She didn't forget that at the nunnery she had met nuns with faith-filled hearts who'd embodied love, joy, and light. She wondered whether she, too, would ever taste that grace.

And Jesus, who was he? She remembered that when she lay in bed bursting with thoughts of heresy, she'd looked at his image on the wall. For some reason, she never blamed him for the actions of the mother superior, who had been so utterly unloving and inconsiderate when she took advantage of Sarah's naivety. In

Sarah's mind, Jesus was not guilty of the wrongdoings of men.

And he, in turn, harbored no resentment toward her—for her bitterness and frustration—and he continued to accept and embrace her with infinite forgiveness and compassion.

Mature, despite her young age, Sarah knew she must seek help for her wounded soul. She tried several therapists who employed various systems of healing and felt lucky when she'd found Alexandra, a clinical psychologist, who treated her with sensitivity and compassion and played a significant role in her recovery. Alexandra helped her understand that to proceed with her life, she had to let go of her painful past and its subsequent bitter emotions, and forgive those who'd harmed her.

"I want to be like you," Sarah told Alexandra after a few months of therapy.

"Like me?" Alexandra wondered.

"A therapist, a psychologist, I want to help people!"

Alexandra looked at her serious young patient and saw the determination in Sarah's facial expression. "I think it would be a brave direction for you," Alexandra smiled at her. "You could be an excellent psychologist because you went through difficult experiences in your life. You know what suffering is which is why you could have true empathy for your patients."

CHAPTER 4

The Broadcast

"Good evening," said Susan Riley, the popular TXB host, as she smiled at her viewers, who were tensely expecting the special broadcast. They waited for entertainment, for a voyeuristic opportunity to see the lives of the rich and famous in order to catch them at their most wretched moment. The renowned broadcaster had hosted news programs for over twenty years. Her beautiful and friendly face, which knew how to look solemn and severe, was recognized all over the country. She had matured during her many years on the screen but still managed to keep a young and vital appearance, in part due to professional makeup and a carefully styled blond hair. Now she gazed at the camera with eyes that conveyed understanding and empathy, and spoke in a low, warm voice.

"This evening we will see an exceptional film, after which there will be a live discussion in the studio," she told her audience, sitting in their soft armchairs in the safety and comfort of their homes. "We all remember the 'trial from the movies' and its controversial outcome."

She recapped the chain of events that had taken place twenty-five years earlier, when many of her viewers had not yet been born, while familiar pictures were projected on the screen: the car chase after Pedro Gonzales's black SUV and the ensuing arrest. "This evening," Susan Riley promised, "after watching the film, the controversy is likely to be resolved once and for all."

Without any commercial break, and after only one sponsored announcement, the film began. Viewers first saw an aerial view of a yard behind a house. It looked like it had been filmed directly from above, and from a great distance—perhaps from an airplane, or maybe a satellite—no explanation was given. For a few moments, no activity occurred which might have increased viewer suspense and expectations. Branches of the trees gently swayed in the wind. A dog ran through the yard and disappeared from the picture's frame. The film was in black-and-white, without sound, and had a mediocre picture quality. Yet, despite the far-from-perfect resolution, viewers could perceive minor details that added credibility to the show: several tables and chairs scattered around, a broom leaning against the wall, and a few gardening tools and a water hose resting on the lawn behind the house.

After a long moment, two people came out of the house: a woman and a man. The woman, her bright hair tossed by the breeze, held a tray in her hands. The couple sat at a small, round table, and served themselves what looked like ice cream or

30

pudding into small bowls. A few minutes passed. They seemed to be talking peacefully and enjoying their desserts. At one point the man leaned toward the woman as if to whisper in her ear, and caressed her shoulder.

A black SUV pulled into an adjacent alley right behind the house and stopped. A person came out of the car. He wore a white baseball cap that hid his face. He nimbly made his way along the fence that surrounded the house and yard, stopped, and appeared to peek through a slit in the fence, examining what was transpiring inside. Immersed in their conversation, the couple didn't notice him.

After a few minutes, the unidentified person leaped over the fence. The couple's attention was immediately drawn to him as he swiftly made his way to where they sat. The woman got up from her chair, walked toward the intruder and confronted him. From the woman's body language and hand movements, it looked like she was very upset and ordered the trespasser to leave. This was evident even though the film was broadcast without sound or a narrator's voiceover.

The invader stood motionless as if listening to the woman. Suddenly, he pulled out a knife; this was clear despite the camera's apparent distance and position. In a swift movement, he charged forward and stabbed the woman in the neck without hesitation. The woman collapsed, her hands clasping the point of injury, as a dark pool of blood spread across the ground.

The intruder turned his attention to the man and moved toward him with quick, confident steps. The man jumped to his feet and lifted his chair in an effort to defend himself from the fast-moving attacker, who now circled around him, with the knife in his hand. The man tried to strike the assailant with the chair, but the assailant dodged it. The assailant lunged forward, and in a fierce movement with his right hand, stabbed the man in the stomach. The assailant then continued thrusting, aiming at the man's upper body, until the man collapsed, drenched in blood.

The murderer spun around and returned to the woman, noticing she was alive and trying to crawl toward the house. He stabbed her several times until she, too, ceased moving. The dog circled around the killer, apparently barking and running amok, but not daring to get closer to the slayer.

The murderer aimed a kick at the dog, then ran in the direction from where he'd come, effortlessly hurdled the fence, and got into his SUV. The vehicle moved forward, out of the film's picture frame. The broadcast abruptly ended.

"We will be back after a short break," Susan Riley, eyes wet with tears, promised her viewers. The program switched to commercials.

CHAPTER 5

Jonathan

Lying on his back under the pickup truck that he was fixing, a long Phillips screwdriver in his hand, Jonathan knew that right there, inside the inner guts of the machine, in a place that most people would find unpleasant—that's where he felt safe and protected from the hostile world.

He remembered that panic attacks could arise without warning and flood him with a deep-seated horror.

For many years, Jonathan hadn't known if his brother Walter, two years older than he, was fond of him or harbored a concealed bitterness toward him. He wondered whether Walter had cause to resent him. Frequently he asked himself whether he bore any blame for the horrible car accident that killed their parents.

Four-year old Walter hadn't been in the car on that fateful drive. Jonathan, who was just two years old, rode in the back seat, secured in a child safety seat. Perhaps he had cried and distracted them, causing the head-on collision?

He had only the faintest memory of the horrific crash. In truth, he wasn't even sure whether it was a credible memory or an early childhood dream. In an image fixed in his mind, he saw himself sitting in the back seat of a car when suddenly he saw a massive object getting closer at a very high speed. In a split-second, he heard his mother scream in panic, and then he felt a terrible blow and sharp pain. Next followed, awful and strange breaking noises, and the indistinct voices of people—frantic, terrified, and agitated.

He had emerged from the accident almost unharmed, suffering only minor scratches, thanks to the specially made toddler seat in which he had been fastened, or so he was told. But he knew that wasn't true. He *had* been harmed, and he carried the emotional damage well into adulthood.

At times he was struck by a strange feeling, an ambiguous sensation that he had a hard time defining. An inner voice somehow related to the accident whispered that the mending of his body and mind was not complete. A tiny gap remained—a narrow crevasse through which he had access to something very different, perhaps to a mysterious, secret world. On occasions, when the world was very still and quiet, he could almost grasp the intangible matter in his conscious mind, but it always evaded him.

After their parents' death, their grandmother took the two orphans into her home. She lovingly took care of them and made sure all their needs were met, until she passed away when Jonathan was seven years old. Now wards of the state, the children were sent to separate foster homes. Walter had been fortunate, as he landed in a supportive family who raised him with love and compassion and adopted him as their son. He received a quality education and learned to play the piano.

Jonathan hadn't been so lucky. He was shuffled from one foster home to another and finally found himself with the Fenwick family, who exemplified the worst traits of a foster family. He ran away from their house time after time and even thought of throwing himself under the wheels of a train to put an end to his misery.

The forced separation estranged the two brothers. Each resented the other. Jonathan felt that Walter didn't defend him, fight for him, and come to his aid when the social workers had separated them and sent him to a foster home with evil people. Walter held a deep feeling of bitterness toward Jonathan, but he didn't know why. He thought it might have stemmed from the accident, from the fact that Jonathan had been with their parents until the end, while he hadn't been able to say goodbye.

Jonathan had met Sarah when he was hospitalized in a mental institution for two months, due to uncontrolled panic attacks that affected his ability to function in the competitive world. Sarah, a clinical psychologist at the institution, took care of him and treated him with unhindered compassion. During therapy sessions, the two had felt a special bond build between them, connecting them with invisible threads. They sensed a great attraction to one another on the physical level, as well as on the mental and spiritual planes. They were two lonely souls who had found the union they had yearned for during many years.

He loved to gaze into her eyes when they reflected the affection and empathy she felt for him. His spirit cried out to her and opened toward her, and he wondered whether the feeling was mutual. Sarah's expression conveyed inner wisdom and insight in a way he had a hard time grasping, feeling at times that he was in the presence of an old priestess. He also loved and was attracted to her sexy body, her shiny brown skin, and her sensuality.

Every day he looked forward to his sessions with her, which filled him with renewed optimism. At night he reflected on their time together and longed to hold her in his arms.

"I feel that life isn't fair," he told her in one of their sessions.

She affectionately looked into his eyes and smiled.

"I know that other people experience difficulties," he continued, "but my life's circumstances are unusually harsh."

"Life is what we make out of the circumstances that come our way," She responded. "Your task now is to let go of what had happened in the past, as harsh as it might have been, and focus on the positive qualities of your life."

"But the circumstances can be overwhelming," he said.

"You don't have to control those circumstances," she said, "just how *you* respond to them."

Jonathan feared falling in love and worried that Sarah was just a sympathetic person doing her job without sharing the same feelings. When he experienced a significant improvement in his condition, he believed it was mostly due to her compassionate care.

For her part, Sarah knew that it was wrong, even unethical, for a psychologist to have a romantic relationship with a patient. For several weeks, she contemplated the issue, considered the possible penalties, and consulted with her sister, who was her best friend in the world. After she had thoroughly examined the unforeseen development, she believed that after everything she had gone through and after the heartbreak she had suffered when her son was taken away from her, she deserved to be happy. She decided to explore that special attraction for her handsome and sensitive patient, regardless of the consequences.

After Jonathan left the institution, the two continued to meet each other and nurture their love. Before long, they moved in together. When they saw that life together was valuable and beneficial for both of them, they decided to tie the knot in a modest wedding.

Jonathan wondered why Sarah decided to bind her life to his because he recognized his instability. He remembered how the girls in high school fancied him for his good looks even when they worried that he was weird. He thought that, perhaps, Sarah did, too.

Both wanted children, but a long time passed since their wedding and Sarah did not conceive. They saw specialists that examined them together as well as separately and underwent several different fertility treatments. The doctors determined that there was no physiological problem with either of them, yet the years passed, and they remained childless. Sarah made it clear that she was willing to get pregnant via a sperm donor, but Jonathan adamantly objected to the idea. He wanted a child of his own blood whom he could love and nurture. He wanted to give his son or daughter everything that he had never had.

CHAPTER 6

The Broadcast

Illinois Police Officer Reginald Tucker of the Springfield Police Department knew the Pedro Gonzales case very well. He had been just a student at the police academy during the investigation and the trial, but he had diligently followed the developments of the affair, mesmerized by the turns of events.

When he sat in front of the TV and watched TXB's special broadcast, he did not doubt the authenticity of the film, despite the mediocre quality of the video clip.

This was important, not because of its implications for Gonzales, but because of what it suggested to Tucker about another case.

About fifteen years after that notorious trial, Tucker conducted a police investigation in a complicated case that had never been solved. In that incident, the body of Scott Jenkins, a wealthy manufacturer and businessman, had been found in his car in a desolate parking lot, with a suicide letter. Police experts determined that the letter was forged, but even with considerable efforts, the police never succeeded in bringing anyone to trial.

Tucker questioned everyone who'd had a conflict with the man or could have benefited from his death. He'd interrogated the beautiful, young wife who had inherited most of the fortune, his son, daughter, ex-wife, business partners, and competitors. He'd tried to find the motive for the murder among the victim's official business dealings and his illegal transactions, about which Tucker had obtained reliable information.

Everyone vehemently denied any involvement in the killing, and all the suspects had produced solid alibis. So the case remained unsolved.

After watching the TXB broadcast, however, it occurred to the experienced police officer that the technology used to shed light on the Gonzales incident might also yield results in the unsolved Jenkins case.

He called the TXB network center, introduced himself, and asked to speak to the producer of that broadcast.

The secretary who answered the call took his details and politely told him that they'd get back to him at the earliest possible time.

The following morning, Tucker received a call at his branch of the police department from a man who identified himself as Walter Lindsey, producer of the much-talked-about televised event. Lindsey asked, in a businesslike yet friendly manner, what the policeman wanted. The decorated officer briefly talked about the circumstances of his past investigation and asked whether there was a chance that, in the same way that TXB had attained a film that documented the Gonzales case, they could get footage that recorded the Jenkins occurrence. Tucker held little expectations of success; but he thought that if TXB couldn't help, at least he wouldn't be worse off.

Walter Lindsey sounded interested and asked a few questions about the different aspects of the investigation and the suspects. He wanted accurate information about the time and place of the murder. He paused after each answer as if taking the time to write down the details.

"I'll check and see whether we can help the police," Lindsey said. "At this stage, I do not promise anything, and I must be clear that, if we do attain the requested documentation, the film will be presented to the public in a televised program."

"A televised program?" The police officer was alarmed.

"Our condition," Lindsey calmly explained, "is that we'll hold a studio interview with you in which you'll present the story and tell our viewers how our contribution helped solve the investigation."

Reginald Tucker was not a public figure and didn't strive to be one, but he saw no better alternative.

"All right," he conceded, knowing that this was his best—and possibly—only option, if he wished to get a break in the unsolved case. He detested the idea that the guarded investigation was going to transform into a media circus, but he was also excited by the chance of seeing the chain of events with his own eyes, after dedicating so many hours in his attempt to solve the puzzle.

A week later, Tucker sat at his kitchen table drinking coffee and going over the weekend edition of the local newspaper, *The State Journal-Register.*

He found an article in which a reporter examined the sensational broadcast of the Gonzales case and tried to analyze it. The reporter wrote:

Points to consider regarding TXB's special broadcast.

a) These certainly seem like satellite surveillance images. How could the TV network have gotten hold of these images from so many years ago? Are they even stored that long?

b) Doesn't this create huge questions about privacy and national security? If these are NSA images, were they leaked? If they're *not* NSA, who has that technology and why doesn't the government know about it?

c) What happens now with the court case that resulted out of this incident? Will it re-open? Or is Gonzales protected by the double-jeopardy clause?

The phone rang. When Tucker looked at the screen, he was surprised to see the name, Walter Lindsey.

"I've got good news for you," Lindsey announced. "I'm in possession of a short film that shows the incident that you investigated."

A seasoned investigator who knew how to keep his composure, Tucker had to exert considerable effort to contain his excitement. "When will I be able to see the film?"

"You'll have to come to New York," Lindsey answered. "According to our agreement, we'll meet in the network's studio, watch the clip together, and film you while you watch the clip for the first time."

The police officer groaned but remembered that these were the conditions to which he agreed. Still, he tried his luck. "I'm in Springfield," he said. "Could you send me a copy for a preview?"

"I'm sorry," came the unwavering denial. "If you want to see the documentation, you'll have to come to us."

Tucker had no choice. He knew he would have to go through the annoying saga if he wanted to achieve his goal. That same day he cleared his schedule, entrusted assignments to his deputy, and booked a flight to New York.

***

Reginald Tucker arrived in New York that evening and checked-in to a modest three-star hotel, which he knew from his last visit to the city, courtesy of a police conference. He ate his dinner at an inexpensive diner, a small effort not to waste taxpayer funds. Before he went to sleep, he called his wife, updated her on his schedule, and asked her to kiss their three kids for him.

The following morning precisely at 9:00 a.m., he entered through the glass doors of the TXB network central building. Ready for the meeting, he approached the reception desk and stated the purpose of his visit. Within a few minutes, Walter Lindsey walked toward him, smiling, and shook his hand.

"In the first session, you'll watch the clip, and we'll record you watching it." The producer reiterated the process as they made their way through the corridors and elevators of the immense building. "We will also interview you, but at this stage, none of the materials will be aired. We don't want to jeopardize the investigation, which we expect to resume following the incriminating findings that you are about to encounter."

"I can hardly wait," the police officer said.

"Once the investigation ends," the producer continued, "we'll conduct another televised meeting with you in the studio, during which you'll tell our viewers how our documentation helped you."

Tucker nodded, and he thought that if the new information helped him solve the case, then it would justify another trip to New York, despite the trouble involved and his dislike of the mass media.

"Just one thing before we proceed," Tucker said, deciding to clear up what was bothering him. "Could you tell me where you got the film?"

Lindsey smiled at him and replied, "I'm not at liberty to discuss this issue."

Lindsey took his guest to a small, round studio, where the famous host, Susan Riley, sat. She got up from her chair, smiled, and shook the police officer's hand. Tucker sat on the couch as directed. Between them, a small glass table held a jug of water and glasses.

The host asked Tucker to tell viewers at home about the case that he had dealt with—the Jenkins case.

Reginald Tucker didn't feel comfortable exposing the details of his unsolved investigation, but he reminded himself that he had agreed to the terms set by Lindsey. To get the breakthrough information that would finally solve the case that had disturbed him for more than a decade, he was willing to bend a few rules.

The host treated Tucker with her familiar cordiality and asked him several intelligent questions in her warm, empathic voice. The police officer thought that she must have been a professional actress, because he couldn't tell whether her intimate friendliness was authentic or faked.

At Susan Riley's signal, the video started. Reginald Tucker noticed two cameras recording his every expression and twitch while he watched the big screen in front of him.

At first sight, the footage looked similar in quality, style, and angle of filming to the video documenting the murder of Melisa Robinson Gonzales: black-and-white, without sound, and of mediocre resolution. But despite the imperfect quality and the unusual angle, straight from above, viewers could perceive even minute details with certainty.

A car drove down a straight, two-lane highway. Traffic was sparse. Tucker identified the vehicle: the luxury Mercedes owned by the murder victim. The car turned onto a side road and, after a short while, stopped at a small parking lot that Tucker recognized. It was where the body had been discovered. In the parking lot, there was just one other vehicle, which looked like an SUV, and the Mercedes parked close to it. Tucker didn't recognize the SUV. The door of the Mercedes opened on the passenger's side and a woman got out. Tucker identified her as Jenkins' young wife. An unidentified man stepped out of the SUV, approached the woman, politely shook her hand, and apparently exchanged words with her. The unidentified man then approached the driver's side window of the Mercedes, bent over, and appeared to talk with the driver, still sitting in his car. After a few minutes, the unidentified man suddenly drew a gun and shot the man in the Mercedes at point-blank range.

The woman ran toward the gunman, waving her hands, apparently shocked and hysterical. He caught her in his free arm and held her against his body. She beat her fists against the shooter's chest. The shooter rubbed his hand up and down her back, as though attempting to calm her. When she appeared to have quieted down, the two stood motionless, hugging each other for several moments.

They separated, opened the doors of the Mercedes, and got busy, probably working on making the murder look like a suicide. At one point, the gunman entered his victim's car and the woman remained outside. Upon exiting the vehicle, the murderer looked upward for a split second.

"Stop!" the police officer called out. The film was immediately paused. "Rewind please," Tucker said impatiently. "I want to look at this guy's face."

His request was obeyed, and the picture froze on the shooter's face. Even with the mediocre quality of the footage, the police officer identified the murderer with certainty. He was the senior partner in the victim's company. Tucker had questioned him intensely for hours, but the man provided a solid alibi, as his wife swore that they were together in their house at the time of the murder.

When the film continued, the man and the woman entered the SUV, and then the vehicle traveled out of the picture's frame. The film ended, and the lights were switched on in the small studio.

Blinking against the sudden brightness while digesting the disturbing images, Tucker heard the producer stating that the interview would begin. Tucker nodded.

"Well," Susan Riley prompted. "Does the film help in your investigation?" The tone of her voice was friendly and caring.

"Yes," Tucker confirmed, his expression somber. "Actually, the film reveals the details that I needed to solve the case."

"Do you know the identities of the individuals who were shown in the film?" the host asked.

"Yes," he replied. He thought that this was just another movie to these TV people, entertainment for the masses, no different than any police series they broadcast daily. But not for him. A man had lost his life, apparently because of greed. Tucker struggled with mixed emotions. He was grateful to these shallow media representatives for providing him access to incredible technology and helping him solve an old, vexing case. However, their pointless questions kept him from his work. He needed to act on what he just saw and arrest the despicable murderer and his accomplice.

CHAPTER 7

Michael

Ever since early childhood, Michael wondered whether he was normal. He didn't appear different than the other children in his kindergarten. He liked the same computer games and TV shows as his friends. However, deep inside, he felt foreign, an outsider. He wondered if other kids also had those odd feelings.

He was smart, serious, diligent, and disciplined most of the time, but every now and then he experienced outbursts of anger that bordered on a loss of control. He didn't know where that rage came from, surely not from his emotionally restrained parents. After these eruptions, he always felt sorry, regretful and ashamed of his behavior, of insulting people and saying things he didn't mean to say.

His parents loved and accepted him unconditionally, and he loved them with all his heart. But occasionally, a deep-seated worry crept into his mind, a concern of an unknown origin, and as hard as he had tried, he couldn't ignore or suppress the bubbling suspicion that he had another family.

He felt that way even before he noticed, much to his dismay, how different he looked compared to his parents. His father and mother had light skin, while he boasted a swarthy complexion. He also perceived that his hair was black and wavy, whereas theirs was blond and straight.

He would stand in front of the mirror examining his reflection, looking at his blue eyes, and wonder where he came from.

When he was six years old, they told him. Michael never forgot the day when his parents sat with him in the living room for that conversation. He, who always loved their focused attention, felt uncomfortable. He sensed that something was wrong that day, which came after the happy day when they bought him his first bicycle, the blue one he wanted so much.

"We love you, Michael, very, very, very much," his mother said. The dread inside of him grew.

His father nodded and smiled at him affectionately. Then the smile faded, and his expression turned solemn. "We have to tell you the truth because it is important that you know."

Michael squirmed with discomfort. His parent looked equally uncomfortable.

"When you came into the world," his mom said, and stopped. She stroked his curls, took a deep breath to steady herself, and tried again. "You came to the world in the belly of another woman…" Tears welled up in her eyes as she took a deep breath and continued. "That woman loved you very much, but she couldn't take care of you. We could, and we wanted you to be our son so much. We love you."

"You being adopted doesn't make you any less our son," his father said, voice cracking. He reached over to hold his mother's hand, and then leaned forward to take Michael into their shared embrace.

Adopted!!!

The dreadful sound of the word hit him hard and then it remained hanging in the living room's space. Once expressed, it sealed little Michael's faith, and there was no turning back.

Finally, he understood why he felt so … different. He tried to be brave, but tears still trickled down his cheeks. He wasn't utterly surprised, but he felt a profound sadness because he wanted, hoped, and yearned to be an unseparated part of them. And now, despite their assurances of love, apprehension crept into his young mind. He worried that events over which he had no control might separate his parents from him.

"Wouldn't you want to meet your *real* mother?" One of his friends at school who was also an adopted child once asked Michael.

"I see her every day," he replied without hesitation. Michael recognized that his parents loved him and took care of all his needs. But deep inside, he admitted to the need to meet his birth mother and knew it would never go away.

In his mind, there was a faint memory from his early life. In fact, he wasn't sure whether it was a credible memory or a primordial dream. In his vision, he saw himself at his mother's bosom a short time after birth. He was cuddled and embraced by her soft, warm body, feeling a connection of endless love engulfing them together, while they drifted into a deep and intimate sleep.

In a successive vision, he awoke alone, surrounded by strangers, strong, blinding lights, and scary noises. He cried, yelled, and screamed for his mother, desperately longing to return to the warm and loving place from where he'd been brutally pulled. The end of his vision always brought with it a primitive resolution: to always search for his mom and strive to return to her.

***

When Michael was three years old, his mother became pregnant for the first time in her life, and subsequently gave birth to a baby girl. Apprehensive about the change in the family's composition, little Michael expressed his worries to his parents:

"Are you still going to love me?"

His parents did their best to assure him.

"Our hearts are big enough to love both our children," his mother promised, and his father nodded.

Michael soon got attached to his little sister. Even when envious of her resemblance to their parents, his affection for her remained strong. He loved to play with her and thought it was his duty to protect his little sister.

The parents did their best to divide their love and attention between their two children, but at times, they dedicated a little more of their time and energy to Michael, to compensate him for not being their biological son.

One time, when Michael was about eight years old, he quarreled with Raymond, the neighbors' son, usually his good friend. They played on the lawn in front of the house. Frustrated about losing in soccer, Raymond provoked Michael by saying, "Lily is your parents' *real* daughter."

Michael lashed out at him and furiously pounded Raymond with his little fists. He didn't stop even when Raymond's nose bled.

Hearing the sounds of the brawl, Michael's mother rushed out of the house to separate the young fighters, and she had a tough time pulling her son from his wounded opponent. She was very angry at Michael; but, when he told her the reason for his outburst, she immediately softened, hugged him, and said, "Oh Michael, I love you so much. You don't have to take to heart stupid comments like that. He probably didn't even mean it."

At the age of twelve, Michael learned to play the guitar, and two years later, he started a band with a few of his friends. They liked to perform old songs from the Sixties and Seventies. Michael also tried his hand at songwriting, lyrics as well as music. He didn't sing because he didn't believe in his vocal capability, so his friend Raymond became the lead singer, enjoying the spotlight.

Michael preferred his place in the back, slightly in the shadows. He liked to watch his songs and the sounds of his guitar being released into the world. The songs he wrote mostly expressed a longing for love and unity, sometimes revealing feelings of alienation from the world and strangeness among people. From time to time he also wrote songs that reflected a tendency to rebel against conventional thinking.

His father, Ruben Evans, held a managerial position in a bank, and his mother, Rose, was a high school history teacher. In their spacious house in a suburb of San Diego, California, they led a comfortable life. Michael knew that his parents would do anything they could to meet his needs and fulfill his wishes.

More than once he surprised his parents with his sharp thinking, his excellent grades, and his considerate manners. His teachers appreciated his diligence. They were somewhat apprehensive about his outbursts of rage, but these faded as he matured.

He became the editor of his high school's newsletter. From time to time, he sent astute articles to a local newspaper, where he expressed a solid liberal point of view. He was handsome, with his blue eyes, black hair, and athletic body, and as he neared high school graduation, he started to think about a career in journalism, perhaps as a TV news broadcaster.

CHAPTER 8

The Broadcast

In a series of previews and trailers, each more sensational and titillating than the last, the TXB network presented their plan to air a special TV exposé in which a 10-year old murder case would be solved.

"They thought they could kill and escape unpunished," said the announcer of the trailer in a dramatic tone, "but they were wrong."

Producer Walter Lindsey expected high ratings, but he knew there was no chance he'd recreate the success of the first broadcast, the one that documented the murder of Melisa Robinson Gonzales.

***

"Good evening." Susan Riley, the popular host, looked at her viewers, through the camera's eye. As in the previous broadcast, TXB aired the program at 10:00 p.m., and once again, they warned that the show was not intended for children's viewing.

"This evening," Susan Riley said, "I would like to welcome our guest, investigative police officer Reginald Tucker of the Springfield, Illinois, Police Department."

The camera zoomed out to include her guest, who nodded and flashed a nervous smile.

"Officer Tucker," she turned to him, "please tell our viewers about the incident that you investigated about ten years ago."

Reginald Tucker turned to the camera as previously instructed and recited the story of the case he had investigated: the murder of the manufacturer and wealthy businessman, Scott Jenkins. He listed the reasons why the case had never been solved. The few viewers who knew the humble and dedicated policeman could tell that the TV studio was not his natural surroundings and that he preferred to be somewhere else.

"Please tell us about the breakthrough in the investigation," the host said.

"After I saw the broadcast of the Gonzales case, I approached TXB and asked if they could use the same technology to get documentation of the case I investigated years ago. They indeed succeeded in obtaining the material, which led to solving the case."

Sharp-sighted viewers noticed the police officer's reluctance to divulge details regarding an ongoing investigation.

He gave his side of the story as if against his will. He seemed somewhat annoyed and didn't make an effort to hide his lack of enthusiasm for cooperating with the voyeuristic media.

"We are now going to watch the footage," Susan Riley said, "and then we'll come back to talk to the officer, whom we thank for being with us here tonight."

The film rolled, while Tucker explained in clipped, clinical words what was occurring on screen. "This is the car of the late Mr. Jenkins. And that's his wife, Mrs. Helene Jenkins," he added, when she was seen stepping out of the car. "And this is the murder suspect," he said when the man came out of his vehicle. "And here he shoots Mr. Jenkins to death."

The film froze at a point where it was possible to see the face of the shooter, and Tucker indicated in a dry tone, "And here you can see the face of the alleged murderer."

"We will be back after a short break," Susan Riley promised her viewers when the clip ended.

After the commercials, Officer Tucker updated viewers on the case: both suspects had been arrested. The victim's business partner was charged with murder and perjury; and the victim's wife also faced charges for her role as an accomplice.

"At first the suspects denied any involvement in the killing," the police officer said. "But when they were shown the film, they broke down, confessed, and also participated in a police recreation of the incident."

Reginald Tucker concluded by saying that the suspects were under arrest, and the trial was scheduled for the following month.

***

Law enforcement officers all over the United States watched the broadcast. Many considered the possibilities that TXB's new technology offered and how it could assist in cracking unsolved cases on which they had labored for years.

Many viewers thought the TV network should reveal the source of the broadcasts and refute emerging charges that the films were fabricated. In the press, a limited number of commentaries alleged TXB's lack of ethics in the immoral manipulation of viewers and intrusion upon people's privacy by photographing them without their consent.

CHAPTER 9

Jonathan and Sarah

The low price of the property made it possible for Jonathan and Sarah to become homeowners when they were only about thirty years old. At the time, it seemed like fate had been kind to them.

Most of their property was rough, mountainous, and forested. A small creek flowed between the mountains and hills. During the summer, the water flow in the creek was shallow and calm, and in the course of the rainy season, its level rose, and the current grew forceful and dangerous to pass.

On weekends, they liked to take long hikes in the forests of their land. Here they were, masters of the land, touring around their territory with their loyal dog. At that time, they only had one dog, a female Doberman named Princess, who always waited for their hikes with great enthusiasm.

It wasn't a hospitable environment. Trees blocked direct sunlight almost everywhere, and the mountainous location forced them to climb steep trails and go down slippery slopes. Despite the tough terrain, the couple loved their land. Sarah felt that it was her duty to preserve and protect the trees from loggers who coveted the timber and offered them a lot of money for a permission to cut the trees.

They enjoyed their hikes and continued with the weekly activity even when tensions arose in their relationship and hung like dark clouds over their heads. Those walks were their time together, away from the din and turmoil of the world that threatened to invade and undermine what they had managed to build together.

The forest had its magic. Walking through the woods, they observed how lights and shadows blended with the soughing of the wind through the branches overhead and the calls of birds warning of intruders. The forest inspired introspection, caution, and a sense of being close to something unknown, which might hide in the shrubberies, concealing dangerous possibilities, unresolved secrets, and unrealized opportunities. They felt that the forest dictated circumstances in which a person had to blend in with nature, to become part of the whole with sharp senses and alert reflexes.

By the creek, Jonathan and Sarah looked for sunshine spots where they sat down for a picnic. They watched the fish swimming in their separate world and listened to the relaxing sound of flowing water. Sometimes they spread open a blanket and made love.

***

On one such hike, they climbed a steep hill. Sarah noticed, and drew her husband's attention, that Princess was unusually reluctant to walk further with them. Princess usually ran forward in front of them, excited and enthusiastic.

"Leave her be," Jonathan said. "She'll follow if she wants."

Sarah shrugged and said nothing more on the matter.

As they climbed up the hill, the forest became thicker, denser, and almost impenetrable. Before long, the two had a hard time passing through; still, they pushed through the brush, because they thought they should get to know all the corners of their land, even the less friendly locations. Near the top of the hill, they noticed that the trees grew in a straight line, without the slightest curve. The trees were so close to one another that they created a natural wall. Both Jonathan and Sarah got the impression that the trees were doing their best to protect something and prevent passage from anyone who was not allowed.

All at once, the vegetation ended. They stepped from the forest into a glade, an exposed, round clearing of about forty feet in diameter. The sun was directly overhead in a blue sky, gently warming them. The place was very quiet, with just a minor breeze soughing around, as if shielding the spot.

About halfway to the middle of the circular clearing, a big rock protruded about four feet above the ground. Obviously chiseled, it looked like a megalith.

They realized, without needless talking, that they had reached an ancient worship site, and they felt that the spot was somehow different from their everyday reality.

"What is this strange place?" Sarah whispered.

"I once saw a rock like this," Jonathan said.

"Where?"

"I'm not sure. Perhaps in Machu Picchu."

The dog cautiously peeked from behind the trees but didn't dare enter the glade. Jonathan paced around, examining every step, attentively surveying every piece of land that might point to the purpose of the odd site.

Sarah sat on the ground facing the big rock. She crossed her legs, stretched her back, and closed her eyes, trying to feel the mysterious place and connect to it. She recalled their trip to Peru.

***

After their wedding, Jonathan and Sarah experienced the happiest time of their lives. They were young and optimistic, despite their past difficulties. Their love blossomed, and the pregnancy issue had not yet mushroomed into a central worry that would threaten to suffocate the light they shared. They enjoyed financial stability since both of them worked, and their cost of living was minimal. So, they allowed themselves to fulfill old wishes and go on trips abroad.

The first trip was to Peru since Jonathan wanted to see the famous Nazca Lines and the site of Machu Picchu. After arriving in Nazca, they boarded a small plane that took them on a flight over the mysterious desert geoglyphs.

Jonathan's fascination for the Nazca Lines stemmed from the book *Chariots of the Gods*, by Erich von Däniken. The Swiss writer claimed that intelligent aliens from other worlds significantly influenced human civilizations.

"The Nazca people never saw their creations in full," Jonathan excitedly told Sarah, "because the only way to observe them is from above. That's why it is a mystery, how were the drawings created and for what purpose?"

Sarah had also found the lines intriguing. "I don't think the lines are related to extraterrestrials," She said. "I assume they were created for some ancient spiritual practice."

"It would have been quite difficult to draw those figures without help from above," Jonathan said.

"Difficult," she said, "but not impossible."

The journey to Machu Picchu, an ancient city from the time when the Inca civilization had thrived, was more challenging. They arrived at the town of Aguas Calientes on a train and spent the night in a motel that wasn't especially clean, not far from a raging river. Sarah wanted to arrive at Machu Picchu early in the morning because her sister, Julie, had told her before the trip that "to see the sunrise at Machu Picchu is a spiritual experience." Sarah promised

Julie to make an effort, although she thought that every sunrise could be an uplifting experience.

They got up at 4:00 a.m. and climbed over winding trails and numerous stairs, on their way to the famous site. Panting, they arrived at the lost city in time to witness the sunrise over the snowy peaks and the vibrant green forests. Indeed, it was a marvelous sight.

They toured the site and listened to explanations by a native guide who spoke English in a heavy local accent.

Although he listened to the guide's patter, Jonathan did not need it. He had prepared for the trip and conducted his own research.

"The Inca people perceived time differently than the conventional Western point of view," he remarked.

"In what way?" Sarah prompted. She knew that he'd studied the subjects they might encounter on the way and would enjoy expounding about them.

"In the West, the perception of time is linear," Jonathan began, seizing the opportunity to show his knowledge. "That means that time exists in three consecutive planes: the past, the present, and the future." Jonathan paused, to let her grasp his point, and continued. "According to the Inca, the past, present, and future do not happen consecutively, but in parallel and exist simultaneously." He looked at the valley spread below, then added, "There was a time when this concept was considered strange and even stupid, as could be expected from uncultured natives, but today, modern science doesn't completely discount it."

Sarah looked at the mountains around them. "And you? What do *you* think?"

"I think," he said, "that there is something to this point of view, although I have a difficult time comprehending it."

Sarah didn't always understand Jonathan's detailed explanations. Although attracted to metaphysics, Jonathan never followed spiritual teachers, participated in meditation workshops, or practiced yoga or Tai chi. His fascination with the sublime was cerebral and expressed through self-directed study.

A couple who arrived at Machu Picchu by bus brought their little boy with them. The child, who looked about four years old, was sleepy, complained that he was hungry, and demanded his breakfast.

"This is not a place for kids," Jonathan whispered.

Sarah looked toward the rising sun and the breathtaking scenery, and thought about her long-lost son, Daniel. Where could he be? And why couldn't she stop thinking about him?

***

Something, a noise perhaps, broke Sarah free from her stream of memories. She looked around. She still sat in front of the massive, partially chiseled rock. The clarity of her memories lingered, powerful and vivid as though she had just relived her experiences in Peru.

The earth trembled. Living on the San Andreas Fault, Sarah and Jonathan had adopted certain resilience to the phenomena and gave that latest rumbling little heed.

Sarah said, "That was interesting."

Jonathan nodded, agreeing with her.

"Let's go," Sarah said, "It is a powerful place, and we should come here only on special occasions."

They made their way down the hill. Immersed in their thoughts, neither spoke.

Jonathan thought about his parents, and how he hadn't been fortunate enough to know them. He wondered if the feeling of guilt he carried was justified.

Sarah thought about her son, Daniel. In her mind, she cried out for him to search for her, so she could hug him and embrace him into her heart. Without him, she was not whole.

That evening, Sarah talked on the phone with her sister Julie, who lived in San Francisco. "Did you feel the earthquake?" Sarah casually asked.

"No," Julie answered. "It must have been only in your area."

CHAPTER 10

Sarah

It started after a Christmas party in the clinic where Sarah worked. Colorful ribbons decorating the largest meeting room created a festive vibe. Members of the staff ate cakes and raised a toast for the New Year.

When the modest celebration ended, Sarah helped to clean and rearrange the room, while staff members were saying goodbye to one another, and wishing each other a good holiday vacation with their families.

Sarah took her time, in no rush to leave the clinic. When asked, she cited a desire to wait out the nagging rain. She would not admit she had no reason to hurry. At thirty-one years old, Sarah still had neither children nor family waiting for her: only her husband, who tended to be withdrawn, especially during the holidays.

As they did in previous years, they had plans to spend Christmas in San Francisco with Julie, her husband Edmond, and their three kids. Julie always invited her sister and brother-in-law.

Sarah thought Julie pitied them.

So, Sarah delayed her departure from the clinic, and perhaps she knew what she was really waiting for. Young Dr. Morgan also hung around, supposedly to finish some paperwork in his office. And when the clinic's door closed and only the two of them remained, they looked at one another and knew that they both desired the same thing. There was no need to waste time and words.

Sarah loathed herself for betraying her husband. She justified cheating as a lack of choice: if Jonathan couldn't give her a baby, she would find someone else who could.

She must get pregnant; she told herself, so that she could remain sane.

Sarah blamed the lack of children on her husband, particularly his continued opposition to artificial means. She refused to give up on motherhood. She convinced herself that, if she succeeded, it would bring happiness to both of them, and Jonathan would forgive her betrayal.

Dr. Morgan looked hesitant, like he was still weighing whether to follow his desire, knowing it was wrong to have sex at work, and with a married woman. Sarah saw that she had to take the lead.

Inching close to him, she gently hugged him. "It's OK," she whispered and smiled into his shy eyes. She tenderly stroked his chest. "Breathe deep," she said.

He obeyed and filled his lungs with air, and she felt how his body awakened and responded to hers. They stepped together into one of the treatment rooms. Sarah swiftly dropped her clothes, knowing that the young man would not be able to resist her charm. Sarah was no longer as thin as she was in her youth, but she thought her womanly curves were ripe and attractive.

She was honest with herself and didn't try to hide her desire for him, coveting his young and innocent body.

He was inexperienced and his response clumsy. While overwhelmed by her aggression and expertise, he expressed appreciation for her body and sexual skill.

Sarah's affair with the young doctor lasted a few months. During that time, she would slip away from her house, making different excuses so that she could meet him. She never fell in love with Dr. Morgan, but she loved the excitement of the affair's forbidden nature.

Worried about the consequences of sex with a subordinate in the workplace, the young doctor ended the relationship. Sarah was not disheartened about ending the affair. She was, however, disappointed by having failed to reach her goal of getting pregnant.

Afterward, she continued to cheat and to feel tormented and hate herself. If the relationship with Dr. Morgan had occurred with some spontaneity, the following affairs came as a result of Sarah's deliberate initiation. She did it as if she were on a mission, fulfilling an undertaking that had nothing to do with love.

Dressed in sexy outfits that emphasized her femininity,

Sarah started going to bars, positioning herself as bait to lure her prey. She didn't go with just anybody but waited to be approached by someone she found appealing in some way.

She assumed that Jonathan knew: she saw it in his eyes, in his behavior, in his constrained rage, and in his withdrawal from her. But he didn't say anything, and Sarah wanted to believe that he understood her, accepted that she wasn't really betraying him.

She regretted making Jonathan sad, hated hurting him—and herself—and she worried that he would find a way to get his revenge. However, the desperate need to have a baby was stronger than her will to resist it. She persuaded herself to think she had no other choice.

Her son, Daniel, had been viciously taken from her a short time after he was born. She still called him Daniel, wondering if it happened to be the name he received from his adoptive parents. She spent much time thinking of him, aching to know where he was, praying he was happy, and wishing the day would come when he would search for and find her.

She must feel it again; she kept telling herself, the immense happiness she fleetingly experienced when she held her child to her bosom. When she would once again embrace that complete, unhindered love in her arms, she vowed she would never give it up. *Nobody* would be able to steal her baby away from her. She would fight to the death to keep her child, and she was prepared to live a life of lies in order to attain that singular goal.

Sarah was keenly aware of her condition. As a psychologist,

she knew she should have sought treatment; otherwise, she was a hypocrite. But she couldn't think of anyone of her peers whom she could trust.

Despite the laws of adoption which she knew very well, she once drove to an adoption agency in San Jose, after scheduling an appointment. Her heart raced as she sat down across from the agency representative. She read the representative's name from her badge: Denise.

"I'm sorry," Denise said after Sarah explained the purpose of her visit. "What you're asking for goes against our strict adoption policies," she added.

"I was a minor," Sarah argued, "and I didn't know what I was signing. My parents made the arrangements without consulting me." For a moment, Sarah felt like the helpless teenager she once was.

Denise's piercing look made Sarah's stomach turn. "You must understand that it could be devastating for your child if you showed up at his door and tried to snatch him from his adoptive family."

Tears rolled down Sarah's cheeks. She saw her world crumble once again, her expectations shattered.

"I'm afraid the law is not on your side," Denise continued. "You just have to wait and hope that one day *he* will look for you."

She reached a low point one night when she met a stranger

in a bar at a nearby town. He bought her a beer, and they had a short conversation in which they got slightly acquainted with one another. He drove to his home, and she followed him in her car. They entered the bedroom which was on the second floor. The sex was short, unexciting, and meaningless. After he finished, the guy—whose name she never bothered to learn—turned to his side of the bed, and immediately fell asleep. She lay there, naked and filled with self-loathing.

As she lay immersed in unproductive self-castigation, she heard the sound of a baby crying. She left the bed and peeked into the adjacent room where she saw a baby in a crib. Entering the room, she wondered, *how could I have not noticed him before?* She cradled the baby against her chest. A wave of sensations, familiar and chilling, flooded her. The baby continued to cry.

She carried the baby back into the man's bedroom, woke him, and said, "The baby needs to be fed."

"What? The baby?" The man spluttered as he came to his senses. "Oh, yeah. There's formula in the fridge. It has to be warmed up."

All of a sudden, Sarah heard the sound of the front door being slammed, followed by the telltale sound of high-heeled shoes on the hardwood floor.

"Oh my God, it's my wife, I thought she's working the night shift," the baby's father whispered in panic. "You've got to run!" He grabbed the baby from her, and led her, or rather pushed her, into a narrow staircase that went from the bedroom's balcony outside into the yard.

Sarah's one-night stand tossed her belongings after her—clothes, shoes, and handbag. With tears of shame in her eyes, Sarah dressed, disgusted by her own actions. She wondered how she had sunk so far; but, she also knew she had no intention of stopping that downward trajectory of shame.

CHAPTER 11

Jonathan

Cars and all their components fascinated Jonathan from an early age. He understood automotive machinery better than people, whose behavior often seemed strange, unpredictable, and vicious.

The challenge of repairing a broken-down vehicle never failed to capture his attention, be it his own vehicle or a car of friends or acquaintances. He knew how to take apart complex components to reach the very root of the problem, correct the problem, and restore the car to an effortless operation, its engine singing a melody that only he could hear.

Cars obeyed him. Their response to his skilled hands contributed to his teenage popularity, especially with high school girls. There were times, when girls who ran into car troubles pleaded with him, "Jonathan, be sweet and help me with my car." He usually agreed, without setting conditions for his services or asking for money. If a girl wanted to compensate him in some way, he gratefully accepted.

After high school, he studied automotive mechanics and

electrical systems. He parlayed his profession into a source of steady income at various repair shops, whose owners always appreciated his contribution, his diligence, and his expertise.

After about ten years of making a living as a car mechanic, a new interest attracted and magnetized him: computers. He liked to solve computer problems, in both software and hardware. He enjoyed taking a computer completely apart and then putting it back together. The computers in his house worked partially dismantled because that way he felt closer to the heart of the wondrous box that produced letters, numbers, and complicated calculations. His computer became an extension of his mind, an elaborate machine that allowed communication, pictures, and sounds, and had at its core a small unit that had only two positions: one and zero, on and off, light and dark, heaven and earth, male and female, life and death… He often let his inquisitive mind explore the possibilities.

In Jonathan and Sarah's estate, inside the big barn near the house, Jonathan built himself a wooden inner chamber to be his computer room. He had an extensive collection of computers, from "ancient" computers running the DOS operating system to state-of-the-art technologies.

Jonathan wanted to implement the computer's abilities and work with sophisticated and powerful programs. From the possibilities that the field of computers offered, he chose to focus on graphic design and introduction to animation. Accordingly, he signed up for evening courses at a college in Soquel, a small town located about half an hour's drive from his home.

He found the studies interesting and challenging, especially the classes on animation. He comprehended the materials easily, and high grades reflected his hard work and talent. The programs obeyed him, as did the instruments when he fixed cars. Within a short time, he was able to create realistic animations with the new tools in his hands. Nevertheless, he realized that while his command of the computer and programs surpassed that of his schoolmates, and even his teachers, his creative ability left much to be desired. His work tended to be very precise but lacked vision and artistic imagination.

At the age of thirty-two, he was noticeably older than most of the students. Even though the youngsters treated him in a friendly manner, he felt out of place—a dinosaur, superannuated. The curriculum was designed for young adults who aspired to develop careers, not for someone who had a genuine interest in the subject matter but none in a diploma. He disliked spending time preparing for exams, and he realized that the commute robbed him of precious time.

After deliberating the issue, he withdrew from college at the end of the second semester and continued to develop his education and skills on his own. He purchased the programs that interested him, as well as instruction books, and persevered in the development of his expertise.

Despite the lack of a degree, Jonathan found a job as a computer technician in a mid-sized factory called Excel-Part, which manufactured parts for the auto industry. The plant was situated outside San Jose, about a thirty-minute drive from his home.

He loved his work, where he isolated and solved complicated problems in software, hardware, networking, and communications. He also responded to simple issues that the users encountered, which he easily solved, patiently and with a smile, and went on his way to the next station, to help users who awaited his help and were always glad to see him.

With time, he gained expertise and proficiency, and his supervisors considered him a loyal, dedicated, and responsible employee.

Jonathan noticed that appreciation from his bosses didn't result in salary increases, and from time to time he felt displeased and bitter. Still, he preferred to focus on his work, to fulfill his duties, and not let frustration affect his work.

"They're taking advantage of you," Sarah commented. She earned more money than he. "With everything you put into the company, the hours of overtime and the responsibility you take, your salary should be much higher."

Jonathan didn't know whether the financial issue diminished his worth in her eyes. Every time he found the courage to ask for a raise, he was told that he could easily be replaced by younger people who were faster and more educated than him. Since the market was indeed saturated with young individuals looking for jobs in his line of work, he accepted that he would have a tough time finding a job elsewhere.

***

When Sarah started to slip away from the house, making different excuses, he knew she betrayed him. Her infidelity deeply saddened him. Sadness turned to fury, and he looked at ways to get revenge, even considering divorce.

He rehearsed his speech. If he could control his anger, he would say, "Pack up your stuff and leave by the end of this week. There's nothing to talk about." If not, then he would say, "Get the hell out of here! You disgust me!" Or something like that.

But always at the dinner table when he intended to confront her, he would look into her eyes and see the love she felt for him, and he sensed her remorse. So, he remained silent.

Sarah understood his conflict; she felt the constrained rage within him and even identified with it. So, she filled dinner time with light conversation about routine matters.

Since she betrayed him, he thought that he, too, was free to break his vows. It didn't happen often, but when opportunities came his way, he felt unconstrained by his marital vows. He spent time with a few women whom he met at work, women who were attracted to his good looks that hadn't waned over the years, to his innocent-looking eyes, and to his ability to help them at a time of need, be it with fixing a computer or with car troubles. They accepted him, rewarded him, made love to him, and for a short time, made it possible to forget how his world was being swept into an uncontrolled whirlpool.

But the affairs didn't fill his heart with joy. They left him discontented, so he sought healing in a world where he felt safe and protected. He turned to the computer, to the internet, and to chat rooms.

In the evenings he sat in front of the screen for hours, spending his time in lengthy chats with foreign women. He looked for someone special but didn't know what characteristics might answer his yearning. He would chat with two and even three women every night, women from all over the US and Canada. Each exchange began with great anticipation and enthusiasm. He examined the information the women online offered about themselves and looked at the pictures they chose to present. He tried to figure out who they really were. Perhaps lonely souls like him?

With time, the charm started to diminish. He wearied of wandering through the chat rooms. Just when he was ready to give up on the fruitless search, he met someone.

He had found her, or perhaps she had found him. When they chatted, it was as though invisible threads united them through their computers, bridging the distance between them. It wasn't love, or so he told himself, but a deep and rooted connection that made him feel that she was the sister he never had. He wrote a line, and she completed it; she developed a thought, and he knew immediately where she was heading. He rejoiced so much about finding her that he even thought of telling his wife about his new friend. After further consideration, he decided not to.

Her name was Irene. She was a married woman with a Ph.D. in computer science, who taught at a university in Minnesota. She had two children, a boy and a girl. Irene spent her nights alone after she put her kids to bed. Her husband, a slippery sales agent whom she no longer loved, respected, and hoped he would change his ways, was absent from home most weekdays due to business trips and random adulterous affairs.

She'd been raised by a single mother. Like Jonathan, her father had been killed in a car accident when she was little, so she had been told. She didn't know her father at all, didn't remember anything about him, and had almost never been able to extricate any details about him from her mother.

Jonathan and Irene spent hours in the chat room and communicated daily. He examined photos that she'd sent him and saw that in spite of her maturity—she was about four years older than him—she possessed traces of exceptional beauty, and her face maintained a youthful appearance.

Over time, they moved to telephone conversations, moving closer to one another. He loved to hear her soothing voice, which carried her sympathetic and comforting intent. Their conversations flowed smoothly, in an unhurried pace. They felt that they could open up to one another, expose themselves, and talk almost about everything. Like Jonathan, Irene also suffered from panic attacks. She was afraid of the dark and always made sure to leave a small nightlight on in her bedroom. There had been times when she awakened from strange dreams breathless and scared. Fortunately, she managed to gain control of her condition with the help of prescription medications.

Jonathan openly told her almost everything that came to his mind. He felt that he found himself an ally whom he could completely trust. He told her about his unfaithful wife whom he couldn't stop loving and about their failed attempts to bring a child into the world. He talked about the orphanage and the foster homes where he had yearned for love, about his work and his affinity for fixing machines and computers, perhaps as a compensation for his inability to heal his wounded soul. He told her about his fascination with the more unusual phenomena of the world, the ones that didn't obey common logic.

He allowed himself to open up like he didn't do even with Sarah. He didn't know if it was the distance that made him feel so safe, or maybe the attentive, nonjudgmental way in which she listened. The way she allowed herself to open up to him moved him to trust her with the deepest parts of his soul.

He told her that like her, he suffered from panic attacks, but unlike her, he chose not to treat them with medications.

The one thing Jonathan didn't mention in his conversations

with Irene was the unusual site that Sarah and he had discovered in the forest.

CHAPTER 12

The Broadcast

Investigative police officer Roger Lambert, of the Los Angeles Police Department jumped at the opportunity to use the unusual technology, hoping to solve a case that had troubled him for about eight years. In that incident, which gained huge media coverage, a young and promising movie actress disappeared. The twenty-year old beauty seemed to have a bright future in the entertainment industry. Her body had been found after three weeks of searches, rolled inside a carpet in the city's dumping grounds.

Roger Lambert, who headed the investigation, faced a complicated challenge because her friends and colleagues agreed she was a charming young lady whom everybody loved. All of them appeared genuinely shocked and devastated, and they couldn't think of any enemies who would do such a horrible thing.

As he delved deeper into the investigation, he discovered that the young actress, Dianne Gillis, was not as pure and innocent as her friends, the media, and the public portrayed. She knew well how to manipulate people to achieve her goals and had no problem using wicked methods.

She started her successful career at the age of seventeen when she had a tumultuous love affair with a leading Hollywood producer. She then threatened that she would publish details of the affair, including secretly filmed, erotic clips documenting their sexual encounters. She told him that the first person to get to watch the footage would be his wife.

Following the blackmail, Dianne Gillis received her first significant role, her breakthrough into the public spotlight. She earned rave reviews from critics who hailed her excellent performance and ability to embody the character. Hollywood's newest star caught the eyes of influential industry professionals who began to court her and offer her major roles in their movies.

After she had achieved fame and wealth, the young star found it difficult to cope with her great success. She turned to alcohol and drugs, which started to influence her work and personality. She had a wild love affair with her drug dealer, a tough criminal; but despite his pleas and demands, she refused to be seen next to him in public. Instead, she attended formal soirees and media events accompanied by the young male co-stars who played at her side in movies and TV productions. Her drug-dealing boyfriend dealt poorly with the insult, and he was furious about her photographs with other men in gossip sections of tabloids.

Furthermore, Dianne Gillis alienated herself from her Catholic family, who refused to accept her immodest appearance in movies and magazine pictures. In her family's view she brought shame on them, so they cut off all ties with their daughter. After her murder, family members isolated themselves in grief and refused contact with the media.

The investigative team, led by Roger Lambert, identified three main suspects who all had solid alibis. The criminal boyfriend claimed he was at a nightclub at the time of the murder. Witnesses confirmed his whereabouts. The producer whom she had blackmailed claimed that he'd been in Miami at the time of the homicide. The third suspect, although the least likely, was the victim's father or someone hired by him.

During a visit to New York, Roger Lambert called the TXB network, introduced himself and his role in the police, and managed to arrange a meeting with producer Walter Lindsey.

"You are filming from above, right?" asked the police officer when they were sitting face-to-face.

Lindsey neither confirmed nor denied, and he didn't even nod his head in response to the question. He merely prompted, "Go on."

The ambitious officer expressed his concern. "I'm worried that there could be a problem in documenting a case like this, because according to the police report the murder was committed late at night in the apartment of Ms. Gillis, and not outside in the open air." He paused to examine the producer who listened attentively, then continued, "The previous two incidents documented by TXB, occurred outside a house and during daytime, a fact that enabled outdoor filming, but in our case, the conditions are quite different."

"I remember the incident," Walter Lindsey said in a sympathetic tone. "It was an intriguing affair with an unfortunate, tragic outcome, and you've correctly identified the limitations that we face. I need the fine details of the occurrence. If you could submit the facts as accurately as possible, I'll check to see what we can do to help the police."

Lambert recited the details and Walter Lindsey wrote down the information. He asked several clarifying questions; he was particularly interested in the exact time and location of the murder, and the models and colors of the cars of the suspects. The investigative officer delivered the details as precisely as he could.

Lindsey explained that if TXB obtained a film that documented the event, Officer Lambert would have to participate in a televised production and agree to the same terms as Officer Tucker of Springfield, Illinois.

Officer Lambert had no problem accepting the conditions and signing a document that reflected his willingness to cooperate with TXB. "I know you have to make a living," he said with a small, cynical smile.

Lindsey assumed that televising the broadcast resolving the popular celebrity's murder would translate into media gold.

Two weeks after their meeting, the New York producer called the Los Angeles police officer. "It seems I have a clip with which you'll be able to solve the case and arrest the murderer."

The announcement excited Lambert. "When will I be able to see the footage?"

"When you get here," Lindsey said.

Once again, Roger Lambert flew from California to New York. After the unusual documentation that was shown in the two previous broadcasts, he was curious, and could not wait to see what the mysterious technology revealed in his case.

Roger Lambert liked the spotlight and enjoyed sitting and chatting with TXB's famous host, who treated him in her familiar warm and caring manner. Officer Lambert wanted the fame that would accompany solving this murder case.

As with the previous broadcasts, there was a preliminary filmed session in the studio, after which the police had time to advance the investigation. During the interview, Officer Lambert discussed some of the issues his team confronted, explaining that all the main suspects had solid alibis.

Two cameras followed the officer as he sat with Susan Riley in the small studio and watched the recording. It showed a parking lot he recognized as being near the victim's mansion. The parking lot was well lit, and there was no difficulty in seeing what was happening.

A dark, mid-sized station wagon pulled in and a man got out of the car. He walked to the actress' front door and knocked.

In a different clip timestamped about an hour later, the same man was seen leaving the house, carrying with him what looked like a rolled carpet, inside of which was probably the dead body. He shoved the carpet into his vehicle in a hurry and then looked around to verify that nobody had noticed him. For a split-second, he gazed upward.

"Stop!" yelled the police officer, and the film froze on the man's face, which was lit by a streetlight.

"My God," said Roger Lambert.

"Do you recognize this man?" Susan Riley inquired.

"Yes," the officer answered. "He was not one of the main suspects."

"Who is he?" the host asked.

"One of her friends," answered Lambert. "He's an actor who worked with her on the set of a TV show. We saw no motive for him, and we interviewed him just in order to shed light on her personality."

Following the new information, the police arrested the man. Now thirty years old, married, and the father of two small children, he initially denied any involvement in the homicide. When shown the film, he broke down and admitted guilt. He said he had lost control of himself and killed Dianne Gillis in a fit of rage and jealousy.

When TXB aired the report, it won huge ratings, which came close to the viewership of the broadcast that portrayed the Gonzales incident.

CHAPTER 13

McPherson and Hensley

Investigative reporter Stewart McPherson was known as an honest journalist who examined the facts in front of him methodically and without bias. He was endowed with an analytical capability and knew how to separate the important details from the insignificant ones.

He gained national recognition when he investigated the well-publicized Mayfield story. Residents of Mayfield, a small town in Tennessee, reported that during about three years, many of them were abducted by unfriendly aliens. The reports shared many similar details, and a few of them were accompanied by blurry photos and video clips, hastily taken with cell phone cameras.

The typical report concerned the victim driving at night. A strong, blinding light surrounded the car, and then the engine shut down. Subsequently, they found themselves inside a mysterious spaceship, lying on a bizarre apparatus, paralyzed, while strange-looking aliens examined them and conducted painful and humiliating experiments on their bodies.

After hours of torture, they were returned to their cars, while according to their clocks, these events lasted only a few minutes. The victims were checked into local hospitals. Doctors found that they had indeed undergone traumatic mental and emotional experiences, but, except for shallow cuts and bruises, they suffered no real physical damage.

The story received a great deal of media coverage, and a stream of enthusiastic UFO pursuers poured into Mayfield from all over the US. Typically, such stories would be confronted by skepticism, not to say laughed at and deemed ridiculous; but this time, they gained unusual credibility because they didn't come from fringe people and UFO fanatics. The majority of the reports came from respected community members, conservatives, law-abiding citizens, including the mayor himself who also reported a particularly frightening experience.

Stewart McPherson investigated the matter. He sent assistant researchers to the town disguised as enthusiastic UFO seekers to gather information from the residents. He also transferred the out-of-focus photos and videos to professional crime scene investigators. After a few weeks of thorough investigation, he arrived at a clear-cut and unequivocal conclusion: the whole story was a fraud. He found that, due to a change in the route of a major highway which passed through the town and supported many of the local businesses—hotels, restaurants, gas stations, and retail commerce—many of the county's people had run into financial difficulties and bankruptcies.

They concocted the plot with the intention of luring alien seekers and curious tourists. Eventually, they planned to publish a book and a movie, thus generating new income for the district and fill their dwindling pockets.

"It started as a practical joke," one city council member later recalled. "But then it was picked up by the national media and grew beyond our expectations."

The investigative journalist published his findings and consequently gained national recognition as a methodical investigator who adhered to the facts and diligently found creative ways to obtain proof for his assumptions.

McPherson was convinced that the films that TXB broadcasted were also fraudulent, and on a much larger scale than the Mayfield hoax. He wasn't sure whether the people of the network collaborated with the scheme or if they were victims of the deception.

The journalist assumed that the three broadcasts were only the preview for a complete series that would air during a whole season and maybe more.

He assigned himself the challenge of investigating the story and hoped that exposure of the sham harvested a prestigious Pulitzer Prize.

McPherson sat at his desk in an old Manhattan office building and planned his moves. He needed to expose the origin of the filmstrips, and that wasn't a simple task. How could he infiltrate the network's center, located at a huge, guarded building in the center of New York? Although not a known television personality, he enjoyed wide recognition among journalist circles. The employees of TXB would recognize him as soon as he entered the building and suspect his intentions.

It appeared he had to plant a spy in the network's center or hire the services of an employee who was already there—perhaps a bitter and disgruntled worker or a novice intern. He had to convince that person to work for him and actually betray his employers in the name of journalistic integrity. He would guide that person to get close to the central people behind those broadcasts, to win their trust, and to leak valuable information.

The network shrouded the broadcasts under a veil of secrecy, leaving little information McPherson could use to determine what was going on behind the scenes. From watching the shows, the journalist learned only that the three broadcasts ended with one credit: producer Walter Lindsey. The producer was the only one who released short statements to the press.

Therefore, McPherson thought, he should find out everything about Walter Lindsey. What were Lindsey's position and role in the production? Where he got the unusual materials from—if he didn't produce them himself? What his background was, and who he spent his time with?

McPherson concluded there were two directions to take to begin his exposé: 1) learn everything he could about Walter

Lindsey, and 2) search for a candidate to plant in the offices of TXB.

For years, McPherson worked with a private investigation firm that collected information for his research and secretly traced, observed, and followed people for him. He knew he had to approach them because they had the resources and expertise he needed to investigate Walter Lindsey. He could not do it on his own, certainly not in the required time.

He called Howard Hensley, the man behind the investigation firm, and arranged a meeting for the following day. Hensley's office resided in an old and neglected-looking office building in the Bronx. Upon entering the place, there was no signboard that might indicate the name of the office or its purpose.

Stewart McPherson did not like to work with Howard Hensley. The man disturbed him, so much so that McPherson doubted himself and questioned his own motives. There was something dark and wicked about Hensley, reinforced by a large, ugly scar on the left side of his face, a remnant of a severe injury from the time he served as a police officer.

Hensley's clients received the feeling that he had contempt for anyone needing his services. But despite the negatives, McPherson knew that Hensley was the best in his profession and that he always delivered the goods in a reasonable time.

***

Private investigator Howard Hensley lived in the shadows. Maybe that's why his name was hardly ever mentioned. People who knew him referred to him as HH.

Once a decorated policeman and investigator with twenty years on the force, he believed his expertise was worth much more than a cop's salary and turned to crime, collecting payments for powerful crime organizations. He took advantage of his scary appearance and his connections in the police force to apply pressure to the people he threatened and extorted.

The FBI finally caught him. He was convicted of extortion and racketeering and sentenced to six and a half years in prison. When he got out of prison, he put his skills and connections to work as a private investigator.

HH dictated tough conditions to his clients. He required that the entire fee for service be paid in whole, in cash, and in advance. He offered neither guaranteed results nor a cash refund if a client were dissatisfied. Despite these tough conditions, Stewart McPherson knew that HH would do the job and acquire most of the information that he needed in a reasonable time.

***

Stewart McPherson sat in HH's dimly lit office. The bars over the closed windows made him feel like he was in a prison cell.

Although tall and wide-shouldered, in front of Hensley he felt as if he were back in elementary school confronting the playground bully.

Hensley lit a cigarette and offered one to McPherson who declined. It had been some time since he'd quit.

"So what kind of elaborate deception are you trying to unearth this time?" Hensley asked, lips curling in a sneer. His narrow eyes probed McPherson in a calculated and sinister look that sent chills down the journalist's spine.

McPherson steeled himself and looked directly into his interlocutor's eyes.

"Walter Lindsey," he said.

"The producer from TXB?" HH wanted to clarify.

"Yes," McPherson confirmed, "I want to know everything there is to know about his professional and his private life."

Hensley nodded and looked like he was considering whether to accept the gig. With a curt nod, he said, "It will take a few weeks."

"OK," McPherson said.

HH thought for a minute. "So, you suppose that the films are fabricated."

Stewart McPherson was surprised. HH didn't usually express interest in needless conversations with his clients, nor did he like to waste words. He replied, "I have no doubt that it's a deception. With the information you'll get for me, I'll be able to prove it."

CHAPTER 14

Michael

Michael finished high school and chose to pursue studies in journalism. His adoptive parents did not hesitate to contribute to the education of their beloved son and made it clear that he could go to any school he desired. He benefited from his good grades and diligence; when he submitted applications to higher education institutions, he received favorable answers from most of the universities that he approached. He chose the New York University School of Journalism in Manhattan. It was an old and prestigious private university where the tuition was quite high.

He managed to finance most of his tuition through student loans, and his parents covered other expenses, including his stay at the students' dormitories.

Michael knew the expense put a heavy financial burden on his parents. He was grateful for their unstinting support and looked for ways to minimize his cost-of-living, so he found a part-time job as a clerk in the college bookstore.

He loved his studies—news and documentary reporting, media criticism, literary reportage, magazine writing, electronic and digital media. He especially loved conducting and editing investigative reporting.

He delved into the subject matter in his serious and diligent way, and good grades reflected his dedication and his sharp mind.

Every so often, he spent an evening with friends. They liked to visit a bar near the university named Sullivan's Place. Sitting in the dimly lit pub drinking beer and listening to live jazz music, they indulged in long conversations.

His two best friends, Randy and Greg, entertained very different viewpoints on most things, which led to friendly debates.

One evening Randy declared, "Most people are immersed in a meaningless life, existing only for materialistic purposes, and their lives are not very different from those of animals."

Michael wasn't surprised by Randy's conversational provocation. Randy came from a wealthy family and had never worried about money.

Randy took a sip of his beer and continued, "A worthy life requires continual spiritual growth and development. If you're living without evolving, you're just wasting oxygen."

Greg, chubby, clumsy, and familiar with financial hardship, looked at Randy with skepticism and rebutted with good-natured certainty, "The meaning of life for me can be found in a good steak, drinking beer, and sex."

The quiet one of the three as well the uncrowned leader,

Michael smiled at Greg's words and found the middle ground. "I think we have to know how to enjoy the good things in life, but also strive to develop and expand our understanding of ourselves."

Although closer to Randy in his opinions, Michael preferred Greg's unpretentious attitude. He thought that daily existence was complicated and mysterious enough already. He saw no need to look for intricate philosophies of some greater significance. It was enough to better understand himself and try to solve the mystery that shrouded his birth. The yearning to meet his biological parents never subsided, nor did the motivation to ask them the questions that never stopped bothering him, like why did they give him up for adoption rather than raise him by themselves?

Michael enjoyed life as a university student. He loved being with people of his age, most of them were filled with optimism and joy of life, and he especially liked to spend time with the female students.

The women liked him, appreciating his intelligence, wit, good looks, and athletic build. Some of them giggled when they said he reminded them of Jesus, and he wondered why his appearance evoked such a strange association.

He had a few girlfriends, but none of the relationships matured into the deep, long-term connection for which he hoped.

"So, how is your love life?" Randy asked him once, an annoying question from someone who hopped from one girl to another.

Embarrassed, Michael shrugged his shoulders and said, "I'm waiting for the right one."

Randy replied by quoting John Lennon: "Life is what happens to you while you're busy making other plans."

Still, Michael was not overly concerned by the lack of a permanent female partner, because his focus was on his studies and acquiring a profession.

However, Michael felt like he was living in a bubble. The city was cold and foreign to him, and alienation ruled the somber streets. He missed home, where people tended to make eye contact and acknowledge each other. Back in the affluent San Diego suburb, the sky was blue, the sun did not hide behind dark clouds and tall buildings, and the beach invited him to play or relax as the mood struck.

The big, urban environment took him back to the feeling of strangeness entertained in early childhood, when he was unsure whether he was a child like all children. Michael wondered if he would ever feel like a normal human being, and he pondered whether there was such a thing as being normal.

Nonetheless, he sensed promise in the Big Apple. He felt that he was at a point in which a clue would be revealed, a sign which would lead him toward his destiny. Inside the foreignness and gloom of the enormous metropolis, he'd be exposed to a narrow path that would lead him to what was missing in his life, without which he couldn't feel whole.

After getting his Bachelor of Arts in journalism, he felt no hurry to pursue a graduate degree. He wanted first to experience being a journalist. He needed to confirm that this was indeed his calling, and he also wished to lighten the financial burden laid upon his parents. Michael knew that his sister Lily was about to finish high school. He assumed she would pursue higher education, which would increase the financial strain on the family. Although his parents never expressed any reservations regarding his finances, he had an idea of their limitations and understood that they were probably struggling.

Michael spent the summer vacation searching for a job. He submitted his resume to a few newspapers, as well as radio and TV stations. He hoped to find a job conducting journalistic research, perhaps exposing the corruption he knew plagued the political system. He dreamed of a career-making opportunity to investigate an affair like Watergate. During job interviews, he made sure to tell interviewers that he would like to be involved in significant research. He was told they would call him if they required his services. In the meantime, he looked for an apartment to rent, a task more difficult than anticipated.

In their favorite bar, he continued to spend time with Randy and Greg where they enjoyed long conversations in their attempts to figure out the best course for their lives. Wealthy Randy wondered why he'd left the protected and comfortable university, while Greg also debated his next steps and considered moving to

San Francisco.

Michael felt lucky when he received two job offers. The first one was from a radio station that focused on airing local and international news, interviews, and commentaries. They needed a field reporter, but their hiring manager informed Michael that he would start out in traffic reports.

The second offer came from the TXB television network. They needed a field researcher for a weekly news magazine called *Around the Clock,* which conducted investigative articles in different areas of interest, like politics, science, medicine, consumer issues, and entertainment.

Michael chose the TV network, even though the starting salary was slightly lower than the radio station. He saw it as an excellent opportunity to make his first steps in the field that fascinated him. He hoped to follow in the footsteps of brave journalists who exposed corruption and were not deterred by powerful politicians and wealthy tycoons.

After an exhaustive search, he found a reasonably priced small apartment in Brooklyn. The elderly landlady, Mrs. Rinaldi, treated him with a kindness that bordered on nosiness. More than once upon arriving home, he wished she wouldn't stop him at the entrance with her wearisome questions. For the most part, he recognized that she was lonely and had nothing to do all day; so when he was there, she wouldn't stop complaining about her husband who had left her prematurely and moved on to the next world. She frequently repeated herself, saying in agony, "My time to die already came, but God forgot me."

Michael spent much of his time on public transportation, on the way to work and back. The bus and subway afforded him an opportunity to see a new face of his country, hard-working people, somber, tired, and trapped by their daily obligations.

For him, however, it was an exciting time filled with optimism. He knew he was one of the lucky few who got to work in the occupation they loved.

The tasks handed to him by the producers of *Around the Clock* were simple. He was primarily conducting background checks on interview candidates, either by phone or by talking and probing around the candidate's neighborhood, at their workplace, or contacting friends and acquaintances, present and past.

Michael had to report his findings to his superiors, but nobody looked over his shoulder to micromanage his time. They only expected him to obtain accurate information within a reasonable amount of time. He felt an obligation to justify his employer's trust in him. His modest salary covered all of his expenses and even allowed him to save some money to repay his parents for their unstinting support.

CHAPTER 15

The Broadcast

Police departments all over the country reexamined their unsolved case files in the hope that TXB's mysterious technology would assist them in shining a new light on the occurrences.

Requests for assistance flooded Walter Lindsey and his team. What started as a one-time, sensational airing turned into a weekly program that aired every Wednesday at 10:00 p.m. The program was given the simple and somewhat pretentious name, *The Broadcast*.

Police detectives understood that the technology could not assist in solving every crime. It performed much better in cases that had occurred in open spaces and during clear days than in events that happened inside houses, at night, or during cloudy weather.

Still, the system showed its strength and capabilities also in solving incidents in which it was seemingly limited. When a crime occurred inside a building, it allowed a look at a nearby street, the yard, or the parking lot, making it possible to draw vital information from observing cars and passersby.

With time and familiarity, public interest in the unusual show subsided. TXB's ratings hit a plateau, and then settled. Nevertheless, the exclusive show continued to generate great curiosity and attract viewers across generations and demographics. Corporations vied for the limited number of advertising slots, which yielded a high income for the network and its affiliate stations. The show was, in short, a goldmine.

Walter Lindsey and his skilled team filtered the many requests that came from police investigators from all over the US, and also from Canada and Mexico. Most of the time, they selected the incidents that had the highest commercial potential.

Lindsey, the clever producer, understood that in order to attract and magnetize viewers, TXB had to develop the storylines behind these lesser known incidents and gradually changed the show's structure. Viewers were now exposed to the personal backgrounds of victims and their families, as well as the circumstances of the alleged criminals.

The regular host, Susan Riley, interviewed the families of the victims, who usually agreed to participate and air their loss and agony. They brought photographs and video clips documenting their loved ones in beautiful moments. They spoke about the tragedies and usually expressed hope that the criminals would be identified, caught, and punished—perhaps even executed.

The families of the alleged criminals were not shy about participating in the program either. They usually talked about the unforgiving circumstances that influenced their relatives to commit crimes. Often, they argued that the criminals were inherently good people who'd fallen into the world of crime due to circumstances beyond their control. They always expressed deep remorse and apologized for the crimes their relatives committed.

Despite the uniqueness of the program, there was a gradual descent in national viewership. The program had a tough time maintaining its lead in the ratings as it competed against movies and original TV series aired at the same time slot. The rival networks not only had expert writers, they also helped stoke a growing chorus of voices who doubted the credibility of the TXB's films.

***

Sitting comfortably in their rural house, near the small town of Corralitos and close to the San Andreas Fault line, Jonathan and Sarah Lishinsky liked to watch *The Broadcast* each week.

Each of them had a favorite seat. Jonathan preferred the wide recliner, with his feet propped on the footboard. Sarah liked the old-style armchair she'd purchased in a second-hand store and had re-upholstered. The dogs sprawled on the carpet at their feet and ignored the television.

Sarah made an effort to be home for *The Broadcast*, even when she was involved in yet another affair. She knew how important it was to Jonathan that she sat with him while they watched the show that his brother produced.

With time, Sarah started to lose interest, because despite TXB's attempts to vary the shows by introducing different cases each week—one week an unsolved murder, and on the next one a sophisticated robbery—eventually, the programs seemed similar to one another. And although the network searched for the juiciest stories and added dramatic and tragic perspectives, Sarah still thought that the program no longer looked much different than other investigative reporting shows. Sarah harbored a secretive and unexplainable wish; she hoped that *The Broadcast* would somehow air footage that corresponds with her personal life story. But she saw how that possibility diminishes with every new episode.

One evening, as they sat down to watch the show; the host presented a shocking murder incident that took place in Ohio.

Sarah didn't feel like watching another gruesome episode. She looked at her husband, who appeared riveted to the TV, and commented, "I think it's time that TXB uses the remarkable technology they possess to document other events, not just crimes."

"They're getting justice for crime victims and their families," Jonathan retorted without taking his eyes off the television.

"There are other events that they could expose," she said.

"Like what?" he wondered, "Do you mean news events? I could talk to my brother."

"Not news," she said. "The news is already covered by plenty of cameras."

"What are you getting at?" he asked, agitated.

"Maybe history?" She suggested.

"Are you serious?" Her suggestion surprised him. Jonathan didn't think that his wife was especially knowledgeable in history, but he recalled that she'd expressed great interest in the history of places they'd visited.

"I'm not sure," she said, thinking aloud. "But I wonder if there is a way the technology could go back in time and show events that happened before cameras were even invented." Sarah was not sure whether her line of thinking made sense.

Jonathan muted the television. Looking at her with a thoughtful expression, he said, "That's an interesting idea." He raised a glass of water from a table next to him and took a sip. "I'll talk to Walter and suggest it, let's see what he thinks and whether it's technologically feasible."

"But do you think such broadcasts would interest viewers?" Sarah asked. "After all, it's a commercial network."

"I don't know," he said. "From what I've read, almost all the cops in the country are currently watching our show. Who would watch the historical broadcasts that you suggest? History teachers?"

"Jonathan," she said softly, "you said *our* show."

"I meant Walter's show," he corrected himself.

CHAPTER 16

Stewart McPherson

The investigative reporter examined the content of the stuffed package that was delivered to his office by special courier. While spreading the 3-ring binders and various papers on his large wooden desk, he had the impression that the shadows man, the private investigator nicknamed HH, had done a thorough job, as always. McPherson received two binders: one dedicated to Walter Lindsey's professional life and one to his private life. In addition to the binders, the package contained several other pages that looked like they were added at the last moment. Most of the material was printed, but there were also quite a few hand-written comments. McPherson had paid plenty of cash for the information, and he was pleased to see that HH was not sloppy in collecting the materials about the TXB producer.

Now, the diligent journalist had to dive into the minor details, assemble the puzzle, and build a big picture. He learned that Walter Lindsey lived in Scarsdale, a quiet and prestigious suburb. A picture of Lindsey's house was attached to the documents and McPherson had the impression that it was a nice but not an ostentatious house.

Lindsey was happily married to Monica, a senior accountant. The couple had two daughters. The older one, Melanie, studied law at Stanford University in California. The younger one, Carolyn, was a high school student.

McPherson learned that, when Walter Lindsey was four years old, his parents had been killed in a fatal car accident. Walter was not in the car at the time of the accident, while his little brother who sat in the backseat, had survived the crash. The brother, Jonathan, lived in California, and by all appearances, the two brothers were estranged. Lindsey's father was Jewish, and his original family name was Lishinsky, which Walter had changed because he worried that a Jewish sounding surname could hurt his chances of advancing in the media world.

The successful producer had three good friends with whom he liked to play music in their rock-and-roll band. Every once in a while, he would meet with one or more of them for lunch, either in a good restaurant or at a small park located behind the TXB building. On weekends, the whole group met at Walter's house, and they played together or watched football, if it was playoffs time.

HH's thorough report included details about the three friends, their occupations, and even the instrument that each played in the band.

Julian, a talented director who worked at TXB, played rhythm guitar and was the band's lead singer. Alex, a high-tech expert, specializing in animation, played drums and percussion. Eric was a literature and history professor; he played bass guitar and sang backup vocals. Walter was the band's keyboard player, and he also contributed with backup vocals.

On rare occasions, the band played at family events. Usually, however, they played for their enjoyment, preferring to keep their music a hobby. *"They sound pretty good,"* HH added a hand-written comment.

How does HH get this detailed information? Stewart McPherson wondered. He decided the how didn't matter. He was pleased to recognize an existing pattern for the deception. The journalist went to the coffee maker, mulling over the information. It seemed likely to him that the members of the band were not content with just making music, so they concocted this magical broadcast scheme to make money. Or perhaps it was a sophisticated hoax.

With the fresh data in his hands, McPherson tried to piece together a basic theory of the system. He assumed that they performed a thorough research of the documented incidents, probably conducted by the history professor. It seemed likely that the clips were created by the film director and the animator. McPherson presumed that they intentionally created videos of mediocre quality, so viewers would not notice that they watched animated films.

He considered it possible that participating law enforcement officers collaborated with the ploy. If it were so, he needed proof of such collusion. McPherson embraced his conjecture as a starting point likely to change once more details were factored in.

At the same time that McPherson approached HH to gather information about Walter Lindsey, he also contacted a young hacker that he employed on occasion. The hacker's mission was to break into the computers of TXB's human resources department and extract the names of all the employees, their positions, wages, telephone numbers, and how long they'd been with the company.

With the detailed list in his hands, McPherson looked for someone who could be his "eyes" in the network's offices, someone who could get close to Lindsey and his accomplices and expose the source of the films. It wouldn't be simple. The man McPherson looked for had to be skilled and capable, but not wholly committed to his job—perhaps a disgruntled employee, frustrated with his salary or failure to receive a promotion. Such a person might be interested in taking revenge on his employer and making money on the side.

He considered another option: maybe someone who had only been at TXB for a short time, someone new to journalism and still idealistic. *Actually*, McPherson thought to himself, *I'm looking for a person who would be willing to betray a media corporation in order to clean the system of journalistic dishonesty.*

Three potential candidates caught McPherson's attention, and he penciled them into his notebook. One was a veteran reporter, not particularly known and not very noticeable, who had been with the network for many years. McPherson had the impression that he had not advanced up the corporate ladder and his salary was significantly lower than could be expected for a man with his seniority. But did he fit the profile of a disgruntled employee willing to sabotage his employer? McPherson wasn't sure.

Next was a young female researcher who worked part-time in the news department so that she could finance her tuition at a prestigious performing arts school. After brief consideration, MacPherson dismissed her. She'd have neither the opportunity to infiltrate Lindsey's group nor the time, considering the demands of her course of study.

The third candidate was also a new researcher, who had a degree in journalism from New York University.

After deliberating between the two remaining candidates, McPherson chose the young researcher, Michael Evans. He hoped the young man might still hold on to idealistic values of pure journalism that wouldn't deceive people for ratings and money. He guessed that, due to the short term of his employment and his low, entry-level salary, the young man was not yet committed to the network.

In a search on social media, McPherson found several photos of Michael. *Handsome kid,* he thought. He saw that Michael grew up in San Diego, California. Michael provided little information for public viewing, but that little was enough for the investigative journalist. He especially liked that Michael was a musician and a guitar player.

CHAPTER 17

Michael

The phone rang. Michael glanced at the screen and saw an unidentified number. He answered the call, hoping that it wasn't from a telemarketer or pollster.

"Am I talking with Mr. Michael Evans?" a man's voice inquired.

"Who wants to know?" Michael replied.

"My name is Stewart McPherson," the caller introduced himself. "May I have a few minutes of your time?"

"Stewart McPherson, the famous journalist?" Michael was surprised.

"It's me," McPherson confirmed. "I'd like to meet with you. Are you available?"

"It would be an honor," Michael said, excitement and curiosity building. "What's this about?"

"I'll tell you when we meet," McPherson answered. "In the meantime, I'm asking that you don't tell anyone about our conversation."

"All right," Michael said, intrigued. "I have a free hour around noon."

McPherson gave Michael the address of his office, which was located about ten minutes away from the TXB center.

***

At noon, Michael hurried out of the building and waved down a yellow cab. He gave the driver the address and sat in the backseat, wondering why the esteemed journalist had summoned him. Michael was familiar with McPherson's work. He saw him as a courageous investigative reporter, righteous, and worthy of being a role model.

The cab dropped Michael in front of a large, nondescript office building. Michael walked into the entrance and checked the signboards of the residents. The building housed lawyers' and architects' offices, as well as some firms that Michael didn't recognize. He identified "McPherson Journalism" among the names on the third-floor directory. He took the elevator to the third-floor and had no difficulty in finding the door with an identical sign to the one in the lobby. Michael rang the bell while still wondering why he was invited to the unexpected meeting.

The man who opened the door looked familiar from pictures that Michael had seen in newspapers and from the journalist's appearances on TV panels. A tall and wide-shouldered man, McPherson had a mane of dense, gray hair over a wrinkled forehead. He looked like he was in his fifties. He examined Michael with a penetrating look, offered a friendly smile, and extended his hand.

"Hello, Michael. Come in, please," McPherson said as his young guest shook his hand.

Michael followed him into the office and sat opposite the famous journalist at a large, heavy desk. He was engulfed by an unusual feeling that this was a distinct moment in his life. Could it be a turning point?

"Would you like anything to drink?" McPherson asked. "Coffee? Soda? Water?"

"No thanks," Michael answered.

Michael looked around the room, noting walls with peeling paint, and windows that lost some of their transparency. Still, the office smelled clean and looked tidy. A computer monitor, keyboard, and scattered papers occupied the desktop. Metal bookshelves screwed into the walls held many 3-ring binders. Bringing his attention back to the journalist, Michael also noticed a framed photo of a smiling young woman holding a small, serious child on the desk. He wondered if they were McPherson's wife and son.

"What's this about?" Michael asked.

"I need your help in investigating a case in which the media is deceiving the public," McPherson said, looking into Michael's eyes.

"The truth is," Michael said, "I already have a job, and I don't have time for more work."

"Your work is the reason I contacted you," the journalist said. "I'm investigating an act of deception taking place at TXB."

"You want me to spy on my employers?" Michael's voice revealed surprise and apprehension.

"I am offering you the opportunity to join me in an investigation of a large-scale, journalistic deceit," McPherson confirmed with a nod.

"Look," Michael said, perplexed, "I know your work, and I have a great deal of respect for you, but I'm not comfortable with what you request. Besides, I don't know of any deception taking place at TXB."

"And what if you found that there was a broad scale deception and they are leading the public astray?" McPherson questioned. "You're a new hire," the journalist continued, "do you really think that the higher-ups perpetrating an enormous hoax on the public would tell *you* what they're doing?"

Michael had to admit that, no, TXB management wouldn't tell him any such thing. "I don't see how I could be of use to you in exposing any such thing." Michael said, "What you're hinting at me doing will get me fired."

"Well," McPherson said, "I'm only looking for information related to the deceit. Nothing else. I don't want you to betray your employer's confidence, unless it becomes obvious to you, beyond the shadow of a doubt, that they're falsifying evidence and misleading innocent viewers."

Michael looked at McPherson and pondered the request. Was it moral? What it ethical? Was it honorable? Should he accept the path that the journalist outlined for him? Or maybe, in some mysterious way, it was already decided for him, and he couldn't pass on the exceptional opportunity to work with the renowned journalist.

"I have to think about it before answering," Michael said.

"Take your time," McPherson said, "but not too much time."

***

The remainder of the day, Michael performed his duties in a somewhat mechanical manner, unlike his usual committed approach. His mind was preoccupied with thoughts of the earlier events.

In his work as a researcher, he had to conduct a background check on a black woman who came to the US from Jamaica as a penniless immigrant, and in time, founded an empire of self-service laundries. Michael called a few of her relatives as well as acquaintances and competitors from the business world. He also went to one of the laundromats to wash the clothes that he'd brought with him in preparation for the assignment.

But he couldn't stop thinking about the unexpected meeting, and what McPherson offered him. He did not like the idea, either of spying on his employer or that TXB deceived the public—

definitely not. By nature, Michael was a loyal person, so he was not fond of the possibility of betraying the trust that was placed in him. Also, betrayal of a large corporation like TXB could blackball him from future employment in the media industry.

On the other hand, McPherson's question continued to trouble him. "What if you found that there was a broad scale deception and they are leading the public astray?" Letting a hoax continue when he might have the means to stop it sat ill on his conscience, too.

If such a thing became apparent, would it not be a betrayal of the public's trust if he *didn't* report it?

Michael considered that a respected journalist like McPherson wouldn't investigate without probable cause for suspicion.

That evening, Michael made his decision. He would collaborate with McPherson, but only if he knew with absolute certainty that there was indeed a severe public deception. He was not going to report on any other activity occurring at TXB, and he would honor the confidentiality agreement he'd signed as best he could. Furthermore, he would not accept any money in exchange for the information he'd provide, if in fact, such information came into his hands.

***

The following day, he called McPherson and notified him of his decision.

"Excellent." McPherson felt relieved at the young researcher's acceptance. He appreciated that Michael had not come to his decision easily: that testified to his being a trustworthy young man who understood what loyalty and secrecy meant.

At noon, Michael took a taxi to the journalist's office for a second meeting.

When Michael sat down, McPherson wasted no time getting down to business. "Are you familiar with the series called *The Broadcast*?"

"I watch the show, but I'm not connected to that department in any way."

"Do you know the show's producer, Walter Lindsey?"

"I've seen him a few times in the cafeteria, but we've never met."

"I am convinced," McPherson said, "that the footage they air while refusing to reveal its source, is produced by animation experts or staged to make it look like it was filmed from a distance. They conduct thorough research of a specific incident and most likely have sources within the police or the FBI."

Michael pondered the journalist's words.

"Otherwise, I would have to believe," McPherson continued, "that there happened to be a reconnaissance aircraft or satellite in the sky at exactly the right time and in exactly the right place and that the films were kept hidden for years. Does that make sense to you?"

"I don't know," Michael admitted. "But I know that the show generates plenty of interest and makes a lot of money."

"Money!" McPherson exclaimed. "That's exactly what they're making."

"But how do you expect me to get the details?" Michael asked. "I hope that you don't think I'm going to sneak in and search the producer's office at night, rummaging through files with a flashlight and camera. I'm not a spy, and I don't want to become a secret agent or anything like that."

"You're not a spy, but you are a musician." McPherson smiled.

"I don't see the connection," Michael said. "And the truth is that, during the last few years, I've hardly had the time for music."

"Well, I just happen to have a superb guitar," McPherson said. "It was bequeathed to me by a good friend, an amateur musician who passed away. I don't know why he willed it to me of all people because I've never played any musical instrument. We used to go to rock concerts together, and we loved the same artists."

McPherson got up from his chair, went to the closet, and pulled out what looked like a top quality, hard guitar case. He set it on his desk and opened it. Michael rose to his feet for a better view and gaped at the superb acoustic Martin guitar, used, but it looked meticulously maintained. Michael's fingers itched to pick it up and start playing. He'd never possessed such a fine instrument and certainly couldn't afford one on his meager salary.

"So, you want me to play spy with a guitar?" Michael asked, amused.

"That's the plan," McPherson somberly confirmed. "Musicians are drawn to one another, and through music, I'm hoping you'll manage to make friends with Walter Lindsey."

"And how exactly am I supposed to accomplish that?" Michael still didn't comprehend McPherson's plan.

"All you have to do at this stage is play. That will attract Lindsey's attention. Don't approach him. It's better if he initiates the meeting. That way it won't look suspicious. Do you know the small park located behind the TXB building?"

"Of course."

"Then you know that many network employees spend their lunch break there, including Lindsey. Find a suitable corner and just play. That's all you need to do right now. Let me know once the connection is made."

"With this guitar, I'll enjoy my mission," Michael said. He was relieved that McPherson did not require him to lie, pretend, or become a mole, at least not yet.

Michael shook McPherson's hand and carried the guitar with him.

"Keep the guitar as a token of my appreciation for your assistance," McPherson said as the young man departed.

On the following days, Michael bought his lunch at the network's cafeteria and hurried to the small park to eat his meal and play for his own delight.

The guitar didn't respond to him right away. After fumbling the strings the first few days, he realized he'd gotten rusty over the past several years when he focused on his studies. But before long, he started to sense that the right feel was returning to him. After about ten days, it was just like yesterday that he had put down his guitar, left his band, and made his way to the Big Apple.

He found a hidden corner in the park, so it would be clear that he played for his enjoyment and not to beg for money. He played different melodies, mostly rock and roll classics from the Sixties and Seventies as well as the old songs he'd written for his band. Playing in the open air calmed him, connected him to that place in his soul he'd almost forgot about; and to the vast world around him—the sky, the trees, the birds, and also to people who passed by.

Some passersby stopped and listened for a moment before going on their way. Others sat nearby and enjoyed the free concert. Sometimes, his audience held a majority population of young women who worked at TXB. They cast flirtatious glances at the handsome young guitarist who, absorbed in his music, never seemed to notice them.

On rare occasions, he caught Stewart McPherson out of the corner of his eyes. In his heart, he thanked McPherson for pushing him back to a world that had once been an inseparable part of him, returning him to an old love, to music. The possibility that Walter Lindsey might approach him triggered his curiosity, even though he hoped that it wouldn't happen. Just thinking about it had caused him a great deal of discomfort.

Michael loved spring days when the sun warmed him and his guitar, and the world woke up to life after the freezing New York winter. On hot summer days, he sat beneath shade trees, played, and improvised, and felt that he was reaching levels and depths he had never known when he was a young teenager and a member of a rock band. New melodies formed in his mind and poured through his fingers without effort. The music surrounded him and pulsed deep within his soul.

CHAPTER 18

The Broadcast

The senior managers at TXB appeared nervous. Although they approved Walter Lindsey's request to change the direction of his popular show, they did not understand the need for such change. The managers knew how to read spreadsheets, and they recognized the slow decline of viewership. However, the show still captivated millions of viewers all over North America every week and remained number one on the rating charts for its time slot.

Even Walter Lindsey wasn't sure whether the new format would work. In a weekly management meeting convened to discuss routine issues like financial turnover, marketing strategies, and proposals for new shows, he argued that *The Broadcast* needed a breakthrough. Lindsey asserted that he could produce films such as never been seen on television.

"It will be a journey back in time," he said. "These videos will enable viewers to see historical events as they truly happened."

Lindsey also argued that the switch to a historical

perspective would deflect public debate about the show's invasion of people's privacy by filming them without their consent.

***

"History." Susan Riley opened another episode, assuming a somber facial expression. "What do we *really* know about history? Of course, we know what they taught us in school, and what we've read in books. And who wrote the books?"

Reading the teleprompter, she continued to stoke viewer interest. "They say history is written by the victors but is their interpretation correct? Were they affected by their personal opinions, by their political agendas, and by their beliefs and ideologies? What *really* happened?"

Riley knew that people all over the country speculated about the announced change of direction taken by *The Broadcast*. Many people, on radio shows and printed and digital forums, expressed discontent with having to depart from their favorite police investigation shows. But there were also positive comments and praises for TXB's courage to pursue less sensational and less voyeuristic stories.

"We at TXB would like to show you history as it *truly* happened. We will take you to periods before the invention of cameras and movies. Until today, it was unthinkable, so we relied on written records and dramatic reenactments, but with the amazing technology that is exclusively in the hands of TXB, now it is possible."

She took a short pause and then continued. "We will start our journey back in time in the twentieth century and focus on the two world wars in which millions of soldiers and innocent citizens were killed. Our guest tonight is Professor Bernard Robertson, from Harvard University. Dr. Robertson is a world-renowned expert on the history of the twentieth century. With his help, we will look at what happened with as much objectivity as possible."

The camera zoomed out, and the viewers could see the two people present in the studio. "Good evening, Professor Robertson." The host smiled at her guest. "Thank you for coming."

"Good evening." The silver-haired professor smiled back.

"Please," Susan Riley said. "The microphone is yours."

"We will start with World War II," the professor declared, slipping easily into classroom lecture mode. "Some say it was the bloodiest conflict that humanity has ever experienced, a war in which millions of innocent people were murdered. We in the United States understand it—justifiably, in my opinion—as a war against the evil that Nazi Germany embodied, which was joined by fascist Italy and imperial Japan. Against the threat of global tyranny, racism, cruelty, and evil stood the free world, aiming to defend the lives of the victims and the values of liberty, democracy, and free society."

"Professor Robertson," the host interjected before he could lecture too long, "what are we going to see?"

"We will watch some of the most important events of World

War II," he answered. "Although humanity already had cameras and we have plenty of documentation from newsreels and war propaganda, I admit that these clips have indeed given me a new angle of observation that I never expected to come my way. I must mention that I have no idea where you got the footage; but, in my humble opinion, it correctly reflects the events as I have researched them.

Clearly, in the short time we have for this program, I cannot convey an in-depth explanation of the materials. Therefore, we'll highlight some of the most important events of the war."

The film started, and the professor explained what was displayed on the screen. For thirty minutes, he followed the progression of videos and briefly spoke of the key battles of the different arenas.

As TXB had promised in trailers, the special broadcast aired without commercials. Short sponsored announcements played at the conclusion of the program.

Once again, viewers saw the unusual filming angle, straight from above. They watched black-and-white video clips, grainy and without sound. Apparently, the footage was filmed from a great distance, thus creating a sterile atmosphere, isolated from the horrors of the war—the dead soldiers, the screaming of the injured, and the blood.

While showing the Battle of France in which the Germans defeated the French Army and the British Expeditionary Force, the recording showed the German armed forces as they crossed the

Ardennes and penetrated French defense lines.

"From this angle," Susan Riley contributed, "the German tanks remind me of a massive swarm of giant insects, and the Luftwaffe airplanes look like birds of prey."

Then, clips of Operation Barbarossa showed the huge forces of the Axis Alliance marching toward the Soviet Union. Due to the time constraint, the professor could dedicate only minutes to a few monumental battles. He presented clips of the fierce fighting in Stalingrad, after which he went on to show footage of the Pacific Ocean Theater, focusing on the battle of Iwo Jima.

Professor Robertson ended his presentation by showing documentation of the Allies' invasion of Normandy.

"It was only a short visual overview demonstrating the most prominent events of the war," the professor said, "deeper understandings of the monumental campaign would require much more time."

"And now," Susan Riley said, "we will turn the spotlight to World War I, which claimed the lives of about nine million soldiers and seven million civilians. Please, Professor, the microphone is yours."

Professor Robertson cleared his throat before speaking. "As far as I'm concerned, the films that I received from TXB documenting the First World War were even more remarkable than those of the Second World War. I say that because photographed documentation we have of the years 1914 through 1918 is limited and incomplete, so actually, I saw some of the events and the fierce battles for the first time. These videos show events that have passed beyond all living memory—unless you're a tortoise." He chuckled at the lame attempt at wit, coughed, and continued.

"Although neither the angle of filming or quality of the video is ideal, it is still outstanding documentation. We will start with the monumental event that was the pretext to the opening of the war: the assassination of Archduke Franz Ferdinand, heir presumptive to the Austro-Hungarian throne."

The film started, and the professor explained what took place. A motorcade of six vehicles rolled through the streets of Sarajevo. The archduke and his wife, Duchess Sophie, rode in the third car. They progressed slowly through the cheering crowd. A bomb thrown in the direction of the archduke's car hit the back of the vehicle, rolled down, and exploded under the next car in the motorcade. The crowd scattered in fright, and the convoy sped away toward the town hall.

"After the reception at the town hall," said Professor Robertson, "the archduke continued on his way."

The video followed the archduke's open car leaving the town hall. Just after turning a corner, the car stopped, then backed up, apparently because it took a wrong turn. The film showed a man approaching the right side of the vehicle. He raised a pistol and shot twice, killing the archduke and his duchess.

"The murder of the heir presumptive of the Austro-Hungarian Empire," explained the professor, "had serious repercussions and served as the reason for the start of the Great War, as it was called."

The professor described who the two fighting opponents were. He took a breath and a sip of water before continuing. "The war started as a consequence of idiocy, and millions of soldiers were killed because of the stupidity of their leaders and commanders."

The professor then described the film footage of one of the bloodiest battles in human history, the Battle of the Somme, in France, where nearly a million soldiers from both sides were killed during about four and a half months of fighting. In one of the films, viewers saw British troops charging from their trenches and storming the well-fortified German lines. German fire cut down most of the soldiers in the charge.

The professor ended his brief overview of World War I with what American President Theodore Roosevelt called "the greatest crime of the war." An unsettling video showed the Turks forcing hundreds of thousands of Armenians to walk without food and water to their death.

"During those death marches," the professor somberly said, "starved, exhausted, and frost-bitten Armenians were massacred, and many of their women were raped."

The film ended, followed by a pause of somber reflection. Susan Riley's warm and sympathetic voice then broke the quiet.

"This brings our special broadcast to an end. I hope you found it beneficial and thought-provoking. Next week, we will

CHAPTER 19

Michael

Summer's heat passed to winter's cold. Michael no longer went to the small park to eat his lunch and play the guitar. He ate most of his lunches in the TXB cafeteria to avoid going out into the frigid weather. Michael, who had grown up in a small suburb of San Diego, was not used to the intense cold that penetrated the bones, the wet snow, or the weak sun, which lit the sky but didn't succeed in warming the earth.

One day he ate lunch in the cafeteria with one of his colleagues, Spencer, with whom he had a friendly relationship. His friend finished his meal and went on his way. Michael stayed at the table, slowly drinking a cup of coffee while going over some work-related information on his tablet.

"Excuse me, may I join you?" Michael heard a man's voice.

"I was just going to—" Michael started to answer, raising his head to look at the man who spoke to him. Much to his surprise, he saw producer Walter Lindsey in front of him, the target of his information-gathering mission.

"Do you mind if I sit with you a few minutes?" Lindsey

asked, his tone friendly.

"Go ahead," Michael said while wondering at the unexpected development.

Michael examined the man who now sat in front of him: in his forties and good-looking, with a mildly receding hairline and a small paunch. In Lindsey's clear green eyes Michael saw no sign of the cunning he might have expected to find, given McPherson's suspicions.

"What can I do for you?" Michael asked politely.

"You play the guitar, right?" Lindsey inquired.

"Yep, that's me."

"You're very good," Lindsey said. "I listened to you in the park a few times. I didn't want to bother you because you seemed so immersed in your playing."

"Thanks for the compliment," Michael said, ducking his head in shyness. Looking at Lindsey, Michael got the impression of unpretentious honesty. In his year as a researcher at TXB, Michael had interviewed many sources and learned to discern their level of credibility and sincerity. Walter Lindsey didn't give off the vibes of a liar, of someone who had plotted and deceived the whole country; but perhaps he was a professional pretender.

"I also play from time to time," Lindsey said.

"Guitar?" Michael asked.

"No, when I was a child I learned to play the piano, and now I play piano as well as synthesizer," Walter answered. "I also participate in a small band, just friends who gather at my house on weekends. Did you ever play in a band?"

"Yes," Michael answered, "during high school. I truly loved playing with my band."

"What did you play?" Lindsey was interested. "Lead guitar or rhythm guitar?"

"Usually lead guitar," Michael replied. "I also wrote songs."

"Lead guitar is exactly what our band is missing," Lindsey said with a nod of approval. "Would you be interested in visiting my house this weekend to see if you might fit in with our band?"

"I'd be happy to do that," Michael replied.

"Great, so we'll be in touch." Lindsey smiled in a friendly manner and held out his hand. "I have to go."

"See you," said Michael, who was moved by the warmth that Lindsey extended toward him.

Michael remained sitting, processing the unexpected development. He knew that he got closer to the objective that McPherson had assigned for him. With that, Lindsey had charmed him with his straightforward approach. Michael realized that he was much more enthusiastic about the prospect of playing in a band than about the chance of advancing McPherson's mission. He was quite uncomfortable with the idea of becoming a mole. But he reminded himself that at this stage, he was merely going to play music, not to betray anybody.

The phone call from McPherson came as expected. The journalist called Michael for an update at least twice a week.

Finally, Michael could honestly confirm that he had formed a connection with the producer.

"Excellent." McPherson was pleased. "Will you continue to meet?"

"This weekend, probably at his house. He wants me to play with his band," Michael said, reluctant to divulge the details.

"Well done," McPherson said. "It appears that my plan succeeds. I knew that music would bring you two together. Musicians are drawn to each other."

"There's also plenty of tough competition and jealousy among musicians," Michael pointed out. "They all want center stage."

"You're right," McPherson agreed in a mild tone, "but, in this case, both of you see music as a hobby. You're playing for personal enjoyment, not for the spotlight. I see no reason for competition here, but rather creative musical cooperation."

"I hope you're right," Michael said. "I'm looking forward to making music as part of a band."

"Just don't forget your mission," McPherson reminded him.

"I won't forget," Michael said without enthusiasm.

CHAPTER 20

Jonathan

Jonathan and Sarah continued to function as a married couple, assisting each other with household tasks. Together they went shopping, and together they fed the animals—the three dogs, eleven cats, the chickens, ducks, and the geese.

They held a joint bank account and shared the burden of mortgage payments and other ongoing expenses. Together they watched TV and exchanged their impressions of the different shows. They also continued to make love regularly. On the surface, nothing had changed.

But both of them knew that their relationship lost the deep, mutual caring, and they sensed the absence of the romantic spark. It was clear to the two of them that the breaking point had started to develop following Sarah's betrayals.

Sarah wanted to atone for hurting her husband, so she continued to prepare their dinners, but without the joy of creativity, and mostly because her conscience was bothering her.

She no longer prepared the meals with love as before, and

she recognized that the taste and the quality of the food were affected. Meals passed with fewer conversations and longer, heavier silences.

Sarah didn't stop going on her empty affairs. Already over forty, she knew her chance of getting pregnant was minimal. Nevertheless, she continued with her adventures, perhaps because she became addicted to the excitement, to the tense anticipation, to sensing increased vitality brought on by danger. She craved feeling attractive, desired, and young. She liked controlling men who were perhaps lonely and lost like her, letting them hunt her while actually, she hunted them. Inside of her sizzled a dusky need for revenge, a desire that possibly arose from a time when, decades ago, an unidentified man had taken advantage of her.

On rare occasions, she saw distant acquaintances, or even patients, while lurking at a bar waiting for prey. But they never recognized her. They knew a prim and proper psychologist, buttoned to the neck, hair tightly arranged. The woman sitting at the bar was immensely different. She dressed in tight, sexy, revealing outfit and wore heavy makeup, with loose hair that covered a part of her face, conveying a mysterious and challenging atmosphere around her.

Jonathan was hurt. As far as he was concerned, Sarah had pierced the delicate fabric they had carefully woven over the years with a sharp knife. While the relationship with his wife grew continue our journey back in time and turn the spotlight to the nineteenth century. We'll watch events from the American Civil War and the battles of Napoleon Bonaparte in Europe. Good night."

colder, his connection with Irene continued to develop. She was the woman he'd met over the internet, and now he enjoyed daily phone conversations with her. They discovered they had a lot in common. The two of them had lost parents in car accidents; they were both attracted to computers and shared an interest in the latest developments in the field. They shared sincere caring for each other. Both felt that the connection between them compensated them for the lack of love in their deteriorating marriages. Strangely, Jonathan felt that his attraction toward Irene, as good looking as she was, didn't carry the potential of becoming a romantic love affair. In his heart, Jonathan wished she would be the older sister he never had.

Jonathan longed for a family. He didn't know what the nature of a relationship between a brother and a sister was, so, he may have romanticized it. He imagined deep understanding and affection for one another, a sense that he could always trust her and she could count on him—on her little, strong, and loyal brother.

Irene informed him that she'd be in San Francisco for two days for a technology conference. She suggested it could be an opportunity to meet face-to-face.

Jonathan liked the idea. He decided to be straightforward with his wife. He wouldn't meet his special friend behind Sarah's back.

During dinner, he said, "I'm going to San Francisco for two days."

She looked at him with a questioning expression, understanding there must be a reason for the unexpected trip.

"I have a lady friend," he continued.

She shuddered and looked down at her plate, knowing this was the consequence of her actions.

"It's not what you're thinking," he added. "I met her on the internet, and we've become very close, but I don't see our relationship as a romantic connection. I see her as a good friend, kind of a big sister."

Sarah gave him a skeptical look, and he got the impression that she suspected he was not entirely candid with her, and maybe not with himself. Both knew that he had no reason to lie and that she couldn't blame him for disloyalty.

"I think it would be good for you to get away from the house every once in a while," Sarah said. She doubted her husband's new connection was indeed platonic and still, she breathed in relief when he said he did not intend on having a romantic affair.

"I somehow hope," Jonathan carefully revealed, "that, in some miraculous way, Irene is really my biological sister, maybe a half-sister."

Except for knowing that Irene's father was killed in the same year that his parents died, he had no knowledge on which to base that hope.

"Maybe it's not so important," Sarah said after a moment of silence.

"What's not important?" Jonathan wondered.

"If the connection between you is that special, is it so important if she is a biological sister or a soul sister?" With piercing regret, Sarah remembered that he used to see the connection with *her* as a connection between two souls.

***

Irene suggested that they meet during her lunch break in a park next to where the conference was held. Jonathan agreed; meeting in the open air suited him.

While driving his car to San Francisco, he was abruptly overcome by panic, when suddenly the whole story seemed delusional and irrational. Here he was, driving to actualize a connection which was not a love affair, out of a yearning to find a woman who could be a soul friend; but she? What were her expectations? Did she see him as a potential lover? And that wasn't his intention, was it? Maybe he was dishonest with himself like his wife probably thought? He knew he had made it clear to Irene that he did not intend to have an affair, but perhaps he wasn't explicit and unequivocal? Maybe it would have been better to leave the connection in the virtual plane? He kept driving, telling himself he must not give in to his fears.

When he finally saw her from a distance, she looked slightly taller than he pictured her. He walked toward her and stood in front of her, his heart pounding. She looked into his eyes, smiled, and shook his hand. She didn't hug him. His doubts subsided.

Irene looked just like in the photos she'd sent him, and he liked finding that she didn't pick photos in which she appeared particularly good, or younger than her age. Her face was pretty and gentle, despite minor wrinkles at the corners of her eyes. She had blonde hair interlaced with some gray. She was thin and just a little shorter than him. She dressed in a simple manner, yet, he thought that her clothes showed good taste.

As Jonathan suggested, they took a walk in the park; and while they conversed, the connection established over the phone clicked into place.

"If you like," Irene said, "I can get you into the conference's lecture hall."

"The conference is open to the public?" he wondered.

"No," she answered, "but I could get you an entry tag as an exhibitor's guest. I think you'll find the material interesting."

"That would be great," Jonathan said. He was always curious about new developments in technology, and his schedule was certainly free. He wasn't in a hurry to go anywhere.

He sat in the back of the large conference hall, in an area that was kept for visitors, glad for the opportunity to get a firsthand update in the field that so fascinated him. The presented material was indeed intriguing, and he was particularly interested in a revolutionary development that allowed, through advanced components and sophisticated algorithms, the sending of large amounts of data at much higher speeds than the current technology could. Irene was right: he found the material informative and interesting.

That evening, they decided to go to a restaurant located on a promenade near the ocean. They walked slowly along the wharf, letting the breeze flutter their hair as they talked about hazy childhood memories. At a restaurant on the pier, they sat next to a window overlooking the water and ordered a meal of fish, noodles, and vegetables. It turned out that they had similar tastes in food. In no hurry to go anywhere, they lingered after dinner and ordered coffee and cake as they watched the lights of the bay.

Jonathan related a distant memory: "I loved my grandmother. There was an old tattoo of a number on her arm. She said that the Germans marked her that way when she was in the camp. I was little, and I didn't understand why they had to mark her. She said that her son, my father, was Jewish, which is why I have a Jewish family name, Lishinsky. But she also said that my mother wasn't Jewish, which is why I am not Jewish. It was quite confusing."

"Oh my God!" Irene said.

"What happened?" Jonathan was worried he might have said the wrong thing.

"Suddenly I remembered something," she said slowly, as though looking at a forgotten memory that surfaced from the obscurity of her subconscious.

He looked at her and patiently waited.

"It's really strange," she said, "I didn't think about it for years, and, suddenly, while you were talking…"

"What was it?" he quietly encouraged her.

"Whenever I mastered something in school, my mother used to tell me, 'You are clever, just like your father.' I remember being surprised every time because she hardly ever mentioned him. One time, she added, 'He was a smart Jewish man.'"

"So, your father was Jewish too?" Chills ran along Jonathan's spine. He wasn't sure if doing so was the right thing, but he asked the question that burned in his mind: "Tell me, is it possible that my father and your father are the same man?"

She blinked in surprise and said, "A DNA test could solve that, but I don't see a reason to rush out and get one done." "There's no reason to hurry," Jonathan agreed.

CHAPTER 21

Sarah and Jonathan

Sarah came home from work early and took the dogs for a walk in the forest. She took Bono, the aggressive Doberman who was the son of Princess, their first dog; Bucky, the easy-going wolfdog; and Narla, a small, old female dog whose previous owner had left with them five years earlier when he'd gone to work in Alaska. The dogs loved these excursions, loved to poke around and discover the magical world concealed among the forest's trees. Still, they didn't like to venture into the woods by themselves, but only if one of their two-legged owners accompanied them.

Sarah led the dogs on a trail bordering the neighbor's estate. The dogs were excited as they dug between the tree trunks and disturbed small forest animals that were busy with their daily routine.

Every once in a while, Sarah heard the crows warning of intruders. When they neared the creek, which at that section was the border between the two estates, Bono suddenly charged forward and, furiously barking, he stormed down the hill in the direction of the creek. Bucky ran after him, barking and wagging his tail. Sarah ran after Bucky. Last was old Narla, plodding along, barking and trying to look irate.

"Bono!" Sarah called, "Stop! What's the matter?"

Bono stopped when he reached the bank where the creek was quite deep and difficult to cross.

Panting, Sarah arrived at the creek, where she saw the reason for the dogs' commotion. On the other side of the creek, which was usually deserted, stood three men, who were busy tying yellow ribbons around the trees.

Sarah silenced her excited dogs so she could talk to the strangers. The three men turned to face her but didn't look pleased about being disturbed.

"Hi!" she called.

"Howdy," responded one tough-looking big guy, as he examined Sarah and her dogs. The Doberman pressed his body against Sarah's leg, bared his teeth, and growled. The normally easygoing wolf hybrid stood nearby, ears pinned and hackles raised. Narla just panted and wagged her tail.

"What are you doing?" Sarah inquired in a suspicious tone of voice, taking confidence in the dogs' ability to protect her.

"The landowners are planning to log the trees on their property," the man answered. "We're conducting a survey for them."

"To log?" She was disheartened. "My husband and I know old Bruce Jensen, and there's no chance he would agree to such a horrible action."

"Lady," the big guy politely responded, "old Bruce Jensen died three months ago. His son Kevin now owns the property and wants to cut the trees. We were just hired to conduct the survey."

He turned his head to his colleagues and muttered, "Women—they get all emotional 'bout some darned trees."

Sarah heard him and bristled. "That's right!" she yelled, "and freaking guys like to chop 'em down for money!"

Sarah worried. She loathed forest logging and considered it a crime against innocent and helpless living entities. She thought it was her duty to protect the forest. She knew the wide sequoia trunks were worth a lot of money, and the landowner stood to make a fortune from harvesting them.

She committed herself to recruit their other neighbors to fight this desecration of their environment.

***

That evening, Jonathan came home from work to find his wife upset. With tears in her eyes, she told him about the incident by the creek.

"We'll fight it," Jonathan assured and hugged her. "They need to get a permit from the county, and we'll be there to protest. We'll get the neighbors involved, too."

Later, Sarah called neighbors and other Corralitos residents whom she thought might sympathize with her cause.

Two weeks later, residents near the property destined for logging received a notice detailing the wide-scale logging plan at the Jensen's estate, and the time of the hearing at the county offices.

Sarah and Jonathan met with those neighbors who supported environmental issues. They planned their moves and thought of all the reasons why the project must not get underway.

Sarah and Jonathan became the leaders of the opposition to the logging plan. They wished the threat did not exist but recognized that the joint struggle unified them. Once again, friendship, appreciation, and affection characterized their marriage.

***

About thirty people came to the meeting that took place at the county offices. Most of them attended via Jonathan and Sarah's invitation and sided with their point of view. Several people represented Kevin Jensen, the landowner who wished to execute the logging.

When the floor opened to public comments, Jonathan asked to address the meeting. He went up to the small podium and held the microphone stand. Although his conduct conveyed self-confidence, when he started to speak, his voice trembled.

He said, "My wife and I have been worried ever since we learned about the plan to log the parcel next to our land.

If allowed to proceed, the logging would have a devastating impact on the vegetation, as it will take decades to replace the current old growth."

Jonathan paused to look at the crowd, who was attentively listening to his words. Taking a deep breath, he continued.

"Logging will also have a harmful effect on wildlife, especially birds when their habitat would be ruined." He looked at his audience and, seeing mainly support, grew enthusiastic. "And let's not forget the destructive effect on life in the creek, because the roots of the trees filter the rainwater flowing into it. We know from examples around the state that the fish have disappeared in rivers running through clear-cut areas."

Jonathan looked in the direction of the county representatives and concluded, "Logging requires heavy equipment and heavy trucks. Our roads are not built to withstand that traffic. Who is going to pay to fix them?"

Sarah avoided speaking. She knew that if she tried to express her opinions, emotion would overwhelm her, she'd start crying, and probably say things she'd regret, and that wouldn't serve the cause.

The council members recorded both sides' arguments and announced they'd send their decision in the mail in about six weeks, after checking all the aspects associated with the plan.

In the following days, Sarah prayed the trees would survive, and Jonathan recognized that the threat of clearing the forest was troubling him as well. Sarah thanked him for supporting her, despite the difficulties in their relationship. Jonathan appreciated the devotion and totality that she showed toward the helpless trees and her focus on something besides her own problems.

But six weeks later, they received the disheartening notification that they lost the fight. The logging plan would commence during the upcoming dry summer season.

***

Large, heavy trucks rumbled on the roads around their property. During the first phase, the trucks carried bulldozers and other heavy equipment. Later, the trucks drove on the dirt and paved roads transporting their prize, the boles of the felled trees which had been sawed without mercy. Some of the trees were hundreds of years old; their trunks were so wide that a truck could not carry more than three logs at the time.

The noise was horrible. Electrical saws roared from the early morning hours, rattling nonstop, followed by the sounds of the helplessly falling giant trees, crushing in a muffled bang that echoed their outcry over long distances.

Sarah left for work early in the mornings to minimize her exposure to the awful noise. The destruction brought tears to her eyes and filled her with rage, directed at the injustice that men were committing against nature—against Mother Earth.

One morning, before Jonathan and Sarah went to work, they noticed the silence that prevailed all around.

"Could it be they've already finished?" Sarah wondered. She was relieved that she could sit comfortably and drink a cup of coffee, without the rattle of the saws and the pounding sounds of the falling trees.

"Maybe they took a day off," Jonathan suggested.

"Yeah," she said, "a day off from their eco-terrorism."

When they returned home, blessed quiet still blanketed their land. Sarah enjoyed listening to the birds as they were busy preparing for their night's sleep. At about 7:30 p.m., a police car quietly rolled into their parking area. The dogs immediately burst with loud barks and furiously ran toward the intruders. Sarah ran after the dogs to catch them before they bit someone.

"What's the matter?" Sarah said, approaching the car while holding the Doberman's collar and quieting the other two dogs. Two officers got out of the vehicle.

"Good evening," said one cop, "Are you Mrs. Lishinsky?"

"Yes." She answered, and looked at the two policemen suspiciously.

"I am Officer Frank Shaver, and this is Sergeant Brent Workman. We're investigating the massive sabotage of the logging company's equipment last night. We need to question your husband."

"What is this about?" asked Jonathan, stepping out of the house.

"Honey, they claim you sabotaged the logger's equipment!"

Jonathan trembled because it had been a long time since she had called him honey.

"Sir," said Officer Shaver, "we can ask our questions here, or you can come to the station."

"Here is fine," Jonathan said as he gestured toward the front door. "I have nothing to hide."

The policemen followed Jonathan and Sarah into the house, observing the interior. Jonathan led them into the dining room, and they sat across the table from him.

"Where do you work?" Officer Shaver asked.

"At Excel-Part," Jonathan answered shortly.

"In San Jose?"

"Yes."

"What do you do over there?"

"I maintain computers and related accessories."

"Did you sabotage the equipment of the logging company?"

"No."

"Do you know who did it?"

"No."

"Where were you last night?"

"At home with my wife." Jonathan tried not to show hesitation, although he hadn't been entirely truthful. Sarah had yet to come home when he went to bed.

"You'll have to come with us to the police station to take a polygraph test," said Officer Shaver with a somber facial expression.

"Now?" Jonathan asked.

"Yes," the officer replied. "According to the law, you are not obligated to take the test; however, let me advise you that if you refuse, it might look like the behavior of someone who has something to hide, and can intensify the investigation against you."

"I have nothing to hide," Jonathan reiterated as he stood. "I'll come with you, but you're wasting your time. If there was sabotage, it wasn't me."

The law enforcement officers escorted Jonathan to their vehicle.

Sarah spent the evening alone, overwhelmed with worry. She wondered how she'd manage on her own if Jonathan were sent to prison. She realized how much she needed him, understood how important he was to her, and how much she appreciated his quiet manners and their life together—the life she was destroying.

Jonathan returned home a bit past midnight. He told his wife, who breathed with relief, that the polygraph test hadn't taken long. But afterward, the cops continued to interrogate him. They claimed that the polygraph results were inconclusive.

Jonathan assumed that the polygraph provided the police with an excuse to interrogate him more intensively. After failing to draw a confession from him and without sufficient evidence to charge him with the crime, they had to release him and drive him home.

Sarah admired her husband's stalwart nature. She thought that, if she were in his place, she couldn't have endured the ordeal with such bravery. She did not ask him if he had anything to do with the sabotage. In her private thoughts, she hoped he had and that he'd done it for her.

CHAPTER 22

Sarah

Her father was dying. Julie persuaded Sarah to accompany her back to St. Louis to visit with their father before he passed away.

"You need to forgive him," Julie said. "Besides, *I* need you there to keep me from killing somebody. They're all wacko."

Not having seen her parents since she left for California, Sarah consented to keep her sister company.

Sarah went alone to her sister's house in San Francisco, because Jonathan had no interest in joining.

"This is your time and your memories," he said.

Sarah didn't argue; she knew her husband didn't cope well with emotional stress.

When she arrived in San Francisco, she learned that Edmond, her sister's husband, would join them on the long journey. That disappointed her. She hoped to spend the time during travel with Julie, to prepare for the complicated family meeting that lay ahead of them.

At the airport, they learned that their flight was several

hours behind schedule. Edmond immediately lost his patience, harangued the ticket agent to get them on another flight right away, and then complained nonstop when the ticket agent apologized and stated that all outgoing flights were fully booked.

"I'm going to sue the airline company," Edmond announced.

Sarah tried to ignore him.

Finally, they boarded. Sarah had a window seat, far from her sister. She tried to remember the good times she'd had with her father: how he had taught her to ride a bicycle and how he used to take her with him when he went fishing. Her fondest memories were of him sitting by the bed and playing the guitar until she fell asleep. Little Sarah loved listening to his playing and watching him strumming and fingerpicking the strings. Now she wondered if her long-lost son had inherited her father's musical ability.

Upon arrival, they took a taxi from the St. Louis airport to her childhood home, where her parents still lived, to meet her mother and older brother. Sarah wished she could delay the family reunion. She wondered if she had the mental strength required to deal with intricate family dynamics. For a moment she envied her husband who didn't have a family and didn't have to deal with unrealistic expectations.

As expected, she felt like an outsider and had difficulty contributing to conversations.

Her mother, big brother, nieces and nephews identified

themselves as Protestant Christians. They held conservative opinions.

Sarah sat in her parents' crowded living room, among family members and friends she hardly knew. The atmosphere was gloomy as everyone knew these were Leonard Sanders' last days. The conversations veered from solemn to light with moments of shared laughter. They talked about the dying Mr. Sanders and political issues.

Sarah wanted to remain unnoticed in the background and held her silence. It wasn't a time for confrontations.

"These darned liberals just want to take away our guns," her brother said, "They don't want people to have the ability to defend themselves."

She listened and nodded, supposedly agreeing.

"The gays and lesbians—all those perverts," her born-again niece chirped when a new conversation tackled social justice, "they choose this lifestyle of abomination, and are surely going straight to hell."

Julie nudged Sarah and stifled a snort. Sarah blinked and realized how much she and her sister had changed.

She visited her father in the hospital. His appearance disturbed her. Scrawny and withered, connected to life support equipment; it looked like the life force had already left his body. Not recognizing her, he asked her to light a cigarette for him.

She looked at the thin piece of meat which used to be her

strong, energetic, and admired father.

Why can't I forgive him? She asked herself. *I should remember him in his good days, but I can't forget how he and Mom betrayed me. They betrayed me; there's no other way to look at it. They sent me to a faraway monastery so that their darned friends wouldn't see me, wouldn't see the embarrassment. They had no compassion for me, just when I needed them the most. So, no, I won't blame myself for not feeling compassion for him.*

Her brother and sister, standing next to her beside their father's bed, wept. Sarah just wished that it would all end. The hospital environment made her feel gloomy and reminded her of the painful experience in the hospital in Phoenix. Feeling claustrophobic, she badly needed fresh air.

She excused herself and took a walk in the old neighborhood near her parents' house. She looked around. Old memories filled her. They hurt.

She wandered to the park and sat on a bench, ignoring the overcast sky and cold wind. This was the place, she knew. *It all started here, the event that changed my life and tore it apart—and I can't even remember it. Did I suppress the memory?*

She got up and started walking toward her parents' house, on the trail she used to take as a young girl. She walked slowly, assuming this must be the path she took on that day, so many years ago. A sudden cold gust hit her face and blew off her hat. She ran after it. The hat landed on the edge of the pavement, next to the street, as if hinting at something that escaped her. As she got close to the cap, the wind picked it up again and tossed it further and further. Sarah ran after the hat, amazed at the naughty wind's play. Panting, she finally managed to reach down and grab her disobedient hat, when suddenly something struck her mind.

The hazy memory didn't materialize immediately. It was a flicker, crude and shapeless, a vague sensation that hinted at a breakthrough, like she was about to recall something that eluded her all these years. What was it? Standing on the sidewalk, she closed her eyes, trying hard to concentrate. A car drove by. *Yes, there was a car.* Not now, but then, on that long-ago day. A car followed her, slowed down, and the driver rolled down his window. He turned to her, spoke to her, and she wasn't afraid of him.

Sarah trembled. Who was he? What did he look like? Was he a teacher at her school? A friend of her parents? A relative? She knew him; he was part of the environment where she grew up, someone who conveyed friendship, someone she could trust. Then the memory dimmed.

***

At the funeral, Sarah allowed the tears to flow. She stood by the open grave and wept for all that she had lost: the innocence of childhood, her youth, her son, and her husband's trust. She cried about her life that was passing without her realizing her deep desire to become a mother.

After the funeral, Julie and Edmond started to prepare for their return to California. In a last-minute decision, Sarah informed them that she would make her way back in a rented car. Edmond looked surprised, but Julie nodded in agreement and sympathy. Her sister understood that Sarah had gone through a storm of emotions following their father's death and her return to her childhood's scenery. She saw that Sarah needed time to relax, collect herself, and think about her plans.

"Take care of yourself," Julie whispered as they hugged.

The next day Sarah rented a mid-sized Chevy that seemed comfortable and suitable for the long journey. She bade her mother and brother goodbye and felt nothing more than relief in leaving them. She called Jonathan to tell him about her plans, and he sounded supportive and told her not to worry; he understood she needed time for herself. *Is he being supportive or just likes being there without me?* With a sigh, Sarah realized she had no right to bear a grudge against her husband, even if he were having an affair in her absence.

Sarah went on her way, and when she saw St. Louis in the rearview mirror, she breathed with relief. Alone on the road, she felt freed from her troubles. She tuned the radio to an oldies station and sang along. When Steppenwolf's "Born to Be Wild" started playing she turned up the volume.

She headed southwest on Route 44 and spent the night at a roadside motel near Tulsa, Oklahoma. She woke up the following day feeling refreshed and hopeful. Passing through Oklahoma City, she took Route 40 westbound. She didn't turn on the GPS, preferring to let the road take her.

Route 40 took her through Texas and to New Mexico. Sarah only took short breaks for gas, food, and some stretching exercises. When she saw a signpost pointing to Santa Fe, she turned the wheel onto Highway 285, even though it wasn't leading back to California. In Santa Fe, she rented a room in a small hotel. After a short rest and a relaxing bath, she went for a walk along the picturesque streets. The lively sounds of Salsa lured her inside a small club where a band of four musicians played. She ordered supper and a bottle of beer. A guy sitting by the counter smiled at her, but she ignored him. She felt light and free as if she had cast off, even temporarily, the burden of time and regret.

At night she lay in bed and mulled over the old, partial memory that came out of oblivion, trying to tease out more detail: the car driving next to her and the driver…

He talked to me, maybe asked something, and I answered him without fear because apparently, I knew him. But what happened after that? Did I get into his car? Did he force himself on me? Did he take advantage of my innocence? There was something about him that inspired trust, but what was it?

Her memory refused to relinquish answers. She knew she must let go so she could fall asleep.

The following day she had a light breakfast and continued on her way. This time she listened to relaxing music as she drove. A heady sense of freedom entertained her with the possibility that she could go anywhere she chose. All she had to do was turn the wheel. She could cross the border into Mexico and disappear…

She drove from Santa Fe to Albuquerque, returning to Route 40 westbound, which led into Arizona. When the road sign appeared showing a left turn toward Phoenix, she knew she had to go back there to revisit the convent, a place that had both healed and hurt her many years ago. Twenty-two years, she calculated in her head, meaning her son was already twenty-two years old, older than she was when she had given birth to him. The convent was the place where she arrived as an innocent young girl, only to leave more mature, and mentally hurt. That was the place where she had lost her naiveté and her trust in human beings.

Feeling tired, she navigated to a small hotel. She had dinner at a restaurant nearby and went to sleep early.

The following day she got up early, entered the car, and turned on the GPS. She remembered the name of the convent, *The Sisterhood of the Holy Cross*, and typed it in. The system announced, "Drive safely, turn right." She went on her way and followed the directions. She made a right turn and a left turn, she passed through traffic lights and roundabouts, and after about half an hour she reached her destination. She recognized the place and saw that the main gate was closed, but a service door next to it was open. She parked the car.

Now what? She sat in the car and wondered what she was looking for. Should she enter? Would they recognize her? She stepped out of the car, walked through the open door, and entered a beautiful and well-maintained garden. A long time ago, she had worked there, gardening and cleaning. She saw a fountain that she didn't remember. "Fountain of Blessing" read the engraved sign on the rockery. She sat down on a bench and listened to the trickling sound of the water. A feeling of peace and calm settled upon her.

A young nun passed by, smiled, and asked, "Do you need help?"

"I'm OK. I just came for a visit," Sarah replied.

The nun nodded and went on her way.

Thoughts and memories engulfed her. *Would I be happy if I'd stayed here? It is undoubtedly a protected environment, although the nuns lead an austere life.*

She recalled a distant memory, from when she thought being a nun might be the right path for her life. One day, she'd prayed with utmost devotion and called Jesus to come into her heart. That night, she'd been exposed to an extraordinary Christian experience.

She'd awakened in the middle of the night, eyes wide open. A few seconds passed before she could grasp the astonishing scene revealed to her. She saw a huge cross that radiated an intense, blinding light. It dazzled her eyes.

And then she knew. *I am in the presence of the divine. God has revealed himself even to a person of such weak faith as myself.*

Her heart pounded. Fear filled her mind and soul. Her hair

bristled. Thoughts ran through her mind at lightning speed. *I didn't believe it could happen, and here it's happening. What does it mean? Do I have to become a nun for my entire life?*

She didn't know how much time passed, perhaps twenty seconds, perhaps an eternity. Then the picture cleared, and she understood the reason for the spectacle. Her eyes adjusted to the light and the vision faded. Sarah told herself she had merely seen an optical illusion. She relaxed and felt relieved. Now she saw things as they were.

The powerful lantern in the convent's yard projected a strong light. Its beam penetrated the window, hit the metal cabinet locker next to Sarah's bed, and reflected straight into her eyes. It was a standard, 4-pane window. The muntin and mullion cast a shadow creating the cross.

Sarah understood that the vision stemmed from an optical illusion; still, she reflected on all the unique variables that had to come together for her to experience that magic.

She wondered if living in the convent was a way to escape the challenges of life. Really, would she want to live without men? They could be unbearable, true, and still, how was it possible to live without them? And wasn't it a waste to go through life without sex? Making love? Wasn't sex a natural, God-given energy?

Sarah recalled the time after her son was taken from her, when anger and thoughts of heresy filled her. She had lain in bed, looked at the crucifix on the wall, and wondered who Jesus really was. She'd assumed he was a human being, a Jew, who probably didn't look like the many paintings and statues that decorated the convent. He probably looked Mediterranean with black, curly hair. But was he righteous? Honorable? Had his status corrupted him like the mother superior? Did he have a lover? Mary Magdalene?

Looking back at her feelings during those days with a more mature perspective, Sarah wondered about her attraction to Jesus' magnetizing image. Maybe it had been transference? As a professional psychologist, she pondered whether the nuns' love for Jesus, and even for the Virgin Mary, stemmed from the repression of natural urges.

She heard the nuns singing in harmonious voices and wondered if her friend Mona was still there.

Sarah knew that she wouldn't have found harmony in monastic life. She remembered the mother superior and her secrets and how the head nun had cooperated with robbing her of her son. *Only painful memories remain here.* She decided to go back home, to the challenges of life.

CHAPTER 23

Jonathan

About two weeks after Jonathan and Sarah discovered that strange glade on the densely wooded hill, Jonathan went back. Princess, their female Doberman, was happy to accompany him on his way through the forest. Jonathan crossed the creek, leaping on rocks that protruded above the water while Princess joyfully paddled in the cold water right behind him. But when they arrived at the bottom of the hill, Princess refused to proceed, so Jonathan continued alone. This time he carried with him a hoe, a pickax, and a shovel, which he had recently purchased at a garden supply store. In a backpack, he had a water bottle and a small gardening spade.

Jonathan wasn't one of those people who felt transcendental energies. He didn't connect to New Age teachings, and he never hugged trees, as his wife could have. Not believing in any pagan faith; still, he was immersed with a strange sense of reverence and his heart pounded when he moved the last branches out of his way and stepped into the protected site. Inside the circle, he felt how stillness prevailed; it was an unusual, powerful quietness like the silence in the eye of a storm.

A tiny hiss spun through the surrounding trees, although he didn't notice any wind. The sun shone from a clear sky.

Jonathan thought the site might have served the early inhabitants for ancient rituals. Perhaps it served as a prehistoric astronomical clock or a star observatory.

Driven by curiosity as well as a gut feeling, he wished to explore and excavate the place. However, he kept his plan secretive and didn't share his intentions with Sarah.

Strangely, he felt an urge to ask permission before starting his work. Whose permission? He didn't know. He sat on the earth, turned his face toward the partially chiseled rock, and tried to feel the energy of the place, as his wife would probably do. He sensed nothing out of the ordinary. His ears caught the sounds of birds coming from the forest. He stood up and laid both palms on the massive rock. The rock was warm to the touch, possibly because it absorbed the sun's rays. There was something unusual about the rock's texture; Jonathan wasn't sure if he connected to something, or perhaps he just imagined it. Intuition hinted that the rock was part of a much larger structure, like the tip of an iceberg that had gotten covered by soil over many years. He felt that the structure called him to unearth it.

Using the hoe, he carefully dug around the rock. The hard

soil resisted his efforts and kept progress slow. Jonathan had never studied archeology, but he had watched several TV documentaries that showed the excavation of historical sites. Digging close to the rock, he exchanged the hoe for the small gardening spade. That slowed him even more, but he wasn't in a hurry. He felt calm and enjoyed the challenge that he had taken upon himself.

After a few hours of rigorous and meticulous labor, in which he only paused occasionally to drink water, he managed to expose two feet of the rock, which now was about six feet tall. With the shovel, he scattered the dirt among the forest's trees.

Shaded by the trees, the place cooled off rapidly. Jonathan left his tools on the hilltop, next to the edge of the circle, and made his way back home. The dog waited for him at the bottom of the hill.

CHAPTER 24

Michael

On Friday, Walter Lindsey called and invited Michael to come to his house on the following day, at 4:00 p.m., to meet his friends and see if he could participate and fit into the band's playing.

"We decided not to be professional musicians," Walter explained, "but we're not amateurs. We treat music with utmost seriousness and also as a source of great enjoyment." Lindsey sounded casual when he added, "come and play with us for fun, and we'll see if we're good enough for you."

On Friday evening and Saturday morning, Michael practiced diligently. He'd never been to an audition because the high school band in which he'd played, was *his* band. This time was going to be different. He also remembered that, if he wanted to investigate the films of *The Broadcast*, he probably wouldn't get a better chance. He was excited and more than a little nervous.

Michael arrived at the producer's house at the allotted time, using the old car that he received from his parents when they'd purchased a new one. On weekdays, he didn't drive the car and used public transportation instead. That way, he avoided the heavy New York traffic and having to deal with finding a parking space.

Walter Lindsey's house was in Scarsdale, a quiet suburb and a wealthy community north of New York City. It was a nice-looking house, large and spacious, but not extravagant, and not much different in size from Michael's parents' house. The band gathered in a wooden cabin in the backyard behind the house, and Michael noticed that the walls were lined with a special noise-proofing material, so as not to disturb the neighbors. Walter introduced Michael to his friends, who welcomed him with polite handshakes and kind words.

He met Julian, the TV director who was the lead singer and played rhythm guitar; Alex, the technology expert who specialized in animation and played drums and percussions; and Eric, the literature and history professor who played bass guitar. Michael brought the Martin acoustic guitar he had received from McPherson, but it turned out that Walter had prepared a quality Fender electric guitar for him.

The band's musical preferences matched Michael's. They played mostly old songs that he knew and loved, songs he'd played numerous times before with his high school band. As a lead guitar player, he had to play known solo parts of tunes by Led Zeppelin, Deep Purple, Pink Floyd, Eric Clapton, The Beatles, and more. While tuning the guitar, he felt excited about returning to his old love of playing music as part of a band.

But when the band started to play the first song, "Layla" by Eric Clapton, Michael was dismayed to find himself struggling like never before. It was as if there was an interruption in the connection between his head and his fingers. He looked at his stiff fingers, which looked like they belonged to someone else, and attempted to tell them to relax. But nervousness engulfed him, perhaps because he knew that much was at stake, and he wasn't used to the distinct interpretations the band gave the songs.

He was the new guy, while they were old friends who had played together for many years. At once, he felt like the outsider, the different one; like he used to feel as a child who yearned to blend in and wondered if he was like the other children.

The meeting lasted about two hours, during which they took short breaks, drank beer, and discussed trivial issues. Lindsey and his friends gave no indication of impatience regarding his nervous fumbling, so Michael wasn't sure to what degree they noticed his mistakes. Only near the end of the session did he finally let go of the anxiety and get into the groove. He even started to enjoy.

When the musical gathering was over, the musicians patted Michael on his shoulder in a friendly manner and went on their way.

"It wasn't my day." Michael felt the need to apologize when only Walter and he remained in the cabin. "I was nervous."

"You were fine," Walter said. "It's understandable that on the first time it's not easy to blend in with musicians who have known each other for years. We all noticed that you made a serious effort, and, at the end, you played 'Hotel California' beautifully."

Much to Michael's surprise, Walter invited him to stay for supper. Walter locked the cabin's door and Michael followed him as he entered the house through the back entrance.

Walter's wife, Monica, just returned from visiting her sister, and Walter introduced her to Michael.

"Michael is a promising reporter working for *Around the Clock*," Walter said, and Michael was perplexed. "He is also an excellent guitar player," Walter continued, "I hope he'll become a permanent member of our group because we need a lead guitar player."

Elegantly dressed, Monica Lindsey cordially shook Michael's hand. She looked like she was in her early forties, a woman of medium height, slightly stocky build, and short brown hair that emphasized her delicate facial features.

"I would be delighted if you would stay for supper," Monica said with a polite smile.

Walter busied himself with holiday lights. He plugged in the cable to illuminate the large Christmas tree which now flickered with many tiny colorful lights, and he lit candles in the Hanukkah menorah which stood next to the tree.

"My father was Jewish," Walter explained, gesturing toward the holiday symbols of two faith's rituals, "and I like to keep the tradition."

Michael liked Christmas, especially the season of Advent preceding Christmas Day. He noticed how the holiday had a certain spirit that inspired strangers to smile at one another. He also liked how the windows of houses and stores were decorated in the holiday tradition, and beautifully wrapped gifts were scattered beneath the Christmas tree.

Michael knew little about Hanukkah, but he found the combination of the Christmas tree and the menorah interesting. He liked how the menorah's candles spread warmth, and not just cold, electric light.

Walter and Monica's younger daughter, Caroline, joined them for supper along with her friend. The two girls were in their last year of high school and had plans to study for an exam and then go shopping. Walter mentioned that his older daughter, Melanie, was a law student at Stanford University, and she would soon come home for a holiday visit.

The warm, pleasant ambiance in the Lindsey household reminded Michael of his beloved family. He missed them.

After supper, Michael thanked his hosts for the lovely hospitality and departed. On his way home, he remembered Stewart McPherson's assignment with feelings of shame and regret. He realized he just met good people who treated him with kindness and affection, and he wasn't honest with them. He was pleased Walter and his friends said nothing about *The Broadcast*, so he wouldn't have to betray them.

CHAPTER 25

Jonathan

Jonathan continued to excavate the site, which turned out to be a source of great excitement for him. Over a period of about one year, he went to the mysterious hill as often as possible. It was *his* project. Sarah didn't return to the glade and never inquired what he was doing over there.

After cleaning the soil around the rock, it reached about six feet in height, with a width of about four feet. As he assumed, the rock was not singular but part of a structure. He worked very carefully, so as not to harm the large rocks, which were gradually being exposed.

He uncovered a stone circle of about twenty feet in diameter, composed of big rocks; each placed about four feet apart with their chiseled sides facing the center.

After he finished excavating the circle of large rocks, he started digging outside of it. He discovered another ring, composed of smaller rocks in the same configuration as the inner circle.

At that point, the site contained two circles of rocks. The place looked very similar to another site, far away, where he had once visited, Stonehenge, in England, although much smaller in scale. Jonathan recalled a magazine article theorizing upon the similarity of civilizations which seemingly had no geographical connection; for instance, the existence of pyramids in Egypt, Mexico, and Indonesia.

***

Jonathan remembered his visit to Stonehenge. For one of their vacations, Jonathan and Sarah went to England, where Jonathan went to visit the famous site on a day that Sarah chose to stay in London. He told his wife that he would like to continue to follow *Chariots of the Gods,* the book that captured his imagination and visit some of the sites that author Erich von Däniken mentioned.

Jonathan knew that not all the theories that von Däniken suggested correlated with scientific research. Still, he was drawn to the possibilities suggested by the Swiss writer: primarily the assumption that some of our religious beliefs stemmed from ancient encounters with aliens that came from distant worlds.

He boarded a bus to Wiltshire, the county where the famous prehistoric site was located. Stonehenge was surrounded by grounds of green grass and contained huge, heavy rocks, which were standing in pairs and created a circle of about eighty-five feet in diameter. Above each pair, another massive rock was laid. The entrance to the ring was in the exact direction through which the sun shone on the twenty-first of June, the longest day of the year.

Jonathan knew that much about Stonehenge was shrouded in mystery, that it was not clear how it was created and for what purpose. How were such massive rocks brought there, carried over a distance of about twenty miles? He learned that the rocks could have weighed over forty tons. Did the ancient people who created the place, between 3000 to 2000 BC, have the capability for such a complicated engineering operation? And if not, then who helped them? And what purpose did it serve? Was it for the sake of some ancient pagan ritual for the sun god? Or maybe as a huge astronomical clock that would help in predicting lunar and solar eclipses?

The questions had been on Jonathan's mind as he walked through the visitors' center and paid for the admission ticket. He faced disappointment. It turned out that visitors were no longer allowed to reach out and touch the rocks, which were surrounded by a fence, to protect them from getting harmed by humans. Still, he was moved by the enormous dimensions of the pillars, which emitted a sense of power and stability. He tried to imagine the primitives gathering for a ceremony for the sun's god and recalled that they might have practiced human sacrifice.

He was not in a hurry to leave the site, and he stayed there until it was dark and the site closed to visitors. There was something about the place that attracted him, engulfed him with a feeling of belonging, a sense that he was part of a whole and not cut off. He tried to grasp what it was that made him feel closer to himself and his concealed destiny.

***

In the glade of his property's unusual hill, surrounded by the wall of trees, Jonathan felt protected from the harm and mischief of the world. At the site, he felt that he was at an extraordinarily powerful location, and it occurred to him that the site was bringing him closer to a destination that was yet to be revealed to him. When he was at the glade, he sensed that there was a deep, hidden meaning to his life, which was not merely passing and futile, as he sometimes felt it to be. On that hilltop, he was able to review his memories and see past events with unusual clarity and acuity.

After he completed excavating the outer circle of rocks, he focused his attention on the navel point of the site. He worked slowly, diligently, and with extra care. He laid down the pickax and the hoe and worked with the little gardening spade and with his bare hands.

He was driven by intuition because he didn't have anything to refer to. Slowly and gradually, one more rock emerged. It was about forty inches squared and about twenty inches tall and reminded him of a table, or perhaps an ancient altar.

On the day that he completed excavating the site, Jonathan cleaned the place and spread the extra soil among the densely growing forest trees.

Basking in a feeling of accomplishment, Jonathan sat on the center stone, crossed his legs, and let his eyelids drift nearly shut. Although he was not interested in Far Eastern methods, here on the rock, it was the most reasonable way of sitting.

After some time, he opened his eyes and looked to the west. He saw the sun setting over the distant hills…

But how was that possible? Didn't the trees block the view? He watched attentively and perceived a gap between the trees, a narrow strip through which the sun's rays penetrated without hindrance.

He looked in the opposite direction, eastward and perceived another strip clear of foliage, and he understood that had he been there in the early morning hours, he would have seen the sunrise. He remembered the date, the twenty-first of June, the summer solstice. The tiny space that the trees opened up was utterly incomprehensible. He thought that it was highly unlikely that someone has recently visited the site and cut the branches with electric pruning-shears.

The descending sun continued on its way and left a golden trail in the sky. Usually, he headed home at dusk, but that day he decided to stay a little longer and ponder his discovery. The strange occurrence excited him, and he knew that he wouldn't get lost on his way back home, as he was very familiar with the land.

The sight of the sun setting between the trees was an unexplained wonder. He sat on the rock at the center of the site and waited. He sensed that something was going to happen. The sound of birds flapping their wings arose behind him, between the forest's trees, but he didn't turn his head to watch the birds.

An old memory flashed through his mind, passed on its way like the sun. But unlike the sun, over which he had no control, he was able to stop the passage of the memory, examine it attentively, with incredible clarity and acuity. He saw it as if he were there, at the most crucial event of his life. The accident.

He saw himself as a small child, buckled in his toddler seat. He looked forward and saw the heads of his parents, who sat in the front seat. His father drove the car. His mother had long and wavy blonde hair. The ride was smooth. Then things happened within a split second. His mother screamed. In the past, when he had run the event in his mind, there were times when he thought he heard her frightened scream, but this time it was close, frightening, and unnerving.

"Robert, watch out!"

His father tried to dodge the big truck approaching fast. Then there were horrible noises of clashing metals and shattered glasses, and there was a sharp pain, and… nothing more. Little Jonathan must have lost consciousness.

Jonathan stood up for a while, and then walked slowly to the circle's perimeter. Glancing back, he left the site with a feeling of reverence. He walked down the hill at a moderate pace and had no difficulty in navigating his way. It was as if his body knew the trails so well that he could have made his way with his eyes closed.

At the bottom of the hill, he was happy to meet his dog who had waited for him during his time at the site. "Princess!" Jonathan joyfully called and hugged her. The two crossed the creek while the moon reflected from the water.

"Where were you?" Sarah asked when he arrived home. She saw from his expression that he had undergone a profound experience.

He told her.

CHAPTER 26

The Broadcast

Greg called.

"Greg, how's it going in San Francisco?" Michael was glad to hear from his old friend from the university.

"Pretty cool," Greg said. "I'm on a short visit to New York, and I thought of meeting with you if you're not busy."

"I'll have time after work," Michael said. "I could meet you at seven o'clock at Sullivan's Place, like in the good old days."

"It's a date." Greg laughed. "And it wasn't so long ago."

Michael liked Greg, who was an easy-going person. Greg had often acknowledged that he was a lazy and uncompetitive person who didn't like to exert himself unless he had no choice. Michael felt that Greg had a good heart and that he was one of those people who didn't turn their backs on their friends.

"So, what brings you to cold New York?" Michael patted Greg's shoulder when they met at the bar next to the university. They sat at a small table and ordered their favorite beers.

"A situation of no choice," Greg sighed. "Mom's in the

hospital. She fell and broke her leg and her reading glasses."

"She's Okay?" Michael was concerned.

Greg held off answering as the glasses of beer arrived. He took a sip from his cold glass of beer, set the glass on the table, and sighed again.

"She'll be fine," he answered. "But you know, I'm wondering if getting old is worth the effort."

Michael smiled. "There are some things over which we have no control."

"Okay, let's drop the heavy stuff," Greg said, "How is it at TXB? Do you like working there?"

"I do," Michael answered. "I think I made the right decision when I left university."

"Tell me," Greg said, "do you have any connection to *The Broadcast*?

"Not really," Michael replied. "Why do you ask?"

"Well, come on," Greg said. "It's the most interesting thing on TV. The program amazes me, even though I don't know if it's real."

Michael nodded. "The show airs tonight. If you'd like, come to my place later, and we'll watch the show together."

"Great idea," Greg said. "We could order pizza."

"And if you don't feel like driving late," Michael said, "you can crash on the sofa in the living room."

"Sounds like a plan," Greg agreed.

***

"Good evening." Susan Riley looked directly into the camera's eye. "As we promised, we will continue our journey back in time, and we'll watch some of the principal events of the nineteenth century." The camera zoomed out, and viewers could see the small studio and those seated there. "This evening, we have two special guests in the studio. From the prestigious Yale University, we have Professor Stanley Baker. Good evening, Professor."

"Glad to be here," the professor replied with a nod.

"And Professor Natalie Péllissier," the host continued, "who came here from the Sorbonne University in Paris. Good evening, Professor Péllissier."

"It is an honor," said the guest in a charming French accent.

"The nineteenth century saw the spread of the Industrial Revolution," Susan Riley read from the teleprompter. "Under the rule of Queen Victoria, Great Britain became the most significant global power. With the assistance of our guests in the studio and, of course, with the help of TXB's exclusive films, we will turn the spotlight to two of the most important occurrences of the nineteenth century: the Napoleonic Wars in Europe, and the American Civil War. This evening, we are privileged to watch amazing footage of events that occurred before the invention of moving films."

Riley paused to let that pronouncement sink in.

"We'll start with Napoleon." The host turned to the French

professor who sat to her right. "Who was Napoleon Bonaparte?"

"Good evening," Professor Péllissier opened. She looked about fifty years old and dressed with the panache one expected from a Frenchwoman; the professor met Riley's gaze with a small smile. "So, first, let's correct a small historical inaccuracy—Napoleon was not short. In fact, he was slightly taller than the average Frenchman. The reason for the mistaken perception stems from the difference between the English and the French measuring units." The French guest's expression sobered as she continued, "Napoleon came to power in a coup that ended the short period when France was democratic, after the revolution. In the year 1804, he crowned himself as the French Emperor."

"Professor Péllissier, what are we going to see?" Susan Riley asked.

"I have watched the impressive footage," said the professor, "and picked three of the most important events of the Napoleonic era. Choosing was not easy, and I hope to obtain further access to the films to use in my lectures. I must admit that I was skeptical about the authenticity of the footage, but the films match what we know from history and what I've learned in my many years of research."

"Do you believe it's authentic?" Greg asked Michael when the video started to roll.

"We'll talk later," Michael responded. Riveted to the TV screen, he did not want to miss a word.

The film started, and the French professor launched into an explanation of the footage which looked similar in style and quality to the previous clips.

The guest elected to start with the Battle of Austerlitz, which took place in 1805 and was considered Napoleon's most significant victory. In the battle, Napoleon defeated the combined forces of Russia and the Austrian Empire.

Despite the apparent distance between the battleground and the camera, viewers saw the cruelty of the war, in which large forces of cavalry and infantry clashed and slaughtered each other using artillery bombardments, gun salvos, swords, and bayonets.

Viewers watched the various tactics taken by opposing commanders who tried to surprise, encircle, trap, and inflict the enemy with as much damage as possible—in body and equipment losses.

Professor Péllissier continued with a film showing some of the events from the bloody Battle of Borodino, in 1812, when Napoleon invaded Russia. Ending her presentation, Péllissier showed a clip that, in her opinion, exhibited Napoleon's most dramatic moment, when he landed back in France after a short exile on the island of Elba.

"We could further elaborate about Napoleon and his wars," said Professor Natalie Péllissier. "To conclude our segment, I would say that he was a gifted army commander, but his megalomania caused France the death of about one million soldiers and eventually brought about his own demise."

"Thank you very much," said Susan Riley. "These were fascinating and illuminating materials. After a short break, we'll return with the American Civil War."

"So, what do you say?" Greg asked. He took a slice of pizza and stretched out comfortably on the sofa. "The fact that your network refuses to reveal where they get the films makes me doubt their authenticity."

"It's a matter of press immunity," Michael said. "You remember that reporters in this country have the right to protect and hide their sources."

"I understand that," Greg said. "But I'm getting the impression that this is way too fantastic. I'm starting to think that they're duping us."

"I'll remind you," Michael said, "that the TXB footage helped crack quite a few unsolved crimes."

Greg nodded. "That puzzles me. The truth is, I hoped that since you're working at TXB, you could shed some light on what's going on behind the scenes."

"Greg," Michael said, "you know that if I had such information, I wouldn't give it to anybody."

"Yeah, I know," Greg said and took a bite from his pizza.

"Nevertheless, I will let you in on a little secret." Michael smiled as his friend became all-attentive. "It just so happens that I know the show's producer. He hasn't revealed anything about what's going on behind the scenes, and I haven't asked him, but I got the impression that he's an honest man and not someone who would participate in any sort of conspiracy."

***

"As promised, we will now turn our attention to the American Civil War," Susan Riley said after a long commercial break. "Once again we'll say good evening to Professor Stanley Baker." She smiled at the knowledgeable guest, "Professor, welcome to the program."

"Good evening," the professor replied. About sixty years old, he was beginning to bald and wore glasses with thick black frames. "First, we have to refute the widespread notion that the issue of slavery was the main cause of the war."

"Really?" the host exclaimed in surprise.

"The war broke out after the union faced secession by eleven Southern states," the professor answered. "In the beginning stage of the war, President Lincoln—who adamantly opposed slavery—made it clear that if he could preserve the union without freeing even one slave, he would do it. Today, most historians agree that economic and political issues were the cause of the cruel war, the bloodiest in US history, in which more than six hundred thousand people lost their lives. It also brought about enormous destruction and financial damages."

"May I say something?" Professor Natalie Péllissier interjected.

"What would you like to say?" Susan Riley looked annoyed at the interruption.

"I disagree with the point of view brought forth by Professor Baker, which is revisionist history," the French professor said with confidence. "While there were certainly other factors at play, slavery was definitely the underlying cause of the economic, political, and moral conflict between the North and the South."

"Thank you, Professor." Susan Riley clearly wished to avoid an academic debate. She turned back to Professor Baker, "What are we going to see today?"

"I received exceptional films showing the Battle of Gettysburg, which took place in Pennsylvania and is considered to be the turning point of the war." Professor Baker chose not to respond to Professor Péllissier's remark. "During the campaign, the Union forces, led by General George Mead, managed to withstand attacks by Confederate forces, led by General Robert E. Lee who sought to invade the North."

The film started, and Professor Baker expounded on what it showed. In one clip, Union forces held a well-fortified position on the Cemetery Ridge. The Confederate forces assaulted their position, one attack after another, but without success.

Professor Baker explained General Lee's tactical errors. Under his direction, Confederate troops attacked four times from an inferior position. Lee refused to listen to General Longstreet's opinion when he recommended outflanking Cemetery Ridge and advancing toward Washington, DC. The mistakes cost the

Confederate forces thousands of casualties. On the fourth attack, the Confederate soldiers passed about a mile where they were exposed to heavy artillery bombardment. The footage showed the tragedy of the failed assault, with Lee's soldiers crushed by the cannons' fire.

As usual in TXB footages, the pictures were projected from a distance and without sound, which only highlighted an eerie contrast between the somewhat sterile video and the horrors of the war, the killed soldiers and the screaming of the injured.

Professor Baker concluded his presentation. "Following the decisive victory of the Union army and the Emancipation Proclamation led by President Abraham Lincoln, three and a half million black slaves living in the Confederate territory were liberated and went on to live their lives as free human beings."

CHAPTER 27

Michael

At the second musical session with Walter and his friends, Michael managed to free himself of anxiety. He enjoyed playing the solo parts that were expected of a lead guitarist and was encouraged by the band members' smiles of approval. In his heart, he thanked Walter for giving him the opportunity to once again play as a member of a band.

Over time, the friendship between Michael and Walter deepened. The two discovered much in common between them, in particular, their childhood circumstances and their love of music.

Occasionally, Walter spoke with Michael's supervisors at TXB. He was glad to hear that they were very pleased with his work. They trusted him and thought he had a promising future with the network. Michael wondered if Walter's warm attitude toward him stemmed from the fact that he had no son. Of course, Lindsey and his wife had their two beloved daughters.

Lindsey's home gradually became a second home for Michael, and he often stayed for dinner after the weekly band sessions. One Saturday afternoon, after the other band members left, Michael asked Walter if he would like to listen to one of his original songs.

Songwriting held the most significant place in Michael's musical world, but he was apprehensive about playing his songs to the group. Michael assumed that the band members preferred to play cover versions of known hits, and that they would be reluctant to learning songs written by the newest member of the group. He remembered that even in his high school band, where he was essentially the leader, there were players that expressed reservations about playing his songs, and preferred to perform covers of their loved hits. It was a delicate issue, and Michael, who drew a great deal of gratification from playing in this new group, did not wish to impose upon their good will and risk making the other musicians uncomfortable.

Walter agreed to listen to his song. Michael, after apologizing for not being a skilled singer, chose from his many songs one that he especially liked, "Follow Your Dream."

He concentrated, took a deep breath, and then played and sang his song, letting the music pour forth:

> *You know they say that miracles happen,*
> *though distant starlight may appear to look dim.*
> *I'm going through,*
> *you're going through,*
> *we're going through the changes.*
> *Blessed are those following their dreams.*

As the last notes faded, he looked toward Walter, heart pounding as he curiously waited to hear Walter's opinion. Michael knew he had allowed himself to expose his innermost world, and he understood that his connection with Walter had reached a degree of trust that he couldn't have anticipated when he first met the producer.

"What an amazing song." Walter seemed genuinely appreciative. "Such a beautiful melody with honest lyrics. I would like to add it to our band's repertoire. And you know what? How would you feel about singing it for my family after supper?"

Michael was moved and worried his performance might not impress. "But I'm not a singer."

"Your voice isn't bad," Walter said. "You can carry a tune, and you sang with true feeling. It was touching."

"Okay," Michael hesitantly agreed.

Later, during the evening meal, Walter announced the evening's entertainment. "I've asked Michael to sing his song for us, and he's agreed. So, this evening we have a short artistic program."

"We would love to hear the song!" Monica enthused. The two daughters nodded.

The family adjourned to the living room. Michael took a moment to tune the acoustic guitar McPherson had given him. He concentrated, and, for a split-second, remembered the distant day when the song flickered to life in his mind.

It was a winter day. Michael woke early to the sound of the wailing wind. At first, he wished to go back to sleep. Then suddenly, he heard the whole melody in his head, as well as some of the lyrics. The song, which apparently was born in his dream, reflected the issues that were on his mind at that time, mainly the question of whether he would accomplish his life's goals. He forced himself from the warm bed, picked up his guitar, and started to play the tune. Afterward, he wrote the song in his notebook.

Sitting in the Lindseys' living room, he played the opening chords and sang the first verse with his whole intention. He then continued to the second verse:

We know not everything in life works as planned.
We also know how beautiful life can be.
Just follow through,
Yes, keep on through,
Break through your limitations.
Blessed are those following their dreams."

He tried to pronounce the words clearly as the melody flowed through him. After the second verse, he played and sang the chorus, followed by a short instrumental section that he improvised on the guitar. He then took a deep breath and continued to the third verse, aware of the people in the room who were listening attentively. He returned to the chorus for the second time and then finished. After strumming the last chord, he waited. For a moment, he felt like he was in a courtroom waiting to receive

192

the judge's verdict.

"Oh, Michael," Monica responded. "What a charming song!" She walked over to him, leaned down, and embraced him. Walter's older daughter, Melanie, who came for a visit from Stanford University, nodded in agreement. Michael perceived the sheen of tears in Melanie's eyes. Surrounded by warmth and support, Michael thought that he might not know his biological parents, but he was privileged to have two adoptive families.

***

Later that night, Stewart McPherson called.

"Anything new?"

"No," Michael replied. He thought the journalist sounded impatient.

"You've known Lindsey and his friends for several months now," McPherson said. "All this time you haven't heard anything about *The Broadcast*? Have you asked?"

Michael understood McPherson's discontent. He knew he hadn't made a serious effort to do the job he agreed to do. He hadn't even formed an opinion regarding the source of TXB's films, which he liked to watch. During his weekly visits to Walter's house, he mostly focused on music.

Michael noticed that he was always the last one to arrive for the weekly jam sessions, despite making a point of punctuality. He wondered if the other members of the band came before him—

perhaps hours before the allocated playing time—to deal with issues pertaining to *The Broadcast*.

One time when he arrived, he noticed a large map of Europe and the Mediterranean basin hanging on the shed's wall. He was certain that the map wasn't there before. Nevertheless, he neglected to ask about it, and the following week, the map was gone.

Despite some doubts, Michael already knew that, even if he came across incriminating facts, he wouldn't betray Walter.

Squirming with discomfort, Michael said, "Look, the truth is I haven't heard anything regarding *The Broadcast*, and I haven't asked. I'm confident Walter is an honest man, and I doubt that he's capable of the things you suspect. If I'm wrong and Walter is knowingly deceiving the public, then there must be a reason for it—and I have no idea what it might be. Anyway, at this stage, it's clear to me that I can't continue with this assignment. I was probably never the right person for the job. I thank you for trusting me, and I'll return the Martin to you."

"You know what?" McPherson said after a pause. He was disappointed but appreciated Michael's honesty. "I don't play music. I understand firearms more than musical instruments. Keep the guitar as a gesture of good will. I'm sure it will be much more useful to you. If I keep it, it will just collect mildew."

"Thank you very much!" Michael said. "I'll take good care of the guitar, and if you ever need it, just call me."

"Good night," McPherson said. His sharp senses told him

that it might be worthwhile to keep in touch with the honest young man, and that he might use Michael's help in the future.

CHAPTER 28

Jonathan

Excel-Part, the car parts manufacturer where Jonathan worked, fell on hard times. The mid-sized plant specialized in producing parts for luxury cars. Operating its complex machinery required skill and experience. The employees heard threatening rumors of layoffs, perhaps intentionally spread by management to prepare people for the inevitable. The issue preoccupied the workers, and many expressed worry about losing their income.

Nobody was surprised when all the employees received a personal letter from Richard Tater, the CEO whom the workers privately called "the Dictator." In his message, the CEO reviewed the difficulties facing the company:

"Dear team.

Over the past few years, Excel-Part has faced tough competition from Far Eastern manufacturers, especially in China, along with changes in currency exchange rates which affected profitability. These and other hardships influence our ability to navigate our company in the complex economy of the twenty-first century. The impact on our revenues led to three consecutive quarters operating at a loss. This hasn't happened to Excel-Part since it was founded in the last century. Our dedicated staff is our most valuable asset, which is why I regret to inform you that the Excel-Part family will have to let go of some of its dedicated workers."

The letter left employees worried and bitter. Many of them had invested many years in the company without their efforts and loyalties rewarded by fair wages. They dismissed the mention of the "Excel-Part family" as nonsense. Hardworking employees on the factory's production floor knew that senior managers received huge salaries and generous bonuses. The top managers drove luxurious company cars, and went to all-expenses-paid business conferences in expensive hotels and exotic resorts, along with their spouses or lovers.

Jonathan talked to Sarah about the pending layoff and expressed his concerns. Sarah tried to put his mind at ease, saying she had always had the impression that his employer appreciated him.

"And besides," she said, "they need a computer technician, don't they?"

He knew he wasn't immune from the layoffs, because he'd heard the human resources manager say explicitly that an external company could easily replace some of the service personnel. He also knew that he could be replaced by a younger person willing to work for a lower salary.

He survived the first wave of layoffs, which targeted mostly unskilled production line workers who had been with the company for a relatively short time. A month later, the financial situation failed to improve, and Jonathan was among those called to the office of the human resource manager.

"I have always appreciated you for your dedication and loyalty," the human resources manager told him. She was in her mid-fifties, had a short, and bleached blond hair, sunken eyes, and an overall tough appearance. She had a reputation for being a trickster who advanced up the corporate ladder due to her ability to manipulate the people around her and pull the right strings. She also pushed her way up by demonstrating utter loyalty to the top managers, which was expressed in her willingness to carry out any policy and do their dirty work. "I always personally liked you," she added, "but what can we do? These are hard times."

Jonathan sat in front of her, his expression frozen, and didn't respond.

"Of course, you'll receive a generous severance package that contains unemployment benefits, as well as a letter of recommendation. I wish you all the best."

Jonathan shook her hand and left the office. He collected his personal belongings and then stepped out of the factory's door for the last time. He was surprised not to find anger or frustration within him, only a faint cloud of worry hovering over the horizon. In the trees of the parking lot, birds were busy with their daily routine, unaware of the struggles of people. He took a deep breath and felt as though a heavy load had been lifted off his chest. He felt free.

He had several months in which he could receive unemployment benefits. After that, he would probably have to return to repairing cars. But for now, he was free, and he would have time to spend at his site in the forest. That was the place, more than any other, where he felt whole and connected to something larger than himself. Perhaps the layoff was the first step on the way to a positive and necessary change? He started the car, which responded with a quiet and smooth sound.

When Sarah heard the news, she tried to remain calm.

"We'll manage," she said. "Luckily, your health insurance comes through my job."

That evening, he talked with Irene on the phone. As usual, she listened patiently and sympathetically.
"With time the layoff might turn out to be a change in the right direction," Irene unknowingly echoed his earlier thoughts.

"I'll have some free time," Jonathan said. "How would you like me to come and visit you in Minnesota?" He immediately reconsidered his suggestion, worrying such a journey could trigger his anxieties.

Irene was not enthusiastic about the idea. "It would be better if I visited you in California," she answered. She contemplated for a moment and added, "I would like to meet your wife."

CHAPTER 29

Irene

Jonathan told his wife about Irene's upcoming visit. He didn't try to hide his excitement at the idea that his wife would meet his good friend, who was possibly his big sister.

Sarah had reservations about that. She thought the whole story of "the missing sister that her husband had found on the internet" seemed groundless and delusional, bordering on the insane. Nevertheless, she was curious to meet the woman who had so charmed her husband.

Sarah believed Jonathan when he said that he was not having a romantic affair; however, she couldn't help but feel threatened. She understood that this strange relationship would not have happened had she been faithful to her husband, so she couldn't blame him. In fact, she was even thankful for him finding this platonic connection, and not following in her despicable ways, looking for love and sex with other partners.

Irene freed three days during the semester break for a visit, a time when her adulterous husband would be home and could take care of the children.

"You have to be back on Thursday," her husband emphasized, "because I'm flying to an important convention."

Irene no longer needed to know about those "important conventions." She no longer loved or respected the man and she actually felt comfortable with his long absences. She did, however, require of him to be present in their children's lives, so they wouldn't be raised by a single mother as she had been. And for the sake of the children, she continued to maintain the appearance of married life, despite being fed up with the man and his lies.

She flew from Minneapolis-Saint Paul to San Francisco, where Jonathan picked her up at the airport. After leaving the city, they took a winding highway, where cars drove at fast and dangerous speeds. Jonathan was not bothered by the driving conditions, but his real worry slipped out when he said, "I hope when you meet my wife…"

"It will be fine." Irene smiled in his direction. "From what you've told me about her, I don't foresee a problem."

Irene hoped to calm his worries, although she had concerns of her own.

"I just hope she'll accept you as a friend and not a rival," he muttered.

She looked at the curved road ahead of her. "I'll make it clear that I don't mean to come between you."

They arrived at the property in the afternoon. Jonathan

introduced Irene to the three dogs, who accepted her with excited barks, jumps, and tail wags. She met the cats, the chickens, the noisy ducks, and the hostile geese.

Jonathan took her for a tour of the property, accompanied by the dogs, and showed her his computer room and the cars he restored. They went to see the vegetable garden where Sarah spent a lot of her time and effort. Irene expressed her appreciation for Jonathan's wife, who worked hard so they'd have fresh and organic vegetables.

***

Sarah met Irene when she returned home. The women shook hands politely. Sarah usually prepared dinner, but on this day they chose to order Chinese food from a restaurant in town.

Irene thought that dinner might be a good time to get acquainted and asked, "Where do you work?"

"I'm a psychologist at a clinic in Watsonville," Sarah answered shortly. She still had a hard time accepting that her husband had brought another woman into their life. Sarah, at least, had kept her affairs outside their home.

"I have a good friend who's a psychologist," Irene said in an effort to ease the tension.

"I understand you have kids," Sarah said. She didn't see what her husband saw in his guest, who was older than he.

"Yes," Irene answered, "a boy and a girl, whom I love very

much."

Sarah nodded. She started to suspect that her husband's fascination with the other woman stemmed from her being a computer expert and a university lecturer with a Ph.D., while Sarah did not excel in that field.

"Are you on vacation?" Sarah questioned.

"Yes, a mid-semester break," Irene answered. "My husband is at home with the kids."

"And he doesn't object to your trip?" Sarah probed.

"He only requested that I'll be home by Thursday," Irene responded patiently.

"From what I hear, college professors get plenty of vacation days during the year," Sarah muttered with discontent.

"It's true," Irene acknowledged.

"I wish I got so many days off," Sarah said.

"What do you ladies think about Joan of Arc?" Jonathan interjected.

"Joan of Arc?" The two women looked at him, wondering at the non-sequitur.

"Yes," he smiled, "I heard that *The Broadcast* is going to do a piece about her in an upcoming program."

The women understood that he sought to diffuse the tense situation.

"From what I know," Irene said, "she was a courageous woman."

"Today she would be forcibly confined to a mental

institution," Sarah said.

"Yes, but does that mean that she was really insane?" Irene asked, looking at Sarah. "Couldn't she be a woman of an incredible, supernatural capability?"

"It's possible, I guess, but we'll never know," Sarah concluded.

***

The following day, Sarah went to work at the clinic. Jonathan took Irene for a long tour of the woods, and the three dogs joyfully accompanied them. He chose a path that wasn't very difficult and tiring, but also not too easy. They took a break by the creek and ate sandwiches. Jonathan debated whether to take Irene to his special site. He had never mentioned the place during their long phone conversations, and even Sarah hadn't visited the glade since he'd started excavating. Would he show Irene the unique spot where he felt most connected to himself and the world around him?

"I like your land," Irene said, "The sound of the flowing water is so relaxing."

"Once, I came here with a recording device, to record the sounds of the creek," Jonathan said. "But then I realized that listening to it at home doesn't have the same effect as actually coming here."

"At home," Irene said, "I like to take my kids outdoors whenever the weather allows."

"I like to take walks outdoors," Jonathan said, "and ponder the mysteries of the universe."

Irene stood up, stepped toward the creek, and looked at the flowing water below. She saw small fish swimming in their separate world and the sun reflecting off the water. She then turned her gaze up to the sky and said, "I don't think it's possible that we are the only civilization in the universe. With so many stars and galaxies, it just doesn't make sense."

"Do you think that aliens visited our planet and affected our cultures and beliefs?" Jonathan asked.

Irene smiled. "According to Erich von Däniken, they did."

"There's a place I'd like to show you," Jonathan said somberly, "but I'd like to ask you not to talk to anybody about what you're going to see."

She understood from the solemn tone of his voice that he was about to reveal something very meaningful to him.

"Sarah was there once, but it was a long time ago," he mentioned.

"I promise," Irene said. "It will remain between us."

They crossed the creek and continued on a winding trail until they reached the bottom of the hill. When they started to climb the hill, Jonathan wasn't surprised the dogs refused to come along. As they continued, the path became steeper and the trees grew denser, almost blocking their way.

"What a strange place," Irene whispered.

He liked that she expressed herself quietly, as if understanding and respecting a sacred place. They moved the last branches out of their way and stepped onto the dome of the hill, which after Jonathan's excavation work resembled an archeological site.

"Wow, Jonathan," she whispered. "What is this place?"

"This is the site."

"What an amazing place," she marveled. "It's like your own private Stonehenge."

"When I'm here," Jonathan said, "my thinking is clear, and I feel connected to the world and not detached from it."

The earth rumbled and sounded a deep and muffled growl. Frightened, Irene looked at Jonathan who appeared unaffected.

"Relax," he said, "That's how it is here. I think this site is an energy center or a gate of some kind. I don't really know."

"Jonathan, I'm scared."

"Do you want to go?"

"In a little while," she said, knees shaking. "May I sit down?"

"Sure."

She sat on the ground near the square rock in the center of the circle and tried to calm her racing pulse with deep breaths.

When she managed to relax, she felt at one with the calm that prevailed in the place. The sharp contrast between the frightening rumble of earth and the serenity that followed put her in mind of having passed through an initiation process.

She gently closed her eyes and felt like she was on a boat, floating in the ocean. Her mind drifted to childhood memories. She saw herself as a little girl with her mother in a small house. The paint on the walls was peeling. There were two beds in the room, one large and one small, and toys scattered across the floor, especially dolls. She heard the wind wailing outside in a terrifying rustle, and the rain was irately beating against the windows. She shivered and felt lonely.

"Do I have a father?" she asked her mother.

Her mother embraced her warmly, "Oh, sweetie, everyone has a father. It's just that yours is already in heaven."

Irene opened her eyes and tearfully looked at Jonathan. "Now I understand," she whispered. "This is indeed a powerful place. I wonder who built it, and what purpose it served." She looked around. "Do you come here often?"

"I know I have to respect this place," he said, his voice also at a whisper, "so I try not to come here for mundane reasons."

The wind whistled gently in the treetops. "Thank you for bringing me here," she said. "Please let's go, because right now I can't take any more."

They walked slowly down the trail, immersed in their thoughts. When they reached the bottom of the hill, the three dogs rejoined them.

"Are you okay?" Jonathan asked.

"Recovering," she said, taking a deep breath. "It was an intense experience."

***

That evening, Jonathan suggested dining at a restaurant.

Irene looked at Jonathan and said, "I would prefer if just Sarah and I go, so we can get to know each other better."

"I agree," Sarah said. "It will be a girls' night out."

Jonathan shrugged and said, "Have fun. I'll find some leftovers or make a sandwich."

Sarah drove Irene to a small and intimate restaurant. They remained silent during the drive, as if learning to feel and respect each other's private space. At the restaurant, Sarah ordered fish and Irene ordered a vegetarian entrée.

"I'm glad to see that my husband has a good friend," Sarah opened the conversation, "but I have a hard time believing that you're siblings. It sounds groundless and even delusional to me."

"When Jonathan brought up the idea, I was quite reserved," Irene said. But, I've started to accept that there is a chance he might be right."

"What facts do you base that on?" Sarah asked.

"We discovered that his parents, as well as my father, were killed in a car accident in the same year," Irene said.

"Many people died that year," Sarah pointed out.

"Then we discovered that we both had a Jewish father."

"That still doesn't mean that it's the same man." Having seen no evidence of romantic feelings between Jonathan and Irene,

Sarah accepted the idea that her husband had a special female friend. However, she was bothered by the thought that two rational adults harbored such unrealistic delusions.

"We don't have more facts," Irene acknowledged, "but we understand each other in subtle ways, and we think alike."

For a moment, Sarah felt pity for the woman sitting across from her. She knew Irene's background as a single daughter to a single mother. "Tell me," Sarah asked, "do you know what your father's profession was?"

"No, I never thought to ask my mom. She didn't like talking about him."

But perhaps, following the intense experience that Irene went through when she visited the site with Jonathan, there was still a channel that was left partially open, a canal that wasn't closed all the way, a conduit that she normally couldn't access. She strained her mind, trying to remember if her mother had ever said anything that could point to her father's profession. A small wrinkle appeared in the center of Irene's forehead as she made an effort to remember. A memory floated in her mind.

"I think he was an architect," she said slowly as an ancient, hazy memory rose from the depths of her mind. She saw herself as a ten-year old girl showing her mother a drawing she had created in school. The children were assigned to draw the houses where they lived.

"This is really an architect's sketch," her mother complimented. "It appears you inherited your father's ability."

Sarah looked at Irene with amazement. The wrinkle that appeared at the center of Irene's forehead looked like the wrinkle that appeared in Jonathan's forehead when he was deep in thought.

When they returned home, they asked Jonathan if he knew what his father's profession was. "I don't know," Jonathan said, "but maybe Walter does."

CHAPTER 30

Sarah

At the clinic, Sarah befriended a nurse named Heidi O'Neil. Heidi was in her mid-thirties and had recently moved to California with her husband and their two little boys. The family lived in a trailer in a densely populated trailer park.

Sarah and Heidi liked each other and enjoyed spending time together. Heidi looked younger than her age. She was red-headed with her hair usually tied in a ponytail. She had a freckled face and a small pug nose.

Sarah visited Heidi's home on a few occasions, and Heidi's kids won her heart. Heidi visited Sarah's house and met Jonathan. She thought him handsome and a little strange.

Heidi was a vegetarian and attracted to the spiritual teachings of the Far East. She invited Sarah to join her at weekly meetings with an Indian guru who had a thriving community of followers. Sarah was curious to meet the guru and hoped that the spiritual experience would prove to be beneficial for her. Years ago, she had experienced Christianity, and even if her time at the convent hadn't ended traumatically, she thought she would still have drifted away from the Christian faith. Her free spirit couldn't accept the way of thinking and rigidity she'd found there.

Sarah felt that Heidi's invitation came at the right time because lately, feelings of sadness and hopelessness crept into her heart and mind. Often, she asked herself what the purpose of her life was and whether she just wasted her time on earth.

The guru, Baba Shree Ramayana, always dressed in an impeccably clean white robe. His hair and beard were long and anointed with oil. During meetings, the guru sat on a chair in front of his disciples who gathered at his feet, on the carpet and on pillows, as he patiently answered their questions.

The guru explained in his sing-song accent: "one's consciousness usually identifies itself with the physical body; but, during yoga practice, it expands and spreads to more transcendental and subtle realms."

He also said: "Beyond intellectual grasping there is infinite knowledge, as well as power, peace, and joy."

He emphasized: "People don't have to search for God beyond themselves, because everything is divine, including people."

The guru's pronouncements fascinated Sarah. She practiced the new techniques in her house, in the early morning hours. Through yoga, breathing exercises, and meditation, a sense of renewed optimism filled her mind. According to her new perceptions, she stopped eating every kind of meat.

Sarah didn't try to share her new world with Jonathan, knowing he was not attracted to Far Eastern teachings. Jonathan was, after all, an intellectual person who wouldn't want to give up thinking and researching. She also thought that he'd refuse to stop eating beef.

Jonathan noticed the joy of life returning to his wife's eyes and spirit, after an extended period when gloominess and bitterness had taken control of her. And not only was he glad to perceive the positive change in his wife, but he was also pleased to see that she stopped her sexual adventures outside the house.

Baba Shree Ramayana invited Sarah to a retreat held in the ashram on his land, and she gladly accepted the invitation. She signed up for the retreat despite the high participation fee, because she was flattered by the personal invitation.

In the retreat, she deepened her studies and practices. She learned to sit for long periods of time without thinking. Or she watched her thoughts as they arose and let them pass by without getting attached to them. She learned to focus her complete attention and observe mental processes in the mind that were utterly unfamiliar to her.

Years after her stay at the convent, and she enthusiastically returned to the spiritual realm. New insights contributed to an improvement in her mood. More than that, she was glad to be back on a path that promised redemption from suffering and offered serenity and hidden knowledge.

But after a few months, she started to observe cracks in the beautiful and clean image of the guru in his white robe, and his community leaders, who were organized in a clear hierarchy.

Sarah couldn't avoid noticing that they ran their financial dealings with cunning and a lack of transparency. She saw how the organization offered various courses to the public for a high tuition fee and assured participants peace and good health for the rest of their lives in return for their "investment." Sarah considered such claims as unfounded sales talk. She was also upset to find aggressive marketing techniques and unrealistic promises emblazoned across glossy, colorful brochures. She thought such an organization ought to act with environmental awareness.

She was especially dismayed when she saw how some of the guru's disciples—those who came from wealthy families—gained preferential privileges, became the guru's cronies, and received central roles in the organization. They were urged to contribute large sums of money to the Guru's foundation for a momentary glory and a promise of spiritual redemption and enlightenment.

Sarah sensed rebelliousness rising within her. Deep discontent and bitter disappointment replaced profound appreciation. It connected to the disappointment she'd experienced years ago with the mother superior at the convent. Sarah believed that a spiritual teacher should provide a personal moral standard of the teachings that he preached. She didn't find that kind of example in Baba Shree Ramayana.

"I'm leaving," Sarah announced as she and Heidi sat in a playground where Heidi's kids played.

"Leaving?" Heidi wondered. "Leaving what?"

"The guru, the organization, everything!"

"But Sarah," Heidi said. "Aren't you a bit harsh on Babaji? So, he's got some money issues. He's not perfect. It just shows that he's human and he has weaknesses like the rest of us."

"It's not about the money, Heidi," Sarah muttered.

"Then what is it about?"

Sarah didn't answer. Although she always encouraged her patients to say what was on their minds, she had difficulty expressing her own innermost agonies.

"Come on Sarah," Heidi said, "you can tell me."

"Okay," Sarah relented. "It's about betrayal... I just can't take it anymore when the people I trust betray me. I've been betrayed too many times." Sarah felt how she was suddenly becoming all emotional and could no longer hold her tears.

"Oh, Sarah," Heidi, who was surprised at Sarah's outburst of emotions, embraced her. "I didn't know..."

Sarah told her. She spoke about her parents, who betrayed her when she needed them the most. She talked about the mother superior who'd deceived her. And she told Heidi about Daniel, her lost son.

Sarah didn't know why she felt she could trust the young nurse who she had just recently met. She continued to talk with tears in her eyes, honestly telling Heidi about her own betrayals—

her disloyalty to her husband.

***

Melancholy returned to Sarah's heart, and she resumed her affairs, which became riskier and more desperate. Heidi understood her disappointment but disagreed with her actions.

Heidi was also unhappy with Baba Shree Ramayana and his organization. She disliked their ways of handling the finances, but she chose to concentrate on the guru's positive messages and on the path that he offered.

Heidi convinced Sarah to give the spiritual world another chance. Together, they signed up for a series of discourses with a Japanese Zen master named Nipo Shiaku. After many years of meditating, Nipo told his listeners that they didn't need to spend time and effort practicing meditation. They could simply live the moment, here and now.

Nipo, whose head was completely shaved, wore black robes. He said in a heavy Japanese accent: "We perceive the world through our senses, and, in our consciousness, we form concepts of the events and issues that we encounter. Our thoughts give us an interpretation of the world and don't allow us to experience reality *as it is* at any given moment."

Nipo looked amused at his students' bewildered expressions as he continued: "The paradox is that we honestly strive to understand the world with our minds, but in order to arrive at a real knowledge of reality, we have to use direct experience, and not our mind's thinking processes."

As Sarah got closer to the teacher and became familiar with his way of life, she found no dark and shady facets in him. The man was honest, lived modestly, and was wholly faithful to his path and his teachings. That gratified her. But the series ended, and old Nipo held very few public appearances. He had no interest in creating an organization around him or expanding his activities.

Heidi invited Sarah to accompany her when she went to a lecture and a meeting with a Tibetan lama.

"The topic of the discourse, *The Tibetan Book of the Dead*, interests me more than any other matter," Heidi said, smiling.

Sarah agreed to come along. She was interested in any activity that got her out of the house, which recently became boring, empty, and gloomy for her. She continued to look for meaning in her life, and she was open to any diversion from the sordid affairs that threatened to ruin her.

Sarah and Heidi heard a fascinating lecture. The lama, who wore a maroon robe, said: "We, in the Tibetan form of Buddhism, have intensely researched the subject of death. Leading lamas mapped the stages that the soul goes through from the moment of death until rebirth. Those stages are called *Bardo*."

The lama looked over the crowd and continued: "After death, we are exposed to a barrage of hallucinations; some of them calming, while others could be startling and terrifying.

It is essential to remain peaceful during the dying process, which we all undergo. We must recognize these mirages as coming from our own subconscious, and we must not be afraid.

Staying calm in the presence of these frightening images leads to a more evolved birth and even to the possibility of complete liberation from the cycle of birth, death, and rebirth."

After the meeting, Sarah and Heidi went out for pizza. "Amazing, wasn't it?" Heidi said around a mouthful of mushroom pizza.

"Outstanding," Sarah agreed. "But I'm wondering if these are issues that we should concern ourselves with, in our daily lives. In my opinion, it's better to focus on the here and now, as Nipo taught."

"Here and now, I'm focusing on my pizza," Heidi quipped. She sobered and added, "In my opinion, we have to remember that death could catch us at any second. We could drive home and get killed in a car accident."

"Since when did you become so optimistic?" Sarah asked while tucking into her olive pizza.

"It's not a matter of being optimistic or pessimistic," Heidi answered. "It's an honest look at reality."

Sarah regarded her young and serious friend with affection and said, "I'm glad we met."

Sarah knew that the Lama's ideas might occupy her mind in the coming days. Despite being unsure about the concept of reincarnation, she couldn't help but wish that in the next life cycle she would fulfill her deep yearning and become a mother.

CHAPTER 31

Michael

The phone rang while Michael chopped onions for a quick stir-fry. Cooking wasn't his favorite hobby, so he tended to prepare quick and easy dishes, soups, and salads.

He found that engaging in food preparation relaxed him. While slicing, chopping, and stirring, he thought about the day's events and examined their effect on him.

He didn't recognize the caller's telephone number.

"Hello, Michael?" said the voice of a young woman. "This is Melanie, Walter's daughter."

"Hi, Melanie," Michael answered warmly.

"Are you busy?" She asked.

"Not especially," he answered. "What do you need?"

"I'm calling because …" She paused. "Well, it's because I like you. I asked Dad to give me your number. I'd like to go out with you sometime."

Michael took a deep breath as he absorbed her surprising words. He perceived Melanie as a beautiful woman, and he knew she was studying at a university out west.

"Am I embarrassing you?" she asked, filling the pause.

"A little bit," he acknowledged. "I didn't expect it."

"If you're uncomfortable, then I—"

"No, wait!" He quickly came to his senses. "Are you in town? Would you like to go to a movie or something like that?"

"That would be great," she joyfully agreed. "I've moved back to New York, and I'll take my internship here. Right now I'm on vacation, so whenever you—"

"Tomorrow?" he suggested.

"Excellent," she accepted.

"Would you like me to pick you up after work?" he asked. "I happen to know where you live."

"Sounds good," she said. "That way we could eat something before the movie. Choose which movie you want to see."

After he hung up, Michael returned slowly to cut vegetables while contemplating the unexpected development. He was surprised, though he remembered that during his high school years, not once had a girl called and invited him to go out with her.

And Melanie?

On the occasions that he and Melanie met during coinciding visits with her family, he was drawn to her. Yet, he never entertained the idea of embarking upon a relationship with her, because he worried about infringing on the trust that her parents had in him. Would a romantic relationship with Melanie change his warm connection with her parents? And would he be risking playing with Walter's band?

Knowing the relationships within the Lindsey family, he could assume that Melanie had been open with her father when she asked for Michael's phone number.

But maybe she just needed someone to accompany her to a movie, a sort of big brother? He hoped not.

Michael could not stop thinking about the surprising phone call. The more he thought about it, the more Melanie's image grew in his mind and pulled him toward her with invisible threads, while all the other considerations faded in the background. A positive expectation started to fill his heart, along with the recognition that he was hungry for a meaningful relationship with a woman.

The following day, Michael tried to concentrate on his work, but thoughts of Melanie intruded. He didn't see Walter anywhere and felt it was better that way.

He left work earlier than usual and hurried home to take a shower and change clothes. Since he didn't know how heavy the traffic was going to be on the roads and bridges leading northbound to Scarsdale, he departed earlier than necessary.

Michael knew that he was fortunate. He was blessed with intelligence, good health, good looks, and a wonderful family who supported his ambitions. The Evans family, who adopted him with much love, had given him a good life and the opportunity to fulfill his goals and wishes. At this stage of his life, he had started to contemplate settling down and having a family of his own. But a tiny worry hid inside him, a fear that one day—for some unknown reason—his whole world would collapse and turn out to be an illusion.

He also had a deep-seated longing to meet his biological parents and ask them the questions that continued to bother him: why had they given him up for adoption and not raised him as their son?

Maybe destiny was in his favor? Maybe his biological parents would have turned out to be awful parents: alcoholics, drug addicts, poor and uneducated? Perhaps they understood that they had to give him away in order to give him a chance at life. But maybe they had changed their minds over the years? Perhaps they were looking for him?

These thoughts ran through Michael's mind as he made his way north, to the wealthy suburb, for a date that could change the course of his life.

He decided to put the thoughts aside when he arrived.

Somewhat embarrassed, he rang the bell to Walter's house.

Monica opened the door and was as cordial as always. "Hi Michael, it's nice to see you." She welcomed him.

"Melanie!" she called to her daughter, "Michael is here for you!"

Melanie leaped down the stairs, luminous, prettier than he remembered her.

"Bye, Mom!" Melanie cheerfully said and kissed her mother lightly on the cheek as she stepped out of the house.

Excitement filled Michael's heart as he looked at his companion. Her face was very beautiful, sweet and doll-like. Her hair was dark, straight, and shiny.

He noticed that she had taken care of her appearance. She wore a stylish, brown velvet coat, a short, cream-colored skirt over tight black leggings, and brown boots.

The weather cooperated: cold, but clear. Bright stars seeded the night sky. In the car, Michael inhaled her light perfume.

During the day while he should have been working, he'd checked to see what movies were playing and picked a critically acclaimed, suspenseful drama. He hoped she approved of his choice.

"Are you hungry?" he asked. She smiled at him, eyes bright, and nodded. He followed up with, "What are you hungry for?"

"Do you like Japanese food?" she asked.

He did and asked if she preferred a particular restaurant. She directed him to a small Japanese restaurant where they ordered miso soup and sushi, discovering similar tastes in cuisine.

"So, were you surprised that I called?" Melanie asked.

"I was."

"You shouldn't have been." She smiled.

He looked into her round, brown eyes and thought she had a charming smile.

"You know," he said, "the connection with your parents is

important for me."

"That's obvious," she said. "They love you, too, Michael."

"So, let's be cautious, okay?" he said. "We have a lot to gain, and a lot to lose."

"Life's not without risk, and we have to take chances," she responded. "With all due respect to my parents, I'm a big girl, and you're not a child either."

He nodded and changed the subject. "Tell me, are you going to be a lawyer?"

"It's interesting that you asked," she answered. The truth is that I have a lot of doubts. It's clear to me that I don't want to be a legal representative for some greedy corporation. I'm thinking of working for a battered women's organization or perhaps for an environmental group."

Michael discovered that he liked not only her beauty, but also her way of thinking and her personality. "You surprise me," he said.

"For the better, I hope." She blushed and averted her gaze.

"Definitely," he said.

"I wanted to tell you," she said and met his gaze, "that the song that you sang at our house charmed me."

The affection in her eyes touched him deeply and echoed back to her.

They finished their dinner and headed for the cinema. Michael wasn't disappointed with the film as suspense-drama was his favorite genre and he didn't like action movies that had too much violence. But he'd found himself wondering if his companion was enjoying the movie as well.

The movie ended, and they stepped outside and breathed cold, open air that didn't smell like buttered popcorn. "Did you like the movie?" Michael asked.

"A lot," Melanie answered. "But I was a little disappointed when the hero and the heroine didn't get their happily ever after and went their separate ways."

"The filmmakers probably wanted to avoid an ending that was too sweet," Michael said. Remembering his manners, he opened the car's door and waited until Melanie seated herself before taking his place behind the steering wheel. He started the car and drove at a sedate pace, continuing their conversation. "It seems to me that they left a possibility of the protagonists meeting again. They left the story open for a sequel."

"I like more closure," she said.

The conversation continued in a discussion of movie preferences until he stopped the car in front of the Lindsey residence.

"Good night," Michael said, feeling awkward. "I really enjoyed spending the evening with you. The truth is, lately I've forgotten to get out of the house after work."

"You're allowed to kiss me," Melanie prompted. "Remember, we're big kids."

He leaned across the center console and kissed her, sensing the sweetness of her lips. His heart overflowed with joy and promise.

***

From time to time, Michael experienced difficulties at his work. He encountered people he wished to interview for *Around the Clock* who were impolite, rude, or even hostile, and perceived him as a representative of a voyeuristic and invasive media.

The job got him rougher days when a few of his colleagues identified him as a rival and treated him with direct or hidden hostility. Michael especially disliked when the competition unbalanced his emotional equilibrium, prompting him to lose control, get angry, and say harsh words to someone who might have insulted him or treated him with disrespect. He expected better of them and himself.

On one of those difficult days, Michael failed in his attempt to bring a young woman to the show, after she had accused her boss, a famous political figure, of sexual harassment, verbal and physical.

"Your bravery will set an example for others that man harmed," Michael urged her. "You'll inspire them to come forward with their stories, so that justice can be done."

But the young woman refused. "The exposure will hurt my family," She claimed. "The media will dig up every little piece of trash about my life and smear it all over the tabloids."

Michael knew there was a certain truth in her assessment; still, he was upset. His colleague, Spencer Stair, with whom he usually had a friendly relationship, annoyed him by commenting that Michael approached the woman with the wrong strategy.

In a manner unlike his usual restrained composure, Michael snapped, "Don't stick your nose where it doesn't belong!"

Offended, Spencer retorted, "You think you're smarter than everyone here and that doors will open for you if you just suck up to the right managers!"

"Go to hell!" Michael growled, stomping from the room and slamming the door behind him.

He went home earlier than usual, wishing for nothing more than a warm shower and dinner. At the entrance to his apartment building, he saw his landlady, Mrs. Rinaldi, waiting for him. *Just what I needed,* he thought to himself.

"Michael, when will I get to meet your mother?" asked Mrs. Rinaldi. "I would like to tell her how pleased I am with my tenant."

Michael couldn't restrain himself. "When will you stop nagging people?" he muttered, going around her and continuing to his apartment.

He immediately regretted his rude behavior and turned back to apologize, but the old lady, who was deeply offended, refused to open her door.

***

From the day that he was recruited to his spying mission by Stewart McPherson, Michael disliked being in a situation in which he might have to betray people who trusted him. Still, he developed a certain curiosity regarding *The Broadcast*: the program's findings, and the mysterious technology that allowed the show to broadcast its unusual films.

He wondered if it were possible for that technology to assist people like himself to uncover their hidden pasts. Was there the slightest chance that the enigmatic technology could show him the events from his early childhood, such as the day he was separated from his mother?

Michael watched televised news reports regularly, but he almost never watched made-for-TV movies and series. Neither did he like game shows and so-called reality TV.

But after the incidents with Spencer and Mrs. Rinaldi, during which he'd lost his temper and said things he ought not, he knew that he would have a hard time relaxing and focusing on anything. So, he ordered pizza and spent the evening on the sofa, watching whatever was on TV to distract his mind. On the TXB affiliated station, he saw a game show, and then a reality show, a slew of commercials, and a news flash.

Later as he was falling asleep, *The Broadcast* started. Michael, who always eagerly waited for the show, had a hard time following the events, which blended with his dreams.

The Broadcast turned the spotlight to the seventeenth century and focused on the English Civil War fought between Parliament supporters and Royalists.

The regular anchor, Susan Riley, hosted Professor Arthur Wilson from Cambridge University. The English professor explained the background and reasons for the fierce fighting. He showed TXB footage, filmed as usual from directly above, which documented battles in the year 1645, when the forces commanded by Sir Thomas Fairfax defeated the army of King Charles I. The professor told the host and viewers at home that, following defeat, the king was brought to trial for treason, found guilty, and beheaded.

Horrified as he watched the execution, Michael's sleep-addled mind couldn't understand why it was not the king who was beheaded, but his colleague, Spencer Stair, with whom he'd quarreled a few hours earlier.

"And now," Susan Riley cheerfully said, "we will say good evening to Michael." She looked at him directly from the TV screen. "How are you doing this evening, Michael?"

Michael was stunned, and his heart pounded. "Are you talking to me?" he hesitantly asked.

"Of course, Michael," the host answered. "It's been some time since you approached us and asked us to help you find your mom."

"I approached you?"

"Indeed, and now our show is dedicated to you," the host smiled at him.

He was startled by the idea that the whole country watched his deepest secrets. As shivers went up his spine, a film started, and he could not look away from the pictures on the screen.

The film was different from previous TXB footage. It was on a level with the action and in full color. He saw a newborn baby cradled in its mother's arms. Both of them slept. They appeared to be surrounded by a halo of love and tenderness, utterly serene. The bed and furniture indicated they were in a hospital room.

A woman in white clothing entered the room and walked toward the sleeping mother and baby. She pulled the newborn from his mother's arms and carried the baby from the room. Neither mother nor baby woke at the separation.

In another film that might have been the continuation of the same occurrence, Michael saw the same baby in the back seat of a car, held in the arms of another woman. Michael recognized her as his adoptive mother. She tenderly embraced him and then buckled him into a toddler's seat. His adoptive father drove the car. It was a smooth, quiet night drive.

Sweating, Michael woke up, still on the sofa where he'd fallen asleep. He blinked at the television. Disoriented, he looked around, trying to grasp where he was. He quickly came to his senses, grabbed the remote control, and turned the TV off.

A glance at the clock informed him of the late hour. He took a deep breath, stretched, and stood up. He then went to the kitchen to make himself a cup of tea, while reflecting on the vivid images that he just saw. The dream was so real that for a moment, he wondered whether he experienced a vision, something that had never happened to him before.

He contemplated that if there were any truth to the dream, it could suggest that his adoptive parents had driven their car to get him. If so, then he was born not far from his hometown, possibly in the Los Angeles area, or perhaps in neighboring Arizona.

CHAPTER 32

Stewart McPherson

The investigative reporter was disappointed. All his attempts to break into TXB in order to uncover the veil of secrecy shrouding *The Broadcast* came up empty-handed. The hacker who worked for him broke into the archives of the network's human resources department. Consequently, McPherson knew who all the employees of *The Broadcast* were, including editors and technical staff. But when the hacker tried to access the internal files of *The Broadcast*, he encountered a series of encrypted levels that he was unable to decipher.

Seeing no other way to advance his inquiry, McPherson returned to the office of Howard Hensley, the private investigator nicknamed HH whom he loathed. This time he requested general background information on all the employees of *The Broadcast*.

He also requested of his hacker to search for further information on Walter Lindsey's three friends. McPherson hoped that the hacker would dig evidence, perhaps in a secured police archive, that would shed new light on the personalities of

Lindsey's buddies.

Henley delivered first. When McPherson went over the details for which he'd paid a lot of money, he focused on one technician with a questionable past. Years earlier, the technician had been arrested for theft and had been sentenced to a short time in prison. Due to the technician's low wage, McPherson thought that the man might be inclined to cooperate with him for the right fee.

McPherson acquired the services of a young female private investigator with whom he had worked in the past. He assigned her the task of connecting with the presumably corruptible technician and extract valuable information out of him.

After several months, the young P.I. managed to get close to the technician but collected no relevant information from him.

McPherson's biggest hope for getting the necessary evidence rested upon Michael Evans, the young TXB researcher. McPherson's plan had succeeded when Michael befriended Walter Lindsey after attracting his attention with his guitar playing.

However, Michael hadn't discovered anything either from Lindsey or his friends, whom McPherson suspected were also involved in the conspiracy. It frustrated him beyond measure.

When Stewart McPherson was a child, his father had disappeared in unclear circumstances while serving in the American army in the Vietnam War.

Young Stewart had invested much effort trying to find out

what had happened to his father, but he had bumped into a wall of silence and cover-ups regarding the unit where his father had served and the mission in which he had disappeared. Stewart learned that it was an undercover operation in which an elite force had been sent to China, with the aim of sabotaging the supply lines providing weapons to the Viet Cong. The unit had stumbled on a Chinese Army ambush, and five of its soldiers, including his father, had been killed or captured by the Chinese. McPherson had been unable to discover more details, and his father's burial whereabouts remained unknown. Those warriors of the unit who returned home remained faithful to their oath not to expose any information about the operation or the unit.

"But one thing I can tell you," said one of the veteran soldiers who returned from the mission. "Your father was the best military sniper I have ever known."

Longing to follow in his father's footsteps, McPherson started to go to a firing range on a regular basis, and like his father, he excelled in the practice.

"Why are you doing that?" His wife was upset with him. She hated guns and strongly supported increased gun control laws. "Do you really want to kill somebody?"

"Maybe if I'll become an expert sharpshooter, I won't have to kill my enemy." He responded.

"How so?" she wondered.

"If I neutralize my opponent, I won't have to kill him."

Stewart McPherson became a central activist in an organization striving to bring back soldiers missing in action.

Over the years, he had managed to attain a few more bits and pieces of information about his father's last mission. He had learned that the mission had been considered too risky and doomed to fail, and thus had never been authorized by the high command. Still, it had been executed by a field-commanding captain who had ignored orders and had been anxious to make a mark, so he could advance up the ranks. The captain had survived the ambush and he had become known for his determination and courage. With time, he had been promoted to the rank of general.

Maybe that was why McPherson had spent years fighting for increased transparency in government institutions and large corporations. He detested cover-ups and had made exposing corruption his life's mission. McPherson especially despised acts of deceit by the press and electronic media. He perceived the media as democracy's watchdog and was angered when journalists didn't faithfully do their job or even collaborated with powerful and wealthy institutions that misled the public.

Stewart McPherson had been married for five years, but his wife, whom he'd loved very much, had left him and taken their son with her.

"You don't need me," she had claimed. "You're already married—to your work."

After that, he had been involved with a few women but didn't succeed in finding the great love that he yearned for, a woman with whom he would feel safe, knowing for certain that she wouldn't run away from him. He wished to find a woman who could share his destiny and could understand his path and his mission.

He only saw his son on rare occasions because his ex-wife moved to Oregon, on the other side of the country, while he remained in New York, where he conducted his investigations.

McPherson had been frustrated after Michael turned him down, telling him unequivocally that he didn't intend to betray the trust of his friend, producer Walter Lindsey. Still, McPherson appreciated Michael for his honesty and integrity, and didn't rule out the possibility of collaborating with him on a future undertaking.

Stewart McPherson called TXB, introduced himself and asked to speak with producer Walter Lindsey. His call was immediately transferred to Lindsey's office.

"It's an honor to talk to you," Lindsey said on the phone. "How may I help you?"

"I would like to interview you," McPherson said.

"I'm quite busy these days," Lindsey was suspicious. "What do you want to know?"

"I'm interested in learning about the source of films of *The*

Broadcast," McPherson said directly. He didn't expect that the producer will agree to collaborate with him, but he had to try.

"My sources are protected by press immunity." Lindsey's response was short.

At that point, all that was left for the journalist was to openly come out against the show. He chose to publish an article in the weekend edition of the *New York Times*. Due to McPherson's prestige as a courageous fighter for truth in reporting, the piece received a prime location in the newspaper, the first page of the entertainment section.

"DON'T LET THEM FOOL YOU," was the title. The body of the article read:

"The American public is fascinated by The Broadcast, which airs weekly on TXB affiliated stations. The program shows supposedly real films which document events from the near and more distant past. All recordings have the same mediocre quality and unusual filming angle, from straight above.

TXB officials, including senior producer Walter Lindsey, refuse to reveal the origin of the unique footage, claiming they are bound by a confidentiality agreement and have an obligation to protect their sources.

In my opinion, the show is based on a large-scale deception. It is one thing to publish a science fiction movie, an artistic creation for the sake of entertainment, and quite another thing to claim that the movie is an authentic documentation of a real event. They are exploiting our yearning to believe in fantastic possibilities to generate high ratings. I know for a fact that nowadays it is possible to produce films like that in a well-equipped studio, through the use of advanced animation, 3-D, and virtual reality programs.

The information and footage that they broadcast on their journey back in time could be achieved by anyone. All you would need is the willingness to invest the time and conduct a thorough research, go to libraries, to the internet, and talk to historians. Of course, you would need an access to an animation studio which no doubt TXB has.

TXB wants us to believe they have some means of going back in time with a spacecraft or shooting films across some split in the space-time continuum... Well, I don't buy that, nor do I believe in the tooth fairy.

I must admit, I had a tougher time figuring out how in the first season, they successfully solved crime cases. There could be two explanations: First, the people of the network somehow came across a secretive police archive that was concealed from police officers, perhaps because it was obtained illegally by the military. Second, the programs were staged with law enforcement officers' collaboration in order to resolve open cases. At this stage, I do not accuse police officers of any wrongdoing; I merely speculate about the cases that were supposedly solved by the films.

The most significant argument that I can bring to my claim that the films are fabricated animation is that if the films were authentic, then the network would not have a reason to protect their source.

I call on the managers of TXB and the show's producer to stop hiding behind the excuses of journalistic privilege and source confidentiality. The law that allows reporters to avoid exposing their source of information is designed to protect journalists from lawsuits and persecution, not to give the media permission to spread false information, deceive innocent viewers, and make a fortune from advertisers."

The article received a great deal of public attention. Many journalists joined their esteemed colleague's call for disclosure, while a few still thought the journalistic privilege must be maintained at all cost. Public debates arose on TV forums, radio shows, and on the internet. Most people agreed with McPherson's opinion that the network should reveal its sources. The pressure on TXB increased.

CHAPTER 33

Sarah

Gradually, Sarah saw how sadness was taking over her world. She felt sluggish, as if surrounded by a dense, murky shroud. She yearned for lucidity and clarity, but it appeared as though she had lost the key to the door of the walls that enclosed her.

Sarah knew that her depression impacted her work, and that her patients weren't getting the quality care they deserved. In the past, she had treated many patients who suffered from depression, and exercised effort to empathize with them; however, she hadn't *really* known how they felt.

Now, she battled an urge to share her depression with her patients, to agree with them and scream together, "It's a shitty world!" But she stopped herself and managed to keep a professional façade.

"What kind of psychologist am I?" Sarah criticized herself in a conversation with her sister, Julie. "If I'm not capable of helping myself, how could I expect to help my patients?"

"You are going through a rough time," Julie responded. "Everyone goes through hardships in their lives, and that includes you and me."

"But I don't see the end of it," Sarah agonized. "I have no idea how to pull myself out of this. I just want to crawl into a hole in the ground and disappear."

"About a year ago," Julie confided, "I went through a rough patch. Edmond fell in love with a young client whose house he renovated, and he moved in with her."

"Really?" Sarah was surprised. "Why didn't you tell me?"

"I wanted to tell you," Julie answered, "but I was afraid of bothering you with my troubles."

Sarah thought about her wonderful sister—always willing to lend an ear but worries about being a burden and exposing her own difficulties. She gently probed, "And how are things between you now?"

"He came back home," Julie said. "He claimed he did it for the kids, but I suspect that she either dumped him, or they just broke up."

"Oh, Julie," Sarah said, "you are the most precious person in the world to me."

"Same here," Julie replied. "Now believe me when I tell you that you'll manage to pull through. One day you'll look back, and you won't understand why you felt so bad."

Sarah wiped her eyes. "I sure hope so," she said. "But in the meantime, I'm having a tough time at work. With Jonathan laid off, I can't simply quit while I work this through. My salary covers most of our living expenses."

"Jonathan's not working?" Julie asked.

"He still gets unemployment," Sarah answered. "And he has a few clients whom he fixes cars for. Most of the time, though, he is in his own world."

"So how about…" Julie contemplated. "Why won't you take a vacation and come to visit me in San Francisco?"

Sarah pondered the suggestion for a little while. "If you're… I really do need a change of scenery. I'll check with the clinic to see if they can manage without me for a week or two. Thank you for the invitation."

Sarah approached the clinic's director and asked for an immediate unplanned vacation. The director approved her request and somberly said, "Go and recharge your batteries. I've noticed you struggling and not fulfilling your duties as you should. I was going to order a leave of absence if your performance continued without improvement."

Sarah understood that Julie's offer had come just in time. The clinic's director hadn't threatened dismissal, but Sarah could read between the lines.

***

Sarah liked living out in the country, far from urban noises and smells. When she had lived in the city, she was especially disturbed by the strident sirens of ambulances and fire trucks. The sirens were a constant reminder of the transience of her existence, and she knew that sooner or later, the sirens would screech for her…

But coming to San Francisco for an occasional visit filled her with excitement. She sensed how the big metropolis, with its hundreds of thousands of pulsating souls and unrealized possibilities, waited for her.

Julie took two days off work, so she could spend time with her sister. The two of them were best friends as well as sisters, and they knew they could count on each other in both good and troubled times.

Julie suggested a trip to the island of Alcatraz, where once, a notorious prison housed dangerous criminals. Sarah didn't care where they were as long as they were together. She needed her sister's company and counsel.

Sarah enjoyed the calm ferry ride. She liked seeing the city from the sea. The wind, the seagulls, and the water granted her a momentary feeling of freedom.

It ended when they arrived at the island and the prison, where the convicts were once jailed, most of them for cruel acts of murder. Sarah and Julie toured the historic jail.

"You see?" Julie said as they peered through rusting bars into a dismal cell. "Your life isn't so terrible in comparison to this place."

"I understand why there were so many escape attempts," Sarah responded. "This place gives me the creeps! It could give you a different perspective on things."

Julie sensed her sister's distress and guided her out to the open air. Returning to the city, they toured the colorful Fisherman's Wharf, where they stopped at a waterfront restaurant for lunch and placed their orders.

"So, what's bothering you?" Julie asked directly and affectionately looked at her sister.

"You know," Sarah sighed and looked out of the window at the rolling waves, "I'm at a point in my life when I have to accept that I won't have children. I'm having a tough time dealing with it. I hoped that my son would search for me, and it's not happening, and I feel hopeless."

"You must not lose hope," Julie said. "I'm sure the time will come when he'll look for you and find you."

"I miss him so much," Sarah uttered sadly.

"And what's going on between you and Jonathan?" Julie asked, understanding that her sister's low spirit was probably affected by the main relationship in her life.

Sarah looked down at the table and pushed her plate aside. "The situation is not good," she said, "and it's my fault."

"Why is it your fault?" Julie was surprised.

"Because I cheated on him. A lot. Then he closed himself off to me. And to complicate matters, he found himself a half-sister on the internet."

"Whoa. You cheated? A sister?" Julie took a big gulp of her wine.

"I wasn't happy, maybe because I wanted to have a child so

badly, so I started to fool around. At first, I hoped to get pregnant. Then it became a habit and a destructive addiction."

Julie sat back, stunned, trying to comprehend her sister's words, delivered in a simple manner and without an attempt to hide or to justify.

"So, I don't really blame him," Sarah continued, "for looking for women on the internet and finding a sister."

"Is this for real?" Julie asked and wondered if Jonathan had retaliated by having affairs, too. "An actual sister or someone who's like a sister to him?"

"At first, I thought it was weird and delusional, but now I just don't know," Sarah admitted. "I met her. She's not some nutcase. She teaches computer science at a university in Minnesota."

"Wow, what an amazing story," Julie said. "Compared to you, my crazy life looks like smooth sailing."

"I still love him," Sarah said. "And I believe that he still loves me, but we live in two separate worlds."

Julie took a bite of her salad. "I remember when you told me about him, right after you met. You were excited about your forbidden love. I never saw you as happy as during that time. You were shining, surrounded by an aura when you told me about the love that had come into your life as a sensitive patient, who was also strong and handsome. I thought that you deserved happiness after everything you went through."

"Jonathan has a place in the forest," Sarah said, veering off the topic. "He spends a lot of time there and thinks that the place was an ancient transmission station."

"What is a transmission station?" Julie asked.

"I don't really know."

"Have you been there?"

"Only once," Sarah said. "We discovered the place together. It's... unique, but I never went back. Jonathan excavated the place by himself and showed it to Irene."

"Irene?"

"The alleged half-sister."

"By the way," Julie changed the subject, "do you watch *The Broadcast*?"

"Yes," Sarah smiled sadly. "It's one of the few things that we still do together."

"They took an interesting turn," Julie said, "when they stopped the crime shows and went to historical events."

"Indeed," Sarah agreed. She kept secret her pride in knowing that it was she who initiated the change in direction for the New York-based network. She added, "Jonathan is totally into that show. He's the one who got me hooked on it. It's strange, but I feel there's a connection between my life and *The Broadcast*."

"What do you mean?" Julie wondered.

"I don't know," Sarah said. "I'm still trying to figure it out."

Edmond, Julie's husband, came home in the evening. Remarkably, he kept to himself and didn't nag Sarah with personal questions. The children behaved well too. Sarah thought that Julie must have cautioned them not to bother their aunt.

On the following day, Julie took Sarah for a tour of Chinatown. They walked around and curiously examined the unusual stores, taking a particular interest in the unique herbal displays, which offered a cure for every illness and pain. Sarah told Julie about the spiritual teachers that she had recently encountered. About the Indian guru who had let her down, the Zen master who had talked about looking at the world *as it is*, and the Tibetan lama who had spoken of the *Tibetan Book of the Dead* and the journey that the soul travels after death.

"Do you think those experiences helped you?" Julie asked.

"I think that I didn't give it a fair chance," Sarah admitted. "Practicing yoga definitely improved my mood, but I couldn't continue on that path after the guru and his community leaders let me down. I'm convinced that the teacher must serve as an example of his teaching. After I stopped practicing, I found myself sinking into a depression. Maybe in the future, I'll continue to look for my path, and I'll find a spiritual guide who speaks to my heart."

"Don't give up, sis," Julie said, "and when you find someone worthy, let me know."

***

The following day Julie had to go back to work. Sarah thought she'd enjoy touring the city by herself. She rode a cable car with no specific destination in mind, letting herself be carried along the streets. She walked down a street called Church Street, where she saw a group of nuns. A long time ago, she had dressed like them and lived in a convent. But… wait. There was something odd about this particular group of nuns. They were… men, or perhaps transgendered.

Approaching them, she asked, "Are you nuns?"

"We are the sisters of perpetual indulgence," one of them answered in a deep, masculine voice.

That's how most people are, she thought to herself. *The nuns in drag are at least honest about it.*

Sarah decided a picnic out in the open air would be a good idea, so she entered a grocery store and bought herself fresh bread, vegetables, yellow cheese, and freshly squeezed orange juice. She waved a taxi over and asked the driver to take her to the Golden Gate Bridge.

She got out of the cab at a park near the bridge and picked a shady spot with a good view of the tourist attraction. She spread a piece of cloth on the lawn and proceeded with cutting the bread and vegetables. She then enjoyed a tasty meal in a pleasant environment. As she ate, she watched children play under the supervision of mothers who chatted with each other.

All of a sudden something was wrong. She looked all around her, suspiciously, wondering at the strange sensation that descended upon her. What was it? The food was tasty, and the environment was pleasant, and still, she felt weird, heavy, and sluggish. *What is wrong with me?* She recognized that a thick fog surrounded her for so long that she had forgotten when she last felt good. *When was the last time I laughed with joy? It's been ages that I've been a ghost, a walking shadow of myself.*

She looked at the Golden Gate Bridge, with its metal cables connecting its huge towers when unexpectedly, a ray of light broke through, a clearing in the dark cloud that covered her world. The solution appeared, and it was so simple that she didn't know why she hadn't conceived it before.

Sarah knew what she had to do and how she could solve all the problems of her life and the whole world, once and for all. She looked toward the bridge, an enormous mass of concrete and steel calling her seductively. Little white clouds hovered far away, friendly, hanging in a blue sky. The sun was warm, and a gentle breeze cooled her face. The bridge called her. She got up on her feet. Now she knew for certain: all she needed to do was to walk to the bridge, take the pedestrian lane, and throw herself into the ocean below.

Reality faded and the bright light that was coming from the bridge intensified, beckoning her toward it. She advanced in a straight line, seeing herself progressing as if she were looking from outside her body. She walked past a group of Japanese tourists who took photos of the famous attraction. The sound of camera clicks was unbearable.

Setting foot on the bridge, she took the lane reserved for

CHAPTER 34

Michael

Michael's worry that his relationship with Melanie would have a negative effect on his friendship with her parents soon faded. It seemed that Walter and Monica approved. Monica confided with him that she wasn't always happy with her daughter's romantic choices and even hinted that she'd be glad if Michael became an official member of the family.

Within a few months, Melanie moved into Michael's small apartment in Brooklyn. Michael invited his landlady, Mrs. Rinaldi, for a cup of tea, and that's when he introduced Melanie to her. The old lady was happy to receive the attention of the young, sympathetic couple, and used the opportunity to rehash her problems, mostly about her husband who had died and left her by herself.

Showing maturity beyond their years, the lovers nurtured their relationship with care and caution. Their financial resources were limited, and they had to get by on a limited budget. Still, they were grateful for everything they had, and especially for their love and for finding each other. They loved being outdoors when the weather allowed, and every once in a while they went out to movies, concerts, and Broadway productions.

Pleased with Michael's work, the producer of *Around the Clock* hinted at a promotion to the position of reporter. In the meantime, he continued to work as a researcher.

Around the Clock prepared a fact-finding exposé about a known criminal who claimed to have seen the light and found salvation through Christ, and now intended to enter politics. Michael was asked to travel to San Francisco, and talk to the man's ex-wife, as his editor thought she could shed light on the controversial figure.

Michael welcomed the challenge. He called his friend Greg in San Francisco and asked if he could impose upon his hospitality for a couple of days.

"Sure, man, it'll be great to see you," Greg agreed.

It had been a long time since Michael's last visit to San Francisco, and he was glad to have a local host.

Michael arrived at the San Francisco airport at 1:00 p.m., after a six-hour flight. Greg was at work at the time, so nobody waited for him at the terminal. No matter. Michael had a meeting scheduled. He took a taxi.

The former criminal strove to get elected to the Florida House of Representatives, and later, with the help of his substantial wealth, to make his way to the national political arena. His ex-wife,

Mrs. Gloria Rice, agreed to talk to Michael at her home; but, she had yet to decide whether she would speak to the camera.

When Michael arrived, he found a woman in her fifties who lived with three cats in a large house commanding a beautiful view overlooking the bay. Age had already left its mark on her, and Michael had the impression that she had undergone one or more plastic surgeries. He made a mental note to tell Melanie that she didn't need to erase the signs of the passing time. He was sure she would keep her beauty and vitality, even with a few wrinkles.

Gloria Rice offered the handsome young researcher tea and homemade cookies, which he gladly accepted, not having eaten since the puny pack of pretzels and tiny cup of juice on the airplane.

"What do you want to know?" Mrs. Rice asked.

Sitting across from her, Michael met her gaze. "As you know," he said, "your ex-husband, Mr. Charles Rice, intends on entering Florida politics. He is, of course, drawing attention because of his history with the mob and the time he spent in jail for tax evasion. Do you believe that he's changed his ways following his involvement with the Christian faith?"

"Not at all," Mrs. Rice answered unequivocally. "I think the whole religion thing is just a scam. Listen to me, young man, I'm not so young anymore and I know people. In my experience, people don't change, especially people like Charles Rice."

"That's quite a definite assertion," Michael commented.

"Once a criminal, always a criminal," she said.

Michael wrote her words in his notebook; per her request, he used no recording device. "Do you know that Mr. Rice contributed a lot of money to charities in the U.S. as well as in Africa?"

Mrs. Rice scoffed. "He would do whatever is needed to get elected. You know, he's actually perfect for politics."

"Did he pay alimony on time after your divorce?"

"At first he said I wouldn't get a nickel out of him. Indeed, for two years I had to manage by myself. Afterward, he started to pay, probably because he'd planned to clear his name."

Michael asked a few more questions, concluded the interview, and thanked Mrs. Rice for her time. Some of her statements disturbed him. *Is it true that people can't change? Are corrupt people really perfect for politics?*

***

That evening, Michael was glad to meet his friend Greg, who only finished working at 9:00 p.m. The easygoing and stocky man worked at a local radio station, where he hosted his own talk show. His friendly, straightforward and casual style, as well as his proficiency in political affairs, had caused listeners to like him and within a short time, he'd become one of the most popular talk show hosts in the Bay Area.

They went to eat dinner at a restaurant that Greg frequented, where they knew him and listened to his show.

"So, how is it going in New York?" Greg asked after ordering a beer.

"Pretty good," Michael replied. "Except for the lousy weather."

"Yeah, I'm glad I moved out of there," Greg said. The waitress returned with their beverages and Greg took a long gulp. Setting the mug down, he added, "It looks like things are working out for me here."

"Is there a lady in your life?" Michael asked, a glint of speculation in his eyes.

Greg smiled broadly. "There is. What about you?"

"Me too," Michael said. "I'm not alone anymore."

"So, let's have a toast." Greg raised his glass of beer, and they clinked glasses.

Greg leaned forward. "You know, occasionally, *The Broadcast* comes up in my conversations with callers."

"And what do they say?" Michael was curious.

"Most of them side with that reporter, McPherson, and think that TXB should reveal its source. I also get science fiction geeks who suggest all kinds of theories regarding the origin of those recordings."

"That's how it is on the East Coast too," Michael said.

"Do you have any information, a scoop for me?" Greg urged him.

"You know, if I knew something, I couldn't reveal it. But the truth is I'm not connected to that show. I work on *Around the*

Clock."

"Okay," Greg said, with easy acceptance. "Just remember me if the situation changes."

"I won't forget," Michael promised. It occurred to him that he was not entirely truthful when he disavowed a connection to *The Broadcast*. His girlfriend's father, who was first a personal friend, just happened to be the show's producer.

***

Michael spent the night at Greg's rented house. It turned out that Greg hadn't exaggerated when he said that things were working out for him. He had a spacious house with three bedrooms, a large living room, a well-equipped kitchen, and a yard. Greg was free until the following day at 3:00 p.m., when he had a staff meeting. His daily talk show started at 7:05 p.m., after the hour's news.

In the morning the two of them went in Greg's car to visit the city's famous Fisherman's Wharf. It was a sunny day with a cold breeze blowing in from the ocean. Michael looked around as they toured the famous tourist attraction at a leisurely pace. He remembered that he had once visited the site with his family and enjoyed the colorful and lively environment.

As they walked, a strange feeling invaded Michael's mind. There was something different out there, something out of the ordinary, something he couldn't grasp. Perhaps it was in the air or carried from the ocean. Maybe it was in the ships' sirens or the calls pedestrians and bicycle riders and made her way to the center of the bridge where she stopped. Leaning over the railing, Sarah took several deep breaths. Then she climbed on the banister.

"Lady, what are you doing?" someone called, but Sarah ignored him. She arrived at the top of the banister and came down on the other side. Now she stood on a strip of steel with nothing separating her from complete liberation. She looked past her toes to the blue water, far, far below. *That's it. It's over.* She breathed a sigh of relief.

of the seabirds, or in the many people who filled the stores and restaurants. He looked in all directions but couldn't identify anything unusual.

"What's going on?" Greg asked, noticing his friend's restlessness.

"I don't know," Michael said. "I feel like there's something strange going on, and I can't figure out what it is."

"Maybe jetlag?" Greg suggested.

"No. It's something else. I'm trying to find if there's anything weird happening around here." Michael knew his answer didn't make much sense.

"You're probably just hungry. Maybe we should find a restaurant."

Michael shrugged. They found a seafood restaurant overlooking the ocean and ordered lunch.

"Feeling better?" Greg inquired after they ate.

"I think so," Michael answered, even as he wondered about the odd feeling that had overcome him. "Could we go to see the Golden Gate Bridge?"

"Sure," Greg agreed, wondering at the unexpected request. "So long as you remember the bridge is not actually golden but rust-colored."

Michael grinned as his friend meant him to. They paid for their meal and drove to the Golden Gate Bridge.

"You know," Greg said as he navigated the narrow city streets, "that the bridge is a popular site for suicides?"

"Really?" Michael was surprised.

"Yeah," Greg answered. "They come from all over the country. Maybe they think it will set them up with a pass to heaven or something."

They drove through picturesque streets. Nearing the bridge, they passed wide lawns where people enjoyed the outdoors. Greg parked his car at some distance from the bridge, and they continued on foot. Michael enjoyed walking in the serene environment and set a brisk pace. Overweight and panting, Greg tried not to be left behind.

"Doesn't your girlfriend want you to go on a diet?" Michael asked as his friend huffed and puffed behind him.

"She knows that with me it's a package deal." Greg smiled.

They arrived at the bridge.

"Now what?" Greg asked.

"When we were at the Fisherman's Wharf, I suddenly felt a strange need to see the bridge," Michael said. Looking around, he sighed. "Now, I don't know. That feeling's gone."

The frantic movement of people running toward the center of the bridge attracted their attention. "A woman jumped to her death," an excited teenager announced.

"Too bad," Greg joked. "If we'd come a little earlier, we could have seen her jump."

Michael didn't think it was funny. He thought about the anonymous woman that he'd never met, and never would. Their paths had almost crossed. For some unknown reason, she chose to leap to her death. A life deliberately ended. Why? What would cause someone to kill herself? A broken heart? Unfulfilled goals?

Michael's thoughts dwelled on the transience of life.

We are so immersed in our daily routine that we don't stop to ponder the fragility of our being and the possibility that at the next moment, it all could end. And that woman preferred to end her existence on earth; sorrow and suffering must have overcome her.

Michael reminded himself that life was precious, that he should appreciate everything given to him, including hardships and difficulties, and he should try to make the most of every single moment.

CHAPTER 35

The Broadcast

Journalists and other notable media personalities joined Stewart McPherson's call for TXB, to reveal the source of *The Broadcast*'s videos. They claimed the network's excuse of "confidentiality of sources" eroded the public's trust.

Letters from viewers, in newspapers and on the internet, declared their intention to stop watching the show, because they agreed with McPherson and suspected that they were being deceived.

Following the publication of his article, McPherson received a lot of mail, mostly from ordinary people who supported his stance. He also received letters from people urging him to back off because they disagreed with him, and because he was disturbing their enjoyment of the fantastic possibilities that *The Broadcast* offered. McPherson also received mail that attempted to explain the footage, or claim responsibility for it.

One such email read:

"To Mr. Stewart McPherson,

The reason why Walter Lindsey doesn't reveal the source of the footage is that HE DOESN'T KNOW.

He receives it from us, and we supply it anonymously.

Had it occurred to you that the military is constantly filming us from space without our consent? Not only the military of our country but friendly and enemy countries as well? Is it such a stretch to conceive that such information would eventually leak?

Take care,

Your friends at UFGIO.

The Uncensored Free Global Information Organization, the source of *The Broadcast* footage.

McPherson tried to locate the source of that email, but it apparently came through an untraceable server.

The negative publicity, however, didn't hurt the overall popularity of *The Broadcast* and even contributed to a mild increase in ratings. But despite the popularity and profitability, some members of the TXB board of directors started to express concern regarding damage to the network's credibility. The directors' worries increased when a few advertisers voiced apprehension of damage to their good name if it turned out that *The Broadcast* was based on misleading the public. However, the show continued.

In an episode dedicated to the fifteenth century, *The Broadcast* examined Christopher Columbus. The show hosted Professor Sebastian Mendoza, from Universidad Nacional

Autónoma de México, who spoke and showed remarkable films of Columbus' travels.

Professor Mendoza said, "Columbus searched for a way to reach India by sea, and he never realized he had arrived at a new continent." The professor continued, "The Spaniards who followed Columbus brutally enslaved the natives, forcibly converted them to Christianity and robbed them of their treasures. If we look at Columbus himself, though he was brutal and greedy, I can admire him for his courage and perseverance in following his vision. We should remember that, at that time, most people believed that the planet was flat. In order to travel by sea to India, Columbus had to trust the theory that Earth was round. Trust like that is not a simple matter."

In one of the videos, the professor showed Columbus' three ships anchored near the Cuban coast, in October of 1492.

***

Producer Walter Lindsey enjoyed management's support. They praised the risk he took in switching *The Broadcast's* focus from crime to history, which had turned out to be a brilliant move. They saw that the change hadn't hurt ratings and added a dimension of respectability to the show and the network. However, under the prevailing climate, Lindsey also felt the heat when he received a memo from Colin Ingram, the network's CEO, advising him to reconsider the confidentiality policy in view of the public's growing incredulity.

Walter Lindsey stood his ground writing back in an email: "Dear Mr. Ingram, I promised my sources not to expose them, and am bound by that obligation. That was the necessary condition accepted in order to obtain the footage. I would rather cancel the show than disclose my sources, as I do not intend to betray the trust placed in me."

Lindsey gained unexpected support when the *New York Times* published an article by Japanese professor Takeshi Nishimura, in its weekend edition. The professor was a world-renowned scientist who taught physics at the prestigious MIT.

The article, titled "Scientific Points Regarding *The Broadcast*," read:

> Lately, I've followed an interesting debate on several forums regarding the TV program *The Broadcast* which is aired on the TXB network. I am a physicist with no connection to the network or any of its employees.
>
> I must admit that the program piques my curiosity, and I enjoy watching it. I would like to examine a few scientific theories that could point to the origin of the films. I don't know whether the following ideas truly explain how TXB obtains its footage, and I'm aware that some of my hypotheses might seem as if they were taken

from science fiction. Application of these hypotheses would require some advanced technologies currently under development, but to the best of my knowledge, we are quite far from such a level of data transference.

For the purpose of our discussion, let's look at the planet Jupiter, with our naked eyes or through a telescope. Can we see it? The simple answer is no. We can only see it as it was about thirty-three minutes ago, but not as it is at this very moment, because thirty-three minutes is the time the light takes to travel from Jupiter to planet Earth.

Let's continue to examine the hypothesis. If we place a telescope on Jupiter, it cannot see an event on Earth until thirty-three minutes after it has occurred.

If we put a telescope on a spaceship that is stationed, say, four light-years from our planet, then an event that happens on planet Earth would only reach the spaceship after four years. This is a gross simplification because light spreads and disperses. Furthermore, the telescope on the spaceship would have to filter the intense light of the sun. I do hope that in the foreseeable future, we scientists will have access to advanced telescopes and innovative computer technology that will allow us to observe occurrences on distant planets.

We could say, then, that events which happen on planet Earth during daylight hours don't really vanish, even if nobody is watching or recording them. The images travel in space at the high velocity of the light.

In theory, one day, a highly developed technology could receive and record those events.

There are enormous technological hurdles for such an application to be possible. We, the human race, are far away from achieving such capabilities.

There is also the problem of distance and time. If a spacecraft receives and records an event that occurred 20 years ago, then it would require another 20 years for the pictures to return to our planet at the speed of light.

There are scientific theories on how, in the future, it may be possible to transfer data at speeds faster than light. But I won't get into such complicated discussions and mathematical calculations which border on science fiction.

So, could a spaceship located hundreds of light-years from Earth receive and record to video events that took place on our planet? Even with a telescope that is far ahead of everything we know?

I don't have an answer. I can only explore interesting hypotheses, sit back on my couch to watch a TV series, and enjoy the possibilities that it opens.

"Another, even more amazing idea comes from Einstein's Theory of Relativity. According to Einstein, the perceived distinction that we make between past, present, and future is illusory.

When we look at the effect that *movement* creates on the space-time continuum, we see that the laws of physics as we know them become irrelevant. The reality of the past and future does not differ from the reality of the present. The past has not gone, and the future is not nonexistent. The past, present, and future all exist simultaneously: from events that took place in the distant past, to events that from our limited perspective are yet to happen.

"It's interesting, I'd like to mention, that the ancient Incan people, the ones who built Machu Picchu, also thought that the past, present, and future all exist concurrently.

Hence, if there were a technology with fantastic futuristic capabilities, it might bridge the gaps between the past and the present, allowing us to receive and record events from the past. Again, this may sound like science fiction, but I can't rule out that one day we will have access to such a scientific breakthrough.

For anyone who might dismiss these theories as holding no practical applications in our time, I remind you that technologies we take for granted today would have looked like a fantasy to people forty years ago. For instance, having access to a wealth of information on the internet, a video conversation between two people when one of them is on a train in Australia and the other is climbing a mountain in Switzerland, or navigating with a GPS, which uses calculations based on Einstein's theory of relativity.

I do not say that *The Broadcast* recordings necessarily use the theories discussed herein. I only suggest ideas that could explain the enigmatic TV show.

Professor Nishimura's article received wide public attention and went viral on the internet. His reasonable explanations and prestige as a distinguished scientist helped diminish the erosion of public support for the show and silenced voices speaking against the authenticity of the footage.

CHAPTER 36

Sarah

Wind whipped at her hair as Sarah moved another fraction of an inch to the edge of the bridge's steel frame. At that point, all Sarah had to do was to tilt her body forward and let go, allowing gravity to take her home.

The phone rang. *Not now*, she thought. *I'm sorry, I'm no longer here.* It rang again and again. With annoyed reluctance, she pulled the phone from her pocket. She could drop it into the water. She wouldn't answer, not if it were her husband or her sister. She glanced at the screen. It was Heidi. She decided to answer, end the conversation quickly, and then toss the phone into the ocean.

"What do you need?" Sarah asked impatiently. Her voice sounded distant and muffled, as if it belonged to someone else. "I'm busy now," she added.

"I need your help, Sarah!" Heidi sounded distressed.

"What happened?" Sarah heard herself asking.

"They kicked us out of the trailer park, and we have nowhere to go. Could we move our trailer onto your land? We'll pay a monthly rent."

In Heidi's voice, Sarah detected despair as she pleaded for a place for her family.

"Okay," Sarah whispered in a feeble voice, unable to deny her friend a safe place for her family.

"So, we can move?" Heidi's voice was filled with desperate hope.

"You can." Sarah looked down at the sea and noticed with a certain discontent that the moment for release had passed. She no longer had the strength and courage to jump.

"Thank you so much!" Heidi breathed with relief. "You have no idea how you saved me. You won't be disappointed."

Sarah looked backward toward the bridge. The world's din and bustle returned. Curious spectators gathered at the railing, some of them trying to talk her out of committing suicide.

Once again, she looked down at the blue water below. Maybe she could still do it? But no, she missed her chance, her opportune moment. She climbed back over the railing, eyes shedding tears of sorrow and shame. She crossed the group of spectators, walking with a brisk stride, wishing to quickly disappear from the view of anyone who might have seen her on the bridge.

***

Jonathan objected to Heidi's move to their property with her husband and kids. But Sarah refused to back down, reasoning that they needed an alternate source of income since he still had no regular job.

After Heidi's family arrived with their big trailer, Sarah found that the sounds of children playing contributed to an improvement in her overall mood.

Word traveled fast. Within a few weeks following Heidi and her family's move, Sarah and Jonathan received additional pleas from young people who wished to park their trailers in a rural environment at a low cost. Sarah interviewed several applicants and allowed a few to set up residence on her and Jonathan's property.

After years of living on the secluded property, Sarah and Jonathan had to adjust to a communal environment. Sarah thought that the change would benefit her, while Jonathan was reserved and not eager to have other people on his land.

"What if they discover my site?" Jonathan protested, disclosing the real reason for his concern.

Sarah tried to ease his worry. "The hill and the trees won't let anybody into the spot," she said. "And Jonathan, I think that a community is *exactly* what we need."

The new residents were easygoing people. They alleviated Sarah's loneliness, and the kids delighted her heart. Sarah and Jonathan installed connections to running water, electricity, and sewer for six trailers. The financial contribution was significant and helped compensate for Jonathan's lack of a steady income.

Among the new residents were Stanley and Sandy and their

little daughter, Tammy. Sandy had spent a year as a volunteer on a kibbutz in Israel, and she liked the community's way of life. She initiated potluck meals that usually took place in Jonathan and Sarah's spacious house. Sarah was glad to have her tenants' company, and even Jonathan admitted that he liked not being so alone.

The trailers congregated near the area where the forest had been cleared. Mother Nature had quickly reclaimed the land, covering it with new vegetation that concealed the stumps.

The new residents liked the sunshine, and even Sarah had to admit (to herself) that she appreciated the abundance of sunlight in her vegetable garden. Every once in a while, Sarah was asked to be a babysitter during evening hours. She gladly agreed. The children called her Auntie Sarah.

Stanley, Sandy's significant other, preferred to use his nickname, "Nature's Son." He familiarized himself with every place, corner, field, or backyard, in the county and beyond, where there were fruit and nut-bearing trees that were not picked by their owners. He harvested their bounty and sold it as organic fruit and brought some to Sarah and Jonathan's house.

Sarah was delighted when the new residents talked about celebrating the holidays together. She saw that she wouldn't have to be a guest at her sister's house as in previous years. Julie was always glad to invite her sister and her husband, but Sarah and Jonathan were uncomfortable, feeling that they were there because Julie felt pity for them.

CHAPTER 37

The Broadcast

In a sea of controversy, *The Broadcast* continued to navigate its journey back in time. Public debate contributed to the popularity of the show, though a few leading managers still expressed concern regarding the long-term impact on TXB's good name.

Public Relation's Manager Gordon Mayson spoke at a board of directors meeting, stating, "In my opinion, it would be better if TXB would forfeit profits and drop the show immediately."
However, the CEO didn't accept his view, probably because he believed in producer Walter Lindsey's integrity and decency. The show's team and the popular host maintained an appearance of respectability. They made an effort to present chosen events without political or cultural bias and hosted distinguished scholars.

Challengers of *The Broadcast* claimed that the concept of the show made no sense. They were annoyed by the angle of filming, straight from above, which made it difficult to observe occurrences, and by the 'illogical' historical progression, going from near past to late past, instead of the 'normal' movement of time, from the past toward the present.

Proponents of the show claimed that displaying historical events in present-to-past order was consistent with Professor Nishimura's hypothetical spaceship. The farther it got, the earlier the events it captured. A few sharp-sighted viewers even claimed that the quality of the films diminished with the increasing age of the historical events, consistent with filming performed from greater distances. Others argued that they didn't notice any difference in the pictures' quality.

***

The Broadcast continued its inquiry into the fifteenth century and hosted Professor Natalie Péllissier from the Sorbonne University in Paris. Professor Péllissier, who was on the show before when she spoke about the Napoleon era, addressed the topic of Joan of Arc.

"Who was Joan of Arc?" the host, Susan Riley, asked the French guest.

Dressed in a stylish outfit, the attractive professor replied in her charming French accent. "Good evening," she said. "Jeanne d'Arc grew up in a small village, the daughter of a devout peasant family loyal to the French crown. At that time, France was split between warring factions that held claims to the throne, and the king of England took advantage of the internal divisions and invaded France.

"At the age of thirteen, Jeanne d'Arc claimed to hear voices and see visions of different Christian angels and saints. She said the voices told her that God had chosen to liberate her country from the English and coronate Charles VII as the king of France."

"How do researchers of our time relate to her claim of hearing voices?" Susan Riley inquired.

"I suppose today she would be hospitalized in a mental institution and treated as a schizophrenic," the professor replied, "although I, personally, am not convinced that every person who experiences a visionary state of consciousness is necessarily mentally ill, and that includes Jeanne d'Arc."

"Anyway," the professor continued, "Jeanne d'Arc proved to Charles VII that she was not insane when she identified him in a crowd, even though he ordered one of his servants to dress like a king, while he was dressed as a commoner."

"Charles VII put her in command of a small army which she led from horseback."

The recording played. As usual, the angle of filming was straight from above, and the quality of the picture mediocre. It showed Joan of Arc riding ahead of her army while holding a banner, entering into the city of Orleans which was under English siege. In subsequent short clips, viewers saw Jeanne d'Arc leading her army in fierce battles.

"I've watched the films several times," said Professor Péllissier while the footage ran. "What strikes me is that Jeanne is seen leading, rallying, and encouraging the French soldiers, but not killing any enemy soldiers with her own sword. That is different from the way she is portrayed in movies."

The professor noted that Joan of Arc won significant battles, conquered towns and fortresses, and coroneted Charles VII as the king of France. She earned her soldiers' admiration and gained mystical stature among her loyalists. People in the towns that she liberated viewed her as a saint.

Professor Péllissier continued, "In a battle near the city of Compiegne, which was under siege by the English and their Burgundian allies, she was defeated and captured. She was put on trial in front of a tribunal staffed by pro-English clergy, was found guilty of heresy and wearing men's clothing, and sentenced to death. Consequently, she was tied to a tall pillar and burned alive in the city of Rouen."

Host Susan Riley looked into the camera's eye and said, "TXB has a film that documents the burning of Joan of Arc, but our editors chose not to air it."

***

Occasionally, Sarah overheard her colleagues talking about *The Broadcast*. Most expressed amazement and appreciation and remarked on how it incited their interest in history. They also speculated how far back in time the show would go and wondered if they would get to see events described in the Bible or the Trojan War. Sarah never mentioned she had initiated the history focus of the show.

In contrast, some of Sarah's colleagues commented that the show had become boring and they preferred the previous format when it assisted in solving crimes.

***

The Broadcast hosted Professor Kadir Sankar from Istanbul University. The Turkish professor was a short, stocky man with a swarthy complexion and luxuriant mustache. He expounded, with the help of accompanying video clips, upon the conquest of Constantinople, the capital of the Christian Byzantine Empire, by the Muslim Ottoman Empire.

"A feverish religious belief motivated the attackers," the professor said, curling his mustache. "The Ottomans had huge cannons that fired half-a-ton shells, which opened wide gaps in the wall of the city and exhausted its defenders."

Indeed, in the film, viewers observed the massive cannons and their lethal impact.

Professor Sankar added that, following the fall of Constantinople, leadership of the eastern section of Christianity moved to Moscow.

***

In a critique published in the *Washington Post*, culture reviewer

Gerald Brooks wrote:

> *The Broadcast* focuses on wars in the Western world. It neglects other parts of the globe, and it ignores events that are not related to fighting. Watching the show, one might get the impression that nothing significant happened in China, Japan, Africa, Australia, or the Americas before the arrival of the white man."

The *Washington Post* also published an article by human rights activist Pamela McKenzie, who attacked the program on issues of invasion of privacy.

> With all due respect, TXB's *The Broadcast* has managed to solve a number of crimes, but isn't it time that we turn our thoughts to human rights issues? What about innocent people who cannot know when somebody records videos of them without their consent?

***

In an episode dedicated to the thirteenth century, *The Broadcast* hosted Professor Ankjargal from the University of Mongolia in the city of Ulaanbaatar. Short, with a typical Chinese appearance, and radiating enthusiasm, he fascinated viewers with stories and short films of Genghis Khan.

"Genghis Khan is considered to be one of the greatest

conquerors of all times," Ankjargal said. "At the beginning of the thirteenth century, he unified all the Mongolian tribes under his rule. At its height, the Mongolian Empire held the largest contiguous territory in history, from China to the Caspian Sea."

"Is the myth of Genghis Khan's cruelty based on fact?" Susan Riley asked.

"Genghis Khan embodied the brutality that characterized his native culture," the professor answered. "He and his warriors symbolized uncompromising malice. They were fierce fighters who traveled on horseback and left horror and destruction in their wake.

"It is possible that they used extreme cruelty as a form of psychological warfare; however, I think that it's hypocritical to apply modern attitudes to thirteenth-century warfare. Remember, in the twentieth century, our so-called advanced society used chemical weapons. During World War II, whole cities were bombed from the air without discriminating between soldiers and noncombatants, and two atom bombs were dropped on civilian cities. In fact, most cultures are guilty of horrible cruelty. So it seems to me that the human spirit, which can reach incredible achievements, is also capable of diving into abysses of hatred and darkness."

CHAPTER 38

Stewart McPherson

The phone rang at McPherson's office. "I got something that you might find interesting," McPherson was surprised to recognize the voice of the hacker that he employed on occasions.

"What is it about?" The journalist asked.

"Lindsey's pals! You've asked me to dig up information about them."

"Did you find anything?" McPherson was interested.

"Come to my house," said the hacker who rarely went outdoors. "I'm free this afternoon at 3:00 o'clock."

McPherson knew the hacker, whom he knew only by his first name, John—and wasn't sure whether it was his real name—was a recluse who hardly ever invited anyone to his place, in an old apartment building in Queens. When the journalist knocked on the door he brought with him a large Submarine roast beef sandwich; he knew it was John's favorite.

"Long time no see," McPherson said and shook John's hand.

"Have a seat," John formally said and pointed to the couch

in his small living room. "I've found some interesting stuff."

"I can't wait," McPherson admitted.

"I followed on your request, and tried to find if any of Lindsey's friends had a police record," The hacker said. "Well," he smiled, "none of them had one."

"So?" McPherson wondered.

"But one of them had a record when he was in college; only his rich father managed to get the whole story buried."

"Who?" McPherson didn't try to hide his curiosity.

"Alex!" The hacker exclaimed. "Today he is a software engineer who writes animation programs, and he makes quite a bit of money. In Walter's band, he plays the drums."

"Go on," McPherson urged him.

"When he was younger, he was sent to a little-known school in Chicago, a place that attempts to rehabilitate young geniuses who have run-ins with the law. *The Chicago Institute of Art and Science* is a private institute which takes a very high tuition fee and specializes in music and computers. Well, our friend Alex had once stolen the school ..." The hacker smiled.

"Stolen the school?" McPherson was baffled. "What do you mean?"

"Well," John said while chewing on his sandwich. "Obviously he didn't actually steal anything; but he managed to create an alternate computer environment, which substituted the school's entire system. I mean, information, finances, everything. For a whole week, he ran the school as his own, changed student's grades, gave promotions and salary increases to his favorite teachers, and sent official written reprimand to staff members he disliked."

"Quite a capable guy," McPherson noted, "though he must have had accomplices. But why create this whole elaborate scheme? Why not simply hack into the existing system?"

"He was probably drawn to the challenge, and you see," the hacker explained, "all the school's personnel were his accomplices as they operated within his alternate environment. I think it was after all just a sophisticated prank. He knew that they would be on to him and that his rich daddy would bail him out. Still, what's interesting is that somehow they managed to completely erase the whole affair from his personal record and the school's archives so that he wouldn't have a problem finding a job later in life."

"Quite interesting," McPherson said. "So he knows how to create a faked reality …"

"That's not all," the hacker grinned. "While working on his "project," he also continued to play drums in a band. Here, have a look." The hacker handed McPherson a photo. "Alex is on the drums but take a close look at the other members of the band."

McPherson examined the photo. "Well I'll be damned," he said in amazement. In the picture, he recognized young Julian and Eric, two other members of Lindsey's band. Walter Lindsey, however, was not in the picture.

CHAPTER 39

Jonathan

On more than one occasion, Sarah pleaded with her husband to initiate a connection with his brother, his only living blood relative. Fearing rejection, Jonathan avoided the issue.

Shortly before Walter aired his sensational broadcast documenting the murder of Pedro Gonzales' ex-wife, Walter came for a surprise visit. The two brothers spent hours together, getting to know each other and catching up on thirty years of estrangement.

***

Walter called and invited Jonathan to come and spend Thanksgiving with him and meet his family.

It had been a long time since Jonathan had been aboard an airplane. He also tried not to drive far away, and just thinking about long distance traveling set off an irrational panic in him. He used to feel quite safe on drives within a certain range, which included San Francisco, but he did his best to avoid longer journeys.

When Walter called, he immediately accepted the invitation. Only after the call ended did the fear start to creep into his mind. Nevertheless, he remained determined and didn't yield to his anxiety. He did not intend on missing the meeting with his brother and getting to know his family.

Sarah, who was aware of the fears he faced without him having to explain, offered to drive him to the San Francisco airport. Ever since her near-attempt at suicide, she made an effort to focus on the good things in her life and accept the reality that she wouldn't realize her childhood dream, to be a mother. And as for her son, whom she called Daniel, she settled for patiently waiting for him to search for her and hoped that the chance for reunion would carry her through future difficulties. She returned to loving and appreciating her husband and avoided further adultery.

They hugged each other affectionately, before Jonathan entered the airport's security line. He chose to sit in an aisle seat and not next to a window, feeling safer where he could get up and move freely without disturbing those sitting next to him. His heart pounded when the airplane's engines awoke with a mighty roar, and anxiety threatened to overwhelm him. He concentrated on calming himself with deep breathing and distracting his mind by reading a book.

The takeoff was particularly challenging. Jonathan was

overcome by panic and dizziness, his breathing became shallow, and for a moment, he wondered whether he had made the right decision in accepting his brother's invitation. But later during the flight, he managed to relax, his breathing returned to normal, and he even enjoyed peeking through the window, watching the clouds passing under the plane and the United States far below.

Jonathan wondered why his anxieties and panic attacks were so easily triggered by airplane flights and car driving, while he could stroll in the woods alone, and even when it got dark, and not have the same reaction.

He thought it was better that he was invited for Thanksgiving and not Christmas, because otherwise he would have had to bring presents—and he dreaded having to buy gifts for people he didn't know.

Upon deplaning in New York, Jonathan looked for his brother. He saw a signboard with his name, held by a young lady.

"Hello," he said as he approached her, "I'm Jonathan. Were you sent here by Walter?"

She looked him up and down, extended her hand, and grinned. "You're my uncle. I'm Carolyn, Walter's daughter. My parents are busy, so I volunteered to pick you up, 'cause I like to drive."

Thoroughly charmed by his cute niece, he followed her to the car. Shortly after she started driving, she turned on the radio and cranked up the volume as her favorite music blared.

the back. He introduced Jonathan to his wife, who expressed her pleasure in finally meeting him. With an apologetic smile, Monica excused herself, saying, "The kitchen calls! I've got a lot of food to prepare for tomorrow."

His brother escorted him to the guest room where he would stay and said, "Take a minute to get comfortable, then join me downstairs."

Jonathan nodded and did just that. First, he unpacked, then he phoned Sarah to report an uneventful flight and safe landing. She replied that she and Heidi were busy with holiday meal preparations. The conversation ended, and he headed off to find his brother. He made a few wrong turns before finding Walter ensconced in his favorite recliner.

Because Monica was preoccupied with preparing the Thanksgiving feast, Walter ordered pizza delivery for supper.

During the meal, Jonathan felt awkward and foreign, despite Walter's family treating him warmly and casually.

After eating, the brothers sat by the fireplace and talked.

Jonathan broached a subject that had bothered him for a long time: "Is it possible that we have a sister that we never knew about?"

Walter seemed surprised. "Not that I know of. Why do you ask?"

"I met someone on the internet," Jonathan said, "and we've found a few interesting similarities between her father and ours. For instance, her father was killed in a car accident in the same year that our parents died, and he was also Jewish."

"Hmm," Walter murmured. "Still seems like a very remote chance."

"We think in a similar way," Jonathan continued, "and we have the same areas of interest. She teaches computer science at a university in Minnesota."

"I remember," Walter said, "that Grandma once mentioned our father had another woman before he met our mother, but she didn't say anything about children."

It occurred to Walter that his childless brother was lonely and yearned for a family, which explained why this irrational idea of a missing sister fascinated him. Walter resolved to build a closer connection with Jonathan.

***

Walter and Monica's older daughter, Melanie, arrived the following day with her boyfriend, Michael, a handsome young man. Jonathan saw that his brother and sister-in-law were very fond of Michael, treating him like a family member. Walter performed the introductions and told Jonathan that Michael was a promising television reporter and a talented guitar player. Monica's sister also joined them for the holiday meal, along with her husband and three children. The combined families made for a noisy gathering filled with laughter and energy.

At the holiday table, Jonathan once again felt a bit awkward, because everyone else had known each other for quite some time and he was the obvious newcomer. Still, he was more comfortable with Walter and Monica's family than with Sarah's sister Julie and her family. He always suspected that Julie invited them out of pity.

Before everyone began eating, Monica suggested that they go around the table and each person will speak on something from the past year for which they felt thankful. Familiar with the practice, Jonathan always found it artificial, coerced, and exhausting. He used to dread the moment his turn to speak would come and he wouldn't know what to say. Typically, he made up something insincere, like, "I'm grateful for whatever life throws my way." This time, however, he was more comfortable than in previous years. When his turn came, he took a deep breath and said: "I'm grateful to be celebrating Thanksgiving with my new family."

Jonathan noticed that Michael said similar things.

On Black Friday, Jonathan accompanied Walter on a shopping trip.

"I'm not crazy about buying presents for the extended family, especially if I don't know them well," Walter confessed as they pushed their way through a crowded shopping mall. "But, that's part of being a family man."

On Saturday, Walter invited his brother to join the band. Jonathan never had the opportunity to learn a musical instrument, but once in a while, he liked listening to live music. Jonathan joined his brother, Michael, and the other band members in the shed behind the house. He enjoyed their performance, especially Michael's guitar solos.

Something about the serious young man intrigued him. Jonathan looked at Michael's face and thought that it displayed inner wisdom. For some reason, Michael looked familiar, although Jonathan was certain they'd never met before.

CHAPTER 40

Sarah

Sarah celebrated Thanksgiving with the small community of friends living on her property. Julie called, as she did every year, to invite her sister and Jonathan to join them for the holiday, and was surprised when Sarah explained she intended to spend the holiday at home with her neighbors.

"Why don't you, Edmond, and the kids join us?" Sarah invited.

Julie noticed the joy in her voice, but couldn't change her plans because she had already invited guests from her husband's family.

"Is Jonathan all right with celebrating at your place with the new people?" Julie inquired, remembering Jonathan as a somewhat withdrawn person.

"He's not going to be with us," Sarah answered. "He's visiting his brother in New York."

***

An autumn sun warmed the land as Sarah and her tenants set a long table outside the house, next to Sarah's vegetable garden. Residents of the trailers, mostly the women, had invested time and effort in preparing many dishes, mainly vegetarian, and they baked desserts. The atmosphere was festive, and Sarah felt grateful for the friendship and brotherhood that she sensed among the participants. Even the children behaved.

After a sumptuous potluck dinner, they proceeded to give thanks for the good things that had happened during the past year. Like her husband, Sarah usually detested the practice imposed on her. That year, however, she had no difficulty counting her blessings: "I'm thankful for having new friends living here with us." She took a pause and added, with a small nod toward Heidi, "And I'm grateful for being alive."

Sarah wished Jonathan were present; she thought that he would have liked the friendly gathering. But she knew he'd made the right decision when he'd chosen to spend the holiday with his brother and his family.

That night, Sarah lay awake in her bed and looked at the moon as it reflected through the window. Her thoughts took her to the Golden Gate Bridge. Now she couldn't understand the despair that had taken hold of her and grabbed her so tightly that just a tiny step had separated her life from death. *If Heidi didn't call me, I wouldn't be here*, she thought.

"How long are you here for?" she yelled over the noise.

"Just for a few days!" he yelled back. "For Thanksgiving and to meet the family!"

"Cool!" she shouted and sang along with the radio while driving at high speed.

"Could you turn down the music?" he yelled.

She immediately complied, turning down the music until it was barely audible.

He breathed with relief.

"Sorry," she said. "It's really great music; I thought you'd like it."

"Perhaps if I were younger," he said tactfully. "Do you go to school?"

"I finished high school, and next year I'll go to a university. What do you do?"

"Right now, I'm unemployed," he admitted. "I was laid off from my work as a computer technician."

"That's not so bad," the young lady sympathized. "You're for sure gonna find something more interesting."

Sitting next to her, he felt old and cumbersome, assuming that was how she saw him. He realized that he hardly associated with people her age, which contributed to his lack of awareness of his advancing age.

The green lawns and spacious parks of Scarsdale improved his mood. Walter welcomed his brother with a hug and a pat on

Suddenly she remembered something—a scene that had flickered for a split-second while she was on the bridge. During those last few seconds on the ledge, her whole life flashed through her mind, and in those seconds, she had seen … She gasped. She *knew* what happened in St. Louis when she was sixteen. She recognized who drove the car.

Once again, she made an effort to remember. She squeezed her eyes shut, trying to bring back the memory. Sarah needed to know who the villain that had taken advantage of her was. Moreover, she thought that she *must* know what had happened on that distant day, so she could liberate herself from the scars that the harsh experience etched in her.

But the window that had opened on the bridge was once again closed, and Sarah couldn't find the latch to open it again.

***

The following day Sarah had no intention of partaking in the madness of Black Friday, she didn't understand the madness that took hold of people and made them push their way into the stores for a sale that would save them just a few dollars. She relaxed on the front porch instead.

She slowly drank a cup of coffee while contemplating the two points in time: the event that took place in St. Louis, many years ago, and the occurrence on the bridge.

Perhaps *The Broadcast* could help her find the elusive clue?

Sarah pondered last week's unsettling episode which focused on the Middle Ages. TXB aired footage documenting the Inquisition instituted by the Catholic Church, including prisoners marching in a ceremonial procession to receive their verdict. But what does that has to do with her life?

An idea popped into her mind, and she knew what she should do. She knew where she would find the answer to what had been tormenting her for so long. She didn't understand how come she hadn't thought of it before, because the solution was right in front of her. Or maybe she unwittingly waited for a time when her husband was away.

She packed a sandwich, some fruit and a bottle of water and then headed for Jonathan's site.

Jonathan's site? It was also hers. They discovered it together, and it was on their shared property. She remembered Jonathan had once theorized that the place had served as an ancient relay station. He mentioned that, at the site, he could observe any event from his life with outstanding clarity. Sarah recalled that Irene, too, had experienced a powerful memory when she visited there.

The three dogs followed as she trekked through the forest, crossed the creek, and continued in the direction that she remembered. A few years had passed since they discovered the site, and during that time, she had gone through so many upheavals. Her memory unerringly led her to the strange hill, conspicuous by its uncommon density of trees. At the bottom of the hill, the dogs stopped and refused to accompany her further. Bono looked at her with his smart-looking eyes that told her, "we will wait for you here, we are not going anywhere." Sarah loved all her dogs, but she felt a special connection to Bono, who was smarter and more attuned to her than the other dogs. Sarah remembered that she had that kind of bond with Bono's mother, Princess.

She climbed up the hill, and once again she wondered at the unusual concentration of trees. Oaks, sequoias, and bushes grew in close proximity to one another, as if trying to protect and prevent entrance to the site from anyone who was not meant to be there. There were points on the way where the trees completely blocked the passage. She shifted branches out of her way, squeezed through in some places, and walked around the denser spots. Entering the glade on top of the hill, she felt immersed in a feeling of reverence.

Sarah looked around, astonished at the extent of Jonathan's excavations. She realized that he must have invested countless hours of hard labor. The place now looked like an archeological site.

Two circles of large rocks, chiseled flat on the side facing the center of the circle, surrounded a large center stone. The square rock at the center resembled a table or altar.

Now what? She walked around the site, examining it. As the sun reached its high noon apex, stillness and quiet blanketed the hilltop, broken only by the light rustle of wind passing through the treetops.

She sat on the low, flat rock, at the center of the circle, which looked like an ancient altar. She closed her eyes and waited.

Nothing happened. Employing the techniques she'd learned from the yogi, Sarah concentrated on her breathing, attentive to her surroundings, to transition into a meditative state. The earth shook slightly and made a terrifying low rumbling sound. She remained still and kept her eyes closed. She focused on the question that bothered her, on the gap in her memory, desperately needing to know what had happened on that distant day when she was sixteen, young and innocent—the event that flickered in her consciousness on the bridge. She sat with an erect spine and waited.

Time passed. She started to wonder if the site would provide the long-awaited answer. Maybe it was only an ordinary glade where a primitive tribe had hauled big rocks out of a belief in supernatural phenomena? She continued to sit and wait, determined not to give up.

The stillness of the place intensified.

After a long while, she heard a flap of wings behind her but didn't turn her head and didn't open her eyes to watch the birds. The rustle of the wings continued, increased, and drew near. For a moment, she felt the gentle wind created by the bird's wings, fluttering so close, it almost brushed the back of her neck.

Finally, she answered the call, turned her head, and opened her eyes. She saw a car driving behind her at a slow speed. She identified the driver right away, and his appearance sent shivers throughout her body. He was dressed in a long black robe. She knew him and was even fond of him. Although not particularly religious, she liked listening to the pastor when she visited the local church with her family. He had an authoritative and pleasant voice which emanated compassion and caring toward his listeners as he enticed them to follow in God's way. She liked watching him. She even confided in her friend Megan that Reverend Buckner was really handsome and he reminded her of a Greek god.

"So what, you'd sleep with him?" Megan giggled.

"No way!" Sarah was appalled. "You're really disturbed, you know that? He's a married man and as old as my father."

"Just checkin'," Megan smiled.

"I would never do it with him or anyone that old," Sarah asserted.

He rolled down his window and called to her.

"Reverend Buckner?" She was curious. "What are you doing in our neighborhood?"

"Hi Sarah," he said in his pleasant voice. "Would it be possible for you to help me on a project that keeps me busy?"

"Now?" She was surprised.

"Just for a little while," he said. "I'm coloring eggs for the Easter egg hunt tomorrow, and it's taking me longer than I thought. It would be wonderful if you could come and give me a hand. I know that you're good at this kind of work, while I ... Well, the good Lord did not bestow me with artistic talent."

"Okay," she agreed with a shrug, "but I have to be home

before 11:00. My parents will get mad if I'm late."

"No problem," the pastor agreed. "You paint as much as you can, and I'll make sure that you are home on time."

She got into his car, and they drove to the church, a few blocks away.

Indeed, on a wide table in a back room where she had never been before, there were eggs, paints of many colors, and small paintbrushes. A stereo system played religious music. Both of them proceeded to the task at hand, leisurely painting the eggs, and Sarah allowed her creative imagination to guide her. She enjoyed the simple activity that reminded her of coloring eggs as a young child.

"Sarah, sweetie, would you like a glass of wine?" Pastor Buckner asked.

"Sure," she replied.

He stepped over to a nearby cabinet, opened a door, and pulled out a bottle of wine and two wine glasses. He poured the wine and handed her a glass.

"Cheers," he said, and they raised a toast together. She took a sip from the wine and started to wonder if it was a proper situation that she and the minister, who was a grown-up, married man, were by themselves at such a late hour.

***

After that, Sarah saw nothing, as if the rest of that memory spool had been completely erased from her consciousness. She tried to restart the vision, but nothing showed up, like a movie that had reached its end. Sarah understood that she'd received the vital information she had to have, and she didn't need to see more.

When she opened her eyes, the trees hid the setting sun. The site was very silent, the large rocks stood still, and the evening chill seeped through her clothes.

Now she knew who the villain was, the man who'd taken advantage of her naiveté, the wicked and despicable person who'd abused her, the father of her son.

CHAPTER 41

The Broadcast

A humble man, Walter Lindsey didn't let success go to his head. When he was young, he wanted to become a film director, and he studied filmmaking at UCLA in Los Angeles. During his studies, he realized that he would never be a great film director. He then quit filmmaking and transferred to the University of Pennsylvania, where he studied business management and accounting. That's where he met a fellow student named Monica, who in time became his wife.

After finishing his studies, he wanted to integrate the profession he'd acquired with his old love for the cinema. He looked for work as a producer and managed to land several small projects in which he exhibited significant talent in managing and logistics. He knew how to get results from his people without ruffling their feathers.

Lindsey advanced through the corporate ranks slowly and patiently, and eventually received a permanent position as a producer at the TXB network. Without a doubt, though, his most noteworthy project which brought him a national reputation and enriched his bank account was *The Broadcast*.

With all of his accomplishments, he remained humble and even shy, and did his best to avoid the limelight.

Lindsey was a good-looking man, although not as handsome as his younger brother. At the age of forty-seven, his hair was receding, and he had put on some weight. He tried to maintain his health by going to a spa to swim in a heated swimming pool, whenever his busy schedule allowed.

***

The network's CEO, Colin Ingram, liked Walter as a person and as an employee. Ingram defended him when other senior managers demanded that he reveal his sources. However, following mounting pressure on the network, and public opinion demands for increased transparency, Lindsey received an invitation to come to Ingram's office for a personal meeting.

Walter entered the CEO's lavish office and took a seat in front of his boss.

"Look," Ingram said, "you know that I support you, and I understand your journalistic ethics and loyalty to your informers. However, we can no longer ignore public sentiment and hide behind the principle of confidentiality of sources without further justification."

"So, what are you saying?" Lindsey asked. He shifted

uncomfortably. "As you know, I've assured my sources that I wouldn't reveal them, and I'm not going to break my promise."

"I suggest that you call a press conference," the CEO said. "Don't expose your sources, but explain your motives. At least they would see that we are using a policy of transparency and show we're attentive to our viewer's concerns. By doing that, I hope they'll get off our back a little."

"I could do that," Lindsey said without enthusiasm. He stood and prepared to leave.

"One more thing," the CEO somberly said, "I should tell you that I received an unpleasant call from a high-up officer at the NSA." He paused and held Walter's gaze to make sure he understood the importance of such a call. "At this time the NSA views the show as pure fiction; but, at some point, they might step in and demand explanations."

***

Lindsey called a press conference to answer questions about *The Broadcast*. He intentionally scheduled the event to take place at 6:00 p.m., and not during prime viewing time. The press conference attracted mostly entertainment reporters.

"Good evening everyone," Walter Lindsey said, his demeanor anxious. "I would like to talk to you about *The Broadcast* and how the show came into being. I'll do my best to answer your questions."

Lindsey looked over the crowd of journalists and noticed Stewart McPherson, his face expressing skepticism.

"Two-and-a-half years ago," Lindsey said, "I was fortunate to be offered access to an amazing technology with which it is possible to observe events from the past. I immediately saw immense potential in that technology; however, I was skeptical. I suspected it was too fantastic. I had a hard time trusting that the recordings the technology showed were authentic and not some form of fictional reality.

"To test the technology, I challenged its operators. I remembered how I was mesmerized by the Pedro Gonzales trial. I recalled that when the trial took place, I thought to myself that if there were only a video clip that documented the event, then law enforcement would not be groping in the dark; the truth would come to light, and the guilty person would be punished.

"So, I asked for a video that documented the event. To my surprise, I received it in a little over an hour, definitely not enough time to comprehensively research the incident.

"I handed the video clip to be examined by the professionals at TXB, and they consulted experts who were familiar with the case, including police officers who studied every detail of the footage.

"The conclusion was unequivocal: the footage was an authentic, real-time display of the incident. Following that determination, TXB decided to air the recording after accepting the explicit conditions of the source of the information. The requirements were that we wouldn't, under any circumstances, disclose any information regarding the origin of the film and those behind it. We agreed to the terms, and I personally gave my word of honor.

"At that stage, I thought that we had a one-time exclusive, something rare, unique, and sensational—but still, a one-time deal. As we expected, the film generated enormous interest, but we didn't expect what followed next: appeals from police officers from all over the country asking us to assist in unraveling their unsolved cases. That's how *The Broadcast* was born."

Lindsey paused and looked at the crowd of reporters. "I spoke to you briefly about my show," he said, "and I hope I managed to clear up some of the questions that were asked in different media forums. Now I'm prepared to answer your questions."

"Does your source operate out of New York?" asked a young reporter from a local Manhattan paper.

"As I made clear," Lindsey responded, "I cannot say anything about the source of the films."

Stewart McPherson raised his hand. When Lindsey nodded at him, he said, "I understand that you can't tell us anything about the people who are behind the technology, but could you elaborate on the technology itself?"

"I'm sorry," Lindsey answered. "In accordance with my promise, I can't satisfy your curiosity. However, I can refer you to the excellent article that Professor Takeshi Nishimura published in the *New York Times*." Lindsey saw the skeptical expression on McPherson's face and added, "A few weeks ago, *The Broadcast* dedicated time to Christopher Columbus. To sail on his journey, which yielded startling revelations, Columbus had to accept a concept that, according to contemporary belief, was completely irrational and unacceptable: the idea that the earth is round and not flat. In my opinion, the technology by which the films are received is based on a breakthrough knowledge of great magnitude, nothing less revolutionary than the idea that made it possible for Columbus to go on his expeditions." Lindsey shyly smiled at McPherson.

"I noticed," said a reporter for *New Explorations*, "that your history pieces focus on the Western world as if the rest of the world didn't exist in previous centuries. What about significant events that took place in the Far East, South America, and Africa?"

"You bring up a good point," Walter Lindsey responded. "I hope that in upcoming programs we'll be able to show events from other parts the globe."

"How far back in time will the show go?" asked Jennie Scott of *Entertainment News*, "and will we get to see the dinosaurs?"

"At this stage," Lindsey answered, "we have no intention of going so far back. Due to technological limitations that I won't get into, the current season of *The Broadcast* will go back in time until the year 1 AD."

"Does that mean that we'll get to see Jesus and the crucifixion?" asked Carlos Martinez, a reporter for the *Chicago Tribune*.

"I don't know," Lindsey honestly answered.

"Will we get to see the holy temple in Jerusalem?" Patricia Bernstein, a reporter for the *Los Angeles Times,* asked.

"If there was a temple, then it's likely that we'll see it," Walter Lindsey replied.

***

"Interesting," Sarah commented as she and Jonathan watched the press conference.

"What? Walter's answers?"

"I mean that they're going back in time toward the first century and the temple. Do you remember our trip to Israel?"

"How can I forget?" he replied. "I especially remember the panic attack that I had by the Dead Sea."

"We also visited Jerusalem, and we've seen the holy sites," she said. "It seems to me like ages ago."

"More than fifteen years," Jonathan said. "Those sites were the focus of ferocious wars and bloodshed, and the struggle for control over the so-called Holy Land never ended."

***

The trip to Israel was Sarah and Jonathan's third trip outside the US.

Although Sarah had severed her connection with

Christianity, she remained fascinated by the image of Jesus. She wanted to visit the places where he walked, taught, healed, and died. She detested the preachers and other religious messengers but continued to believe that Jesus, the man, had pure intentions, that he was righteous and compassionate.

Jonathan's attraction to Israel arose from *Chariots of the Gods*, in which author Erich von Däniken used quotes from the Bible to indicate the presence of aliens from outer space in the ancient world. For instance, in the book of Genesis:

"The Nephilim were on the earth in those days, and also afterward, when the sons of God came in to the daughters of man and they bore children to them." (Genesis 6:4, English Standard Version).

Von Däniken also quoted the book of Ezekiel and claimed that the description matched that of a spacecraft:

"I looked and behold, a whirlwind came out of the north – an immense cloud with flashing lightning and surrounded by brilliant light. The center of the fire looked like glowing metal, and in the fire was what looked like four living creatures. And this was their appearance; they had the likeness of man." (Ezekiel 1:4)

Jonathan diligently prepared for the journey, reading about the history of the land of Israel.

The couple flew to Israel in economy class. From the airport near Tel Aviv, they took a bus to Jerusalem, where they checked in to a modestly priced hotel. They stayed five days in the famous metropolis, touring the many sites and absorbing the shades and fragrances of the unique, ancient city. They walked in the Via Dolorosa from the Muslim Quarter to the Church of the Holy Sepulchre. Jonathan mentioned that the actual path of the Via Dolorosa was unknown. They visited the Church of the Holy Sepulchre, where, according to Christian belief, Jesus was crucified.

Sarah kneeled in front of the statue of the crucified Jesus. She closed her eyes, prayed, and tried to sense the sanctity of the place. But her thoughts took her to another being whom she imagined as having blue eyes and curly black hair: her son Daniel, who accompanied her in spirit wherever she went.

They visited the Wailing Wall, where Sarah could not explain why she was overcome by emotions. Her hands trembled when she inserted a note in the cracks between the big rocks, pleading with God to embrace a child of her own.

They joined a tour of the Temple Mount. Impressed by the Dome of the Rock, Sarah asked Jonathan to take a picture of her standing in front of the magnificent mosque.

Jonathan reached for his camera and said, "This is the place where the Jewish temple used to stand."

When Sarah was in high school, she hadn't excelled in history. It wasn't that the subjects didn't interest her; on the contrary, history had always fascinated her, and she used to imagine herself living in different eras. The reasons her grades languished were because the school system and the continuous repetition over the same materials bored her. So, she'd mostly scribbled in her notebook during the lessons, paying little attention to the content that the teacher tried to convey.

"So, if this is where the Jewish temple used to be, how come there are mosques here today?" she asked Jonathan.

"The Jewish temple was destroyed by the Romans years before the Muslims showed up," he answered.

"Didn't the Jews object to the Muslims building a mosque on the ruins of their temple?" Sarah continued to probe into history's complicated turns of events.

"The Romans killed a large portion of the Jewish population and expelled many of the survivors to be slaves in exile. The few who remained were no match for the large Muslim army." Jonathan enjoyed the opportunity to show off his knowledge. "Haven't you ever seen *Ben Hur*?"

"So, why didn't the Jews rebuild their temple after the Romans left and before the Muslims arrived?" Sarah continued to wonder.

"I don't know," Jonathan admitted with a shrug. "Maybe because the Byzantine Christians prevented them or maybe because they believed they should wait for the Messiah."

"It's a pity that humanity didn't have cameras back then," Sarah said. "That way we'd be able to look at the past directly."

His wife's unexpected wish surprised Jonathan. "Historians and archeologists did most of the work for us. To a large extent, they recreated history."

***

After a few days in Jerusalem, Jonathan convinced his wife to visit the Dead Sea. He said that the salty sea was reputed to have distinctive curative qualities.

Sarah was glad to leave Jerusalem. After a few busy days of visiting ancient archeological sites, she began to sense the charged emotions of people of different religions, and the hostility between them.

They made a reservation for two nights at a hotel in Ein Bokek and hopped on a bus.

On the way, Jonathan told Sarah that according to Erich von Däniken, the event in which God destroyed Sodom and Gomorrah with brimstone and fire was actually an atom bomb that was dropped by aliens from outer space.

"And why would they do such a thing?" Sarah scoffed with disbelief.

"I don't agree with all of von Däniken's claims," Jonathan said. "But I'm still curious to see the place. I read that it is the lowest place on earth."

"And I'm looking forward to a relaxing vacation over there," Sarah smiled. "Maybe I can get a massage."

They checked in to the hotel which was located not far from the waterfront. On the following day, they went down to the sea, dressed in bathing suits and carrying towels on their shoulders. At the end of the winter, they enjoyed warm and pleasant weather.

They dipped in the sea and floated on the salty water, enjoying the unique experience. Stepping out of the calm water feeling invigorated, they washed off the salt in nearby outdoor showers. Then they lay in reclining plastic chairs under large beach umbrellas. Sarah rubbed her body with the unique mud, advertised to contain medicinal qualities.

Reclining next to his wife, Jonathan was absorbed by the serenity of the place. He sipped at a bottle of chilled grapefruit juice, grateful for the absence of loudspeakers and loud music.

Sarah pulled out a book to read, a psychological thriller. The sun sparkled at them, sending its caressing light from the sky, the water, and glinting off the salt that accumulated on the shores.

Jonathan took a deep breath, but for some reason, he had a hard time filling his lungs with air. *Could the location of the sea, at the lowest place on earth affect the quality of the air?* He made another effort, struggling to fill his lungs with air but his breathing remained shallow and uncomfortable. Worried, he watched the tourists. Some of them floated on the salty water, while others covered themselves with the unique mud, which is believed to remove toxins from the body and give the skin a renewed, vivid look. Gazing upward, Jonathan saw no clouds in the blue sky, while next to him, Sarah turned a page in her book. Everything appeared peaceful, and nobody was in a hurry to go anywhere.

Once again he tried to take a deep breath but felt like his lungs were not getting filled all the way.

"Is the air here all right?" He hesitantly turned to his wife who was absorbed in her book.

"The air?" she wondered at the unusual question. "It's fine," she casually said without taking her eyes off the page.

Her voice sounded bizarre and muted as if breaking through an invisible wall. His body tensed as he frightfully looked around. Supposedly nothing has changed and yet, he sensed an eerie ambiance that penetrated the site. Were people examining him through the corners of their eyes? Did they have hostile intentions? Did they know something bad about him?

One more time he tried to fill his lungs with air, but his breathing remained shallow. Terrified, he jumped off his chair.

"What happened?" Sarah lifted her head from the book.

"You don't feel it!?" he shouted at her. A few nearby people turned their heads in curiosity.

"Jonathan, what don't I feel?" Sarah laid down her book.

Panic gripped him. A dull pain blossomed in his chest, and a cold sweat covered his body. Now he knew for certain: something terrible was going to happen. He stared into the distance, trying to assess where the catastrophe would come from. *Maybe an enormous water wave will wash us away, here, at the lowest point on earth? Perhaps brimstone and fire would rain from the sky, as it had already happened in this area when Sodom and Gomorrah were demolished.* Addled by fear, he wondered why the place was called "The Dead Sea" if it weren't the place where they would meet their doom.

He suddenly got the message; he must warn them so they

would save their lives.

"Run! Run away!" he screamed, careening through the startled people who were leisurely lying in their recliners. "Run! Save yourselves!"

"Jonathan, that's enough!" Sarah rushed after him, still covered with mud, and wrapped a towel around his shaking body. At her touch, he stilled. "Stop screaming," she softly said. "Nothing is happening, and you are worrying people for no reason."

She gently embraced him. "Let's go back to the hotel," she said. "You just had a panic attack. Try to take deep breaths."

He let her take him without resistance. His breath soon returned to normal as he calmed down, though his body still tingled.

"I embarrassed myself," he said in a subdued voice.

"It wasn't so bad," she said lightly. "They probably think that the American tourist smoked something."

"I don't know what got hold of me." He felt the need to explain himself. "Everything was so peaceful, and suddenly, out of the silence, I couldn't breath and I felt a horrible panic as if something fatal were about to happen."

"Let's get something to eat," Sarah suggested. "I'm sure that after you eat, you will feel much better."

It was the couple's last trip outside the US.

CHAPTER 42

Michael

Curiosity about *The Broadcast* occupied Michael's thoughts even after he quit Stewart McPherson's mission.

Like many in the American public who wondered about the source of the films, Michael continued to ponder the question. More than once he had considered approaching Walter and asking him about the source of the footage; but, he felt that it would be a breach of the trust between them. He hoped that Walter would share with him what he hid from the whole world, but the subject never came up in their conversations. Maybe his band members knew? Perhaps he could extract the information out of them, if only to satisfy his curiosity?

Julian was the rhythm guitar player and lead singer of the band. He was always accurate in singing the right pitch, and although his voice was somewhat raspy, Michael thought that he had the right qualities for a rock singer. Julian worked at TXB and was known as a talented film director.

One day, Michael went to lunch late. The cafeteria was almost empty, and the employees were busy cleaning and organizing the place. After paying for his meal at the cash register, Michael noticed Julian, sitting at a table by himself. Michael decided to take advantage of the opportunity.

"May I sit with you?" Michael politely asked Julian.

"Always," Julian answered and raised his eyes from the paper he was examining, with a wide, welcoming smile on his face. He looked like he was about fifty years old, a tall man, with faded light brown hair, and several deep wrinkles that added character to his face.

"May I ask you about something?" Michael decided to approach him directly and not beat around the bush.

"Always," Julian repeated.

"Do you know what's the source of the videos of *The Broadcast*?"

Julian contemplated the question for a few seconds. "Yes," he said unequivocally and looked directly at Michael.

Michael hoped that he would volunteer more details, but Julian simply held his silence and waited.

"Could you be more specific?" Michael asked.

"No." Julian held Michael's gaze with somber honesty. "My friend, you're asking the wrong person. If you feel that you *must* know the answer, then you should turn to Walter."

"I don't want to take advantage …" Michael said, conscious that Walter was not only a friend and a band member, but also

Melanie's father.

"I understand," Julian said, "but I can't help you." He collected his dishes in preparation to leave the cafeteria.

"Could you just tell me if the films are authentic?" Michael tried a different angle.

"Define what you mean by authentic," Julian stood and looked at Michael. He seemed amused.

"Do they show the events as they took place in real time?"

"Definitely!" Julian put on his jacket.

"Are you involved in the production?" Michael questioned.

"Who said there was a production?" Julian solemnly gazed at him, and then went on his way.

CHAPTER 43

The Broadcast

Walter Lindsey's press conference went over well. When asked, most reporters and viewers expressed favorable opinions regarding the producer's honesty and transparency. They didn't receive answers to all their questions; still, most believed in Lindsey's obligation to remain faithful to his promise and protect the confidentiality of his sources.

The Broadcast continued its journey back in time while the controversy contributed to its popularity. Reporters and cultural reviewers were amazed by the phenomenon. They never expected that a TV program about historical events would attract so many viewers.

***

"Good evening." Susan Riley smiled at her viewers at home and presented her guest, Professor Charles Boyd of Oxford University in England.

"Good evening, Professor," she turned to her guest. "Thank you for coming all the way from England to be with us here this evening."

"Good evening, Susan," the professor said. "It's an honor for me to be here. I must say, though, that I'm here despite some of my esteemed colleagues who warned me that your recordings might be a fabrication."

An experienced TV host, Susan Riley chose to ignore her guest's comment. "Today," she said, "we continue our exploration of history with films from the First Crusade, which took place in the eleventh century."

Professor Boyd cleared his throat and said, "The crusade followed the call by Pope Urban II to liberate Jerusalem from the Muslims. The Crusader army started at around twelve thousand men and shrank during the long journey from Europe to Jerusalem." The professor paused and took a sip of water. "Following a vision by a priest, the Crusaders tried to take the city as in the biblical story of Joshua and the siege of Jericho. They fasted for three days and then marched in a procession around the city walls while praying and blowing horns. The walls didn't fall."

The professor showed the Crusaders' procession around the city walls. Priests carrying crosses marched in the lead; they were followed by knights on horses, and infantry, all blowing different wind instruments. The angle of filming made it impossible for viewers to discern details of the musical instruments.

"After that failed," Professor Boyd continued, "the

Crusaders tried to take the city by more practical means. Five weeks after the beginning of the siege, they managed to break into the city, on the fifteenth of July in the year 1099."

Another clip rolled, and the professor accompanied it with explanations. Viewers watched one of the two huge siege towers that the crusaders built. From that tower, the Crusaders extended a bridge to the fortified city's wall. Over that bridge, a group of soldiers penetrated the city. The invaders then opened one of the gates, through which a large Crusader force entered and captured Jerusalem.

The professor somberly said, "The Crusaders massacred the city's residents, Muslims and Jews alike. They killed soldiers and showed no mercy for civilians, including women, children, and the elderly. Following their success, the crusaders founded 'The Kingdom of Jerusalem' and ruled the land of Israel for about a hundred years, after which the country fell again into Muslims' hands, led by Salah ad-Din."

***

The phone rang in Walter Lindsey's office. On the line was the network's CEO, Colin Ingram, who summoned him to come to his office. Lindsey, who was busy corresponding with one of the advertisers, finished the line he was writing before heading to meet the CEO. He hoped the reason for the unscheduled meeting was a routine issue and not an unforeseen threat to the continuation of the show.

"You may enter; they are waiting for you." Amanda, the CEO's secretary, smiled at him.

With a murmured word of thanks, he opened the door and walked into the plush corner office where the CEO sat with another gentleman wearing ecclesiastical garb.

"Walter, thank you for coming on such short notice," Ingram warmly welcomed him. "I would like you to meet Father Thomas Shelton, who has graced us with his visit."

The bald, elderly priest got up from his chair and shook Walter's hand. He wore a long necklace that held a large cross over his black robe. Through thick glasses, he examined Walter with a piercing look.

Lindsey took a chair as the others reseated themselves. "To what do I owe the honor?" Lindsey asked.

"I understand that you're the producer of a show called *The Broadcast*," said Father Shelton.

"That's true," Lindsey said.

"As I told Mr. Ingram," the priest continued, "we understand that you're broadcasting historical TV programs that go back in time."

"True," Walter responded.

"I also understand that you are in possession of remarkable technology that allows you to air video recordings of previous eras, earlier than when humanity had cameras."

"Yes." Lindsey shot a questioning look at the CEO.

"The Archbishop of New York sent me here," Father Shelton calmly continued. "We are concerned about your plans for the upcoming shows."

"What do you mean?" the CEO asked.

"If I understand correctly," the priest said, "and excuse me for not watching the show; I don't watch television at all, and I prefer to dedicate my time to prayer. Anyway, it has come to our attention that you intend to continue the series back to the first century AD."

"That's the plan," Lindsey confirmed.

"Do you intend to broadcast films from the life and death of Jesus Christ?" Father Shelton asked, turning his investigative eyes directly at Lindsey.

"I don't know," Lindsey replied. "I don't dictate the content of the films. I just ask for footage of specific events and give the operators of the technology the approximate time and place of those events."

"Interesting," Father Shelton murmured and seemed like he was contemplating Lindsey's words. "Anyway, we prefer that events that are written in the Holy Bible remain within the theological realm, and in accordance with the teachings of the holy Church."

"The truth is, sir," Lindsey responded, "that it's unlikely that we'll see events from the life or death of Jesus. Even if that was our intention, we don't have specific dates of his actions and crucifixion. As you know, crucifixion was a common practice at that time and a way by which the Romans executed many of their prisoners." For a brief moment, Lindsey had a strange sensation, as if he was standing in front of a Spanish Inquisitor.

"The problem is," the priest said with a polite smile, "that even if you broadcast videos of that time without showing Jesus, it could still hurt the important message by which Jesus gave his life for us. Because what is that period without Jesus of Nazareth?"

"So, are you asking that we cancel the program?" the CEO interjected.

"That's not what I'm saying." Father Shelton patiently shook his head. "The archbishop is only asking that you don't broadcast films showing the land of Israel in the first century."

The CEO wrote a short memo in his notebook and seemed to contemplate whether to speak up. "I want to be clear on something," he finally said. "I am a devout Christian, I go to church regularly, and I hold a strong belief in our Lord and Jesus Christ. I don't see how a TV show that may or may not show our savior could be a threat to the Church."

Father Shelton looked directly at the CEO. "I appreciate your sincerity and faith. But there are several considerations that you might not be aware of, which I'm not at liberty to discuss at this time."

The CEO glanced at the clock. "We'll consider your request." He rose from his chair to accompany his guest to the door. "Thank you for visiting us. It's been an honor."

Lindsey got up to leave, but Ingram signaled him to stay.

"What do you think?" the CEO asked Walter after the priest left.

"Strange," Lindsey answered. "I would think that people of strong faith would not be intimidated by a TV program that shows past occurrences. On the contrary, why wouldn't they welcome the chance to see the most significant events of their religion with their own eyes?"

"And still," Ingram solemnly said, "we must be attentive to their worries. The last thing we need is a large group of rich, powerful, and influential people who feel that we pose a threat to their faith. Although our visitor was a Catholic, I'm mainly concerned about the Evangelical Protestants of the Bible belt."

***

"Good evening," Susan Riley opened a new program. "We continue our journey back in time and turn our attention to the religion of Islam which originated in Medina and Mecca in the early part of the seventh century. With us in the studio is Professor Kadir Sankar from the University of Istanbul, who was already on our show not long ago. Good evening, Professor, and thank you for agreeing to be with us again."

"Good evening, Mrs. Riley." The Turkish professor politely nodded.

"Professor," the host said, "in Western countries, Islam is often portrayed as a religion of violence and oppression. Would you say that's a misunderstanding?"

"I would," Professor Sankar responded. "I am honored to be a Muslim. Islam is essentially a faith of peace and love for our creator, which requires that believers pray to Allah to guide them on the path of righteousness."

"So, let's start from the beginning," the host said. "Who was the Prophet Muhamad?"

"Muhamad, according to our belief, is the last prophet and the most important of them," the professor said. "We don't know exactly when he was born, but historians estimate that it was around the year 570 AD, in the city of Mecca in what is now Saudi Arabia. Tradition tells us that, when Muhamad was forty years old, he went to a secluded cave where the angel Gabriel was revealed to him, handed him verses of God, and instructed him to read them. Following the revelation, Muhamad started to preach to the people of Mecca, and Angel Gabriel continued to reveal messages to him. A group of believers gathered around him, and they documented his words. Later, those words were assembled into the Quran, which is Islam's holy book. We believe that the Quran comprises the words of Allah, not the ideas of people."

"Professor," the host said, "what are we going to see?"

"We will watch the Battle of Yarmouk," answered Professor Sankar, "in which the Muslim forces defeated the army of the Christian Byzantine Empire. The Battle of Yarmouk, which spanned over six days, is considered one of the most important battles in history.

The video clip started, accompanied by the professor's explanations. The two armies lined up for battle along eight miles on both sides of the Yarmouk River's steep banks, which served as a natural defensive barrier. In footage showing the second day of the fighting, Byzantine forces attacked the Muslim army's flanks with heavily armored cavalry as lightly armored cavalry followed with bows and arrows.

In a film documenting the last day of warfare, the Muslim forces were seen breaking through Byzantine lines and winning the battle. Defeated in the clashes, the Byzantine soldiers found themselves surrounded and unable to withdraw. Some tried to escape, while others tried to surrender. The Muslim forces took no prisoners. They killed those who surrendered, and chased, hunted, and slew those who fled.

"Following the overwhelming Byzantine defeat," the professor concluded, seeming pleased, "the Muslim army conquered Syria and turned its main effort to the Holy Land. In the year 637, Jerusalem was conquered after a prolonged siege."

***

Walter Lindsey sat in front of the computer screen and went over emails addressed to the editors of *The Broadcast* and which could not be answered by corporate secretarial staff. He read a letter from a retired high school history teacher. She praised the show that allowed her to observe events she never thought she would get to see, and from such an unusual angle. Along with that, she expressed the now-familiar discontent regarding the order of the programs. "It would be better," she wrote, "if you would advance according to the logical progression of time, from the year 1 CE to our time, and not the other way around."

The phone rang. "Walter," his secretary said, "someone wishes to talk to you on behalf of the Islamic community. He's already called several times."

"Ok," Lindsey said, glancing at the clock. "Put him through."

"Hello," said the man with a slight Arabian accent. "Do I have the honor of talking with Walter Lindsey?"

"Yes," Lindsey answered. "To whom am I speaking?"

"Let me introduce myself: my name is Hasan Antar, and I work in the Islamic cultural center of New York."

"What may I do for you, Mr. Antar?" Lindsey asked.

"With your permission, I would like for us to meet in order to express the concerns of our community regarding *The Broadcast*."

"I am swamped," Lindsey said in an initial impulse to deny the request. Then he paused and reconsidered. "If it is very important, I can meet with you in my office, tomorrow at eleven thirty."

"Thank you, Mr. Lindsey. We shall meet tomorrow."

On the following day, Hasan Antar arrived at Walter's office exactly at the appointed time. He presented a polished appearance wearing an elegant three-piece suit and his black hair meticulously slicked back from his forehead.

"What is this about?" Lindsey asked without preamble. After his meeting with the Catholic priest, he hoped that this was not another plea from a religious faction, worried about possible controversy springing from portrayals of historic events.

"First of all," Antar said, "let me tell you that I've been watching your show from the beginning, and it is one of my favorite shows."

"Thank you," Lindsey answered, and peeked at the computer screen.

"Correct me if I'm wrong," Antar said, "but I understand that your history series would continue back in time until the first century AD."

"That's the plan," Lindsey confirmed.

"As a representative of the imam of New York, we want to know if you intend to show the Jewish temple in Jerusalem."

"At this stage, I don't know," Lindsey echoed his earlier reply to Father Shelton. "I haven't received the footage for that period."

"We respectfully request that you don't air footage that shows the temple."

"Interesting," Lindsey murmured. "The Archdiocese of New York made a similar request."

"So, you have double the reason." Antar seemed pleased with the unexpected support.

CHAPTER 44

Howard Hensley

The seasoned private investigator, Howard Hensley, followed the development of *The Broadcast* ever since Stewart McPherson visited his office and requested information about Walter Lindsey.

Watching the producer's press conference, Hensley sneered at the screen, not believing the producer's words for one moment. Like McPherson, Hensley thought that the show was an elaborate scheme that Lindsey and his friends concocted with the sole aim of achieving high ratings and making money.

Howard Hensley was not a nice person. Moreover, he didn't believe in niceness. His opinion was that all the people in the world were conducting utilitarian wars with the goal of attaining assets, whether material, emotional or intellectual. Niceness, as far as Hensley was concerned, was only one tool on the road to acquire those assets. Another tool was money.

Years earlier, before he'd lost his faith and deviated from morality, he had been a promising police officer, married, and a father of two children, a boy and a girl. And then, within one terrible year, he lost his son to an illness, and in a failed police operation, his partner was killed right in front of him. Hensley himself was badly injured in the incident. Although the doctors managed to save his life, a large, ugly scar remained on the left side of his face.

A review board charged that he was to blame for the death of his partner, who'd been his best friend. They accused Hensley of not following protocol and not taking adequate precautionary measures in the operation for which he was in command. They claimed that he'd hurried recklessly and hadn't ensured that he had sufficient support and backup.

In the internal police investigation, he stood alone, and his superiors turned their backs on him.

In that year, he lost his faith in the goodness of the world, in God—who in any case, he didn't really believe in—and mostly in people and their motives. And in a corrupt society in which hypocrisy rules, he chose to leave the police force and turn to the side of crime. At least criminals didn't piously pretend to be good, he told himself.

His wife tried to understand him, even when she knew that he'd become a notorious criminal. She saw that he was hurting and attempted to support him. But after he was caught, she sat at his trial where she was stunned by the actions he was blamed for, and the brutality and cruelty he was accused of. She finally gave up on him and accepted that he had no hope. In the six years that he was in jail, she didn't visit him once. The most she did was send him occasional pictures of their daughter so that he could see her grow up.

The loneliness he experienced in jail toughened him and cemented his perception that he was a lone wolf, alone against the whole world. He despised mainstream people, whom he perceived as merely surviving and doing what society expected of them. *They*, those unidentified people in the crowd, obeyed the law, but were actually hypocrites, just pretending to be good people while inside they were selfish and conniving, looking for an opportunity to manipulate the system.

With all that, he aspired to prove to those faceless individuals, to society, and to himself, that he was better, more talented and capable than them. He strove to show them that they needed him and couldn't make it without him.

His daughter, Janet Hensley, was a significant factor in his life. He vowed to watch over her, protect and support her, no matter what she said or thought about him. Among all his investigations, he always found time to follow her, from afar, to make sure that she was safe. He was present, without anyone seeing him, in the main events of her life, like school plays and end-of-year parties.

Janet Hensley didn't understand why, when she was a second-year student at Long Island University, her boyfriend suddenly disappeared without leaving a trace. He only left a short letter pleading with her not to look for him. She didn't know that her father had investigated and found that the boyfriend was a scumbag with a history of taking advantage of women. Howard Hensley ordered his men to abduct the boyfriend, then Hensley made it clear to the young man, in an unmistakable way, that he had to disappear from Janet's life immediately and commit to never get in touch with her again. That is, if said scumbag wanted to live long enough to see his twenty-fourth birthday, which was in two weeks.

Long before leaving the police force in disgrace, Howard Hensley won the nickname HH, for his initials and for the acronym of the tough image that stuck to him—the Head Hunter.

He carried the HH nickname through his days as a cop, then as a criminal and convict. He still had it when Steward McPherson came to him about Lindsey and *The Broadcast*.

When Hensley delivered the results of his investigation to McPherson, he submitted, amongst other facts, that Walter Lindsey had a distant brother in California. According to Hensley's findings, there had been a long-lasting feud and estrangement between the two brothers. But Hensley knew from his sources, which included informers, sleuthing, and computer hacking, that the two brothers had recently made peace with one another. Hensley followed his instinct and did not share that piece of information with the journalist.

Although HH agreed with McPherson's opinion that the

producer was creating the films along with his three friends, he thought that it wasn't the whole picture. He sensed that the distant brother, Jonathan, was linked to the affair in some way.

Hensley knew quite well that this wasn't his case, and that his job ended when he submitted his findings to McPherson and collected his hefty fee. But his intuition, on which he'd learned to rely, told him he wasn't really done. He suspected this was bigger than his routine investigations, more significant than McPherson realized, and that this was an extraordinary opportunity for him to prove his capabilities. His sharp senses told him that he could profit from the case, either monetarily, by attaining access to crucial information, or in power and influence. He didn't know how the prospect would come about, but he assumed that the opportunity would present itself down the road, and he would know how to take advantage of it.

HH figured that if he wanted to get the complete picture regarding the source of *The Broadcast's* footage, he had to check out Lindsey's brother in California.

So, he used the opportunity of a business trip to California to investigate the mystery. He rented a car In Los Angeles and drove all the way to Corralitos, where he rented a room in a motel. For two days, he drove around Jonathan and Sarah's land stopping where he could surveil the property, either with binoculars or the naked eye. The presence of several trailers on the Lishinsky's land prompted him to examine records at the county's zoning department. The examination confirmed that Jonathan and Sarah Lishinsky owned the property, and he assumed that the residents of the trailers paid rental fees for parking their trailers and for connection to utilities.

On his second day in Corralitos, he parked his car near the property, after making sure that Jonathan and Sarah left for work. He walked to the trailers' area where he saw a young lady outside her trailer, practicing yoga, or some form of exercise that HH wasn't familiar with.

"Hi there!" He tried to sound cheerful. "Sorry for bothering you, but I was passing by, and I'm looking for a cheap rental space for my nephew."

"You'd have to talk to the landlords, Jonathan and Sarah," the young lady answered. She had a freckled face, a small pug nose, and red hair tied in a ponytail.

"What kind of people are they looking for?" HH appeared interested.

"Generally, they prefer people who have some environmental awareness," she answered.

The young lady smiled at him, apparently not put off by the ugly scar running down his face. It disconcerted him. When did anyone smile at him like that? He couldn't remember. For a split second, he felt a dull pain in his heart.

"Thank you very much," he said to her. "You've been very helpful."

"Good luck to your nephew." She smiled again as he walked

Curious, Lindsey said, "If I may ask, why are you concerned about seeing the temple?"

"I'll be frank with you," Antar responded. "Although I personally enjoy *The Broadcast*, I'm also one of the skeptics who doubt its sources. I read the article by Mr. Stewart McPherson. You are probably familiar with his assertions. Regardless, we Muslims do not accept the assumption that the Jewish temple once stood where the Al-Aqsa mosque stands today. Since this mosque is the third most important mosque in Islam, I assess that such a film could instigate unrest."

"Please explain," Lindsey demanded.

"Look, Mr. Lindsey," Antar continued calmly, "I am one of the moderates of our faith; but, unfortunately, there are extremists who might respond with violence."

Lindsey didn't know whether his guest threatened him or simply stated a real possibility. "Do you really think violence will erupt because of a single episode of this program?"

"Unfortunately," Antar confirmed, "such a film could be interpreted as a plot against Islam."

"As I said," Lindsey said as he rose to his feet to signal the conclusion of the meeting, as he truly was busy, "since I haven't seen the materials for that century, it is too soon to address your request. But I thank you for coming to express your concerns."

away, determined not to let her niceness sway him.

This will be the point of infiltration, he told himself, making plans to plant one of his men in the trailer neighborhood. That way he would have eyes on the ground.

When he returned to New York, he summoned one of his men, a young criminal named Willie Fowler who specialized in car theft and burglarizing old people's homes. In exchange for helping to get Fowler an early release from jail, he delivered packages for HH.

"I have a job for you," HH said. "It's important. Screw this up, and you're going back to jail. Understand?"

"What do you need, boss?" Willie Fowler asked.

"For starters, grow your hair out." Hensley reached out and grabbed Fowler by his short mop-top to make sure he understood.

"What's the hair for, boss?" Willie Fowler blinked his shifty eyes.

"You're going to California to be a hippie," Hensley said with a smile that boded ill for the young thief if he screwed up. "In the meantime, there are two books that you gotta read."

Hensley handed Fowler two books about the environment by authors who took strong stances against forest logging and explained the damages caused by it.

"What's your stand on environmental issues?" Hensley asked.

"Environmental issues?" Bewildered, Fowler rubbed his

nose. "I don't care about stuff like that."

"You do now!" HH raised his voice and Fowler listened. "From now on, these issues are dear to your heart: you support renewable energy sources, and you oppose nuclear energy and offshore oil drilling. You stand against forest logging, and you especially care about the rainforests. You're going to learn these issues and know them inside and out. Am I clear?"

"Yes, boss," Willie Fowler answered, willing to do whatever it took to avoid returning to jail.

CHAPTER 45

Sarah

During her years as a clinical psychologist, Sarah helped many patients examine their memories, re-experience and confront them, so that they could free themselves of past mental and emotional trauma.

But despite tireless efforts, she had never succeeded to witness and deal with her own ordeal, that long-ago event that remained shrouded in mystery.

The intense experience at the stone circle unveiled her repressed memory. She saw, encountered, and re-lived her trauma, and it brought up a flood of mixed emotions. Naturally, the vision that came out of oblivion disturbed her, but it also granted her a certain relief and elation which stemmed from finally solving the enigma that haunted her for so many years.

However, it wasn't enough. Sarah still needed closure. She wanted to confront the villain who took advantage of her innocence when she was just sixteen years old. She strongly felt that he shouldn't get away unpunished.

She called Megan, her old friend from high school who still lived in St. Louis and with whom she'd kept in touch over the years. Sarah asked her to search for the whereabouts of Pastor Mathew Buckner, if he were still alive.

"Why are you still interested in him?" Megan was surprised, remembering that years ago Sarah had liked the minister.

"It was him, Megan," Sarah dryly replied.

"Him... Oh!" Megan immediately understood what Sarah meant.

"He's the bastard who drugged and raped me," Sarah confirmed in a choked voice. "Please, find out about him. It is very important to me."

"I'll do my best," Megan promised. "Give me two or three days."

After two days, Megan called. "Sarah," she said, "I got the details you asked for. I went to the church and told them a story about how, thanks to Reverend Buckner, I've found God. I said I wanted to meet him so I could thank him. It turns out he's retired and lives in a quiet neighborhood with his wife. I have the address. I even drove by his house."

"Thank you so much!" Gratitude brought tears to Sarah's eyes.

"Sarah," Megan warned, "are you sure you want to open those old wounds?"

"Those old wounds never healed," Sarah said.

"So, what are you going to do?"

"Fly to St. Louis and confront him."

"You can stay at my place," Megan said, knowing her friend would not be deterred and would probably need emotional support. "I have a spare bedroom since my children have already left the nest."

"Thank you, Megan." Sarah was touched by the gestures of her old friend.

Sarah flew to St. Louis. Megan met her at the terminal and drove them to the modest house where she lived alone. It turned out she had separated from her husband after many years of living together, and her two grown kids had already left the house and gone their own ways. Sarah and Megan spent the evening talking at the kitchen table. They talked about themselves and about some of what they had gone through over the years. Sarah was interested to hear about a few of her classmates who had stayed in St. Louis and whom she hadn't heard from in years. She shared with Megan some of the significant events of her life, and didn't hide the overwhelming impact that the rape incident had on her.

The next day, Megan suggested that Sarah borrow her car, and Sarah gratefully accepted the offer. She drove to the address that Megan gave her. Using the GPS, she had no difficulty finding her destination.

She parked the car along the curb in front of a large house in a quiet, affluent neighborhood. After taking a moment to gather

her courage and her composure, she walked through a gate in a white picket fence that surrounded a manicured green lawn and a well-maintained flower garden.

Her heart pounded as she made her way to the front door and rang the bell. She hadn't planned what to say, thinking her presence would be an obvious statement in itself.

A nice-looking elderly woman opened the door. "Good morning, young lady," the woman cordially welcomed Sarah. "May I help you?"

"I'm looking for Reverend Buckner," Sarah replied, trying to sound businesslike, not belligerent.

"Please wait," the woman said. She turned around and called, "Mathew! There's a young lady here who's looking for you!"

Reverend Mathew Buckner emerged from the depths of the house. Although his hair had gone silver and his face had several wrinkles, he was still a good-looking man who conveyed solemnity. He saw Sarah and hesitated for a moment trying to recognize her. When recognition dawned, he turned pale and his expression wary.

"Well hello, I haven't seen you in so many years." He tried to put on a smile, "How have you been?"

Sarah didn't know if he forgot her name or just avoided pronouncing it. She sensed her palms tingle, and a rush of adrenaline stimulated her blood circulation. She stood still and waited for him to invite her into the house. She had no intention of leaving if he refused to receive her.

Buckner's wife watched her husband and the unfamiliar woman. She felt the tension in the air and didn't know what to do. Should she invite the mysterious woman in? Or perhaps her husband would prefer that she sent her away? She opened her mouth to speak, but he took charge.

"Gladys!" The minister said to his wife after a moment of perplexity. "The lady and I have a matter to discuss in my office."

His wife nodded and stepped aside to let the visitor pass through the door. Buckner led Sarah to his home office, closed the door for privacy, pointed to an armchair, and sat in front of her. Guessing as to the reason for her unexpected, unannounced visit, he assumed an intimidating expression of disapproval.

"What do you want, Sarah?" he said.

"The truth!"

"We both know what happened a long time ago, and there's nothing new." He tried to evade her.

"I didn't come here to reminisce over old memories," she hissed. "What happened was that you took advantage of me and raped me when I was sixteen. You abused your position of authority and betrayed not just me but also God and Jesus and all those things you preached about. You *impregnated* me."

For a moment he appeared stunned, as if he'd never comprehended the scope of his actions.

"The truth is," he said in a subdued voice, "that I'm really sorry about what happened. I know that I caused you pain, and it tortures me. Believe me, it was a moment of weakness in which the devil overcame me."

He looked like he would burst into tears, but Sarah didn't buy his excuse or feel any sympathy for him.

"If you want money, I'm willing to pay," he muttered.

"Don't you want to know if you had a son, or perhaps a daughter?" she asked in a harsh voice.

"Please, just go," he whimpered. "I'll pay for my sins, to you and the Creator."

"Were there other women?"

"No. I swear it was a one-time stumble."

"So, I request that you confess in front of me, your wife, and your kids," she demanded. She despised the man who'd led a comfortable life while she endured humiliation and exile. She didn't believe that his conscience was bothering him.

"Sarah," he pleaded, "my wife and kids are not at fault."

"Your wife and kids deserve to know what kind of monster you are!"

"But that will ruin them, and they haven't done anything wrong," he begged. "You want to turn them into victims of *my* sins?"

"You probably want to keep pretending that nothing happened," She accused. "So, you can continue this comfortable lifestyle."

"I just want to protect my family. I'm at fault here, not them."

"At *fault*? You're a hypocrite, a despicable creature, and I hope you burn in hell!" Sarah shouted; however, she knew he was right in that his family was not responsible for his wrongdoing.

"Alright, I'll take your filthy money," she conceded, knowing that the statute of limitations for rape in Missouri had passed. Regardless of whatever social consequences he'd suffer, he wouldn't go to prison for his crime. "I'll donate the money to women's shelters. You pay me four thousand dollars a month, or I'll destroy your reputation." Her lips peeled back from her teeth in what was obviously not a smile. "After the pedophile priest scandals in the Catholic Church, you know the media will love this story."

"But that's my entire pension," he protested the blackmail.

"Not my problem!" she responded in an unforgiving voice. She stood and made her way to the door.

"Is everything alright?" Mrs. Buckner asked as she exited the office.

"Just fine," Sarah answered and left the house.

***

Sarah told Megan how the meeting went.

"I admire your courage," Megan said.

"It's something I had to do," Sarah said. "I needed closure."

On the following day, Megan drove Sarah to the airport.

"You know, Sarah," Megan said on the way. "I never forgot what you went through. I often pondered the affair, realizing it could have happened to me."

"Or maybe it was written into my destiny," Sarah said.

"I think," Megan continued, "that the adults in your life—parents and schoolteachers—did not treat you fairly. And I feel that I didn't support you enough either, because I was too busy with my own teenage issues."

Sarah sighed and knew her friend sought absolution from sins she hadn't committed. "Teenagers are self-absorbed, and you've more than made up for any mistakes. I'll be forever grateful for your help."

They arrived at the airport. Megan accompanied her friend into the departure terminal, and their eyes were drawn to the newspaper stand. The front page of the *St. Louis Post* displayed a large photo of Minister Buckner above the fold. The headline declared: "Minister's Body Pulled from River." Below in large, bold text was written: "Murder or suicide? Police investigate." A paragraph above the fold quoted the church's current pastor, who stated that Reverend Mathew Buckner "was loved and appreciated by everyone who knew him. For many years, he led his congregation with love, under the spirit of God."

Sarah snorted with disbelief. *Well, so much for the monthly payments to the women's shelter.*

"Take care of yourself, my friend," Megan said and gave

Sarah an affectionate hug.

"You're a wonderful friend," Sarah whispered with tears in her eyes.

CHAPTER 46

The Broadcast

Pressure on *The Broadcast*, which seemed to subside for a few months, intensified again and with greater fervor. In the past, the pressure came from people, like Stewart McPherson, who doubted the credibility of the footage. New protests arose from individuals and groups who believed in the film's authenticity but were worried about their content.

At the front of the new opposition to *The Broadcast* were Evangelical Protestant communities from the southeastern United States.

Public statements by church officials in Texas, Tennessee, Missouri, and North Carolina, warned that *The Broadcast* might show Jesus of Nazareth in a different light than portrayed in the Holy Bible. Celebrity preacher Nicolas Davis from Montgomery, Alabama even called upon his followers to stop watching the show immediately. Similar manifestos were published in Italy, The Netherlands, Australia, and Canada.

***

In a program dedicated to the fifth century, *The Broadcast* hosted Professor Zoltan Bodrogi of the University of Budapest.

"Good evening, Professor," Susan Riley smiled at her guest. "Thank you for coming all the way from Hungary to be with us tonight."

"Good evening to you and our viewers," the Hungarian professor answered politely.

"We are going to talk about the Huns," the host said. "Professor Bodrogi, who were the Huns?"

The professor responded with pleasure, warming to his favorite topic: "They were nomadic people from Central Asia and the Caucasus who founded an empire and invaded Europe. The Romans described them as terrifying savages who ate raw meat, lived on their horses, and even slept on horseback.

"European history remembers their notorious leader, Attila, as the embodiment of evil and cruelty. The Huns turned toward the Eastern Roman Empire. They defeated the Byzantine army, conquered lands, and on their way, they destroyed cities and showed unhindered cruelty toward their enemies. The Romans agreed to pay Attila an annual tax in return for his withdrawal from Byzantine territories and ending the fighting."

"And what happened next?" the host asked.

"Attila turned his attention toward the Western Roman Empire," the guest said.

Onscreen, viewers watched the Battle of the Catalaunian Plains in ancient Gaul.

"It was a massive confrontation," the professor said. "Scholars consider this as one of the most important battles in European history. The Romans had the upper hand, but a year later, the Huns recovered and invaded Italy. On their way, they looted and destroyed the cities they conquered."

"Professor Bodrogi," the host intervened, "Attila the Hun is not remembered for the fall of Rome, so something must have stopped him. What was that?"

"The emperor sent envoys to negotiate with Attila," the professor answered. "One of the envoys was Pope Leo I. Attila, who believed in superstitions and apparently was very impressed by the pope, accepted Leo's plea and promised to withdraw from Italy. Scholars speculate that his decision was influenced by widespread illness and hunger among the ranks of his army."

Susan Riley stated that TXB had not managed to attain footage documenting the historic meeting between Attila the Hun and Pope Leo. Instead, TXB displayed a digital copy of Raffaello Sanzio's famous fresco titled "The Meeting between Leo the Great and Attila."

***

Walter Lindsey read letters from viewers of his show that administrative staff hadn't the knowledge or authority to answer.

One man wrote, "Dear Walter, I watch your show every week, and I never miss a broadcast, even with the late hour. I do take issue with the way history is portrayed on your show. Watching *The Broadcast*, one might get the impression that the way of humanity consists only of battle and bloodshed. Why don't you also show our greatness, such as Leonardo Da Vinci, Michelangelo, Beethoven, or Van Gogh?"

Lindsey replied, "Dear Edward, I certainly agree with you that the human race is capable of impressive spiritual and cultural achievements, not just bloodshed. Unfortunately, the available technology can't penetrate walls, so we cannot see what goes on inside buildings, such as where Beethoven composed, or Van Gogh painted. Furthermore, we usually need precise dates and locations in order to direct our spotlight to the events we wish to see and show."

Another letter that the secretaries forwarded read, "Dear Mr. Lindsey, I am Dean Wagner with the St. Louis Police Department. I wonder if the technology demonstrated on your show, *The Broadcast*, could assist in solving a recent case. We're investigating the death of a retired minister, recognized as a pillar of his community. According to our findings, Reverend Buckner had no known enemies, and we found nothing that could explain why his body was found floating in the Mississippi River. In talking to his widow, we discovered that, on the morning of his disappearance and subsequent death, Reverend Buckner was visited by an unidentified woman. We have a description, but no name. We don't know what transpired between the priest and the mysterious woman, but we suspect blackmail. I am hoping that your technology could track down the woman's car and discover where she came from. If we could identify her, it would shed light on the investigation, which right now is going nowhere. Sincerely, Dean Wagner, St. Louis Police Department."

Walter Lindsey's reply was short: "Dear Mr. Wagner, our show and our technology are currently focused on the historical journey, not on solving crimes. Sincerely, Walter Lindsey."

On the evening of the weekly show, producer Walter Lindsey used to look out through the window of his twenty-eighth floor office to observe the streets and traffic below. From that vantage point, he often felt like one of the military commanders portrayed on his show, directing his regiments on their unpaved road toward new territories.

Muslim protests against the show were significantly less vocal than the Christian ones. The relatively small American Muslim population kept a low profile; but, since the representative of the community had visited his office and uttered a veiled threat, Walter Lindsey knew he couldn't ignore the religious issues for much longer.

While the American Muslim population kept quiet, articles were published from time to time in large and important Muslim countries, including Turkey, Pakistan, and Egypt. Writers of those articles told their readers about the danger harbored in an American TV program called *The Broadcast*, a seeming entertainment show. Warnings primarily focused on the possibility that the video footage might show the ancient Jewish temple on the Temple Mountain that the Muslim world denied ever existed. The articles urged readers to contact TXB. Indeed, appeals flooded TXB's mailbox. Some letters were very polite, and others carried veiled and even explicit threats.

TXB's CEO, Colin Ingram, maintained the line he'd held ever since the program first aired. He made it clear he would continue to support Walter Lindsey and *The Broadcast* as long as the business was profitable. He warned that, the moment advertisers pulled their commercials or viewership decreased, he would pull the plug.

CHAPTER 47

Michael

Michael sat in front of the computer at work when the phone rang.

"Would you like to join me for lunch?" Walter asked in his usual friendly manner.

The invitation surprised Michael because the producer didn't use to socialize with him during business hours. Walter kept their interaction time mainly for weekends, when the musical meeting and the family meal took place.

"Eric is also coming," Lindsey added. Eric was the band's bass player and a professor of history who taught at a local college.

"Sure, sounds great," Michael replied, curious as to the reason for the unexpected invitation. Michael wondered in silence as Walter drove them to a small Chinese restaurant in the East Village. He hoped Walter would share information about *The Broadcast*.

"It's a really good place," Walter said as he parked his SUV. "The food here is excellent and not too expensive."

The waitress brought them a pot of tea and small ceramic

cups. They looked at the menu; Walter and Michael ordered a business meal of stir-fried shrimp and vegetables, and Eric ordered Kung Pao chicken.

"Do you know Stewart McPherson?" Walter asked and looked at Michael with eyes that reflected inquisitive curiosity, as well as innocence. Eric also examined him.

The question caught Michael off-guard. For a moment he was alarmed and felt like his heart skipped a beat. He quickly reviewed all the possibilities that could have inspired the unexpected question. More than anything, he regretted not being honest with Walter right from the start. Had Walter somehow found out that McPherson sent him to spy on him? He didn't want to think about the consequences of such a development. His relationship with Melanie was probably doomed if he had a falling out with her father.

"I don't mean knowing him personally," Walter elaborated, noticing Michael's bewilderment. "I mean, are you familiar with his work and the things he wrote about my show?"

Michael breathed with relief and tried to get his thoughts in order, fast. "I read the article in the *New York Times*."

"What did you think about it?"

"Well," Michael looked for words that wouldn't offend or incriminate. "I never miss an episode of *The Broadcast*. But I also think that there is something to what he wrote."

Walter smiled. "I appreciate your honesty; people think that I see McPherson as an adversary, but in fact, I truly appreciate the man for his work and his courage."

"So, you're not angry or disappointed about his claim that your show is based on deception?" Michael asked, blinking with surprise.

"I regret the things that he said about my show, and I wish we were not at odds with each other. Anyway, recently I find myself under growing pressure." Walter paused to eat a bite of vegetable before explaining. "Religious groups are demanding that I cancel the show, or at least skip over some specific events from the first century."

Michael felt that, by exposing his difficulties, Lindsey was expressing trust toward him in a way he never had before. "How do they pressure you?" Michael asked.

"Email. Phone calls. I've even received some death threats. They're pressuring the network, not just me."

"What are you going to do?" Michael questioned.

"I won't give in," Walter promised. Then he sighed. "Of course, not everything is up to me. The CEO decides whether the show continues."

"I think," Eric finally cut in, "that religious fanaticism stems from inner doubts. A man who is truly convinced of his faith does not feel insecure and has no need to impose his ideas on others."

"By that reasoning, the religious wars over the centuries originated from inner doubt; that's quite an assertion," Michael said.

"Religious identification is not essentially different from

national identification," Eric explained. "It stems from our need to be a part of a larger group and to know we're not alone in the world. Our egos need the assurance that our path is the only true and righteous way."

Immersed in their conversation, they didn't notice the man sitting at a nearby table eating his lunch and listening closely to their discussion. Had they looked, they would have seen the large, ugly scar on the left side of his face.

***

'Around the Clock' assigned Michael the task of flying to St. Louis, Missouri. He was asked to inquire about a strange incident in which police and city officials stood powerless when confronted by a puzzled community. The disappointed citizens demanded answers and started alleging a cover-up.

As time went by, the story did not disappear, and more and more questions were piling up.

A news article in the *St. Louis Post* tried to sum up the unanswered questions:

What was the real reason for Minister Buckner's death?

Was his death murder or suicide?

If he was murdered, then who would have killed him? Did he have ties to the mob?

If it was suicide, then what was the reason? What secrets did he have? Did those secrets lead to his death?

Who was the mysterious woman who visited the minister on the day he died? Is she connected to his death? Did she try to blackmail him? Was she a victim of misconduct by the reverend?

Why are the police so tight-lipped about the incident? Are they covering up some embarrassing revelations?

The widow, Mrs. Gladys Buckner, refused to talk to the local media. Surprisingly, she agreed to meet with the TXB researcher in her home, although she'd insisted that the first meeting would be held off-camera.

Michael passed through the white gate and noted the manicured lawn and the flower garden as he approached the front door.

Mrs. Buckner, who opened the door, invited Michael to sit with her in the living room. A practiced hostess, she offered him tea, which he gladly accepted.

He noticed that the air in the spotlessly clean house was stale as if there were no open windows. Mrs. Buckner's face reflected her grief. Michael thought that despite her age, silver hair, and wrinkles, she had a pleasant appearance.

"Mrs. Buckner, these must be difficult days for you," Michael said, using the platitude to build rapport with his interviewee.

Mrs. Buckner looked at him and let out a long sigh. "You

spend most of your life with someone, and you'd think you know him."

"You mean you didn't know him?" Michael asked, sensing that she needed to confess something.

"Clearly," she said. "A man doesn't just go and throw himself into the river without reason." She poured herself a small cup of tea. Her hands trembled.

"I understand that you were married for many years," Michael said. "What kind of person was the reverend?"

"Charming," she said. "Good looking, a good husband, but…"

"But what?"

"I think there was another side to him, a dark side that I didn't want to know about. I've been thinking about some irregularities that happened, and I see them in a new light. I realize that I was blind, and it's making me crazy."

"Did you know the woman who visited him on the day he died?"

"I'd never seen her before. She seemed … *angry*, but that's no reason to hate her. As a minister, Matthew counseled a lot of people who were angry for various reasons. She was quite pretty, and there was something … genuine about her."

"Do you have a picture of the reverend?" Michael noticed the photo album on the living room table.

"I do," she said and handed him the album.

He opened the first page which held a large professional

portrait of Reverend Buckner dressed in ecclesiastic garb. Michael saw a good-looking man with a mane of gray hair, his face reflecting solemnity in what might have been a moment of deep prayer.

The photo had a strange effect on Michael. It mesmerized him, and he could not stop staring at it. For some reason, his scalp tingled and shivers raced up and down his spine.

Gladys Buckner noticed the young man's reaction and inquired, "Are you okay?"

"I'm fine," Michael answered, regaining his composure. "It's just that this picture ... I don't know ... the reverend must have had quite an impact on people."

"He sure did," she said, then frowned. "But now, I'm not so sure that he reserved his influence only for good things."

"What do you mean?"

"As I said, I have many things to re-examine."

"Was he unfaithful?" Michael asked, though he knew his question might give offense.

"I saw how women looked at him," Mrs. Buckner didn't seem to mind his prying, "how they adored him. I always felt blessed that he chose me. But now ... I just don't know anything anymore."

She shook her head and started weeping softly. Michael handed her a box of tissues.

The visit with Gladys Buckner left a strong impression on

Michael. He didn't understand why the reverend's portrait affected him so intensely.

The mysterious woman intrigued him. Had she been someone the reverend knew from his past? Was she a victim of his misconduct?

How remarkable was it that Mrs. Buckner didn't feel animosity toward her. Perhaps Mrs. Buckner even displayed a little empathy for her? Like they were both victims of the same man?

The allusion to suicide reminded Michael of the occurrence at the Golden Gate Bridge.

To really know what had happened, he thought to himself, he would need to track down that woman, which could only be achieved if he had access to the technology of *The Broadcast*.

CHAPTER 48

Sarah and Jonathan

Sarah felt as though the trip to St. Louis had lifted a heavy load off her shoulders, a load she'd carried for decades. Joy returned to her heart, along with a fresh and optimistic attitude toward life. At the age of forty, she felt vital and thought she looked younger than her actual age.

Sarah determined to set aside her futile wish for motherhood and find activities that fulfilled her in other ways. She never gave up hope of reuniting with her son, whom she still thought of as Daniel, and prayed that he would search for her and find her.

The first task she took upon herself was to mend and improve her relationship with her husband. She deeply regretted hurting him during those desperate years of infidelity.

Now, she tried to compensate him for his patience and for not divorcing her. She thought that maybe one good thing had come about as a result of her infidelity: Jonathan finding himself a good friend in Irene. Sarah knew that her husband had found it difficult to trust people, and her destructive actions hadn't helped.

In fact, she thought, it wasn't easy for most people to find a good friend who was caring and supportive. Sarah at least had her sister, so Jonathan could have Irene. Sarah decided it made no difference whether Irene was his biological sister or not.

On weekdays, Sarah tried to come home from work at an early hour, so she had sufficient time to make dinner. Enjoyment and creativity returned to her food preparation, and both of them were pleased to find that she succeeded in making wholesome and delicious meals. Sarah did her best to cook the foods that Jonathan liked. Although she had become a vegetarian since her experiences with the spiritual teachers, she was not put off by preparing meat dishes for him.

Jonathan recognized her efforts to atone for "the bad years." He, too, invested in repairing their relationship. He spent more time at home with her, rather than closing himself off in the computer room.

Sarah's efforts to make amends did not skip the bedroom. She made a point of being available and loving, and to accept him whenever and wherever he wanted. On his birthday she came back from work early after shopping at the supermarket. As Jonathan helped put away the groceries, he noticed she had purchased an unusual amount of chocolate.

"What's all this chocolate for?" he asked.

"I'm going to make a chocolate spread," she answered with a sly smile, "and rub it all over my body. Your job is to lick it off."

His physical reaction to her words—the bulge in his pants—

made her giggle.

"Men," she grinned, "You are so transparent."

"Women," he responded in kind, "you are so mysterious."

They returned to hiking together on the trails crisscrossing their property, rediscovering and reconnecting with nature and finding once again the mystery of the forest and the magic of the water flowing in the creek.

Their three dogs accompanied them with their usual canine enthusiasm. They tagged along when Sarah or Jonathan walked separately, but it seemed that the couple's shared hikes made the dogs especially happy.

On one Saturday morning, they went for a picnic in the forest. They arrived at their destination beside the creek, where they sat for a picnic.

"There is something about that TV show, *The Broadcast*," Sarah said between bites of her sandwich, "that, for some reason, speaks to me personally."

Jonathan nodded and looked at her with quiet curiosity. As he expected, she hadn't finished speaking.

"I know this show is important to you," she said. "After all, your brother is producing it. So, maybe it's because of you that I feel connected to it more than any show I've ever watched on TV."

"Well," Jonathan interjected, "it is a unique program, and I also think that there is no other show like it."

"But, beyond that," Sarah resumed speaking, "I feel that, in some way, the program corresponds with *my* life. The same way it goes backward in time … if I, too, could go back in time, I'd be able to acquire insights that would have a direct impact on my life in the present."

"Isn't that true for all of us?" he replied. "You're a psychologist. In psychology, there's always an effort to reconcile the residue of the past with its implications on the present. Maybe investigating history is a kind of psychological process that allows us to understand our behavior as a society."

Sarah pondered his words and said, "I have a strange feeling that my son is also watching *The Broadcast*, and through the show, we could somehow find each other."

"I sure hope that you'll connect with him soon," Jonathan said, then looked down at the water flowing in the creek.

After they finished eating, Jonathan looked for a flat spot of land. When he found the perfect place, he spread a blanket over it, making sure that there were no stones underneath.

"What are you doing?" Sarah asked.

"I would like to make love with my wife."

"I have a better idea," she said, and a spark of naughtiness flashed in her eyes.

"What?"

"Let's make love at the site …"

"Are you sure?" He felt a shiver of apprehension at the idea.

"It's a pagan site," she said. "Let's make pagan love and

dedicate our love to the gods and the universe."

"Okay," he said with some hesitation. "I hope we won't disturb the spirit of the place."

"If we're honest, respectful, and, most of all, loving, then the site will accept us," Sarah promised, looking in the direction of the hilltop. She felt as though the site called to her.

They picked up their bags and made their way to the site. Jonathan wondered whether they were doing the right thing. The more he contemplated the issue, the more he realized that he would deeply regret it if he let his fears stop him.

At the bottom of the strange hill, the dogs stopped, as they always did. Sarah and Jonathan continued climbing, cutting through the densely growing trees and bushes. It wasn't a long walk, but the trail was quite steep, and it required a significant physical effort on their part.

They reached the clearing at the summit where a friendly blue sky welcomed them. Leaving their bags at the edge of the glade, they stepped into the circle with a feeling of reverence as well as a considerable level of excitement.

Sarah walked to the stone table at the center of their henge. She stood still, closed her eyes, took a few deep breaths, and, from her inner being, asked the spirit of the place to grant her permission to do what was in her heart and mind.

The earth shook with a low, muffled rumble in apparent answer to her request. It could have been frightening, but the two of them were already familiar with the expressions of that exceptional place. Their hearts felt no fear, only a sense of veneration.

The sun stood at mid-heaven, warm but not burning. A mild breeze blew among the branches of the trees surrounding the hilltop. Sarah swiftly dropped her clothes and stood stark-naked and barefoot. She looked at her husband, who followed her to the center, but hadn't yet managed to free himself of his hesitations. She understood she had to lead, so she held his hand and pulled him close to her. Embracing him, she looked into his eyes and felt his body respond to hers.

"Take a deep breath," she gently whispered.

He filled his lungs with air, and then slowly exhaled.

She helped him undress and guided him to sit on the rock in the center of the circle. She stood in front of him, her legs straddling his. He wrapped his arms around her, looking into her eyes, and pulled her closer to him. He saw an otherworldly spark in her eyes. She was his beloved and familiar wife, yet there was something different about her. He imagined her as the pagan priestess of the site. Slowly and gently, they joined.

The sexual activity was pleasurable, but not much different and unfamiliar than what they were accustomed to. They loved each other as they had numerous times before.

After some time, Sarah heard the flap of birds' wings behind her. She didn't turn her head. The sound increased and got closer until she could feel the flutter of the wings gently touching her neck. She answered the call, looked around and gaped in awe. The trees curved backward. The usually straight trunks were arched into the shape of petals. Sarah and Jonathan were no longer in a glade, but at the heart of a gigantic flower. She felt how their bodies and souls were uniting. They no longer made love to one another; instead, there was immense love, and they were at its center, breathing as one body. There was a union, and they were there. There was the divine, and they were part of it. The world revolved around them. The trees, birds, blue sky, the earth, and the massive rocks: everything rejoiced and celebrated their love. Time coalesced, past, present, and future merging and flowing together, surrounding them in a circular orbit. They could reach out and touch every place and time in the universe.

They understood. They knew the essence, the source, and the answers to questions that need not be asked. Their hearts filled with gratitude for the world, for creation, and for the blessings of God.

***

Sarah awakened, lying inside the circle of rocks. Her body shivered in the evening chill. She looked around and saw Jonathan lying next to her. She touched him, and he trembled and woke up.

"Come, my love," she whispered. "It's getting dark."

They dressed and made their way down the hill to where the dogs eagerly waited. They did not discuss the sublime experience they shared. It needed no words.

***

In the following days, Sarah continued to fulfill her duties. She nurtured her house, loved her husband, saw her patients in the clinic, and felt that she was lightly floating, a sense of elation filling her whole being. The sensation of awesome well-being did not subside for six weeks. Even bouts of nausea and vomiting did not diminish Sarah's inner joy.

CHAPTER 49

Jonathan

A series of minor earthquakes inflicted several cracks on the bridge leading to Jonathan and Sarah's land. The engineer sent by the county determined that the bridge was unsound and unlikely to survive another rainy season, during which the water flow in the creek becomes forceful. But when Jonathan went to the county offices to find out when the work on the bridge was scheduled to begin, he learned that the county was in a dire financial situation. He was told that they wouldn't be able to help him this year. He would have to reinforce the bridge with his own money, and next year they would try to allocate the needed funds.

Jonathan argued that the loggers' trucks had destabilized the bridge's structure, which was why it couldn't sustain the earthquakes. He reasoned that since the county approved the logging, it bore the responsibility of fixing the damage. At the county, they just reiterated that they had no money.

Jonathan and Sarah faced an enormous financial expense if

they didn't want to run the risk of losing access to public roads. When they checked their income and savings, they realized that they would have to get a loan. They suspected the bank wouldn't approve such a loan with Sarah as the sole provider. Jonathan's occasional automotive repair work brought in some small revenue which he hadn't bothered reporting to the Internal Revenue Service.

The first action they took was to allow more trailer owners to move onto their land. The new tenants included a young man from New York named Willie Fowler, who owned a large, new RV. Fowler presented himself as an enthusiastic environmental activist who participated in demonstrations against forest logging in different states across the U.S. He told Sarah when she interviewed him that the decimation of the rainforests in South America was particularly important to him. Sarah, with the environment dear to her heart, accepted him as a tenant, even though she perceived him to be a flatterer, too eager to agree with everything she said. She also noticed his strange habit of sneaking hasty looks to the side, as if trying to locate a hidden danger.

However, even with the additional trailers, up to the maximum the land could hold, they still didn't have sufficient income to cover the repairing the bridge. Sarah hinted that Jonathan should sell the antique cars, but although his interest in them had waned, he avoided giving her a direct answer.

After a long time in which Jonathan had hardly worked, and mostly spent time in the forest and in front of the computer, he understood he had to return to the workforce. But to do what?

***

About a dozen years earlier, Jonathan had withdrawn from his studies of graphic design and animation in a college. He disliked wasting valuable time driving back and forth to the college, where he sat next to young people who viewed him as an old man, a relic from a different era. He'd also wanted to avoid spending time preparing for unnecessary exams. After his withdrawal from institutionalized studies, he hadn't allowed himself to rest, and he'd actually increased the pace of his studies. Jonathan was not someone who needed external discipline to engage in the fields that attracted him. He'd purchased the graphic design and animation software, as well as instruction books, and diligently immersed himself in studying the applications that interested him.

He started in two-dimensional graphics and progressed at his own pace to three-dimensional animation and virtual reality. He realized that he wasn't endowed with a great creative imagination, but the clips that he created reflected his tendency to strive for perfection and meticulously attend to minute details.

From time to time, he anonymously uploaded works to the internet. The responses were usually positive. Viewers expressed their favorable impression of his talent and ability.

Jonathan never seriously considered turning to animation as

a source of livelihood. He assumed executives were no doubt looking for younger and more creative people than he. But when the financial pressure increased and hovered like dark clouds over his and Sarah's heads, he started to consider the possibility of employment in the field that attracted him, and in which he had invested so many hours.

He feared rejection and ridicule. He dared not try his luck until he convinced himself that he had nothing to lose.

Sarah encouraged him to look for a job in the field that was close to his heart. Both of them knew that if he didn't succeed in finding a job in computer animation, then he could always find a job as an automotive mechanic.

He answered a classified ad published by a large company seeking an animation specialist. Anim-Art was based in the Silicon Valley, a forty-minute drive from his home. The company was headed by the billionaire Barry Dawson, who was its founder and visionary.

When Jonathan arrived for his job interview, he felt a bit awkward and out of place. He sat in a waiting room and waited along with five young people, all of whom were hoping to get the desired position, which assured a high salary. While he was already over the age of forty-five, they looked half his age: ambitious young people, optimistic, driven by motivation and self-confidence.

When they called his name, he entered a room with large windows where a beautiful Asian woman introduced herself as

Mrs. Shirley Chang, the human resources manager.

She asked him the usual background questions regarding his experience and skills. After she recorded his answers, he was politely asked to return to the waiting room and wait with the other applicants.

After about twenty more minutes, a young man dressed in an athletic outfit and sporting long hair tied in a ponytail asked them to come with him.

"My name is Douglas Green," he told the small group. "I'm in charge of examining and assimilating new employees."

Green led them to a large room and directed them to sit in front of well-equipped digital workstations. "I just want to clarify," he said, "that degrees and fancy credentials don't amount to much here at Anim-Art. We want our people to demonstrate remarkable performance capabilities. Your task today is to impress me."

Douglas Green gave them a testing assignment. They had to exhibit their capabilities, using the 3-D programs of their choice, to create an animated clip showing a first-grade student's first day of school.

They had three hours to complete a five-minute video clip. Green left them in the big room to do their assignment. He entered a nearby office that had a big window, through which he could see them and they could see him.

Jonathan was ready for the challenge. He was familiar with the programs and was skilled at using them. He took a deep breath, and with a pencil and paper, he dedicated a few minutes to manually designing the clip. He did that while the other candidates were already working on the computers.

When he finished planning, he turned to the computer and focused on his work. His ideas and thoughts streamed from his mind, through his hands, and became discernable on the computer screen, transforming into lines, shapes, colors, figures, and movements, which took on a life of their own. He progressed rapidly and with confidence, so completely engrossed in his project, that the world around him ceased to exist. There was only his creation, which materialized in front of his eyes. It took him about forty minutes to complete his project. He saved his work, got up, and knocked on Douglas Green's glass window.

"What's the matter?" Douglas asked, assuming the old dude might have encountered some technical difficulty.

"I've finished," Jonathan said.

"Finished everything? A five-minute clip? Douglas Green's face expressed his disbelief.

Jonathan interpreted Green's incredulity as doubt of his competence.

But despite his apparent misgivings, Green treated Jonathan with respect. He invited him to enter his office and sit beside him. Green's computer, had access to all the workstations. He looked at the file that Jonathan created, and then played the clip. Green watched Jonathan's project with utmost concentration. He didn't say anything, just nodded his head from time to time. Several times he stopped the clip and rewound it a few seconds, to look again at particular segments.

Anxious, Jonathan regretted having been in a hurry to submit his work. He worried that he should have spent more time on some of the details or in shaping the characters. Why did he rush so much?

When the clip ended, Green turned to Jonathan, looked at him with appreciation, smiled, and shook his hand.

"Impressive," he said, "truly impressive." Green's phone rang, but he silenced it. "Usually we don't tell our applicants during their first interview whether they'll get the job," he said. "But when I look at your project, which you burned through in forty … dude, you're *going* to be accepted at Anim-Art. Your work is thorough, high quality, with an emphasis on the tiniest details. Your characters are totally vibrant and nearly jump off the screen. I'm especially amazed, 'cause you've got almost no formal education. *Whoa.* I'm wholeheartedly going to recommend that you be hired."

Jonathan heaved a sigh of relief when he left the building. He recognized that he had been under a lot of pressure and that he had put to the test not only his creative and technical ability, but also his mental strength. He was glad that he hadn't let his fears deter him from applying.

Still giddy that night, Jonathan told Sarah that he'd put his capabilities to the test and felt that he'd done quite well.

Two days later, the human resources manager called him

with an official offer to work at Anim-Art, at an annual salary double than what he had ever made before.

CHAPTER 50

The Broadcast

Three programs were left until the end of the season when Susan Riley unexpectedly resigned her anchor position.

"I love this show more than any other project I've worked on," she told Walter Lindsey with tears in her eyes. "But I can't do it anymore. I can't handle any more nasty phone calls and letters."

"I'm sorry to hear that," Lindsey empathized. "I've gotten some too, but I try to ignore them."

"I could handle it when the hateful comments came from strangers," Susan Riley said. "I stood firm even when friends at church snubbed me. But lately, the flow of threats has just … there's no break from the hatred. Just this morning, I received nineteen threats against my reputation, my career, and even my life. Three of those threats explicitly targeted my family. I can't risk my children, Walter. They're the most important thing in the world to me."

"Do you know who's behind the calls and the letters?" Lindsey asked.

"Religious fundamentalists. They're scared that what we're going to show conflicts with what they believe. Many use similar wording and identical phrases, like they've been organized." Susan Riley was clearly upset.

"I made it clear to a representative from the Archdiocese of New York," Lindsey said, "that I doubted we'd get to see Jesus. I know from numerous letters that there are many good Christians who would actually love to see their savior and look forward to the possibility."

"And don't forget the Muslim fanatics," Susan Riley said. "Scared we're going to show the Jewish temple. Their threats are really scary. I didn't sign up for this and my kids sure as hell don't deserve to die in the hands of some crazy extremist. I hate to quit, Walter, but I have to, for my family. I'm sorry."

***

With reluctance, Walter Lindsey accepted Riley's resignation and replaced her with Nancy Whitfield, a good-looking young broadcaster considered to be TXB's rising star.

The first program hosted by Nancy Whitfield focused on the third century. Studio guest Professor Liang Shunyuan from the University of Fudan in Shanghai appeared relaxed, while the host looked nervous. It was obvious she was trying hard to step into Susan Riley's big shoes.

"Good evening, Professor," the young host welcomed her

white-haired guest. "Please tell us about the Battle of Red Cliff."

"Good evening." The professor nodded and stroked his white beard. "It was a famous battle that took place at the end of the Han Dynasty, shortly before the Three Kingdoms era. The northern warlord, Cao Cao, tried to invade the territories south of the Yangtze River, leading his large army. His efforts were blocked by an alliance of warlords who ruled the southern lands."

"What will tonight's footage show us?" the host inquired.

"We shall see the decisive naval battle," the professor said, "that resulted in a conclusive victory for the allies."

The film rolled, and the professor narrated the sequence of events. The clip, like all *The Broadcast's* footage, showed the combat from above. Viewers saw Cao Cao's ships anchored on the northern side of the Yangtze River. The northern army was significantly larger than the opposing force.

"A divisional commander of the southern forces sent Cao Cao a letter feigning surrender," Professor Shunyuan explained. "Then that commander sent a squadron of ships as an indication of his defection and acceptance of the authority of Cao Cao, who fell for the strategic deception."

Viewers watched the squadron make its way northbound from the southern harbor, propelled by a strong wind. When the ships of the south crossed the river's midpoint, their sailors set them on fire before abandoning them in small boats. The unmanned fire ships, which were filled with burning materials, were seen carried by the powerful wind at high speed, and they crashed into Cao Cao's fleet with lethal impact. Most of the fleet was set on fire and destroyed, and many soldiers and horses burned to death or drowned. The northern army was overcome by confusion and was defeated, and its commander, Cao Cao, ordered an overall retreat.

"You see," the professor said in his heavy Chinese accent, "Warfare in the East was not different in ferocity or cruelty than in the West."

Nancy Whitfield nodded and said, "In the West, we have a hard time understanding who fought against whom and for what."

"When we observe your wars," the professor replied, "sometimes we too have difficulty in understanding what people fought for. I think that many people in the West don't know what the First World War was about. It is my opinion that many times, people fought, killed, and died for their leaders' greed and hunger for power."

***

Walter Lindsey sat in front of his computer, busy corresponding with an advertiser who expressed concerns over increased protests by Christians and Muslims.

It seemed it was only a matter of time before a major sponsor withdrew support for the program, and he did his best to postpone that inevitability. He hoped to complete *The Broadcast's* current season. If he could just get past the controversy of the first century, then he figured the religious zealots would settle down.

Lindsey knew he could deflect the pending storm by announcing that the show would skip over the events of the first century AD and pass directly to the first century BC. But despite the logic and safety of that approach, which the CEO strongly recommended, Lindsey refused to yield.

At major crossroads throughout his life, Lindsey had chosen the way of compromise, rather than fighting and sticking to his wishes. Most of the time, the concessions had proven beneficial for him. For instance, when he had given up his ambition to become a film director, or when he'd abandoned his plan to travel the world when he was young, and instead focused on acquiring a profession.

His most significant capitulation had happened when he was nine years old, when he didn't resist the social workers' plan to separate him from his younger brother. The social workers had claimed that they couldn't find a family for the two of them, so they had no choice but to send them to different foster homes. And Walter hadn't fought it. He didn't kick and scream against the verdict.

For years afterward, he'd carried guilt feelings, and abandoning his brother contributed to decades of estrangement.

This time he wasn't going to yield. As long as he got the green light from the CEO, he would continue with *The Broadcast*, despite obstacles and threats.

***

"Good evening," Nancy Whitfield said, opening the broadcast that focused on the second century. "Tonight we have Professor Giora ˜gan, from the Hebrew University of Jerusalem. Good evening, Professor Dagan, and thank you for joining us."

"Good evening, Nancy," the world-renowned researcher and archeologist replied with a solemn nod. "I've been following your remarkable show ever since you embarked on the historical journey."

"Professor, will you please tell our viewers about the Bar Kokhba rebellion?"

"The main factors of the Jewish revolt against the Roman Empire," Professor Dagan said, "were the establishment of a pagan city named Aelia Capitolina over the ruins of Jerusalem, the building of a temple to Jupiter on the Temple Mount, and the ˜˜hibition of circumcision."

"How was the rebellion managed?" Nancy Whitfield asked.

"In the first stage, the Jews employed guerrilla warfare, hiding out in caves they prepared in advance. The Romans sent einforcements from nearby provinces, and their forces amounted to about eighty thousand soldiers, but Bar Kokhba's fighters had the upper hand. Following the successes, Bar Kokhba took control of wide areas and declared the independence of Judea. The three years of Bar Kokhba's ruling in Judea were the last years of Jewish independence in their country until the foundation of the state of Israel in 1948."

"What happened next?" the host asked.

"The Roman Emperor Hadrian mobilized a large army and sent twelve legions to the campaign. He appointed Julius Severus as commander of the forces. Severus, who was considered to be a skilled tactical commander, had served as the governor of Britain. He was brought specifically to suppress the uprising. Severus adopted a wise strategy. He isolated areas that were under rebel control and defeated them one after another. That way he destroyed Bar Kokhba's forces without running the risk of an all-out war. Bar Kokhba's people withdrew to the fortified city of Betar, near Jerusalem. The Romans cast a blockade of Betar and built a dike of about four kilometers, completely cutting off the city from its surroundings. After a prolonged siege, the Romans succeeded in breaking into the city, where they committed a horrendous massacre, killing everyone including women and children."

From its bird's eye vantage point, the footage displayed the sack of Betar. The fighting was seen somewhat distant, but there was no doubt as to the merciless cruelty of the Roman soldiers.

"And what were the results of the rebellion?" the host asked.

"Absolute devastation for my people," Professor Dagan somberly replied. "According to several sources, more than half a million Jews were killed by the Romans, not including those who died of disease and starvation. Most of the Jewish towns and villages in Judea were razed to the ground. Most of the Jews were expelled from their land, and more than a hundred thousand were sold into slavery. Emperor Hadrian wanted to erase the Jewish existence in Judea, and he even changed the name of the province from Judea to Syria-Palestina, a name that's still in use today by the Palestinian Arab movements.

"As if that weren't enough, the Romans issued decrees prohibiting the Jews from practicing their religion. Following the great devastation, leading rabbis banned the Jews from using force as a means of attaining national liberty, and they forbade attempting to bring the redemption before its time. So, without a doubt, the shock of the destruction following Bar Kokhba's rebellion affected the mentality of my people during two thousand years of living in exile."

***

Lindsey was talking to one of the editors of his show when the CEO's secretary called him.

"Colin requests that you join him for a meeting in his office at ten-thirty," she said.

Lindsey got an ominous feeling in the pit of his stomach.

The CEO's office had solid wood interior walls and large glass-door cabinets. When Lindsey entered, Colin uncharacteristically got up from his chair and shook his hand. The CEO's clammy grip indicated distress.

"Thank you for coming on such short notice, Walter," Colin Ingram said and, without further ado, introduced Lindsey to the person already seated in his office: Agent Donald Russell of the FBI.

Walter thought Russell looked more like an accountant than an intelligence operative.

"Walter," Ingram said as he returned to his seat, "we'd better listen together to what Mr. Russell has to say."

Lindsey turned to look toward the guest with disfavor and wondered at the purpose of the visit.

"The FBI does not involve itself in television programming, because these issues concern the FCC," the agent said, choosing his words with care. "Unfortunately, we have an exceptional situation on our hands."

Donald Russell paused and examined the two men, who waited in silence for him to continue.

"It's no secret that recently there were many protests by religious groups, in our country and overseas, against the program *The Broadcast*. As you probably know, most of the protests come from vocal and influential Christian groups that are worried your program might show Jesus in a light that is not compatible with their scriptures. We at the FBI are not particularly concerned with those Christians. We view them as a small and loud minority who don't reflect the majority of Christians in our country. We are much more worried about the Muslims, who up until now have kept a low profile."

"What are you getting at?" the CEO asked impatiently.

"We want to avoid a situation in which your program may provoke violence against Americans and American interests," the FBI man patiently said. "You may remember the demonstrations that followed the publication of Salman Rushdie's *The Satanic Verses* or the riots that followed the publication of the caricatures of the prophet Muhammad."

The two men nodded.

"Our analyses predict that radical Islamists are likely to view a broadcast showing the Jewish temple as an American and Zionist conspiracy, which could lead to terrorist activity against our country."

"What are you asking TXB to do?" Ingram asked with suspicion.

"Of course, we won't tell you what to do," Donald Russell said. "But we ask that you avoid airing materials likely to incite violence."

"We share your concerns," Colin Ingram said, "and will consider your request. Thank you for coming to TXB."

The agent accepted the polite dismissal and left. Walter rose to follow him, but Ingram signaled the producer to stay.

"Walter, my friend," the CEO said after the door closed, "we have no choice. Earlier this morning, I received notice that Ford is withdrawing their sponsorship of the program. I don't doubt that other companies will follow. We can't lose our advertisers; after all, they're the ones who pay the bills. Moreover, I can't ignore the

FBI's request. A little controversy's always a good thing, but provoking terrorists just doesn't make good business sense. I've decided to suspend."

Lindsey was not surprised, and a little gratified that his boss appeared genuinely regretful about his decision.

"I understand," Walter replied, "I'm disappointed, of course, but I agree with you that we don't have a lot of choices."

"I'm not saying that *The Broadcast* wouldn't be able to come back for another season after the controversy calms down," the CEO said. "You know I personally like the show, which has been very lucrative for TXB."

"I appreciate your support, Colin." Lindsey kept a noble attitude. He was deeply saddened, and he worried that tears would disclose his feelings.

Walter returned to his office to notify staff of the decision to pull *The Broadcast* off the air and then look for another project. After all, the public's demand for entertainment never ceased.

TXB released a short statement, announcing that *The Broadcast* was going off the air, effective immediately, and the season's closing episode would not air. The announcement offered neither explanation nor indication regarding plans for the next season.

CHAPTER 51

Michael

"Would you like to spend Easter in California?" Michael asked Melanie while they sat at their small kitchen table, having supper.

She examined him, curious. "You mean at your parents' house?"

"Yes, I'd like you to meet them."

After a pause, she said, "All right. I hope they like me."

"You have no reason to fear," he said. "Actually, I'm the one who's worried."

"Of what?"

"Well, in addition to the important meeting between you and them," Michael talked slowly, as if weighing his words, "I think I'm ready for a conversation with my parents."

"You intend to ask them about your biological parents?"

"I think it's time."

Melanie met his gaze. "I know this has been on your mind for a very long time, and I'm glad you're ready to deal with it. But won't my presence be a distraction?"

"I would like you to meet them, and I need you there to support me."

"I want to meet them as well," Melanie reassured him. "But it seems to me that if you feel ready to bring up the subject of your biological parents, then it's better if I don't come with you. It's *your* journey, and you have to do it by yourself. I'll always be available, just a phone call away."

He pondered her words for a moment, "You're right … as always".

"Next time we'll go together," she promised.

***

Michael boarded the long flight from New York to San Diego to spend three days with his parents. It had been a long time since his last visit. He missed his family, his childhood friends, and the neighborhood where he grew up. He hoped the meeting would go well.

For many years, he worried that his desire to seek his father and mother would hurt the two wonderful people who'd raised him and loved him with all their hearts. Now he saw that his striving to understand where he came from did not conflict with his love of and gratitude for his adoptive parents.

Michael looked out through the airplane's window. He saw the clouds below him and knew that all his life he'd been on this one-way journey taking him to the important meeting ahead. There was no turning back.

The meeting at the airport was an emotional experience, especially for Michael's mother, Rose, who couldn't stop crying. She looked at her son, whom she hadn't seen for two years, and through the veil of tears, she searched for changes in the boy she raised. Did he look older and more mature now that he was living with a woman?

His father was more restrained than his wife, but he too was overcome by emotions when he hugged his beloved son. As they drove to their house in the suburbs, Michael was glad to see that the neighborhood had hardly changed. He also appreciated California's sunny warmth after New York's dreary cold.

"I was hoping that you'd come with your girlfriend," his mother said during dinner. "I'd really like to meet her."

"It didn't work out this time," Michael said. "I hope she'll come next time. It would be nice if Lily visited, too."

"And how is your sister?" his mother asked. "Lately she doesn't say much about her life. She just sends short text messages."

"From what little I hear, she's fine," Michael said without divulging the regular phone conversations he recently had with his sister. He knew she'd broken up with her boyfriend and taken the separation hard but didn't think it was his place to discuss her problems. He treasured the discussions with his sister. Lily was convinced that their parents wouldn't be hurt by a request to find his biological parents; she gave him the encouragement he needed to take that step in discovering his past. His sister, a university student, had wisdom beyond her years.

After dinner, Michael went to meet a few of his old friends, including members of his high school band. They were amazed when he told them he worked at TXB and expressed disappointment about *The Broadcast* going off the air.

Before going to bed, Michael called Melanie and told her that the flight went well. She encouraged him to pursue his plan.

"I love you," she said, her words warming his heart. He knew that Melanie only expressed her loving feelings when she felt them with all her heart.

The next morning, he decided it was time for the conversation he'd delayed for so long. He told his parents he wished to discuss a very important matter with them. So, the three of them adjourned to the living room.

"Yes, Michael," his mother lovingly said. She thought she knew the reason for the meeting, and essentially the purpose of the whole visit. She secretly hoped that Michael wanted to discuss an upcoming wedding, or anything else, but deep inside, she understood that there was only one explanation for his wish to talk with them. It was the topic she'd been afraid of since the day they'd received him.

"Mom, Dad," Michael opened, feeling uncomfortable. "It's

and little Michael, who had always been somewhat a mother's boy, had gotten scared during takeoff, so he'd clung tightly to his strong father.

"We knew the day would come, Michael," his father said now. "We think that it's your birthright."

His mother returned after a few minutes, carrying a large brown envelope. She handed it to him and said, "It's not much, but that's all the information we have. I believe it will help you find your biological mother."

Taking the envelope from her, he noticed that his adoptive mother said that he'd be able to find his biological *mother*. She hadn't mentioned his biological father.

"I'll forever be *your* son. I hope you know that," Michael said.

"We know," his father said, and his mother shed a tear and nodded in agreement.

After the meeting, he retreated to his bedroom. He felt grateful to the wonderful people who had adopted him, had been so good to him throughout his life, and now they granted his plea without hesitation.

Sitting on his bed, he spread out the contents of the envelope and looked at the old, yellowing documents. His heart pounded. According to the documentation, he was born at a hospital in Phoenix, Arizona, on the fifteenth of April, about twenty-four years ago. The name of his biological mother was Sarah Sanders.

CHAPTER 52

Howard Hensley

Howard Hensley examined two issues of the *New York Times* with great interest. In the Tuesday edition, there was a short item at the bottom of the first page. The reporter wrote:

> *In a surprise decision, TXB network announced the immediate cancellation of its popular show,* The Broadcast. *The season finale will not air.*
>
> *There seem to be two reasons for the cancellation: Christian groups who oppose a broadcast that might show Jesus in a different light than in the Bible, and fear of Islamic factions who oppose the showing of the Jewish temple on the Temple Mount in Jerusalem.*

In the Thursday edition of the same newspaper, Hensley found a short item on the last page. The article reported that an unknown internet news site called *Uncensored News* made a surprising announcement. It read:

> *Uncensored News has obtained exclusive rights to*
> *the footage that was initially scheduled to air on*
> The Broadcast's *season finale. The footage will*
> *be broadcast online, one week after the initially*
> *scheduled date. Uncensored News promises a*
> *fascinating show that, among other items, will*
> *show the Roman soldiers breaking into the Jewish*
> *temple in Jerusalem.*

The article made no mention as to whether *Uncensored News* would broadcast footage of Jesus and the crucifixion.

It had been about three years since reporter Stewart McPherson brought the story to Hensley and revealed his suspicions regarding the authenticity of the films. Already then, HH's gut feeling told him that this was not just another routine investigation. Hensley thought that the case carried the potential of a significant gain for him, although he had yet to figure out how to make that happen.

Most of HH's investigations were not truly interesting for him. They typically involved monitoring unfaithful spouses or following business competitors. He conducted his investigations thoroughly and discreetly, meticulously tracking even the tiniest details. But he always preferred the more significant cases, those through which he could prove to the higher-ups of the ungrateful establishment, that they could not function effectively without him and that he was the best in the business.

Hensley liked to feel that he was at the center of matters that most people didn't even know about. He enjoyed meddling in dark affairs and manipulating those righteous hypocrites who pretended to be honest, respectful citizens, when in reality they were driven by ego and greed, like everyone else.

Like McPherson, Hensley assumed that Walter Lindsey was producing the films with the help of his friends who were also members of his band. But unlike the journalist, HH thought that another factor was involved in the scheme: Lindsey's brother in California.

That's why he had sent out a spy, Willie Fowler, the young felon he'd managed to free from jail. Fowler succeeded in getting accepted as a tenant of the little trailer park. From there he supplied Hensley with information on the activities on Jonathan and Sarah Lishinsky's land.

Obeying Hensley's instructions, Willie Fowler broke into Jonathan's computer room, inside the barn. Fowler examined the contents of Jonathan's computer and transferred emails to HH.

Hensley read with interest the correspondence between Jonathan and a woman named Irene, whom Jonathan related to as if she were a big sister. Strange, though, since Hensley didn't remember that such a sibling ever existed in the family.

Of greater importance was a weekly exchange between Jonathan and his brother. HH was particularly interested in the emails that contained encrypted attachments. But despite considerable efforts, he didn't succeed in decrypting those attachments, so he could only assume that those files were the materials that TXB aired in *The Broadcast*.

In his many years as a private investigator, Howard Hensley had learned that it is possible to convert vital information into financial gain and power.

He considered turning to the media, to try to sell the scoop: the sensational revelation that *The Broadcast* was based on falsification. To expose the fact that Walter Lindsey had been manufacturing the materials along with his musician friends and his brother in California, all of them cooperated in concocting the deception. Hensley despised the media, mainstream and tabloids alike. So, he thought he shouldn't be overly concerned about the lack of proof for his assumptions, or about presenting accurate facts. He thought that if he just threw enough dirt in the right direction, something was bound to stick.

Upon further consideration, it occurred to him that his profit could be much higher if he not only exposed the source of the films, but also stopped the broadcast of the last episode altogether. As the only one who could prevent the transmission of the footage that worried the religious factors, he could extort huge sums from those groups.

HH figured that if he could get to Jonathan and Sarah's estate in time, he'd find a way to stop the scheduled transmission.

But which organization would be willing to pay an enormous sum of money for his services? Should he approach the vocal Christian groups who published manifestos against the show? Or perhaps he would get better results if he turned to the Muslim Brotherhood?

He suspected that he would have a hard time convincing them to invest enough hard cash for their cause. And time wasn't on his side.

Wrapped in his thoughts, Howard Hensley lit a cigarette. He got up from his chair to make a cup of coffee.

Then, out of the blue, he thought about Father Thomas Shelton. He immediately knew that he'd stumbled upon the best solution to his quandary. And in what looked like an extraordinary coincidence, at that exact moment the phone rang, and on the line was none other than Father Thomas Shelton.

My prayers are answered, he thought as a sinister smile crossed his face.

***

Hensley had performed delicate and secretive tasks for Father Shelton several times over the years. The first time had been when important to me that you know that I love you with all my heart."

His parents, who knew him so well, waited with patience, giving him the silent support he needed to express himself.

Michael took a deep breath and continued, "For years, I've wondered who my biological parents were, and now I'm feeling ready to look for them. I hope you can give me a lead on where to start my search." Michael stopped speaking.

A weighty silence filled the room. His parents looked at him and at each other. A car passed on a nearby street and sounds of children playing filtered through the window. Michael looked at the familiar furniture in the room, which hadn't changed over the years. He saw the large, dark cabinets, made of solid wood, filled with books that no one read anymore. He remembered being six years old when *that* conversation had taken place ... Right in that same room, when they told him he was adopted. After that, nothing had been the same.

Now he looked at his parents, and for a moment he wondered whether he'd done the right thing. Perhaps he should have delayed his plea?

His mother's eyes glistened with tears. She got up, walked over to him, leaned in and embraced him with love. "I'll be right back," she said, and walked out of the room.

His father remained stoic. Michael looked at him and remembered his first airplane flight. When Michael was four years old, the family had flown for a vacation in the state of Colorado,

With a large cross worn on top of his black robe, Father Thomas Shelton arrived at HH's office a few minutes earlier than expected. "As you might know," he said after dispensing with the pleasantries, "TXB had already dropped the TV series, but the materials are going to transmit on the internet, which is just as bad."

"And you want me to stop the internet broadcast," HH said with perceptive confidence.

Father Shelton examined him inquisitively through his small glasses. "Can you do it?"

"You'd be surprised. I've been following *The Broadcast* for three years. I know what's behind it, and I'm the *only* one who can prevent the last episode from going public." HH spoke that last sentence slowly, even though he wasn't sure if he could really deliver on his claim.

"Do you know what's in this footage?" Father Shelton inquired. "Does it show the crucifixion?"

"Obviously, I haven't seen the films, and I don't know what's in them," Hensley answered, "but I do know that time is not on our side."

"How much?" The holy fire extinguisher asked.

"It's a very complicated operation," Hensley said. "I need two hundred and fifty grand, not including reimbursement of expenses."

The priest didn't appear startled, but he took his time pondering the offer. "It's a lot of money," he finally said.

"Your choice," HH said calmly without attempting to justify the amount, which he'd calculated as expensive, but not extortionate. HH knew that Father Shelton represented an organization with deep pockets and that he had a special budget which was not subjected to auditing.

"Alright, I agree," Father Shelton said, "on the condition that you don't kill anybody."

***

Howard Hensley was pleased with the results of his negotiation with the Roman Catholic Church. Now it was time to widen the net.

Hensley had sources within the police and the FBI. The relationships with his contact people benefited both sides, especially in gathering information on criminals, small fry as well as mighty mobsters.

From his sources, he learned that the FBI had shown interest in *The Broadcast* and advised its cancellation. HH discovered the name of the agent who approached TXB: Donald Russell. He called Russell's office to arrange a meeting.

"What's this about?" Russell asked, not bothering with the social pleasantries. He was familiar with Howard Hensley by name and reputation. The knowledge did not generate an enthusiastic response, especially with Hensley being a convicted criminal, a former cop who'd served time in jail.

400

"The Broadcast," Hensley replied.

Russell was not happy about granting the unexpected request, but he knew time was running out. If he wanted to prevent the transmission of the footage and avoid the unrest it would cause, especially in Islamic territories, he had to use every element that might be able to assist. Donald Russell wasn't one of the law enforcement people who thought that the end justified the means, but he'd learned from his experience that when there was an urgent and important matter, sometimes he needed to employ players who operated in the shadows.

The secretary at the reception desk of the bureau's branch office examined Hensley with a piercing look. Her gaze lingered on his facial scar, and while her facial expression revealed her aversion, she told HH that Russell was waiting for him.

The long hallways, lit by fluorescent lights, reminded HH of the days when he worked as an officer of the law. He knew he'd never return to such a job because his independence was vital to him. Obeying orders from superiors was particularly unbearable; the fact that they outranked him didn't mean he could trust them. He'd already accepted he was a lone wolf; yet, he savored the thought of showing his former colleagues that he was the best detective around, and that the cumbersome and ungrateful system couldn't make it without him.

"What do you have to offer?" Russell asked, getting straight to the point as soon as Hensley walked into his office.

"I can stop the transmission of the last episode of *The Broadcast*," Hensley said, although he was not sure he could succeed in his mission.

Russell looked unimpressed. "You know that airing the footage over the internet won't have the same impact as a broadcast on an institutionalized television network."

"Extremists and fanatics will still see it as an American conspiracy and provocation. They'll look for revenge, instigate riots, and harm innocent people," Hensley said.

"Maybe," Donald Russell said while examining the man standing in front of him. "I'm sure you want payment for your services."

"Of course. I don't work for free."

"What do you want?"

"In my line of business, I need information from time to time," Hensley said.

Russell weighed the ramifications of an agreement. He decided it was worth it, and he could maybe claim a misunderstanding if Hensley's future demands exceeded reasonable expectations. "Do your job, and I'll see to it that you get access to my desk. Just don't kill anybody."

Satisfied with his negotiation, Howard Hensley drove home, packed a small suitcase, and headed toward the airport, on his way to California.

CHAPTER 53

Michael

With the new information in hand, Michael set his mind on finding his mother. Right after the meeting with his adoptive parents, he used his laptop to conduct an extensive search on the internet. He looked for someone named Sarah Sanders, likely in her forties. Thorough as it was, his internet search yield nothing valuable or relevant. He assumed that she had gotten married and changed her name.

Michael realized that he would have to be patient. He might have to hire the services of a private investigator, or go to Phoenix and try to locate the main adoption agencies, where he would have to deal with plenty of bureaucracy.

He called Melanie, who reminded him there was no rush. "You've waited this long, a few more days, or even weeks, won't matter all that much. The important thing is that you made the first big step."

Despite her logic, Michael remained impatient.

He remembered Stewart McPherson. Michael had not heard

anything from McPherson since telling him he would not continue to spy on Walter Lindsey. Although his decision disappointed the esteemed journalist, Michael thought they'd parted as friends, and McPherson had even left him with the superb Martin guitar.

Michael still had McPherson's phone number in his contacts list, so he took the chance and called.

"What a surprise!" the veteran journalist answered in a friendly tone.

A bit embarrassed, Michael continued with the reason for which he'd called: "I need a favor."

"Tell me what it is, and I'll see if I can help," McPherson said.

"There's someone I'm trying to locate," Michael explained. "I have her birth name, but she has probably gotten married and changed her name."

"And who is the lady?" McPherson inquired.

"My mother."

"That is indeed a worthy cause," McPherson said solemnly. "What do you know about her?"

"Only her name, Sarah Sanders, the hospital where I was born, and my birth date." He rattled off the details and listened to the scratch and rustle of pen and paper.

"That's not much," the journalist commented. "I'll check the archives of the hospitals and the main adoption agencies in Phoenix. That shouldn't be too complicated. Let's hope they saved the information."

Father Shelton hired him to check allegations brought forth by a group of concerned parents who claimed that a senior priest had abused his position and molested the children under his care.

Hensley looked into the matter and found that the accusations were true. Consequently, Father Shelton asked him to help suppress media coverage of the scandal.

Later, he collaborated with Father Shelton in a few incidents in which the church wanted to silence damaging publicity. HH privately called Father Shelton "the holy fire extinguisher." Working with the senior church official gave Hensley a unique sense of pleasure. It conveyed the absolute proof of the hypocrisy of the society that turned its back on him—the same society that couldn't make it without him.

***

"Hello, Father, what do you need today?" Howard Hensley asked in a nearly chipper tone.

Hensley listened to Father Shelton as he outlined the danger that *The Broadcast* harbored.

"I can be at your office in two hours," Hensley said.

"I would rather come to your office," Father Shelton replied. "My driver will drop me off outside your building."

"Okay," Hensley agreed, not caring that the priest preferred not to be seen in the company of a scarred monster like him. That might raise unwelcome questions.

"Thank you, Stewart," Michael was grateful and appreciative.

On the following day, the last day of the visit with his parents, Michael received a call from McPherson.

"It seems you're in luck," the journalist said. "My people had no difficulties in hacking the data banks of several adoption agencies in Phoenix. We've found that Sarah Sanders came from St. Louis, Missouri. She was sixteen when she had you."

"Did you find out what happened to her?" Michael's excitement was mixed with apprehension.

"Yes. She did marry, and her married name is Sarah Lishinsky. She lives in a small town called Corralitos, in central California." McPherson rattled off the street address.

Michael's heart pounded as he wrote the details, "I don't know how to thank you," he said.

"That's what friends are for," McPherson replied. "I'm glad I could help, and especially in a case when someone's looking for his parents."

Michael called Melanie. "I'm delaying my return. I have my biological mother's address and I'm going to see her."

"This is so exciting," Melanie said. "I wish I could be there with you, but I know you should continue this journey on your own."

"I miss you."

"Miss you too."

Michael pondered the information that he had about his mother. He thought about the ramifications of having a baby at such a young age and wondered why she delivered in Phoenix rather than her home city. He wondered who his father was and speculated as to what caused them to decide to give him up for adoption.

Something else in the information that McPherson gave him sounded familiar. He wracked his brain and gasped when he remembered. Lishinsky! He'd heard that name before. That was the family name of Walter's brother, Jonathan. In fact, it was Walter's original family name. Was his biological mother married to Walter's brother?

CHAPTER 54

Stewart McPherson

Stewart McPherson navigated his way through journalism trying to maintain high standards of decency, fairness, and impartiality. He detested media channels that were not faithful to the facts, and instead, distorted and exaggerated them to create a sensational story for the sake of high ratings. He also strove to expose the manipulations conducted by wealthy tycoons who were connected to politicians and the media.

McPherson read the announcement about *Uncensored News* intent to broadcast the last episode of *The Broadcast*. It reminded him of an email he received from an organization calling itself UFGIO, the Uncensored Free Global Information Organization, claiming that they were behind the footage of *The Broadcast*.

At that time, he thought the mail was bogus. Now he pondered the possible connection between that organization and the internet site. Upon further consideration, he decided that the similarity of the names was coincidental.

McPherson had unsuccessfully tried to expose the source of *The Broadcast*'s films. The article in which he claimed that the show was based on deception had snowballed, and many joined his opinion and his call for disclosure.

But little by little, McPherson realized that his confidence in the viewpoint he'd established had started to wane.

He watched the entire series one more time, focusing on programs from the first season, when the network broadcast episodes that helped in solving crimes. The reexamination made him change his mind.

When he'd watched the films the first time, he'd thought police officers had collaborated with the network's deception, but that no longer made sense. Now he recognized that one or two police officers could succumb to such a deplorable act, but the program had hosted too many esteemed detectives who'd asserted *The Broadcast* helped in cracking their unsolved cases.

Moreover, over time, McPherson saw that Walter Lindsey and his team demonstrated a level of decency and integrity that he hadn't expected from them. He approved how *The Broadcast's* second and third season shows avoided the sensationalism that characterized the first season.

When religious fanatics slandered the show and claimed that it threatened to reveal information contradictory to their holy scriptures, McPherson thought that those scriptures were themselves manipulative. He found himself siding with the show, and respected Lindsey for resisting the pressure. McPherson assumed TXB canceled the program due to advertisers' demands.

The Broadcast continued to fascinate him, even when he moved on to work on other projects. From time to time he reexamined his facts and wondered why he hadn't succeeded in solving the enigma of the source materials. One day as he was driving his car, an explanation came to his mind: Howard Hensley had misled him.

McPherson had never been comfortable in his collaboration with the private investigator with the dubious past, and he'd had difficulty trusting him. The first few times he'd turned to Hensley, he doubted the information that the man with the scarred face supplied. With time, he saw that despite his suspicions, HH delivered reliable information. Apparently, he had sources, connections, and capabilities that McPherson lacked.

But had he given McPherson *everything* he'd found about *The Broadcast?* The journalist remembered the information that Hensley handed him, every detail. It occurred to him that there was one fact in which HH was *intentionally* not accurate. McPherson was confident that Lindsey produced the films with the help of his friends, but now he thought that this wasn't the whole picture. Another factor must be involved in the story, which up until now had evaded him.

It must be the brother in California, McPherson thought to himself. He remembered HH's assertion of complete estrangement between the two brothers. Really? Now he tended to believe that this point was untrue.

The phone call from the young TXB researcher, Michael Evans, rushed back to his mind. Michael had gotten himself close to Walter Lindsey. Michael was now looking for a mother with the last name Lishinsky, which was the last name of Walter Lindsey's brother. Was it a coincidence or were the two brothers much closer than he was led to believe?

McPherson called the hacker that he employed from time to time. "I need you to check on an important matter," McPherson said. "I want to know whether a man named Jonathan Lishinsky flew from San Francisco to New York in the past year."

"It might take some time," the hacker said. "Many people fly from San Francisco to New York, on several airlines."

"Please make this job a top priority," McPherson said.

After two days, the hacker called back. "I've managed to break into the data archives of several airlines," he said. "Jonathan Lishinsky visited New York on Thanksgiving."

McPherson called Hensley's office to demand an explanation. Nobody answered the phone, and there wasn't even an answering service. He called Hensley's cell phone.

"What do you want?" HH snarled.

"We have to talk," McPherson said.

"I'm busy," Hensley said impatiently. "Maybe next week." He disconnected.

When Hensley talked, McPherson heard distinctive background noises on HH's phone. HH was at an airport. The private detective often traveled for his business, but his disinclination to speak with the journalist who never quibbled about his fees raised McPherson's suspicions.

At that moment, McPherson decided to go to California. It was time to interview Lindsey's brother, Jonathan Lishinsky, to resolve lingering doubts. If it turned out that the brother didn't know anything about the source of the films, then he could at least shed light on Walter Lindsey's personality and thereby assist in solving the mystery.

McPherson drove home and packed a suitcase. From the airport in New York, he called a good friend who lived in San Francisco, a colleague with whom he'd collaborated on several past investigations. McPherson asked him to meet him at the airport and to arrange for a car and a handgun.

CHAPTER 55

Irene

After growing up as a daughter of a single mother, it was important for Irene that her children grew up in a home with two parents, a mother and a father. She kept her marriage despite the many days that her philandering husband was absent from the house and his children's lives. But in her heart, she yearned for a new relationship and with a decent man. She tried internet dating and felt lucky when she found Jonathan. The connection between them was unique and profound, regardless of whether they were half-siblings or simply good friends who understood each other in exceptionally subtle ways.

When her two children became young adults, she felt that she was ready to untie her false marriage and separate from her sneaky bastard of a husband.

She continued to nurture her connection with Jonathan, whom she perceived as a rare, gentle, and honest soul, and she always listened to what he said and to things she sensed, even when they were not said.

Recently, during a couple of weeks, she noticed that Jonathan sounded aloof and withdrawn during their phone calls, as if he were intentionally distancing himself from her. Irene called Sarah to share her concern, and Sarah confirmed that Jonathan appeared troubled and upset ever since TXB announced the cancellation of *The Broadcast.*

"I don't understand why he is taking it so personally," Sarah said.

"I'd like to come for a visit," Irene said, "if you think that I could help him."

"I think you could," Sarah said. "He really appreciates you and listens to you more than me—maybe because you're a computer expert or maybe because he hasn't completely forgiven me."

Irene was glad that Sarah no longer perceived her as a threat. She told her kids that she'd be away for a few days, and they were glad to have the whole house to themselves. She made a reservation for an economy class ticket and flew from Saint Paul to San Francisco. Nobody waited for her when she arrived at the terminal. She rented a car and drove to Corralitos, and with the help of the GPS, she found the Lishinsky property without difficulty.

Jonathan and Sarah were busy with their evening routine when Irene arrived. Jonathan welcomed her with a smile, although he appeared reserved and less friendly than in their previous meetings.

Sarah greeted her with a hug and said, "The final episode of *The Broadcast* airs tonight on the internet. Jonathan's been on tenterhooks waiting for it."

They had dinner at seven thirty. Jonathan tried to be sociable, but the two women noticed that he was tense and restless. Irene talked about technological innovations in her field, which she knew would fascinate him. Jonathan expressed mild interest and asked questions, but remained distant. The women exchanged puzzled looks.

After the meal, Jonathan turned on the smart TV and tuned it to *Uncensored News*.

"I'll be in my computer room," he told the women. "I'll be back about half an hour before the show starts."

CHAPTER 56

Jonathan

Leaving the house, Jonathan saw one of the tenants, Willie Fowler, near the parking area.

"Hey Willie," Jonathan said. "What are doing here?"

"Just waiting for a friend," Willie Fowler answered.

Jonathan shrugged and walked to the barn where he repaired cars and where his computer room was located. He packed his laptop computer into a small backpack and left the building.

Cool evening air swirled around him. He looked in the direction of his unique glade in the forest, and for a moment he imagined seeing a beam of light connecting the hilltop to the sky. Jonathan took a deep breath and headed toward the site, accompanied by his three dogs. For some reason, he felt the need to look around and make sure Willie Fowler didn't see him. *I really don't like that guy*, he thought to himself.

It was dark when he got to the creek. His eyes adapted to the darkness, and he had no difficulty in finding rocks protruding above the water, thus crossing without getting wet.

He reached the bottom of the hill, where the dogs remained as usual, and continued up to the glade by himself. During the past ten days, his visits to the site granted him visions: spectacles of a great fire burning on the altar at the circle's center. He didn't understand the significance of those images and assumed that the meaning would become clear in due time. Following the visions, Jonathan gathered small logs, dry branches, and kindling.

He set his computer aside, piled the collected wood on and around the altar, struck a match, and tossed the lit match onto the wood. The fire ignited immediately, and its flames rose upward. A giant bonfire gushed from the navel of the site, from the altar, and soared up to the sky—although, for a moment, it seemed as if the fire descended from the heavens onto the altar in front of him. The earth shook and rumbled.

Jonathan stood in front of a magnificent bonfire. The glowing pillar of fire hissed and whispered, bewitching and hypnotizing him with its array of colors. He knew that his whole life was channeled into this moment. All he had left to do was step over to his laptop computer and press the "send" button. That action would transfer the last films to *Uncensored News* and from there to the world.

Then, he would be free to move on to a new phase of his life that was yet to be revealed. He waited for a sign.

***

Jonathan and Sarah had discovered the site together several months after they'd moved to their property. Afterward, Jonathan had excavated the place on his own.

Shortly after he'd finished his huge project, Jonathan experienced his first vision: the horrible accident in which his parents were killed.

He'd assumed that it was a one-time vision, but with time, he realized that while at the site, he could observe occurrences from his past with vividness and clarity, beyond what he could ever imagine. He was able to watch every event from his life, including the most negligible and forgotten ones.

Jonathan had an ambivalent attitude toward his visions. At first, he was disturbed by them because they contradicted his dismissal of spirituality, meditation, and Far Eastern teachings. Over time and with repeated experimentation, he started to look forward to the revelations.

Striving to understand the visions, Jonathan learned that only in recent years, scientists had arrived at knowledge that mystics had known for ages. For instance, the understanding that our senses are limited in their perceptions; and grasping of other dimensions that we can't access in our everyday reality.

Jonathan had spent hours probing into his past. With time, it occurred to him to try to see events he had not actually witnessed. So, he would sit on the stone altar and focus his attention on historical incidents that he had found interesting. He was especially interested in notable occurrences from the twentieth century, like the murder of President Kennedy. Gradually, he learned to control his visions—to direct his consciousness until the desired events rolled through his mind like movies.

He noticed a difference between the experiences of his life, which he relived, and the occurrences he never witnessed firsthand, that were seen from a bird's eye view, silent, and in black and white.

Jonathan didn't know what the source of the pictures was. Were they created inside his unconscious mind or outside of it? Perhaps his unconsciousness was connected to another unconsciousness, a collective unconscious, such as he had read in a Carl Jung book.

Jonathan didn't rule out the possibility that in some mysterious way, he had connected to a spaceship that sent him pictures from a great distance. When he read Professor Nishimura's suppositions, he thought that the professor might have been right in his assumptions. According to Nishimura, events that take place on planet Earth, during daytime and when there are no clouds, are drawing away from the planet at the speed of light.

Perhaps, in a way that was beyond his comprehension, Jonathan was catching those images as they were flying through space. It would explain the manner by which the pictures appeared in his mind: from above, and without sound.

and virtual reality software. His ability and skill were so highly developed that he watched his visions and transcribed them to the computer almost simultaneously. It was as if he was in a trance in which the world around him stopped moving, and there were only the events that he saw in his mind and the pictures that appeared and moved on the computer screen.

When he finished his work, he was pleased as he watched the fruits of his labor. The films he created were an accurate reproduction of the scenes he saw in his vision. They looked like video clips that were shot from above, from a great distance.

Shortly after the success of his experiment, Jonathan called Walter. Each of them wanted to break their estrangement and feared making the first move. Sitting by the creek, Jonathan called his brother. He was relieved to hear Walter answering him warmly, like he was genuinely glad to hear from him, and as if he'd waited for the call for a long time.

Jonathan talked candidly with his brother. He told Walter about his life, and about the land he'd purchased with his wife. He spoke about the site, and about the vision of the accident in which he heard his mother screaming, "Robert, watch out!" right before the head-on collision. He revealed his ability to see events from the past, and how he could document those events with advanced computer programs.

Although he was glad to hear from his long-lost brother, Walter worried that Jonathan was utterly delusional.

"Tell me," Walter asked, "could you send me a film that documents the murder of Melisa Robinson Gonzales?" Like many in the American public, and especially in the media, Walter had been curious and riveted to the screen when that famous trial took place twenty-five years earlier.

"Okay," Jonathan accepted the challenge. "I need the exact time and location of the murder."

Walter had no difficulty in handing over the information.

Jonathan climbed up the hill with the laptop computer, sat on the stone altar, concentrated, and focused his attention on the place and time that Walter had given him. The earth shook lightly and sounded its familiar rumble. Jonathan felt how his whole being became attuned, like a channel was opening, getting ready to receive the information.

Soon the pictures showed up in his mind. He spent an hour documenting the visions, which seemed to materialize and come to life on the computer's screen.

Right from the site, he had sent the clip to his brother and asked that Walter would promise not to tell anybody about him and his unique spot. The last thing that Jonathan wanted was strangers roaming around the forest and desecrating his site. Jonathan also insisted that there would be no exchange of money between them, not for the clip and not ever. He feared that money would be a source of contention that could ruin their reconciliation.

Walter agreed, and promised.

When Walter received and watched the clip, he was amazed

and impressed at the professional quality of his brother's work. He couldn't tell whether he was watching a 3-D animated film or a video clip that was shot from a long distance. He then had to find out whether the details were, in fact, true and accurate. So, he showed the film to a few of his colleagues who were familiar with the particulars of the case. Their astonished response encouraged him.

But it wasn't enough. Walter then sent the clip to selected police officers, saying he had received a film that documented the murder of Pedro Gonzales's wife, and he wanted to know if the footage was reliable. Police detectives who knew the minute details of the crime examined the video and responded with the unequivocal answer: the film was authentic.

Lindsey then debated his next step. He wasn't sure that the film could truly be classified as genuine, but when he further examined the issue, he also couldn't disqualify the authenticity of the footage. Walter was convinced that there was no way his brother could have dug up such detailed and accurate information about the event, certainly not in the short time that he was given. Walter concluded that if Jonathan had succeeded in producing this in-depth footage in such a short time, then he must have stumbled upon a fantastic source of information.

Walter never told anyone what the source of the footage was, and he remained faithful to the promise he had given his brother. Seeing the footage, leading managers within the network, including the CEO, were amazed, thrilled, and eager to go forward with what was sure to capture the nation's attention.

Before airing the video, Walter felt obligated to go to California and meet his brother. Both of them were determined to leave the past behind and start a new chapter in their relationship.

They met at the terminal in San Francisco. Tears in their eyes, they hugged and observed the many changes and the traces of time in one another.

"In my mind, you were always my little brother, a child," Walter said as Jonathan drove to Corralitos. He shook his head and chuckled, "wow, you sure have grown."

Jonathan experienced mixed emotions. "Time passes by," he said, "and we can't avoid changing." There were so many things he could have said, like, *where have you been all those years?*

"Sometimes, we have to let go of the past," Walter said, sensing a great deal of perplexity.

"We can learn from the mistakes of the past," Jonathan said.

Walter examined his little brother with empathy, knowing of Jonathan's difficult life. He didn't want the conversation to drift into past failures and old resentments, so he gently remarked, "But it's important not to let the difficult memories control us." So much time had gone by, and Walter still felt that he was the big brother. He bore the responsibility and knew best what was right for both of them. *But did I escape my obligation as a big brother all those years?* The nagging question was on Walter's mind.

Upon arriving home, Jonathan introduced his brother to his wife, who was also deeply moved by the long-awaited reunion.

"I'm so glad to finally meet you," Sarah said to Walter. She warmly shook his hand while looking into his eyes.

The two brothers spent three days together, having long conversations in which they became reacquainted with each other and tried to fill in the gaps from years of non-communication.

They hiked in the forests, and Jonathan took Walter to the site. He wanted to be open and honest with his brother, and not hide where he got his visions.

Walter was amazed by the unique spot. "This place reminds me of Stonehenge," he said.

"I've been to Stonehenge," Jonathan replied, "I think that my site is much more powerful. I can't explain it, but you may notice that we're practically on top of the San Andreas Fault." And as Jonathan spoke, the earth shook and sounded its scary rumble.

Frightened, Walter saw that his brother was completely relaxed.

"That's how it is in this place," Jonathan calmly said. "I believe this site was built by ancient tribes who identified that it was located on a rift that connects different worlds. I think that it served them as a ceremonial place where they communicated with their ancestral spirits or with their gods."

Unnerved, Walter nodded. "Do you come here often?"

"Every once in a while," Jonathan replied. "It just so happens that in this geologically unstable place, I feel the most centered and balanced. For me, it's like taking a tranquilizer."

Walter looked around and admired the enormous amount of work that his brother had invested in excavating the site.

"If you wish," Jonathan said, "you could experience a vision of your own. All you have to do is sit on the rock at the center of the circle, concentrate, and focus your attention on an event from your past that you are particularly interested in."

But Walter was apprehensive. He didn't see himself as someone who followed extraordinary practices. Walter also realized that the reunion had stirred up deep-seated emotions within him. He worried that subjecting himself to an intense spiritual experience was more than he could absorb. "Maybe next time," Walter said.

"That's fine." Jonathan accepted his brother's decision. "I'll be here, and so will the site."

***

Now, three years later, standing in front of the pillar of fire, which seemed to need no fuel, Jonathan felt that his life's work was completed.

He slowly walked over to his laptop computer and pressed SEND, thus transferring the last films into the hands of the people at *Uncensored News*. He returned and stood in front of the giant flames. The intense heat threatened to scorch his face as he looked directly into the fire.

Nishimura had also written that according to Einstein, the distinction that people make between past, present, and future is not consistent with modern scientific observations and calculations.

Jonathan liked the concept that the past, present, and future existed in the same way: everything that had happened and everything that will happen exists here and now.

Was his mysterious site some kind of gate? A focal point? A hub connecting the worlds and the times? And Jonathan, through his visions, could tune into past events that continued to exist?

Jonathan didn't know the answers to the intriguing questions, but he had an easier time accepting his visions when he assumed that there was a scientific explanation for the phenomenon. He found that he more easily connected to past events when he knew the exact place and time of the occurrence, as if he was directing the flow of information into his conscious mind.

One day it had occurred to him that he could document his visions. He brought his laptop computer with him, sat on the rock in the middle of the site, and concentrated. He directed his attention toward an event that had long intrigued him: the Cuban Missile Crisis, a confrontation from the Cold War in which the United States and the Soviet Union came very close to a nuclear war. Before long, images appeared in his mind in which he saw different incidents from the course of the confrontation.

Quickly, employing the proficiency attained during many hours of persistent self-study, he created a clip using 3-D animation

CHAPTER 57

The Broadcast

Irene helped Sarah clean up after dinner, and Sarah assisted her in getting organized in the guest room.

"I don't think that he holds any ill will toward you," Irene said. "There's something else on his mind."

Sarah nodded. "When he's preoccupied like this, I just give him time until it passes. Sometimes he goes to the site, where he renews his energies and finds his balance. But now it's dark outside, so I guess we'll have to be patient, and hopefully tomorrow he'll be in a better mood."

They went to the living room and sat in front of the television. On the *Uncensored News* site there were only commercials, but exactly at 9:00 p.m., a signal heralded the beginning of the special broadcast. The program opened to a studio where a woman and a man sat, smiling at their viewers.

"Good evening," the blonde woman said. "I'm Stacy Gilbert."

"And I am Victor Ortiz," said the man who had a Latin

appearance. "This evening we are presenting a special broadcast."

"We are thrilled," said the female host, "to have been chosen to broadcast the footage ending the exciting season of *The Broadcast*."

The two hosts then commenced an overview of *The Broadcast*, reviewing the previous three seasons.

"Do you think that TXB consented to the showing of these materials?" Irene asked.

"I doubt it," Sarah responded. "But I don't think that the site is in the United States, so they can do whatever they want."

"Do you know where they're located?" Irene was curious.

"Jonathan mentioned they're in the Caribbean Islands," Sarah answered and glanced at her watch with worry. It was after 9:30 p.m. and Jonathan had not yet returned from his computer room.

Sarah heard the front door open and, with relief, turned to greet her husband. However, the man who entered the house wasn't Jonathan, but a hulking stranger with a scarred face.

Irene clutched Sarah's arm in fright, and Sarah tried to sound confident and assertive. "Who are you?"

"Where's Jonathan?" the man said in a quiet voice, which sounded both commanding and threatening.

"Do you know him?" Sarah asked.

"In a way," he said.

"He's ... out," Sarah answered. "He should be here shortly." She hoped there was a sensible explanation for the scary stranger entering her house without knocking.

"I checked the computer room," the man said, "he's not there."

"You checked in the computer room?" Sarah was baffled. *How had he even known there was a computer room?*

"Yeah," he said. "He needs to stop the broadcast. *Now!*"

"What? What broadcast?" Sarah was perplexed.

"The lousy films," he spat. "Don't pretend you don't know that your husband is behind all those damn videos used in *The Broadcast.*"

"Jonathan?" Sarah echoed, puzzled. All of a sudden Sarah understood that the menacing stranger was right. She realized why her husband treated *The Broadcast* as if it were *his* show—because it really was. That explains why shortly after she expressed her wish that *The Broadcast* would stop airing crime shows and move to history-oriented programs, it had happened. Jonathan had done it for her; he made the whole country watch programs that dealt with previous centuries because she had asked. But how?

"Jonathan is not here, as you can see," Sarah said, trying to regain her composure and collect her thoughts. "And if he's not in the computer room, then I have no idea where he is."

"Then call him!" This time he raised his voice.

Sarah managed to maintain a certain level of calm, but Irene trembled in fear beside her.

"I need to find my phone," Sarah said, stalling for time and trying to draw attention away from Irene. "I might have left it by the kitchen sink."

"Bring her the damn phone, Willie!" The stranger ordered. Only then Sarah noticed that her tenant, Willie Fowler, was also in the house.

"Here's the phone, boss," Willie Fowler said, handing it over.

"'Boss,'" Sarah scowled at Fowler. "You pathetic, little liar."

"Now you do what I tell you and nothing else," the scarred stranger told Sarah as he handed her the phone.

"And what will you do if I don't call him?" Sarah stared him down. She decided she wouldn't obey orders from strangers, not in her house.

"Call him," the man said in a quiet voice and pulled out a gun. "Or both of you will die."

Sarah could feel Irene's terror, bordering on panic. However, an unexpected state of tranquility descended on her. She recalled the day when she'd walked on the Golden Gate Bridge, intending to throw herself down. She'd already faced death. She wasn't scared. It would be unfortunate if her life ended today, in the hands of the stranger, now, when she was on the verge of fulfilling her dreams. But still, she could confront her death directly and without fear.

Irene did not feel like a hero. "Please don't kill me; I have two children," she pleaded.

"That depends on her," Hensley said, and pointed his gun at Sarah.

CHAPTER 58

Michael

Michael bade his parents goodbye. His mother felt that ever since she handed him the information about his biological mother, he was restless and anxious to go and search for her. For a moment, she wondered whether she should have concealed the information from him, and then she knew she had done the right thing. All his life, Michael's parents had loved him and cared for him, and they were confident that even if he found his biological mother, he was not going to leave them. His parents actually hoped for his sake that he would succeed in his efforts, and that the meeting with his biological mother would go well.

Michael traveled from San Diego to Los Angeles by bus. The ride afforded him the solitude and opportunity to collect his thoughts. He looked out through the window at the constantly changing scenery. Unfamiliar places passed him by—houses, villages, the ocean, fields, and mountains; green, blue, yellow, and brown; people laboring in their daily routine. He wondered where his destiny was taking him.

Excitement mixed with apprehension. What if his mother didn't want him? What if he didn't like her?

He boarded a flight from Los Angeles to San Francisco and arrived at his destination in the early evening. At the airport, he rented a car and typed: Corralitos, 2408 Oak Road, on the GPS.

As he drove, he received a phone call from Walter. "How are you?" Walter asked.

"I'm fine," Michael answered, "thank you for asking."

"Melanie told us that you're going to meet your biological mother and it's really exciting," Walter said. "Monica and I wish you the best of luck."

"Thanks." Michael felt a wave of gratitude toward Walter and his family. "I've waited a long time for this."

"Do you remember that today, the internet site *Uncensored News* is going to show the last films of the season?" Walter asked.

"Wow, no." Michael replied, "I forgot." In Walter's tone of voice, Michael heard the producer's disappointment about the films being transferred from him to a previously unknown internet site.

"I'm worried about Jonathan," Walter shared his concern. "It's been a few days since I spoke to him and he hasn't answered my calls."

"I suppose I'll see him," Michael said.

"You mean after you meet your mother?" Walter asked, puzzled. "You don't have to. I'm sure you'll be pretty occupied, reuniting with your mom after so many years."

"Um. Yeah." Michael was not sure how to break the news to Walter, then he blurted, "You'll be surprised, but it appears my mother and your brother are married."

After a moment, Walter responded with excitement, "That's incredible! What a small world! So ... we're related?"

"Yep, you're my uncle," Michael said. He paused, remembering his relationship with Melanie, "Well, we're not blood relatives, but still ..."

Walter swept it aside. "When you get to your destination, please see that my brother is all right."

"Of course," Michael responded.

Setting the phone aside, Michael focused on driving. He headed south on a winding highway in a sparsely populated area, where forests grew on both sides of the road.

As it got dark, Michael turned on the car's headlights and continued driving in the foreign environment. The navigation system's female voice gave him the feeling that he was not alone, as well as the assurance that he was on the right track.

Passing the corporate limit sign for Corralitos, the GPS guided him to a gravel road. Michael wondered why the system directed him through such rough terrain. He continued to drive between dark mountains and hills, into a forested area that became thicker as he kept going. He concentrated on driving and following the headlights as they penetrated the darkness. The road became narrow, winding, and bumpy, and suited more for off-road vehicles then rented sedans. He slowed down and drove carefully so as not to get stuck in the wide holes that opened in the dirt road. The GPS continued to call out directions. Michael considered stopping the car and turning around when the system suddenly announced, "You have reached your destination."

Michael stopped the car, looked around, and didn't see any house. Still, he switched off the engine and stepped out of the vehicle to a moonless evening. He stretched his body and deeply breathed the forest's air. While surveying the surroundings, he listened to night birds that awakened a sense of apprehension within him. His ears caught the gurgle of flowing water in a creek nearby. He also heard dogs barking in the distance, so he assumed he must be not far from people's habitation. He wondered where he was.

Michael noticed that the hill near where he parked the car was darker than the surrounding hills, apparently because the trees there grew in a denser pattern.

Looking toward the dark hill, he was surprised to see a huge fire billowing upward. It was a magnificent sight that filled him with reverence and amazement.

CHAPTER 59

Howard Hensley

"Call Jonathan now!" Howard Hensley yelled at Sarah and aimed the gun at Irene, "or I kill her and then I kill you. And I know she's his sister!"

It was nearly 10:00 p.m. and the show was about to begin. *Uncensored News* played the last commercial. Sarah looked at her phone and made the call as she was ordered, but there was no answer. She tried again.

"What do you want me to do?" she said. "He's not answering."

"Call the other number," HH growled, sweat beading on his forehead.

Sarah wondered how the gun-wielding man knew Jonathan carried two phones. She also knew that, had he wanted to, her husband would have answered by now.

"Call now! Your time's running out," Hensley ordered. "These could be your last breaths." Pointing the gun at Irene, he released the safety.

Sarah was at a loss, fearing he was crazy enough to act on his threat while there was nothing she could do. She realized that the situation was completely out of her control.

Sarah heard the muffled click of a door gently closing at the back of the house. A long corridor led from the living room to that back door. Had Jonathan returned? If so, he could be in grave danger, although she didn't think the stranger noticed the sound.

On the TV screen, the show started, which might infuriate the strange man, whom Sarah began to suspect was mentally unstable.

"Good evening." Once again, the host at *Uncensored News* greeted her many viewers, knowing she'd gained a larger audience than ever in the site's history.

"Mute the sound," Sarah whispered to Irene as she again attempted to contact Jonathan.

Eyes wide with fear, Irene took the remote into her trembling hands and obeyed.

In some obscure way, Sarah sensed that the footage running on the screen might somehow be related to the occurrences in her house.

Suddenly, the unexpected voice of another man echoed within the house's walls. "Put the gun down, Hensley, or I'll shoot you!"

Hensley and Fowler tensed and turned in the direction of whoever spoke. Also surprised, Sarah and Irene wondered who might have come to their rescue. Neither woman recognized the new voice.

"Drop the gun now!" The voice sounded like it came from the unlit corridor.

HH crouched, lowering his hand, but he didn't set down his weapon.

Howard Hensley did not easily admit defeat. He took pride in his courage, self-control, and nerves of steel. The voice of the hiding man surprised him. It sounded familiar, but Hensley couldn't immediately identify it.

"Who the hell are you?" Hensley defiantly looked in the direction of the dark corridor and continued to hold onto his gun. "You are not scaring me."

Ever since the death of his friend and partner, Hensley preferred to work alone, but now he regretted not having a reliable partner. He knew he couldn't count on Willie Fowler who looked ready to bolt.

Sarah saw how fearful and shaken Irene was, so she laid a comforting hand on Irene's shoulder and tried to calm her trembles. Both of them realized that they had stumbled upon an unforeseen situation. Here they'd sat comfortably to watch unusual events on television, and suddenly they found themselves in the midst of an intense drama. And it wasn't clear how they would come out of it.

"Your time is running out, HH," said the voice from the hallway. The calm tone conveyed confidence and certainty. "Drop the gun. This is your last chance."

Sarah saw that for a brief moment, the intruder seemed perplexed. Would he drop his firearm as ordered? Would he try to shoot at where the voice came from? He shifted his attention back to the women, seated next to each other on the sofa. Maybe he would point the gun at them? Shoot them?

From where he stood, Hensley couldn't see the TV screen. However, he was smart enough to assume that *The Broadcast* was already underway and he'd failed in his mission. He considered how to salvage the situation. Surrender was not an option.

The unknown man had managed to surprise him and put him at a definite disadvantage. Nonetheless, in the past, he had come out of similarly impossible situations.

The footage of the final episode showed a massive blaze as Roman soldiers stormed into the Temple Mountain and set the temple on fire. The flicker of televised flames momentarily lit the corridor.

HH saw the image of his opponent, though indistinctly, and he recognized the opportunity. In a split second, he raised his hand and aimed the gun at his enemy.

The deafening sound of the shot echoed within the house's wooden walls.

CHAPTER 60

Michael

The earth trembled. Michael sensed that he was in a strange place. Fear engulfed him, and he considered returning to the car and driving back to the main road.

It occurred to him that the GPS had led him to the wrong destination, but upon further reflection, an inner voice told him that he was meant to be in that place at that time. He debated climbing the hill toward the pillar of fire. Would he know what to do once he reached the top? Would he meet his mother?

He took a deep breath and started to climb up the hill. The darkness closed in on him, and the hike wasn't easy. The trees grew unusually close to one another, but they didn't block his way. In sections where the slope was particularly steep, the trees actually assisted him as he could grab onto the branches in front of him and pull himself upward.

He continued his climb on the steep and winding path toward the bonfire, its orange light filtering through the branches. Eager to reach the top, he could feel the blood pumping through his veins making his heart race.

The earth trembled again. This time it also rumbled. Frightened, Michael questioned his decision to climb the hill. Still, his inner voice compelled him to continue toward the fate waiting for him.

He reached the top of the hill, and pushing the last branches out of his way, found himself in a glade illuminated by fire.

He encountered an unexpected scene. Jonathan, Walter's brother, stood facing the heart of the fire that burned on a stone altar. Jonathan's face had a concentrated and stoic expression. Suddenly, it occurred to Michael that Jonathan might cast himself into the fire and disappear.

"Jonathan, don't!" Michael shouted.

Surprised, Jonathan turned in his direction. He recognized the young man from his visit to Walter's house over Thanksgiving.

"Where did you come from?"

"Walter needs to hear from you," Michael said, "and your wife must be really worried about you."

Jonathan nodded in acknowledgment and turned back to face the fire, his gaze captivated by the roaring blaze. For a moment, Jonathan saw in his mind's eye how the fire at his site united with another fire, the ancient blaze that once consumed the temple in Jerusalem. He knew the film he'd just sent to *Uncensored News*, was being watched all over the United States and the world.

Deep inside his soul, Jonathan felt this was an auspicious moment, a turning point. From this point on, his life was going to change, although he didn't know how, so he continued to wait for a sign. He had no intention of jumping into the flames, but if this were the call … he would not hesitate.

Michael understood that he wouldn't be able to stop Jonathan from stepping into the fire and disappearing from the world, if that was his wish.

CHAPTER 61

Sarah

The gunshot was brutally accurate, and it delivered a direct blow to the center of the target's chest. As he was falling down, in that second when the world around him blurred and darkened, HH knew that the physical pain was not as dreadful as the humiliation of defeat.

"I warned him!" Stewart McPherson said as he entered the room with a gun in his hand. He glanced at the body of Howard Hensley, on the floor, gasping for air, then at Willie Fowler who raised his hands in surrender.

The front door slammed open, and cops stormed into the house.

"I called you," Stewart McPherson said to the cops who shouted at him to drop his weapon, "and I shot this man. It was self-defense. Now he needs immediate medical attention."

McPherson approached the dining room table, where he placed his gun, knowing he would have to face questioning regarding what might turn out to be a fatal shooting.

Irene, who was frightened and shaken following the difficult ordeal, got up from the couch and walked over to McPherson. She wrapped her arms around him and wept, even as the police moved in to cuff him. "Thank you," she said, "thank you for saving us from that horrible man."

McPherson returned the hug, and Irene felt that his embrace conveyed strength, caring, and trustworthiness, and that she was safe in his firm arms.

The journalist, who hadn't been intimate with a woman in years, was drawn to the unfamiliar woman who was trembling in his arms. Looking into her eyes, he saw something right and authentic and felt that he wanted to know her better.

The open front door emitted a flickering orange glow that caught Sarah's eye. Ignoring Irene, McPherson, and the police, she rushed through the doorway. Immediately she saw the pillar of fire and had no doubt where it came from. She blinked, the blurry image of the fire momentarily merged with the image of the fire on the television screen. But Sarah was not interested in the horrendous film on TV, which showed the Roman soldiers surging into the Temple Mount's square, killing everyone who was in their way without mercy, and setting the temple on fire.

She made her way in the direction of the blaze. An ominous feeling told her that she must hurry to prevent Jonathan from performing an act from which there was no turning back. She must tell him the news that had recently been confirmed.

Thorny bushes scratched her face on the slope leading down to the creek, but they didn't slow her sense of urgency. She splashed through the water in the creek, ignoring the wet that soaked through her shoes and clothes. The pillar of fire guided her to the strange hill, where at its base the dogs joyfully jumped on her.

She left the dogs behind and started to climb up the hill. Her lungs heaved from the exertion as she raced toward the glade. She noticed that the trees and bushes didn't block her way, as in the past. It seemed like the dense vegetation actually cleared a passage for her, and the firelight that penetrated through the branches illuminated her way.

One more bundle of trees, one more bush ...

She shoved the last branches out of her way and walked into the site.

She only needed a split second to grasp what was taking place. Jonathan stood in front of a huge blaze, mesmerized by the flames. He looked poised to step into the fire.

"Jonathan stop!" she screamed.

He ignored her and continued to stare at the glow that beckoned him to step closer. The earth shook and rumbled. Desperate, she yelled again, "Jonathan I'm pregnant! You're going to be a father!"

He turned his head toward her voice, his expression filled with doubt and hope.

"Jonathan, it happened here, right here, when we made love.

I knew it right away, but I didn't want to tell you until the doctor confirmed it."

He looked back at the fire for another moment and took one step backward away from it.

In response, the blaze diminished to about half its size, but it was still a large bonfire, which illuminated the place for them. The earth calmed, and its muffled rumble turned into silence.

Jonathan started walking toward her. They drew closer to each other until Sarah lunged those last few feet into his arms. He pulled her into his embrace and felt her warm tears moisten his shoulder.

He, too, wept, but without sound or tears. He grieved for the parents he didn't remember, for the misery endured in foster homes, for unrealized dreams, doubts, and fears.

The flames consumed their anger and sorrow; their troubles, evil, darkness, and depression. Sarah accepted Jonathan all over again. She accepted who he was, the man she had always seen in him, the one he could be, and the one he would be. She felt how as she accepted him, he too, accepted and forgave her.

For a long time, they stood in a loving embrace, and the fire continued to illuminate the site for them.

***

Suddenly, Sarah noticed that they were not alone. A

handsome young man stood nearby, affectionately watching them. Patiently waiting.

Looking at him sent shivers through Sarah's body. There was something familiar about him, and also unknown and enigmatic. She parted from her husband and turned toward the young man, who seemed like he had something to tell her. His eyes shone and conveyed complete acceptance.

Sarah didn't know why she felt her soul stir at the sight of him. Her heart pounded and her eyes again filled with tears.

The young man stepped toward her and said the one word that for so many years she had desperately longed to hear: "Mom?"

EPILOGUE

Six years later

Daniel

My name is Daniel and I'm almost six years old.

I live in Corralitos with my parents and I just started to go to school.

I have a few friends and my best friend is Nathan.

He is a little younger than me he's five years old and his parents are much younger than my parents. Actually my parents are kind of old but I don't mind because I love them a lot.

My father's name is Jonathan and my mother's name is Sarah. My daddy works on computers and he drives to work every day in his car.

When he is not working we play together and he likes to teach me to take apart and put together all kinds of things.

My mom doesn't work and she stays at home and works in the garden and also she likes to cook. We have two cute dogs that I really like to play with. One of them is called Nipo and the other is Ramayana. We also have lots cats.

My mom stopped working after I was born. She told me that she was a psychologist but I don't really know what that is.

She said she used to sit in a room and talk to people about their problems, so I think this work is weird.

I also have a big brother and his name is Michael who is a lot older than me. He is like thirty. He lives far away but sometimes he comes for a visit with his wife that her name is Melanie and with their little daughter whose name is Linda. It's funny but Michael still calls my mom, mommy. I tell him he's got to grow up.

Melanie's dad is the brother of my father and he makes movies for TV.

Sometimes we have earthquakes here and it's kind of scary. When I was little I was really afraid of earthquakes but now I'm not so afraid. Only a little and my mom says that it's OK to be afraid.

Sometimes when my mom works in the garden and I play next to her I look at her and see that she's crying a little. I ask her why do you cry mommy and then she comes to me and she hugs me really tight and says because I love you sooooo much.

ACKNOWLEDGMENTS

I would like to thank the kind people who read the manuscript and contributed their illuminating suggestions.

Amanda Safran, Mark Bunyard.
Karen Smith, Terry Hayman, Janet Williams, Kathleen Strickler, Sharon Orr, Loren Hilbert, Jane Hagar.
Lee Ann and Nick of First Editing.

Thank you, Rob Williams, for the cover design.

I wish to thank:

Dave and Kate Workman.
Magy Speelpenning, Erelah Gafni, Laurette Maillet, and Lucia Van-Diepen.
Molly, Nathan, and Eve.
My parents, my sister and my brother.
Jacob, Cécile, and Nathan.

And Linda, who has been patient with me during all those long hours I sat in front of the computer. I'm grateful for your insights, and for your love.

Thank you all,

Liam Fialkov

If you enjoyed reading *The Broadcast*, it'd be greatly appreciated if you leave a review on Amazon.

https://www.amazon.com/dp/B07KDRQ8XN/ref=sr_1_2?s= books&ie=UTF8&qid=1541930064&sr=1- 2&keywords=The+Broadcast%3A+A+Mystery+Thriller

liam_fialkov@outlook.com
https://www.facebook.com/liam.fialkov.77

Made in the USA
Monee, IL
29 November 2020